RED LOTUS

RED LOTUS

Pai Kit Fai

白傑輝

sphere

SPHERE

First published in the United States of America as *The Concubine's Daughter*
in 2009 by St Martin's Press
First published in Great Britain in 2009 by Sphere

Book design by Ruth Lee-Mui

Calligraphy by Archibald Tsui

A CIP catalogue record for this book
is available from the British Library.

HB ISBN 978-1-84744-077-8
C ISBN 978-1-84744-061-7

Printed and bound in Great Britain by
Clays Ltd, St Ives plc

Papers used by Sphere are natural, renewable and recyclable
products sourced from well-managed forests and certified
in accordance with the rules of the Forest Stewardship Council.

Mixed Sources
Product group from well-managed
forests and other controlled sources
www.fsc.org Cert no. SGS-COC-004081
© 1996 Forest Stewardship Council
FSC

Sphere
An imprint of
Little, Brown Book Group
100 Victoria Embankment
London EC4Y 0DY

An Hachette UK Company
www.hachette.co.uk

www.littlebrown.co.uk

For my wife, Phyllis

Hope Dellon

Al Zuckerman

Acknowledgments

When a book takes a while to finish, there's a risk you might forget some of those who were with you at the start. First, it's best to thank those who were beside you every step of the way: My wife, who has lived through a dozen books and never lost faith; an amazing editor, Hope Dellon, who put time and distance aside and shared the journey all the way, including the stony bits; Al Zuckerman, whose calm advice was constant and patience remarkable, and whose incomparable wisdom makes books out of stories and writers out of scribblers.

They would all have wasted their time if it weren't for those brave souls who spoke nicely to my computer when I threatened to kill it: dear, reliable Christine Lenton was always there for a backup and Richard Harvey, a technical giant who was never too busy. A special thanks to my friends Master John Saw, Blake Powell, Bryce Courtenay, and Justin Milne, and they know why; Derek Goh for his unconditional generosity; and Marabel Caballes, who is as beautiful as her name and talked me through some computer glitches but never raised her voice.

So many friends who stopped by to make my day, not least that colossus of the Tasmanian bush, Bradley Trevor "Ironbark" Greive, whose mighty words in little books have put smiles upon 20 million faces and one to spare for me.

PART ONE
CHILDREN OF THE MOON
月亮的孩子

A Thousand Pieces of Gold

Great Pine Spice Farm on the Pearl River, Southern China, 1906

> Seek every hidden happiness. Collect the smallest of joys.
> Each of these is precious as a piece of pure gold.
>
> —PAI-LING

Y*ik-Munn, the farmer, poured* another cup of hot rice wine. His hand shook as though he too felt the agony endured behind the closed doors above. He had heard such commotion many times, and to him the shrieks of Number Four might just as well be the squeals of a sow advanced upon with a dull blade. Even in this small room, chosen for its isolation and quiet darkness, her bleating was an offense to his ears, following him like a demented wraith as he descended the stairs to seek a moment's peace and privacy.

He supposed it was to be expected from the newest and youngest of his women and this, her firstborn. The first always came into the world with much caterwauling, but it opened the way for those yet to come— until they slid out as slickly as a calf from a cow. Still, in the year since he had fetched his concubine from the great northern city of Shanghai to Great Pine Farm—through the mouth of the Pearl River Delta and far into its fertile estuary—he had pondered the wisdom of his purchase on more than one occasion. He pondered it now.

Pai-Ling was barely fifteen when he bought her from a large family escaping the turmoil of Shanghai. The Ling clan had once been rich and powerful, occupying an extensive compound in the old quarter, well away from the foreign devil's cantonments. After the Boxer Uprising, all face was lost; they were at the mercy of the tongs as extortion and kidnapping gripped the city in the name of the I-Ho-Chuan, or "Fists of Righteousness."

The Ling family had been left with no alternative but to return to the humble village of their birth. With their sons scattered, their belongings greatly reduced, they decided to sell the youngest daughter, the child of a favorite mistress and considered dispensable. Better that she be sold to an idiot farmer from the south than be kidnapped for a ransom they could not pay, to become a plaything for the Boxers or meet a miserable death in the hands of triad kidnappers.

Pai-Ling was taller in the way of northern women, more beautiful than the three wives who had serviced Yik-Munn's long and arduous life but had become fat, and tiresome in his bed. She was proud, and her eyes were filled with unexpected dignity. Yik-Munn remembered well when she was first brought before him in the great reception hall of the Ling compound.

As he sat in his well-polished shoes and his best suit of bold check cloth, custom-made made for him in the Western style by a master tailor in Canton, she had glanced at his scanty hair, freshly trimmed and plastered with sweet-smelling pomade, without enthusiasm. His long, high-cheek-boned face shaved, patted, and pampered, even his large ears had been thoroughly reamed until they glowed. Their fleshy lobes were one of his finest features, said by the priests to be a sign of great wisdom, like those of the lord Buddha himself.

That all such careful preparation did not hide the deep-set eyes and hollow cheeks of an opium eater did not bother him. To afford the tears of the poppy whenever he wished was a sign of affluence among the farmers of Kwangtung Province. And to own such a suit, specially made to fit him alone and worn only by the big-city taipan, was proof that he was also a respected spice merchant.

Neither did the hostile look in her eyes discourage him. His only hesitation had been to learn that she had taught herself to read and write. This was unheard of along the banks of the Pearl and its many tributaries, at least among the families who had turned the fertile soils for many generations.

They were Hakka, the peasant clans of the south who knew of nothing but the moon's rich harvests and the blessings of the Tu-Ti—the earth gods—who watch over hardworking families with a benevolent eye. When she was not too heavy with child, a woman's purpose was to plant and follow the plow, to harvest and grind, thresh and bale. Had not Number-One Wife continued to work on the rice terraces almost to the moment of birth after her third time—stopping only long enough to give him a healthy son, rest for the remainder of that day, and have the buffalo yoked to resume plowing as the sun rose the following morning?

Number Two had once made his heart trip like a boy's with the appetite of a whore in the bedroom . . . but she was of no other use and had a whining voice that sawed its way into his soul. True, Number Three could read and write, and her fingertips were fast and light as a cricket as they tripped the beads of the abacus . . . but only to keep tally in the godown. One woman with brains was more than enough under Yik-Munn's roof. An educated female would bring nothing but trouble to any clan.

Wives as sturdy and enduring as One and Two were worthy of their rice and of great value to a struggling farmer. Times were different now. The Great Pine spice farm had prospered; his elder sons were studying in the best schools, one of them running his own restaurant on the Golden Hill of Hong Kong. The younger ones still worked the spice fields, and his grandsons were already able to plant rice and gather a harvest.

So Pai-Ling was a plaything—perhaps to bear him more sons, but he expected nothing more of her and overlooked the unsettling discovery that she could not only read and write but was said to have studied the many faces of the moon and understood the passage of the star gods. This was the forbidden domain of priests and fortune-tellers; a girl child who sought such knowledge could be considered of unsound mind, liable to become rebellious and a danger to those around her. Still, the cost of Pai-Ling's education had been borne by her family, and it was they who had allowed her to consult mischievous imps and pray to mysterious gods.

Yik-Munn had earned a ripe young concubine with a spirit yet to be tamed, who would nourish him with her virgin body and give him great face. He would soon beat the foolishness out of her and change the insolent light in her eyes to one of gratitude and respect; he would draw upon her rebellious sap to nourish his spirit and receive her pure essence like dew from an open flower.

That she had looked at him without fear but with clear distaste, and even seemed to flash a warning, had caused his blood to surge. He had run a bony finger around the stiff collar caught too tightly by a brightly colored tie. His large and splendid teeth displayed themselves in an approving smile. Defiance in one so young gave him a thrill that cast all other thoughts aside; she would be small and tight as a mouse's ear. He would not demand love or affection, or even the friendship of a fond companion; had he not once received such futile sentiments in abundance from wives One, Two, and Three?

He knew what pleased him most in the bedroom, and expected such service from Pai-Ling: the incomparable feeling of ownership and absolute, unquestionable power. In addition, his elder sister, who had once been a part of Shanghai society and had maintained the best of connections, had recommended this fine family. This, she had assured him, was where he would find a suitable concubine—a summer peach to bring endless spring in his autumn years.

Now that the Ling family's fortunes had crumbled along with those of many other wealthy Shanghai families, this was the time to do business, when they were eager to escape and in no position to bargain. That the girl had been sired by the master of the house and a white Russian mistress of uncertain heritage had been considered in the price and otherwise not spoken of. Not only did she promise new adventures in the bedroom and have hips to bear more sons, but most precious of all were what he saw when she was presented for his consideration: her tiny lotus feet, rare these days.

So dainty were her crippled toes, bent until they touched her heel—the deformity of elegance sheathed so exquisitely in embroidered silk—that he could cradle them in the palm of his rough farmer's hand and fondle them like a lovely finger jade. This girl was indeed *qian-jin*—to be compared to a thousand pieces of gold. As with all things costly on Great Pine Farm, the money to pay the asking price had come from the brimming coffers of Elder Sister.

That his wives would not welcome another as young and beautiful as Pai-Ling was certain. They had worked hard to attain power in the House of Munn, to play mah-jongg in the village and enjoy the lavish attentions of the beauty parlor whenever they wished.

Yik-Munn had returned to Great Pine Farm with his proud and willful concubine, younger than his youngest son, dressed in silks of red and gold, carried over the muddy fields in a palanquin. This had given him great face among his neighbors. When she tottered behind him on his frequent visits to the temple, the tilt of her spine and sway of her behind made him the envy of friends and enemies alike. *Yes*, Yik-Munn had thought, *Pai-Ling is well worth the money.*

That was almost a year ago. She had been a problem to him from the start, biting him as savagely as a stray dog on the first night because, she yelled, he was too hasty, too big, and too clumsy for her. On his command, One had gagged her, and Two and Three were told to hold her wrists and ankles while he struck her nearly senseless and planted his seed so violently, her squalling roused the doves from the barn roof.

Worse, the commotion had disturbed Elder Sister, known to the household as Goo-Mah (Great-Aunt), who hammered for quiet with her heavy blackwood stick.

Yik-Munn was afraid of his sister, who lived on and on and had stopped counting the years while she held tightly to the family purse strings. Goo-Mah also possessed lotus feet, no bigger than a child's, but could no longer stand or walk and had not done so for a thousand moons. The feet had rotted so much, their stink escaped her tightly closed door.

Hidden away in upstairs rooms of her own, unable to leave her bed, she was surrounded by the furnishings of a prosperous younger life. On a shelf, proudly arranged side by side like rare and precious toys in the prettiest of colors, stood the tiny silken slippers that once encased her feet so sublimely. She was senile, toothless, and half deaf, her lifeless stumps soaking always in a bowl of steaming herbs to ease her agony, her malignant spirit prowling the house like a phantom.

Goo-Mah no longer feared death or the judgment of gods that might

7

await her; she prayed to be taken every day. Life had become so bleak, her only remaining pleasure was to be as disagreeable as possible to those around her. She could not demand more attention or command more obedience in the house of her brother if she were the great Dowager Empress Tzu-Hsi, who was renowned for her arrogance and cruelty.

Reduced as her life had become, her pride had grown all the greater. Did she not own this farm that had made them wealthy, and the house where they lived with such comfort and security? In truth, her worthless brother would have starved, and his greedy wives with him, if it were not for the endless generosity of the great Goo-Mah.

Was she not, until now, the only one in this family who had feet so splendid they had been glorified by the lotus slipper, stroked like a kitten by a loving husband who showered her with gold? She could have been a courtesan with such delicate feet, while those around her had monstrous extremities fit only to paddle in mud.

Goo-Mah's face was wrinkled as a preserved plum, pale as parchment, and her eyes were filmed by the milky blue of cataracts. To express her dignity and remind visitors of her great importance, she wore the jade and ivory trinkets collected throughout her life—rings on every withered finger, bony wrists laden with bracelets, her scraggy neck hidden by necklaces of gold, silver, and precious stones. Crowning this treasury of memories, skewering her crooked wig, was an array of combs and dangling decorations.

She trusted no one, least of all her good-for-nothing brother. She did not like him, she did not respect him, and she did not trust him. So sure was she that he would not spend enough on the coffin that would carry her to the glittering mansion of her ancestors, she had had one crafted to her grandest expectations, supervising every detail from her bedside. Hewn from the ebony heart of a persimmon tree, it was sheathed in copper, sound as the keel of an emperor's junk, every inch inscribed with sacred talismans to ward off all manners of evil that might waylay her ascent into heaven.

Lined by layers of the finest silk, with hidden pockets for her most valuable treasures, it was kept in the room adjoining her bedchamber, covered by a black silk cloth and surrounded by porcelain images of the appropriate gods. Far too large to be taken through the door and down the stairs no matter how many strong men were enlisted, a crane would need to be used and the window demolished to move her remains to the family cemetery beneath the great pine. It was a comfort to her to know that she would have the very shortest of distances to travel from this life to the next, but would command attention and respect to the very last instant, causing as much trouble as possible even after her death.

Beneath her pillow, in a small, flat box, resided the most important riches to be taken with her into the afterlife: a set of jade plugs fashioned to close each of her nine orifices so that any roving spirit in search of a home might not find a way to enter her corpse. Exquisite to look upon and carved from only the most expensive stone, they differed in shape and color, from duck-bone white and mutton-fat yellow to rose madder, kingfisher blue, and date-skin brown. The matched pair that would close her eyes forever had the sheen of chestnuts and were in the shape of fish, who with eyes eternally open would be forever watchful. The most splendid piece would be placed in her mouth to hold her tongue. It was the color of morning dew on a chrysanthemum and shaped like a cicada, a creature that, through its long periods underground in the larval stage, symbolized a resurrection of the spirit and eternal spring.

Great-Aunt had railed long and loud when told that the new concubine defied her brother's wishes, demanding she be flayed within an inch of her life and denied all food and privilege until she showed proper respect and humility to those who sheltered her and filled her bowl. Did this ill-bred bitch not know how fortunate she was to be chosen to cross the door of this most honorable clan? Her brother, worthless fool that he may be, was the oldest male in her family and deserved respect. Any who insulted him, insulted her, and this she would not tolerate.

So rebellious was Pai-Ling, Goo-Mah declared to her troubled brother, that the women of the household had concluded that she was possessed by a demon. Where else would such defiance come from in so worthy a household as the House of Munn?

In the kitchen, Number One plotted against the impudent Shanghai bitch, convincing Two and Three of the danger. They wished her gone, along with her precious feet; there was no room for one so young in a house already filled with honorable and deserving women. They wanted no more sons to share the family wealth, nor anyone beneath their roof who could awaken their husband's passions. The mistresses he bothered in the village were well known to them, and welcome to keep him occupied as long and as often as they could . . . but a concubine under the same roof was a danger to them all.

If young enough, a clever concubine was capable of grasping power from those who had earned it—those who had served the master of the house in harder times and borne his sons. The women had thought of poison, and secretly paid good money for the deadliest of mushrooms—and more for the black magician's talismans—to see her cursed. But the girl from Shanghai had proved fruitful and was quickly with child before the forces of darkness could find a way to be rid of her.

These were the thoughts and deeds of One and Two, while Three said little. There was nothing she could do but show the lonely concubine what small benevolence she could whenever the opportunity arose. Secretly, by eyes that met without conflict or by tone of voice and touch when unobserved, they had come to know each other as forbidden friends.

Yik-Munn's hand trembled as he placed the brimming cup before the shrine. Why did morbid thoughts crawl through his mind at such a moment? Perhaps they came from his ancestors, unsmiling in an assortment of wood and metal frames. Joss sticks pricked the shadows with sparks of cherry red, beside a bowl of fresh peaches, golden kumquats, and plump pomegranates, their stones and pips assuring many sons. He knew how careful a man with young sons must be. The whim of the gods could be as fickle as March winds. When his sons were infants he had dressed them as girls, with jade anklets, to deceive the evil spirits into thinking they were female and not worth claiming, to be passed over as something unworthy of attention.

He had given them names like Ah-Gow—the Dog—and a silver collar to wear so that they would be protected from the hungry ghosts roaming the skies, ready to snatch them away. He had entrusted each of his sons to Chang-Hsien, whose portrait, bow in hand, hung where they slept, his heavenly arrow ready to shoot down the spirit of purgatory that sought to devour the precious soul.

Threads of incense wound among rows of tablets on smoke-grimed shelves. Slips of wood, bone, and ivory bore the names of the long-dead and the reign in which they had lived. On the altar, in a brass urn, paper offerings still curled in feathers of blue flame. It was not surprising that thoughts of his sister should come to him here.

One day she would join these somber faces, and he prayed daily for it to be soon. Great-Aunt had long outgrown her usefulness and lived only to remind him of his failure. She, who had buried three husbands and accumulated their wealth, was the one who controlled his life and the welfare of his family. When the day came to add her photograph to this grim gallery, he would be a rich man, and a free one.

He felt no guilt at praying for his sister's death, but it brought tears to his eyes to think of the cost of her interment; if it had been left to him, her remains would reside in an empty wine jar somewhere in the spice fields.

For many moons, he had been ready to send her on her way. All preparations had been seen to, and he looked with comfort upon the paper offerings that filled each darkened corner: a splendid palanquin to see that her lotus feet would not touch the ground; her favorite foods and a gourd filled with fresh water; effigies of many servants to wait upon her every need; a magnificent mansion for her soul to occupy on arrival; great wads of heaven money to assure her every comfort in the afterlife—all made of colored paper pasted over frames of split bamboo.

He was a cautious man, and had made generous offerings at the temple for his unborn son. Freshly roasted pig, an abundance of fruit, flagons of good wine, and pyramids of rice cakes as high as his head had been laid upon the altar, then eaten under a tree by Yik-Munn and his family. There was, after all, no worthiness in waste.

This he had done for every month that his son grew in the womb.

Gold and silver paper had also been burned at the shrine of the earth god, and his prayers had been pinned to the sacred banyan in the village to please the tree spirits. There was nothing to say a man should not travel all roads to heaven and call upon many powers when a son was to be born, and he had beseeched them all.

Yik-Munn was wrenched from this reverie as the screaming changed to a choking moan, and the first lusty cry of his son reached out to him like a hand from above. He fell to his knees and kowtowed deeply three times. Seconds later, a wail of despair wrapped the house in loud lament, the words of the midwife clearly heard echoing among the rafters, filling the joyless rooms, and spreading out across the fields: "*Aaaeeeyah . . . lui, ahhh . . . lui, aahhhh . . . luiiii . . . luuiiii, ahh. . . .* A girl, a girl. It is a girl. . . ."

Only then did he know that his preparations and offerings had failed to appease the eight immortals. The dried penis of the wild horse, which he had paid for dearly each week and consumed to increase his issue and assure him of a son, had not been enough. The two duck eggs he had placed so carefully in her chamber pot to attract the precious testicles of a boy had made a mockery of his faith. All gods had turned from him and allowed the beggar spirits to snatch away his son. There would be no new boy child to join the others, to create greater wealth for the House of Munn and add filial piety to a deserving father's old age, to care for his soul in the afterworld. Why had he been cursed with a female?

For a family of wealth and nobility, to have a daughter could bring great luck. She could be tutored in ladylike skills and arts and married into a wealthy house for all to profit. But to a farmer, a girl was just another bowl to fill.

Moments later, carrying a small bundle, Yik-Munn left the house, which was sheltered by the towering pine that gave the farm its name. It was a monkey puzzle pine, the only one of its kind in the district and said to be as old as three centuries. He gazed up into thickly clustered branches spread wide above the house. So tall that its crown could not be seen except from the center of the mustard field, its girth took five long strides to walk around; its bark had the texture of weathered steel with great gouts of golden sap that ran like open wounds. For all his life, the great pine had been a monument to prosperity and strength, the protector of his land, the center of his earthly luck. Now it had failed him.

It has grown too tall, he told himself. *Its energies have turned against me. It casts yin shadows over the house, attracting the shady cool of the female spirit.* Perhaps he would have it taken down, whatever the cost, to bathe his house in the yang of sunlight, brighten his spirit and give heat to his energy. He could give the girl a few weeks to recover and straddle her again. By all gods, he would fill the bitch with sons.

At almost seventy-three years of age, he fought bravely for his potency, paying the village doctor regularly and well to keep him filled with the abundant juices of youth. But his body had never recovered from a boyhood of crippling work and meager nourishment, and the medicines he took were rare and costly.

His backbone curved like a bent shovel, his large head nodded with every plodding step, and what hair remained upon it was dyed the flat black of chimney soot. He was tall and painfully thin, his distended belly, stooped shoulders, and long neck giving him the look of a tired but angry rooster. His face, jaundiced by opium, was beset by moles that dotted his sunken cheeks like beetles. Only his eyes, almost hidden by sagging lids, still shifted as cunningly as ever.

Most prominent in his efforts to remain young and to keep face in the village was his commissioning of a set of perfect teeth from Hong Kong, which kept him forever smiling within an elder community of rotted stumps and shrunken gums, shining proof of his good fortune.

"There are too many women in my house, yet I am cursed with another," he said aloud for the ducks to hear, lighting a cigarette, drawing hard on the acrid smoke with a deep hiss of relish. How unfairly this moment brought back unwanted memories, clear as painted pictures before his eyes. Memories of his first daughter, the one he had kept to serve her brothers, until one bitter winter's day when a party of soldiers sent by the local warlord to gather taxes had ridden across his fields with banners streaming. Times were hard, and Yik-Munn had nothing to pay them and little to offer in the way of food. They had beaten him and

13

ordered him to catch the doves in his barn, then cook them with the last of his winter rice and bring them to the camp on the riverbank. They had taken his daughter, then ten years old, for their amusement, and as his wife prepared the doves, they could hear her screams, like the cry of a curlew on the wind. She had died a week later. He sighed; such were the problems of a girl child.

The bent figure of the midwife scuttled like a spider from the house, the pot containing the placenta—the only payment required for her services. She would sell it in the village to fortify the old ones who needed to digest the essence of the newly born. From the rice store, a tumble-down shed beneath a peppercorn tree, he took the big iron hoe to which he owed all things and waded knee-deep into the field of ripening mustard. He stopped, gazing out across his fields of fennel, hemlock parsley, angelica, chili, and garlic. In their midst was a snow-white field of flowering ginger; closer to the house, a silver sea of foxtail millet beside the rice paddies. The wide hats of his sons and grandsons were dotted among them, his sons' wives stooped along the rice terraces.

How hard he had worked to make all this possible, yet how little his efforts were appreciated. Why had the gods betrayed him? Had he not kowtowed at the feet of Kuan-Yin, the goddess of mercy, and laid gold leaf on the knee of the Buddha? What had he done to displease them so? He dropped the hoe, and proclaimed his misery to unfriendly skies: "Bad rice . . . Bad rice. My fields are bare and my family is hungry. My buffalo no longer pulls the broken plow and pestilence descends upon my crops." He wrung his hands.

"I am a poor man, my harvest is dust, and I cannot fill the rice bowls of my hungry family. Why have you sent me a girl—one who will cost much and return nothing but sons to another clan?"

The bundle under his arm squirmed and kicked; a muffled cry told him that it still lived. He had wrapped it tight as Pai-Ling fought him like a wildcat. She had clawed so hard to save her baby that the wives would not enter the room, afraid of one as possessed as she. He had struck her hard across the face, flung her to the floor, and locked her in. Even now he heard her shouts from the open window of the upper floor, beseeching all gods to save her child. He felt the pain of fresh scratches welling on his face and neck as he waded farther into the field to escape her wailing, cursing the day he had traveled to Shanghai.

When the soil underfoot was soft to his heel and far enough from the house, Yik-Munn dropped the bundle, unnerved by this puny life he had hoped to stifle without the striking of a blow—this uncanny will that jerked and twitched like a silkworm shedding its cocoon. This would be the fifth female baby he had buried in the thirty years since he first acquired the land, sleeping beneath the stars with his hoe as a pillow to guard it from thieves.

The first he had drowned in the rice paddy, but her tiny bones had been unearthed with the spring planting, to be fought over by squabbling ducks. That could bring bad luck, but here in the middle of the mustard field, he could dig deep. He spat on the callused palms of his hands. A dozen times, the broad iron blade bit into yielding earth.

Pai-Ling sprawled exhausted where she had fallen beside the bed. She heard the distant thud of iron digging deeply into sodden earth, striking fragments of shale with great force. The thuds grew louder, reaching through the open shutters. She struggled to her feet in frantic haste, dragging herself upright to stare in terror from the window.

The sound was louder, joining the smell of newly turned sod and the sickly stench of night soil. She saw Yik-Munn, waist deep in the middle of the mustard field, swinging the broad, blunt blade of the hoe again and again. The scream that started in the pit of her belly escaped in a howl of despair so far-reaching it lifted the doves from the barn rafters and echoed through the house. Even Goo-Mah, who was hard of hearing, clucked her tongue in annoyance, rapping the wall with her stick at the violent disturbance.

In the kitchen, wives One and Two did not raise their eyes from their needlework, but Three was jerked to her feet by the wail of torment from the floor above.

"Do not interfere," One said quietly, without missing a stitch. Two could only nod her agreement, equally engrossed in the shaping of a peony. Three's hesitation lasted no more than a second before she rushed up the stairs. She thumped the locked door, calling Pai-Ling's name until, with a frightening suddenness, the terrible cries were stopped.

It took only moments for the narrow trench to be deep enough. Yik-Munn straightened; he was no longer young and was unaccustomed to such labors. He lifted the wine gourd to his lips, spilling the last of it into his mouth. Would he need to use the hoe to end this unearthly squirming? He would wait a little longer for the swaddling cloth to do its work. Moments passed; the bundle no longer moved and was silent.

Yik-Munn looked around. He had no sense of guilt; his neighbors had done the same as he must now do to ensure the prosperity of the family. He dropped the empty wine gourd, looped around his waist with a tasseled cord, to wipe the back of his hand across his eyes and gob his bitterness into the reeking earth.

Through eyes blurred by unaccustomed sweat, he saw the slightest movement, a sudden swirling of yellow flower heads and a drift of pollen. It was the head of a fox—white as a ghost, ears pointed and alert, eyes the color of milky jade, its slender snout feeling the air like a delicate finger. A bolt of terror transfixed Yik-Munn, his eyes commanded by those of the ghostly beast. Then, as suddenly, it was gone, the wake of its passing swept over by a restless breeze.

Sweat broke like a fever to prick his neck with fright. That this was a fox fairy come to claim the life he was about to end was as certain to him as the heartbeat that pounded to the rush of his blood. Trembling, he dropped to his knees, snatching at the cloth with frantic fingers, desperately loosening the tight folds that bound the infant's head.

The tiny face was twisted and turning blue. Finally, bubbles of air emerged as a breath was sucked in and a juddering cry escaped the daughter of Yik-Munn. At that same moment, with a final howl of torment that spiraled through the twisted branches of the pine, her mother leaped from the window with wide-open arms.

CHAPTER 1

The Fox Fairy

A *year later, all* thoughts of fox fairies had faded in the minds of Yik-Munn and his wives. He did not doubt that this was what had visited him in the mustard field. If the girl child had died, the fox would have entered its body and haunted those responsible to their graves and beyond.

But Yik-Munn had gone quickly to the temple and paid the abbot to exorcise bad spirits and to purify his house with due ceremony and with no expenses spared. The priests had come in scarlet robes and black caps to sprinkle chicken blood on the doorposts and hang the Pa-Kua mirror, so that unwanted spirits would be driven away by their own ghastly reflections.

The Lion of Purification had pranced from room to room with choking censers of burning ash, and much banging of drums and clashing of cymbals. Ropes of firecrackers exploded among the peppercorn trees and outside every door with a din that the deepest pits of the underworld could not ignore. The Lions had collected a generous *lai-see*, the fat red packets of lucky money offered with much ceremony to their gaping jaws, and the temple had accepted a donation to the deity that would cause the gods to smile as one.

All was well, the priests assured Yik-Munn. The fox had passed on too quickly to have entered the child's body, and the child had survived. The fox fairy lived only in sepulchers, graveyards, and untended tombs. They were no friend of the living, yet companions of the dead, with the power to become a woman of great beauty to seduce an unsuspecting man.

But the prosperous and lordly Yik-Munn, the fortune-teller announced for all to hear, was still young at heart with the strength of the wild horse—one with great face for whom prayers were regularly said at the temple. He was assured that the female he had sired would bring much to him in return for his compassion. If her hands were small enough and her fingers fast, the silk-weaving factory of Ten Willows might take her. If her hands were too large and her fingers short and strong, she could be sent north to the Yangtze Valley to pick oranges and peaches, apricots and jujube; or downriver to Canton, Macao, or Hong Kong, to be sold to a rich Chinese or Parsee merchant—even to the household of a foreign devil. The prospects of profit for such a girl, Yik-Munn told himself, were many and varied. He was greatly relieved by such propitious omens. He had told his women to feed the child and keep her in an outbuilding.

That Pai-Ling the concubine had accidentally fallen from the window and to her death upon the iron spikes of a harrow was certainly a misfortune, but could not be blamed upon the innocent. He had beaten Number Three for creating such a fuss about it. She also had to be locked away while his sons pulled the concubine's body from the rusty tines that had pierced her body. Waiting until nightfall to see her buried in the ginger field, he had left it to them to wrap her in a suitable shroud and choose a spot unknown to him, where the earth was soft and the grave could be deep. It would cause less trouble for his family if she were disposed of without great ceremony. Otherwise, the story that the House of Munn had been host to a fox fairy and that demons roamed the fields of Great Pine Farm would spread like locusts along the length and breadth of the river.

⛭

Number One and Number Two hated the child. They did not believe the priest or the fortune-teller, thinking them liars who said what they were paid to say. From the moment she could stand, the daughter of Pai-Ling sought the open fields, leaving the house when eyes were turned the other way to hide among the mustard plants, straying ever farther to the edge of the ginger field, crouching silent as a toad on the rich earth while they shouted her name.

Number Three, the youngest of the wives by perhaps ten years, found it hard to forget the death of the unhappy concubine. She had watched the single lantern weaving like a firefly through the fields, to bury Pai-Ling in the ginger field, but she never spoke of it. Nor did she listen to the frightened jabber of those about her.

"She is beckoned by her demon mother," Number Two wailed, afraid of her own shadow. "She tries to lead us away from the house. She cavorts with imps and specters."

"Nonsense," grunted Number One, who feared old age and poverty far more than the presence of unfriendly ghosts. "She is no more than a stupid and willful child who needs to be taught her place. I will find her and beat her till she is afraid to open her eyes."

This she had done when the child went missing one day, dragging the girl from the ginger field through the tangled roots of the mustard field, and locking her in the rice shed. But fear of the fox fairy could not be denied. The child was fed because Yik-Munn demanded it, but the sniveling of Number Two could not be stopped, and the accusing silence of Number Three threatened his peace of mind. The harmony of his household was torn apart. He could not deny that his life had changed for the worse since the concubine had fallen from the window. His face was threatened in the teahouse, where he could no longer boast of owning a concubine with lotus feet who was young enough to be his grand-daughter.

When he could stand no more, he found respite in the warm embrace of the opium pipe prepared by his mistress in the village. But when his winter barley failed and disease broke out among his livestock, Number One went on her knees to her husband's sister, convincing her that this misfortune would ruin them all if the child remained beneath their roof. The great Goo-Mah was an expert on all things of the spirit world. She burned a large bundle of joss sticks to Chang-Hsien, the god of children, and spoke to him of the trouble that had befallen the House of Munn. The result, she claimed, was absolute. "The earthly chi, the life-force of the mother, has entered the child and sought revenge. The child must not spend another night beneath the roof of Great Pine Farm," Goo-Mah announced in a voice that caused Number Two to take to her bed and hide beneath the covers. "The child must be taken to the baby tower outside the village of Ten Willows before another sun has set and left for the wild dogs and the ravens. Chang-Hsien has spoken."

The women watched from the courtyard and the dowager from her window as Yik-Munn laid the sleeping child in a basket and onto the cart and led the donkey out through the paddies to the road. No one spoke of the baby tower that was a mile outside the silk-weaving community of Ten Willows. It was visited only in the dead of night, by those too desperately poor to raise an infant or cursed with an imperfect child.

An hour passed before Yik-Munn saw the ghastly shape of the tower etched against a restless sky, leaning into the night wind, its walls of barren stone harshly scraped by moonlight. The slow journey had given him time to think, to search the corners of his mind with each jolting moment. He stopped at the wayside shrine that marked a milestone to the baby tower, placed there for the offering of final prayers or, for those who may relent, a final chance to turn away. There he burned the painted effigy of a girl child riding the back of a white crane, to give it safe passage to oblivion. Flaming fragments were whisked away by the wind as he continued to the tower, stopping the cart outside the jagged stone gate.

He left the cart on the road and approached the baby tower on foot. It was not without fear that he walked toward this sad and lonely place. It was believed that the spirits of the tiny bodies left there were doomed to forever inhabit the hard stone ledges and alcoves, searching the night sky for their lost souls, the homes they never had, the lives they were denied, returning to the tower as owls return to their nests.

In his arms, the child slept soundly from the glob of opium paste he had fingered into her mouth. In a pot in his pocket he carried more, enough to make her sleep forever. Dark scuttling reached him, rats over fragile bones, a dry rustling of bat wings from a gaping roof open to the sky. Ragged shreds of cloud, driven by wind that moaned through the tower like a hymn, drew apart to reveal a cold, bright moon, round as a newly minted coin.

Rotting tentacles of death reached out to meet Yik-Munn and then, in the sudden blaze of moonlight, a ghostly apparition of the fox, pale and silent, emerged to watch him, its glowing eyes searching the hollow of his heart.

Begging forgiveness in a quailing voice he didn't recognize as his own, Yik-Munn stumbled back to the cart, mumbling prayers for deliverance. He placed the sleeping child under the seat and whipped the donkey into a lather to reach his home alive. There he beat his wives mercilessly, turning a deaf ear to the ranting of his sister, and, with hands that trembled, made himself a pipe, seeking urgent sanctuary in the fragrant realms of paradise.

At sunrise he was at the temple gates with a generous donation. Many times the bamboo slivers were spilled before the altar, and the great table of stars was scrutinized minutely for many hours. That Yik-Munn had again chosen wisely was confirmed by Kuan-Yin herself, who had blessed him and his household.

The girl child was probably possessed by a vixen spirit, but a benevolent one, which would bring great prosperity to the House of Munn. She would grow to be even more beautiful than her mother and would fetch a high price from a rich taipan when sold at the age of eight years. Yik-Munn did not mention the prophesy of Chang-Hsein, knowing full well that his sister frequently spoke to patron saints who said exactly what she wanted them to say.

So it was settled. Having heard everything he could have wished to hear, Yik-Munn gave the little fox fairy the name of Li-Xia (Lee Shee-ah), "Beautiful One." As soon as she was old enough, his wives would give her work so that she could earn her rice. With his confidence restored, he gained a new vigor to his step and his splendid teeth gleamed all the brighter among those who envied Yik-Munn, the merchant of fine spices.

The rice shed Li-Xia was allowed to occupy was close to the kitchen. It was home to many spiders, their webs thick in every corner. But it was quiet and she was alone, making a place that was her own beneath the single window, sweeping it clean. She rubbed the dirty glass until it let in a stream of light that fell upon the rice bins and sacks of dried mushrooms.

Only two things frightened her, and she tried not to look at them: two glass jars, big as washtubs, set high on a shelf, reflecting the light from the window. They contained Yik-Munn's special wine, the wives had told her, and must not be touched. One was Hundred Snake Wine: Coiled inside the jar, in a tangle of yellow, black, and green, were one hundred deadly snakes, steeped in clear liquor, the black beads of their eyes still angry. The other jar held Hundred Mice Wine: in a mass of palest pink, floating in the liquid they were drowned in, were one hundred unborn mice, their eyes unopened.

Each week, Number-One Wife came to the rice shed with a ladle and a pitcher, which she filled with the clear fluid. This was the wife Li-Xia feared the most, always quick to slap her. Each time Number One filled the pitcher, she made the same threat: "Do not touch this wine and do not make me angry, or *you* shall be put in a jar—we will call it Fox Fairy Wine." She would laugh at her cleverness and leave Li-Xia alone to think about it.

When the door had closed with a rattle of the latch and the mutterings of Number One were lost to the carping of ducks, Li-Xia would lie down and watch the diamond specks of dust that floated in the patch of light from the window. She had stuck bunches of wildflowers and leafy twigs into tin cups and containers of every kind to form a screen to block the hideous wine jars from her sight. But she imagined she could hear the rustle of a hundred snakes winding their way across the floor, and the squeaking of a hundred mice scampering toward her. She dreamed that she too was stuffed into a jar, Number One pressing her head down into the bittersweet liquid, laughing at her through the thick glass wall of her tiny prison.

Then Li-Xia found the treasure that would one day change her life. In a dark corner, hidden beneath a pile of empty sacks, she uncovered a broken wooden box filled with scrolls and wads of musty paper of all shapes and sizes, each covered with strokes and squiggles, lines and curves of the calligrapher's hand. She had taken each piece and smoothed it flat, blowing away the dust and scraping off the marks of cockroaches with her fingernail. By the silver light of a moon that sometimes kept her company, driving back the threatening shadows, she studied every page and wished so much that she could read.

The characters were shaped so beautifully, displayed before her in such neat rows, splendid in their mystery. She wanted to understand them, to let them take her to places she could never go, to learn the wisdom of scholars she would never meet. To read and understand would be the greatest of all wonders.

CHAPTER 2

The Happiness Tile

The *fifth birthday of* Li-Xia arrived without further incident. No fox had been seen in the spice fields, and even Goo-Mah had little more to say. Li-Xia was unusually tall for a girl of her age, and obviously strong. Her child's limbs were long and awkward, her long hair thick and shiny as black silk. Her large round eyes were tilted to give them a look of wonder, as though everything she looked upon was made of shining gold.

It had reached Yik-Munn's ears from the kitchen that the child had asked Number-Three Wife to teach her to read for her birthday. Had she been a boy, the gift on reaching the age of five—when a child becomes of value—would have been a miniature silver abacus so that he might be good in business, or a gold chicken leg so that he might one day own a restaurant. For a girl it was a simple plaything, for she would have no need of knowledge. As was the custom in his district, he would not accept a daughter as part of his family, acknowledging only his sons.

Only a mother might value a daughter and teach her to cook and to sew, Yik-Munn said to himself, to train her to help in the kitchen and serve the family. There was no such chance for this one, but she would soon know her place. Teach her to read? Where could she have gotten such a thought but through the demon spirit of her mother?

That the concubine, Pai-Ling, had died in such a violent way no longer disturbed him. She had clearly been mad, but the priests were right; already the child's luck was blessed. The fox spirit had saved her twice—

once from being buried alive in the mustard field and again at the baby tower.

At this moment a comforting light descended upon him, as though the gods had reached down to touch his head. *Lotus feet*. He would give his daughter the dainty feet of a courtesan. It would make her future shine. He smiled to himself. And it would stop her from running away.

❊

Yik-Munn had Li-Xia brought before him, and peered down upon her as he would a fattened piglet. He received her in the room where important business was conducted with all the time-honored rituals of the spice trade; where weight, quality, and price were debated over much drinking of hot rice wine and munching of small chow.

Fans hanging from the high ceilings beat the musty air in broad, soundless sweeps. Rows of chests, great cabinets, and small drawers covered the floor and lined the walls, each filled with the costly herbs and spices that had made Yik-Munn rich. Ground and powdered, shredded and chopped, some were displayed in special jars or open bins, others kept in darkness, too delicate to be exposed to light. Aromatic samples were passed around with much sniffing and tasting from tiny silver spoons, as carefully examined for quality as any collection of precious stones.

He sat in a grand chair, its arms and legs and wide back carved with peaches and pomegranates, the fruits of longevity. In this chair Yik-Munn felt like an emperor. His large slippered feet rested on a single step that elevated the occupant of this magnificent chair at least a head higher than those who sat before him. A robe of kingfisher blue reached from his neck to his white-stockinged ankles. His knees wide apart, a hand planted firmly on each, he attempted a smile, his perfect teeth white as a china cup.

Yik-Munn kept his daughter standing, her head no higher than his bent knee.

25

Females were not allowed in this room except to serve food and drink. The lingering odors of grand banquets mixed with the earthy smells of nutmeg, cloves, and cinnamon. The fox fairy had never been so close to Yik-Munn, and was not quite sure who he was until this moment.

"I am your father. You are five years old today, old enough for me to tell you of your place in my household. You are a girl, but I have decided to fill your bowl for three more years. On your eighth birthday, you will go to stay with a great-uncle upriver and learn the silk trade." He took a tiny bottle from his sleeve, tapped snuff on the back of his hand, and sniffed hard, pinching his nose. "The few coins that I will get for you will never recover your debt to me. You will repay me with your respect and obedience. If you cause no further trouble in this house, you will not be beaten, but you will earn your rice." He reached into the sleeve of his robe and held out a flat, square package. "I have something for you." Li-Xia took it from him with a bow so low she almost fell at his feet.

"You will repay me with your obedience and respect, but take great care; it is costly and not to be broken." She took it carefully from its red paper wrapping, uncovering a colored tile with a single Chinese word upon it, hard and cold but quite pretty. Li-Xia studied it, tracing the shiny character with her fingertips, turning it over in her hands. It was the first gift she had ever received.

"It is a very nice tile, and I like it very much. But I cannot read it."

'The word says 'happiness.' Now take it and be happy. Do not make me or your gracious aunties angry."

"But I cannot read it for myself. Will you teach me to read?" The words tripped from her tongue before she could stop them.

Yik-Munn scowled darkly. She felt her smile snatched away as the happiness tile fell from her fingers and shattered loudly into many pieces on the hard stone floor. The sound of it smashing seemed to echo through the room and beyond its open windows. It seemed to Li-Xia as though the ground shook beneath her feet. Her father shot to his feet quickly, tall as a giant. His voice was loud with anger and shock.

You see? Even the gods are ashamed of you. They have struck the hap-

26

piness tile from your hand. You are a useless girl, a disappointment to me and to the ancestors. You must know your place in this house and in the world. Do not try to rise above it. Books are no business of yours.

These were the words that rang out within him. His arm twitched with the will to strike her, his teeth clenched as he looked down upon her with evident disgust. Instead, he thought before he spoke. Perhaps it was best, he told himself, to make a promise he knew he would never keep. He had found this to be useful when keeping a female in her place—to keep her never quite sure but always hopeful.

"Perhaps one day, when you are a little older, we may speak of it," he said in an easier voice. "But first I have another gift for you—one far greater than the greatest book or the reading of words written by others. A gift that will turn you into a princess. I have decided to give you the feet of the golden lotus, as small and as beautiful as your mother's."

He spread his arms wide, the sleeves of his robe spread like the wings of a peacock. For less than a heartbeat, Li-Xia thought he would descend from his throne and reach for her. But he did not.

Li-Xia looked puzzled. *Has this child no gratitude?* He cupped his hands as though they cradled something very fragile but very, very precious.

When she continued to show no understanding, he waved a hand to dismiss her. "Go now. Perhaps one day, if you are respectful and never run away—if you obey me and your gracious aunties in all things—then perhaps you will be taught to read . . . even to write and count the beads of business."

When she was gone, Yik-Munn sat back in his chair, reaching with an unsteady hand for the long-stemmed pipe carved from pig bone that rested on the table at his elbow. The tile, it seemed to him, had struck the floor with a force beyond the strength of a five-year-old child. He shook his head to clear the sound still ringing in his ears, forcing unwanted thoughts from his mind. From a pot no bigger than an eggcup he speared a small black bead on the tip of an ivory toothpick, fitting it carefully into the pipe's tiny bowl.

Moments later his nerves were calmed, as thick blue smoke curled from his nostrils. He had always considered lotus feet among the most enchanting charms a female could possess. Cheated of such delights by Number Four, he would give them to her child. It would increase her value a hundredfold.

His elder sister would be pleased to hear of his decision—she had first recommended Pai-Ling because she was known to wear the lotus slippers and would bring much-needed dignity to this family of clodhoppers.

He knew the process could take three years or longer to complete, but if the gods were with him, the lotus feet would be perfect—no more than three inches long—by her eighth birthday. They would be truly beautiful, ready to be unbound for the lucky hands of the silk merchant Ming-Chou.

But what if something went wrong in the process? Li-Xia would suffer greatly, with nothing to be done. She might even die, as one in ten did. Sometimes the feet became infected, and some lost toes or feet altogether—but it was well worth the risk. Lotus feet were a sound investment. Any female who had them would be no bother; her father, her husband, and then their sons would have complete control. The pain of walking more than a few short steps would always keep her close.

Yes, Li-Xia would have feet to dance upon the golden lotus, which would make up for the high price he had paid for her worthless mother. It was settled. That some said foot binding was forbidden did not concern him; such laws were made for those who lived in crowded cities and not for simple tillers of the soil.

⁂

The next day Yik-Munn opened the creaking door of the rice shed, the bright sun upon his back, his wives behind him carrying the things that they would need—bandages, a clay container filled with herbs, and a terra-cotta stove.

"Just as I promised, your aunties will make you as beautiful as any princess. You must be still for them and then perhaps I will let Number-Three Auntie teach you to read." He turned away and was quickly gone, along with his promise.

She tried to hide when they came to wash her feet, darting from one pile of sacks to another and squeezing into dark and tiny places, calling loudly for her mother as they chased her as if she were a chicken ready for the pot. When she was finally caught and held, her feet thrust into the container of scalding herbs and grasped by the ankles, her screams drove the sparrows from the peppercorn tree: "Mah-Mah, Mah-Mahhhhh."

"Your mother cannot hear you. She is lost in the wind."

Number One's voice rose high above the others as she slapped her hard across the cheek. Number Two honked like a goose as Li-Xia kicked against their grabbing hands, upsetting the clay pot and splashing the hot brown muck into their angry faces. An hour later, despite her struggles, the first bandages had been wound about her shins, binding her feet so tightly against a wooden paddle that her cries of pain caused the wives to cover their ears. They tied the bandages with secret knots, hard to find and thought to be impossible to remove except by the hands that bound them. The wives of Yik-Munn banged the door shut on grating hinges, sliding the big iron bolt on the outside.

They prayed to have this irksome business done with, yet knew too well it was just beginning. The bandaging of the fox fairy's feet would continue for many months, until the supple bones were slowly bent or snapped, sinew and ligament drawn together ever tighter, until with infinite patience the heel would touch the toe and the bones would re-set themselves to remain forever . . . *such pretty golden lotus feet.*

The torments of the process were well known to the three wives of Yik-Munn. This was not discussed; only the great benefits were considered. Lotus feet gave much pleasure and face to the lucky man who fondled them; the erotic tilt to his woman's stance, the enticement of her tiny steps were pleasing to his eye and to those who envied him. Such a woman could be proud of this enhancement to her beauty in the interests of the man who possessed her. The saying "Lotus feet are lucky feet" was widely believed by those who did not have them.

For the first weeks Li-Xia was bound and gagged, released only to eat and wash and use the chamber pot. Both Number-One Wife and the great Goo-Mah loudly agreed; if she was not tamed and taught her place, all manner of disasters could beset the household.

They dared not let the girl die, to be haunted by her vengeful spirit—or face the wrath of Yik-Munn, so determined to sell her at the highest possible price. He had already been to see the wealthy silk merchant Ming-Chou, a prefect of Kwangtung province and a very important man. Half the price in silver had already been paid, and the family Munn would forever lose face if she were not delivered on her eighth birthday as pure and beautiful as promised.

Still unnerved by the destruction of the happiness tile, Yik-Munn had not been to see Li-Xia since the foot binding began. He had to admit that he was disturbed by the child's presence. Leaving her to the women, he spent his time listening to gossip in the village teahouse, walking his caged songbirds in the public park, playing checkers, or pushing hands in the way of tai chi chuan with old friends. His afternoon pipe became more frequent, and more hours were spent chasing the dragon than ever before. Often he stayed the night in the house of his mistress, who showed such compassion and understanding of his many difficulties, always waiting with tonic wine and his favorite pickles.

But nothing freed him from the spell the fox fairy had cast upon him. He played mah-jongg but lost heavily, and there was nothing his mistress could do to revive his passions. The women began to fear for his mind. So sure was he that unfriendly spirits were abroad on Great Pine, he left the running of the farm to his sons and control of the demon child to his wives. To escape their poisoned tongues, he went to live with his brother until he could be rid of this injustice forever.

CHAPTER 3

Lotus Feet

When the wives came to throw open the door and let in the light, Li-Xia was prepared for them and began squealing as soon as she heard the rattle of the latch, her squeal so loud and shrill it hurt her own ears. She quickly learned to flex her toes inside the binding, to use all her strength against the hands that held her—to fight so hard that they were careless, eager to be done with her. When they slammed the door behind them, she relaxed her feet inside their cruel trap, moving her toes slightly but constantly until they tingled.

Alone in the shed, with the patience of a spider spinning its web, Li-Xia had learned to free her hands and pick at the foot bindings to find their secret. After endless nights she had figured out how to unwind them and rub her feet until the blood returned and the pain eased, then to test them on the floor. This way she could find some sleep. When the first cock crowed, she bound them again but not so tightly.

The wives came only once a week to remove the bindings. They had learned to let the mixture in the herb pot cool a little and were less rough in their handling of her. Li-Xia pretended not to fear them, kicking and crying less, each time asking the same questions.

"Where is my mother?" And every time, Number Three would say the same thing: "She is at rest in the ginger field. You must try to forget her."

"Nonsense." Number One would snort impatiently. "Your mother seeks her lost ancestors. The gods do not see her, just as they will not see you because you are her daughter."

"Where do the gods and the ancestors live?"

"In the spirit room," Number Two would reply as sharply as she could.

Wives One and Two felt little guilt over the terrible death of Li-Xia's mother. There was nothing they could have done to prevent it; the door to her room had been locked by Yik-Munn himself and only he held the key.

Of the three wives, Number Three was the kindest. It was a kindness more felt than shown, a silent pact that built with every visit, so strong between them that Li-Xia began to lose her dread of pain. The throwing open of the door—the gush of air and the blaze of light and sound—became less terrifying. It was clear by the touch and looks of Number Three that she knew the bandages had been loosened, but she spoke no word and made no sign to show it.

She had a name that was never used. Like any respectable man of substance, Yik-Munn referred to his wives by numbers, as he did his many sons. She was from a faraway place and looked different from the other wives. She did not have the broad, flat features of the Hakka peasant, but a smoother brow and a rounder chin and a strong mouth that almost never smiled.

Number Three had been the first to speak to Li-Xia without anger, and had whispered the secret of her name when she came to fill a basket with dried mushrooms.

"My name is Ah-Su. I am from the island of Hainan. Never call my name or speak of it, but keep it in your heart and know that I do not hurt you more than I must. I will help you."

When she had gone, Li-Xia whispered Ah-Su's name many times, then hid it away among the special secrets of her heart.

She found strength in the secrecy and the silence of her solitude. She remembered the cold wet feel of the mustard field beneath her toes and how butterflies had drifted from the ginger blossom at her passing. Soon she could pass through the curtain of pain into the perfumed shroud of white, where she could see her mother cloaked in silver by the moon. Sometimes, as she drifted into sleep, she heard a comforting voice that

32

pushed back the shadows: *You are not alone. Ah-Su is my friend and will watch over you if she can. She will not let them take away your right to walk alone. Without your precious feet, you will always belong to others and never journey through life on your own.*

My heart beats with your heart. Your pain is my pain and your happiness will always be my happiness. We will journey together and share all things.

Although this comfort came only in thoughts and dreams, Li-Xia found herself believing that one day her mother would open the door to take her by the hand. Together they would run far away from Yik-Munn and his wives and the great pine that towered like a watchful giant.

Sometimes, when other eyes were turned away, Number Three would kiss Li-Xia lightly on the head, or squeeze her hand with a swiftly stolen smile. Their secret passed between them like a precious coin, hidden in the palm of her tightly closed fist, glimpsed and then gone but firmly held.

It was Ah-Su who wound the bandages, pushing a finger down so that they were not bound quite as tightly when she pulled it out. She would do this while joining the impatient chatter of the other wives.

"Stay still. You wriggle like a worm under the hoe. A fat hen ready for market could not squawk so loudly. It will be easier if you stay still and keep quiet." It became clear that Number Three could manage Li-Xia with very little fuss. One and Two would stand aside, leaving her to deal with the little demon alone, until after a while they did not even wait until the binding was finished to leave; it had all become too irksome.

One day, Ah-Su opened the shed door quietly and alone in the very early morning. Through the open door the fields were thickly layered with mist, the ducks were still silent, and the cockerels had not yet crowed. She brought warm goat's milk and a pickled hundred-year egg with a steamed bun filled with minced pork. Under her arm she carried a large bundle of rolled-up clothing fastened with a strap.

"These things belong to your mother. You must keep them safe. Hide them well, but if they are found, tell no one that it was I who gave them to you or I will not be allowed to see you."

Ah-Su knelt and held Li-Xia's face in her gentle hands.

"Her name is Pai-Ling. She comes from Shanghai and is very clever—a great scholar who studied the moon and learned to read the secrets of the stars. In this bundle you will find books and papers that she has written and drawings she has made with her own hand. But she has lotus feet, and that is why she cannot come to you. Perhaps she hides somewhere in the ginger field; it is a beautiful place, always fragrant and ever peaceful. She wears a gown of white and breathes the sweetness of ginger blossoms. You need not be sad."

"Will I find her there?"

Ah-Su lowered her eyes and shook her head.

"I don't know. Perhaps she will stay there forever; perhaps sometimes she will visit her mother the moon, but she is very brave and very happy. She has told me that you are as precious to her as a thousand pieces of gold, and that you must always remember this and be strong, as she is strong."

"Number-One Auntie says she is sometimes in the spirit room—the place where all ancestors gather, behind the big wooden door. Will I find her there?"

Ah-Su smiled sadly and placed her arm around Li-Xia's shoulders as she sought an answer.

"Perhaps sometimes she may be summoned there. It is better you do not seek her; just know she watches over you."

Then Ah-Su was gone and the door closed before more could be said.

Li-Xia removed the strap, unrolling the clothing to find many paper pages stitched together into books hidden inside. They were more carefully wrapped in a robe of fine yellow silk. She unfolded the other garments one by one. They were not pretty clothes—brown, dark green, or black, the colors of unhappiness. She could smell traces of her mother—an elusive hint of rosemary oil and powdered spice. She buried her face in each garment, imagining her mother's skin in the heat of summer and bitten by winter winds. But the soft yellow silk in their center nestled like a secret heart, stronger and happier than its drab surroundings, and its scent was of jonquils in springtime.

She held it close, until through her sadness the calming voice told her not to cry, but to be strong and make her ancestors proud. As if to confirm her mother's nearness, something dropped from the folds of silk to glow like a jewel in her lap.

Light from the window fell upon a finger jade of great beauty—milky white with streaks of orange. No bigger than the smallest mouse, it was carved in the shape of a moon bear. Years of contact with her mother's hand had made it silken smooth and a pleasure to touch.

Her joy at the unexpected gift made her search more thoroughly for other hidden treasures. Eagerly, patiently, she felt among the folds of a padded jacket and discovered something hard and square stitched deep in its lining. She unpicked the stitches, revealing a small book, its many pages covered with the strokes and circles, dashes and dots, squiggles and squares of Chinese writing; row after row, each character so small and perfect it made a tiny picture of its own.

It was the most wonderful thing she had ever seen.

✳

After endless days and nights measured by light through the window, Li-Xia could rub her feet and stand up, until enough circulation had returned for her to take a step, and then another, and another. Each night she walked a little farther, first only one length of her bed space, then twice and three times, until she could walk around it ten times . . . then twenty times . . . and, with great patience, one hundred times.

She hid the bundle in a secret place where the wives would have to search to find it. There was little chance of this; they were so anxious to leave her each time, they did not look around, nor did they notice that the fox fairy's feet were not as deformed as they should be. Believing their charge was not able to stand and certainly not to walk—and if she crawled, where could she go?—they no longer bothered to lock the door.

When Li-Xia could walk around her room many times, she unlatched the door, stepped into the night, and, quietly as a fox, entered the darkened kitchen. Crossing the stone floor, the flagstones cold beneath her bare feet, she walked through the passageway that led to the spirit room, until she stood before its great wooden door. This was the place she had heard was occupied by the gods, and where the ancestors dwelled. A fearsome door guardian on either side stared down at her, daring her to enter uninvited.

She did not look at them as, in breathless silence, she lifted the heavy latch and opened the door just wide enough to slip inside. A single red candle burned in a pool of wax upon the altar. "Mah-Mah," she whispered, and waited. When the shadows did not answer, she called again, a little louder, "Mah-Mah . . . Mah-Mah . . . are you in here?"

Trapped smoke made her want to cough and blurred her vision. She rubbed her eyes, and as if by magic, the gods appeared before her in the dull red light from coils of joss sticks burning overhead. First she saw Kuan-Yin, the beautiful goddess of mercy, clasping the vase of compassion, her feet upon a lotus flower. Around her were the eight immortals, fearless guardians of her realm. They glowered at Li-Xia with bulging eyes and bared teeth.

She could see that they were made of wood and painted many colors beneath their coats of sooty dust. The corners were empty, but in the flickering light, stern faces of people long dead looked down at her.

As her eyes became adjusted to the light, they fell upon something more—items of great beauty and in all the colors of the rainbow: a mansion house, a beautiful carriage, many servants, and stacks of paper money. These were the things that were sent to heaven with special prayers to comfort those who had gone away.

First, she took the paper money and the red candle and, with a prayer heard only by herself, burned the heaven banknotes one by one. When they were gone in a tree of sparks, she set fire to the mansion, stepping back from its blaze to watch the paper walls and windows flare and crumble into ash. Onto this she added the carriage, and then the ser-

36

vants, one by one. When the last black crisp had settled in the censer and she was sure no one lived in the spirit room, she blew out the candle and quietly left the sleeping house . . . out through the passageway, to where the mustard field was white with rising mist.

The earth was cold and wet. Her toes squished deliciously in the mud, and she wriggled them for many moments, then started to walk. There was only one purpose to her journey—to place one foot before the other, taking her away from the dark room and the smell of incense and the gods that could not see her, did not hear her, and would not tell her where her mother was. And from the women who brought her cold rice and hurt her feet.

Yik-Munn returned to the farm when he heard of the fox fairy's escape. Sending his sons to search the fields, he entered the spirit room to beg forgiveness for allowing the fox fairy to run away—to find it bare of the offerings he had so prudently set aside for the passing of the great Goo-Mah. He fell to his knees.

It must not be known in the village that the fox fairy was loose and had defied the guardians of the spirit room, or his face would also be as paper, burned to ashes and blown by a thousand winds. A man who could not control his own family was also a man who could not satisfy his mistress or live in his own house without enraging his ancestors. He dared not lose this child and must not beat her as he should. Instead, he beat his wives until they kowtowed for his mercy.

The sons of Yik-Munn trod the furrows, cursing every step until they found her, gone to ground like a fox in the middle of the field.

Having heard of this terrible thing, Goo-Mah had the fox fairy brought before her, mud-caked and shivering.

"You were bad to run from those who feed you. Again, you have made the ancestors angry. You shame the house that gives you shelter, you insult the proud name of this family, and you break the heart of your poor father."

She sat up in her bed, her wig heavy with ornaments, unsteady in her anger.

Li-Xia tried to keep her voice respectful, but felt no regret.

"My mother is not in the spirit room but lost in the ginger field. I must find her."

Goo-Mah flapped her hand as though brushing away a bothersome fly.

"You are an ungrateful little witch. The wives come to bind your feet so that you may one day dance upon the golden lotus—to prosper as I have prospered, to have power as I have power. Do you thank them? You do not; you run from them like a cunning fox."

"Forgive me, Great-Auntie. I do not want a fine gentleman who wants me only for my broken feet. I do not want to be like you. I do not want feet that smell like donkey dung."

Goo-Mah sat forward from her pillows with such a spurt of fury, the heavy wig slipped and fell, rolling to the floor like a severed head. A large brown cockroach, fat with eggs, scuttled from its stiff, matted coils. The gold bracelets and jade bangles clattered on her arms as she tried to salvage her wig, her head as hairless as a newborn bird.

"Take her away!" she shrieked. "Get her out of my sight! To have lotus feet is an honor she no longer deserves. Lock her up and tell my brother to get rid of her. Who knows what this will bring? She is useless as her ungrateful mother, unworthy of this house."

Her screeching followed Yik-Munn's sons as they dragged Li-Xia down the stairs. They did not know that Great-Aunt had choked on her own bile and fallen back in all her finery, her frenzied heart finally stopped like an ancient clock.

When Yik-Munn heard from his frightened wives the news of Goo-Mah's death, the sun burst through the clouds to embrace him with its warmth. He hurried to the spirit room to hug the feet of Kuan-Yin, sobbing his thanks for her great mercy and burning joss sticks as big as bullrushes kept for only the most prestigious of events. He told himself that the life of his elder sister, who had long prayed to join her ancestors, must be the price demanded by the restless spirit that had plagued him since the death of Pai-Ling. That with the passing of the great Goo-Mah came the deed to the farm, a chest full of jewelry he could hardly lift, property she owned in the village, and the sum total of her considerable wealth was proof of his patience and his worthiness as a brother.

Such a large inheritance, however, did not stop him from paying a "loafer"—one who would defy all gods for a handful of coins—to strip the grand coffin of its copper sheath, rifle its carefully hidden treasures and even replace the valuable jade plugs from her various orifices with ones carved hastily from wood.

He looked upon Li-Xia with caution but ordered her to be freed. His heart was not without favor for her role in his sister's blessed departure. He told the wives to feed her well, wash her in hot water before the kitchen fire, make her a new set of clothes, and take her back to the rice shed.

To appease the newly departed spirit, he sent to the village for better paper offerings: a much bigger mansion, a fleet of motorcars, a troop of servants, and a cartload of heaven money to be blessed by the priests and accompany Goo-Mah on her final journey to the afterlife. He also sent for the exorcist to purify the fox fairy and purge the vacated rooms with abundant incense, and for many mourners to receive food and drink, plus a generous *lai-see*.

The following day, the divine being, clad in colorful robes and his official hat, arrived wielding his demon-dispelling sword. A grand feast was prepared to appease the offended ancestors, to be eaten by the family and their holy visitors once it had been offered to the ancestral tablets.

With the last of the roasted pig shared, every bowl empty, and the last rice cake eaten, the ceremony began. Li-Xia had been given an elixir that left her unable to move but conscious of the proceedings carried out around her. With much rattling of the official sword and banging of drums, she was laid upon a hastily erected altar, mystic symbols smeared upon her naked body with the warm blood of a freshly killed cockerel.

Strings of jumping crackers were set off to warn away hungry ghosts eager to pounce upon the crumbs of the living. Incense sticks were burned, together with talismanic inscriptions daubed upon red paper. After many noisy moments of mystic incantation and a great rattling of ritualistic weaponry, the ashes of the talismans were mixed with a cup of pure spring water.

With the cup in his left hand and the all-powerful sword in his right, the exorcist prayed for power: "Gods of heaven and earth, invest me with the healing seal that I may purge this being of all evil that possesses her." He picked up a switch of willow and dipped it into the cup, sprinkling first east, then west, north, and south. To reinforce the spell, he filled his mouth with the magic water and sprayed it over Li-Xia's motionless body. Having banished all malignant spirits properly and eternally to the cellars of the Master of Heaven's palace in far-off Kianghsi, the exorcism was officially and successfully completed.

The divine being then turned his attention to the burial of the great Goo-Mah, accompanying the ravaged coffin to the family burial spot beneath the great pine. This done, the group of professional mourners set up a wailing that could be heard for a mile across the fields, succeeding in rousing the dogs to add their howls of sorrow to this cacophony of lament. This was kept up to the accompaniment of gongs and firecrackers, drums and trumpets, until the divine being accepted his red packet from a tearful Yik-Munn. Then, with a final spray of magic water in the direction of Goo-Mah's grave, he sheathed his demon-dispelling sword. Li-Xia was lifted from the altar, washed clean of chicken blood and ashes, and returned to the rice shed, where she fell into the deepest of sleeps.

Having performed his duty commensurate with Yik-Munn's donation to the temple, the exorcist led the procession on its noisy way back to the village. Yik-Munn did not make it known that in the interests of prudence, he had persuaded the temple to carry out both rituals for the price of one.

⚜

A week later, the fox fairy disappeared for two days and was found even farther from the house. She had crossed the sea of silver millet and the

40

mustard field, leaped the irrigation ditch, and followed the river until her feet were sore and bleeding, but she felt no pain and would have walked for a thousand miles if they had not caught her. This time her brothers did not beat her and their curses were mild. Though they did not say so, they were wary of powers that even the exorcist seemed unable to appease, and could not deny the courage and determination of one so young. She was allowed to walk back unrestrained, and treated with caution on her return.

So troubled was Yik-Munn by the failure of the costly ceremony and the child's continued defiance, he decided her resistance must be sanctioned by powers from above and must be respected more than punished.

Only when the attempts to bind her feet had been stopped altogether, because it seemed the only thing to do, did she cease her caterwauling and settle down. It was a defeat, but at least it brought comparative peace and quiet to Great Pine spice farm.

The irritating news that the Beautiful One from the House of Munn would not have lotus feet was conveyed to Ah-Jeh, the superintendent of the Ten Willows silk farm, who laid it before Ming-Chou. But the great man was tolerant. He would still accept the child, though she would never become a concubine for him or his sons or grandsons. Upon the day of her eighth birthday, he would buy her for one-third the price agreed upon.

Yik-Munn accepted the merchant's offer gratefully; less than one more year and he would be rid of Li-Xia, and his life would be complete. He set her to work in the godown, or warehouse, with orders for the dockworkers to keep an eye on her. The long, low-roofed wharf shed faced the river, its large doors opened wide to invite fresh air, but the mixed smells of peppercorns, nutmeg, black beans, and drying garlic were overpowering. This was where the harvested and winnowed spices were sorted, weighed, and packed to await shipment.

Li-Xia was set the task of filling sacks, bins, boxes, stone jars, and clay pots—three scoops of spice to one scoop of sweepings from the floor—with a rag around her mouth and nose. Yik-Munn had insisted she must wear gloves at all times; if she could not be graced with lotus feet, her hands must be those of a weaver, with hummingbird fingers soft and nimble enough that they might one day caress the lordly limbs of the great Ming-Chou.

Ah-Su, who performed the task of comprador from an office of her own, a hut at the end of the loading dock, commanded much respect and was left to herself, keeping tally of the cargoes that filled the holds of the sampans and junks and other boats on the river.

Recognizing that the godown was no place for the child, she convinced Yik-Munn that Li-Xia would be better used helping her—fetching tea and tidying her office—than risking her health and her precious fingers among the crude boys who labored in the godown. He agreed, on the condition that the girl did not shame him further by trying to rise above her lowly station, forbidding her to be taught the mischief of letters and figures.

Number Three had the child properly bathed and dressed, and gave her a bed to replace the mattress on the boards of the rice shed, as well as a chest to keep her things in and and a bucket to fetch water. She even hung a scrap of pretty curtain at the window, and set a vase of wildflowers on the sill, but most important of all was an old desk with a mended chair, matches, and a box of candles.

She was given a seat of her own in a corner of the small, well-ordered tally office.

"You may sit here if you are quiet and cause me no concern. See that there is fresh tea in the pot, and the water jar is always filled. You will fetch the rice and if I need you to run an errand, I will tell you."

Ah-Su did not smile, but said with firmness, "If you wish to grow brains, you may watch and listen. Learn what it is to be a comprador. In this office I am no longer Ah-Su, Number-Three Aunt—I am your teacher. But this must be our secret." She looked down at Li-Xia with eyes that smiled. "I cannot teach you to read; it will make much trouble and is difficult to hide. But that you will one day learn what it is to be a scholar like your mother is as sure as the rising of the sun."

Li-Xia spent almost six months in the corner of the office, happy to do as she was told, fascinated by the tallying of figures and the transfer of spice cargoes from the wharf to the open hatches and into the holds of river junks. It was a joy to discover that she could keep things in her mind and find answers to questions that she asked herself. Ah-Su was contented with her company, speaking to her often and answering her questions with thoroughness and patience, showing her approval at the brightness of her little assistant's mind.

One morning, she delighted Li-Xia with the gift of a broken abacus: "Take this, and if you can mend it with the right number of beads, you may try to use it, but let no one see you."

Ah-Su was amazed at the speed and accuracy with which Li-Xia learned the abacus with little coaching. "You have the fingers and the brains of your mother."

When Yik-Munn appeared unexpectedly and caught Li-Xia with the abacus, he snatched it from her and trampled it into matchwood. That this defiant creature was idly wasting time seated on a chair and playing with a frame of beads against his wishes made him sick with fury. He would have flayed her to death and buried her beside her breeder, but he dared not. Instead, he sent her to wives One and Two, with instructions to at least see that she earned her rice.

⁂

Li-Xia's days started before the dawn mist had risen, with feeding hens and milking the goats. She spent her mornings gathering wood and sweeping the courtyard, her afternoons planting rice, until it was time to bring in the ducks and geese. She had grown strong, and no work was too much for her to do, but her brothers treated her as cautiously as they did the farm dogs. The wives made sure she obeyed Yik-Munn's commandment to keep her hummingbird fingers covered with gloves, but otherwise kept their distance, as though to look into her strange round eyes might strike them as dead as the great Goo-Mah.

Since Goo-Mah had joined her ancestors in a paper mansion of many colors, Yik-Munn had regained his lost face in the village by generosity in the teahouse and expensive new clothes for his mistress. It was well known that he was now the ruler of his house. He beat his wives more often and for less reason, which among those who shared a pipe with him was proof of his recovery.

Despite her solitude, Li-Xia found that she was never lonely; contentment came with every sunrise, opening her mind to whatever the day brought. She rubbed her feet and wiggled her toes each morning until they tingled, and she ran everywhere, as though to walk was not enough. She discovered that the smallest things could bring the greatest comfort—the softness of a newly hatched duckling, a bumblebee balancing on the petal of a flower, a wren's nest made from tiny feathers and bound with moss, the constant song of larks high above the ginger field.

Because there was no one to talk to, Li-Xia spoke in her heart to her mother, imagining her wise words: *You are already finding your thousand pieces of gold. We enjoy all these priceless things together. There are no adventures too great, no journeys too long for us to share. Call and I will always hear you; look and you shall always see me.*

From the quiet words of Ah-Su, Li-Xia had formed a picture of her mother's lovely face intent on the making of images, the curled tip of her tongue lightly touching her lip and her eyes filled with purpose as each character spilled ever more smoothly from the tip of her brush.

At night, before sleeping, she spoke in whispers to the rising moon, seeking Pai-Ling in the softness of its pure light.

"Is it true that I am *qian-jin*, as Ah-Su has said—compared like you to a thousand pieces of gold?"

She could almost see Pai-Ling's smile and hear her answer clear and steady as the murmur of a gently flowing stream: *Gold can be found everywhere if you look for it . . . sprinkled by sunlight on clear water . . . in the evening sky and the coming of each new dawn. It falls like scattered coins on the forest floor and gilds the leaf of every tree; glitters on every blade of grass after the rain and turns each dewdrop into a precious jewel. You will find gold in kindness; it can be found in the seeking of happiness and in helping others. Try to find your fortune among these things, collect what you can of this real gold, and one day you will be* qian-jin.

"But I am told that I am worthless and do not even deserve my rice."

The shining face of Pai-Ling seemed to brighten the dark room.

Do not reward such foolish words with your precious tears; they are not worthy of your sadness. Carry your dignity with care: The world and its people are not always kind to those who are gentle, and even the gods may pass you by. Gather your thousand pieces of gold wherever you may find them and protect them with all your strength. You will find these words on the very last page of my journal. I wrote them for you before you were born.

Each evening, by the light of the lamp and the fluttering of moths, Li-Xia turned the pages of her mother's precious papers, learning to separate one character from another, carefully copying them with the colored pencils Ah-Su just happened to drop under her bed in the rice shed, then hiding her work beneath the thin straw mat of her wooden bed. The paper journals had no covers and were easily rolled up and hidden in the piece of hollowed wood that was her headrest. Some of the yellow pages were torn, but every one was filled with row upon row of Chinese characters. Here and there, attended by tiny images of gods and goddesses, a drawing of the moon appeared in all its many palaces.

The small book, with its cover of faded silk, was her greatest treasure. On its first page, Ah-Su had assured her, was the perfect image of her mother's name, written when she was a child and surrounded by pale flowers painted by her hand. The last page was so beautiful it took her breath away, showing the lady of the moon dancing upon a carpet of stars. Li-Xia longed to know what was written there. Finally, when Ah-Su found a way to visit her in secret, bringing sticky rice wrapped in a spinach leaf, dumplings, and fried noodles, Li-Xia asked her to read the words clusterered at the feet of the Moon Lady. Ah-Su read slowly and clearly:

Protect the secrets of your heart as others may protect the jewels and riches of a kingdom, share them only with those deserving of your trust. Do not allow your expectations to rise above your reach, but let no one set a limit to your hopes and dreams. Never lose respect for the feelings of others older than yourself, remember courtesy and good manners in the receiving and giving of face . . . but do not waste such wealth upon the undeserving, nor give the treasure of your smile to those without joy. These words you will find are written in my hand and those you do not now quite understand will become clear to you when you can read them and form letters of your own. Seek your fortune and find real gold where you can. Such happiness is *qian-jin*.

Li-Xia had been told little of Great-Uncle Ming, the silk merchant, and the changes in her life that were soon to come about. She was surprised and excited when her father himself appeared in the doorway of the rice shed. It was her eighth birthday, he said, and she would not work today. He brought her a ripe peach and a new *sam-foo*—a pair of trousers and a top the color of an apricot, with birds in flight embroidered on the cuffs and collar. Her porridge on this special day was sweetened, and there was fresh goat's milk to drink, and a sweet bun filled with red bean paste. Li-Xia had never seen such beautiful clothes or tasted such delicious food. The butterfly of hope sat upon her shoulder.

She must eat and then wash herself, her father told her. Number Three would dress her hair and see that she was fit to ride upon the river and be seen by important people. When she was ready, he would come back and take her on a ride in the sampan, to see the willow trees and the frogs among the lotuses. The bucket was fetched specially for her to use; the hot water tipped from the steaming bucket into a washtub was the first real bath she had ever known. Washing herself with soap, fragrant as a petal, and dressing herself in the fresh-smelling clothes, she thought how greatly her fortunes were changing for the better.

When Yik-Munn returned, he looked with interest upon the child he had created, relieved by her mildness of manner. Could it be that the priests were right, the fox fairy had left her completely? She seemed vibrant in health and of quite an engaging disposition. He wondered if he should ask a higher price than the bargain he had struck. Even without the lotus slippers, did she not show promise of the beauty of her mother?

"Let me see your hummingbird hands," he commanded with a twitch of his wide thin mouth and a glimpse of his famous teeth, and she quickly obeyed, placing them in his outstretched palms. He fondled them carefully, inspecting each finger with its perfect painted tip. He bent, lifting them to his broad, flat nostrils, and sniffed each in turn, as he would a fresh-cut flower or the delicate traces of a rare and valuable spice, then held them against the roughness of his sparsely whiskered cheek.

It was the first time Li-Xia had felt his touch, and it both confused and emboldened her. Seeing him look so kindly upon her, she dared to speak in a strong and fearless voice.

"Will my honorable great-uncle up the river teach me to read?" she asked.

He frowned, instantly dropping her hands; then, turning away with an angry snort, he spotted the tip of a paper book under her bed. He stooped to pick it up and for a moment was so silent, she wondered if he had understood her question. When he spoke, each word was cold with accusation. "What are you doing with this? Where did you get it?" She hesitated, shrinking from his sudden burst of fury as he kicked aside her bed to uncover more tightly wound scrolls and loose paper pages of her copied words. He pulled them out, ripping and twisting until they were torn to shreds.

"You defy me and spit upon my kindness. These papers are old and full of rubbish; good only as a home for cockroaches." He flung them at her. "Today you will visit Great-Uncle Ming . . . you will have no need of such nonsense."

He seized her jaw, forcing her to look directly into his eyes. "Never mention such a thing to anyone at Ten Willows—do you hear me?"

His thumb, Li-Xia thought, *is big as a soup ladle, but his eyes are those of a tired old dog.*

Before she could find the words that would stop him, he scooped up the remaining papers and left, banging the door behind him. She watched through the window as he tossed the precious pages onto the dung hill beside the buffalo stall and set it alight. The pages lifted like leaves in the wind to drift and disappear.

Number One nodded wisely when she heard how slyly the fox fairy had deceived them all and tried to teach itself to read. Yik-Munn was quickly bathed and changed, then served with Swatow tea to soothe his nerves. How brave he had been to face this thing alone, and how wise he was to see to it that this unholy being would leave the farm this day, never to return.

Yik-Munn was dressed in his finest clothes for the journey to the Ten Willows silk farm—a plum-colored gown of shantung velvet and his official high-crowned hat trimmed with gold. The prefect must not think that his daughter came from a poor and unimportant family, or the price might go down even further. His wives had fussed about him until he looked the picture of prosperity, a casket of rare spices beneath his arm as a gift for Ming-Chou.

Li-Xia walked behind him to the jetty and to the front of the sampan, well beyond his reach. Why had he taken her papers and burned them? She could find no forgiveness for such a terrible thing.

Watching lotus flowers drifting by, she cherished her few remaining secrets. Hidden under her new clothes and flat against her heart was the book she had kept hidden in its secret place, the story of the Moon Lady, to be remembered forever through her mother's hand. As precious as this was the orange-peel finger jade, sewn carefully into the hem of her *sam-foo*, weighing no more than a baby frog.

These great secrets helped her forget the sight of the pages turning black under a cloud of yellow smoke. As long as these last things were safe, she felt protected too, wondering who rich Uncle Ming could be, and if he would be pleased to see her. She had never felt as pretty as she did today; the apricot *sam-foo* fit her well, and the wives had dressed her hair and dabbed her cheeks with rouge till they were rosy as an apple. Her mouth had been carefully painted red as a rose petal and her eyelashes and eyebrows were black as ink. The wives were nices to her than ever before, but the thought of going far away from the spice farm filled her with a grim determination: She would never return to the rice shed and its jars of pickled snakes and the pink little bodies of baby mice.

When all was done and she was ready for her journey, Number Three

48

returned with a yellow water iris to wind into her hair, and a most beautiful gift. It was a sunshade, which when opened bloomed in the same bright yellow as the iris on a stalk of green bamboo. Ah-Su had found a moment when the others were engaged in readying Yik-Munn. She kissed Li-Xia and said with her secret smile, "I have gathered the rest of your mother's things from the rice shed; I will keep them safe for you until we see each other again. Remember, my Beautiful One, your feet are your freedom. While you have them, nothing is impossible."

CHAPTER 4

Ten Willows

In *the smoky blue* mulberry groves, there were as many trees as there were scales on a snake, or so it was said among the *mui-mui*, the young girls who killed the moths and collected the tiny pearls of silk. The rolling hills of the Ten Willows silk farm were covered with the trees as far as could be seen from the banks of the river.

Unlike at smaller spinning mills, which depended on cocoons supplied by others, Ming-Chou, a man of great prosperity and power, had the advantage of owning his own groves. Established by his great-grandfather, they had made him the richest silk merchant in the Pearl River Delta, living in a world of lordly privilege beyond that of even the city taipans of Canton or Hong Kong.

Here, behind the high, dragon-back walls of his tranquil gardens, he employed one hundred women. Fifty of these were *sau-hai*, "women without men," an ancient sisterhood born to the cult of survival. As hungry children, victims of flood and famine, mauled and molested by field hands for a handful of rice, they had been plucked from the darkest depths of despair. The oldest of them had forsaken the notion of wedlock and motherhood, banding together and welcoming any virgin girl to join their ranks and accept the traditional comb and mirror as she took the sacred oath of *sau-hai*.

The sisterhood cherished and protected its own as surely as nuns in a convent. It had always been the way for a poor woman of China, if her family was unable to feed her but had failed to kill her at birth, to be sold to anyone who would have her. Such lost women had sought the sister-hood and shared its strength for centuries. It offered food and shelter, but above all it promised a measure of dignity, and security from the injustices of men.

The *sau-hai* were much sought after as dometic servants, and any household worthy of its name was prepared to pay a little more for an amah who wore the black *tzow* and showed the white handkerchief of purity, her hair wound into a tight bun and caught by the wooden comb. Thus had been formed a network of secret communications that could stretch from house to house, village to village, and town to town, even from province to province. Members of the sisterhood became a constant source of information on the fortunes of rival clans and competitive households.

Ming-Chou was deeply proud that he had chosen the sisters of *sau-hai* to become his weavers. He paid them well, saw that their conditions were pleasant, and treated them with respect. Most could not read nor write, so questioned nothing. Yet they were intelligently led and there were some among them who were of considerable breeding, whose families had been beset by disaster, or who despised or feared the male sex and preferred the company of women. Some, like Elder Sister Ah-Jeh, the Ten Willows superintendant, had great skill with the abacus, a keen eye for business, and a deep knowledge of healing the sick. The money paid to them at the end of each month was less than half of that given to men and boys, but it was wisely used or carefully saved.

Ming-Chou knew well—and did not challenge—that they created their own laws and enforced them by rules and rituals laid down by the society over the centuries. Controlled completely by the elder sisters, they did not drink rice wine or fornicate. Their discipline was absolute, and their punishment swift and brutal.

The peaceful and efficient running of his mill he owed to Superintendent Ah-Jeh, who oversaw the weavers as diligently as the abbess of a sacred temple watching over her novices. For this, her personal rewards were considerable. What punishment or promotion she meted out was done in private, unseen and unheard. It was she who decided which girls among the *mui-mui* should leave the groves for the more delicate work of the sheds, perhaps to become a spinner or even a weaver if she accepted the comb and the mirror of *sau-hai*.

From this small number, so carefully chosen, if a young girl shone brightly enough among her sisters, she might be selected as a "lantern girl," whose charms would be wasted at the loom and better suited to the master's bed. In this, as in other matters, Ming-Chou relied on the judgment of his superintendent and paid her handsomely if that judgment pleased him.

To attract the eye of the Master of Ten Willows for even an instant was thought to be ordained by kindly gods. When such a child was found, she would be prepared by amahs skilled in the expectations of the bedchamber, dressed in a robe of white, and given a paper lantern, to be carried to the house of Ming-Chou on the night of a propitious moon. If she was found acceptable, she might become part of a privileged few, and join other favorites in accommodations of their own. Neither concubines nor mistresses, these were comfort girls in the Pavilion of Pleasure, called upon when needed and offered as gifts to the mandarins who were sometimes sent to meet with the prefect and gather taxes.

If she was not found acceptable, the superintendent lost much face. The girl might be considered as a sister of *sau-hai*, but if she lacked the hummingbird hands and butterfly fingers and subservient soul of a *sauhai* weaver, she would be whipped and sent back to the huts to live out her usefulness among the mulberry groves.

If a girl resisted, she was deemed to be bewitched and her fate was decreed by ancient laws: She would be beaten and tethered beside a goat for the sport of others. When her humiliation was complete, she would be trussed in a weighted pig basket and drowned in the river. The Master of Ten Willows had never witnessed such a ritual, nor did he wish to hear of it, leaving all things female to the judgment of Ah-Jeh. The conscience of Ming-Chou the silk merchant was as untroubled as his garden was at peace with the universe.

The other half of his female workers were the *mui-mui*, the little sisters; they were thought to be aged from eight to fourteen, but most had no age as well as no name. Among them were many who had not es-caped the abuse of men—their fathers or brothers or those they called uncle—but had found the courage to run away and seek shelter in the nearest temple. The monks fed such children before handing them over to the silk farm or another employer. The *mui-mui* were also fifty in number, some brought to the Ten Willows silk farm by parents who could no longer feed them, accepting a paltry sum in return. Others, whose parents had died or whose families had abandoned them, came seeking the sisters of *sau-hai*. His *mui-mui* were fed well, clothed, and given shelter. For this they worked from sunrise to sunset—feeding the silkworms and harvesting cocoons, and sorting and cleaning them for the boiling vats, the spinning wheels, and the weaving mill.

Some, whose hands were fast and nimble—too valuable to waste in the harshness of the groves—were taken into the spinning sheds to learn the secret of the golden thread. From their numbers, when a loom lost its weaver to illness, death, or old age, one would be chosen for the mirror and the comb. It was the dream of all of the *mui-mui* to spin the golden web and be taken into the lifelong sanctuary of *sau-hai*.

The sun, almost level with hilltops, turned the river into a ribbon of flame as the sampan bumped the jetty beneath the row of towering wil-lows. Li-Xia was the first to scramble from the prow, eager to arrive at this place so different from the brooding shadows of the great pine. Far from the echoing stone-flagged rooms and strident voices, the solitary gloom of the rice shed and the flat muddy fields of the spice farm, she was dazzled by flickering ceilings of leaves, delicate reflections strewn like flowers at her feet. She opened the yellow sunshade among the dancing blades of light, only to have Yik-Munn snatch it away.

"Where did you get such a thing, to cast a shadow on the face so care-fully prepared for inspection? Who gave you permission to pose beneath a sunshade made for wives and concubines?" He snapped it closed and tossed it into the river, to swirl away on the fast-flowing current. Silently, Li-Xia followed her father along the jetty, past a gang of boys who, stripped to the waist, loaded sacks and baskets into the open hatch of a river junk. Some paused to leer at the girl in the apricot *sam-foo*, their skinny bodies slick with sweat.

They passed through towering scarlet doors and into a huge space, its walls lined with shimmering bolts of brightly colored silk. A row of chairs was lined along one side opposite an altar to the Supreme Being Yu-Huang—the Jade Emperor—to assure those he smiled upon of a prosperous life. Li-Xia did not know of such a god and found little comfort in his bloated belly and greedy smile. Before the altar was a high desk holding an open ledger, an ink block, a bamboo cup of brushes, and an abacus. A high wooden stool stood behind it.

After a slow, silent wait that caused Yik-Munn to adjust his hat and smooth his hair many times, nervously sucking his teeth, a short, round woman seemed to roll into the room. She was followed closely by the silent figure of a girl, perhaps twelve or thirteen years old, attached to her wrist by a silken thong. The stout woman, Li-Xia had already been warned a hundred times by her father's nervous whisper, was the all-powerful Ah-Jeh, elder sister of *sau-hai* and superintendent of the mill.

"You must remember your place in the presence of such a worthy person. Do not speak unless you are spoken to. It is she who will take you to Great-Uncle Ming if you do not displease her."

Crossing to the stool, Ah-Jeh hopped with unexpected agility onto its elevated seat, her short legs and broad feet hanging inches from the floor, to look down at Li-Xia with the eyes of one guessing the freshness of fish. She was dressed in a black *tzow*—a high-necked tunic with wide-legged trousers of waterproof twill that shone like the wing of a crow, making a faint swishing noise when she moved. A large white handkerchief hung from a pin on the sloping bulge of her breast.

Her oiled hair was the color of ashes, skinned back like a skullcap and caught in a finely plaited bun at the back of her round head with a simple wooden comb, so smoothly held it gleamed like sculpted metal. The dark worm of a vein beat visibly in her temple; a tear of dark jade hung from a thin gold chain around her short neck.

Her fleshy face was pampered and powdered until it was white as a mooncake; her thick brows drawn together in a frown of expectation; thin, disapproving lips daubed red as a fresh wound. Flat, waxen lids were stretched over eyes that were black and unyielding as spilled treacle. *She hops onto her stool like a crow hops onto a dunghill.* Li-Xia had learned to observe such things without any visible sign on her face or in her eyes. It was, she had decided, the voice of her heart.

The girl behind Superintendent Ah-Jeh, who was dressed in the same oily black, carried a furled black sunshade and a large fan of black feathers. Over her shoulder, a bundle of willow wands—some thin as whips, others thick and heavy as a club—were slung in a sleeve of leather. As though she had done so many times, the girl selected one of them and handed it to the superintendent, who took it in her outstretched hand without a glance.

Li-Xia felt no fear of this woman, who resembled, her heart said now, a fat, shiny black beetle with the powdered face of a festival clown.

"So you are the ungrateful one who disobeys her father and runs away whenever she can."

The tip of the long willow jabbed Li-Xia hard in the ribs. "Is it true that you dare to think above your station?" The willow whacked loudly across the deskop. "Look at me when I am speaking to you."

Ah-Jeh frowned with grim displeasure when this failed to make the farm girl flinch.

"You are the one who refuses the golden lotus slipper, who breaks her father's promise to the most honorable prefect Ming-Chou, great benefactor of us all and savior of our souls."

Accustomed to seeing threatening faces, Li-Xia did not blink an eye as the superintendent wielded the thin wand menacingly, slashing it through the air till it whistled like a tin flute.

"She will not run away from me. You have treated her too well, sir." The superintendent slipped from the high stool to walk around the farm girl. "We have a way to make those who run away wish they had no feet at all to run with."

Yik-Munn looked helpless, raising his hands in a humble gesture of defeat.

As quickly as a conjuror, Ah-Jeh brought the wand down with a solid thwack across the back of Li-Xia's legs, which made her scream inside, but she only blinked her eyes.

"Bow before your superintendent, or feel this across your back," Ah-Jeh hissed, as Li-Xia felt her father's fingers jab hard into her back.

"Bow when you are told. Where are the manners I have taught you?"

You have taught me nothing but how to endure pain and that all promises are meant to be broken, her heart said, sure that her mother heard these words and approved of them. *And this woman with the face of a clown does not deserve my respect.* She bowed deeply, three times, comforted by the secret words of her heart. *I will bow because I must, but you will never know what I am thinking and you will never make me cry.*

"I am told your name is Li-Xia, the Beautiful One." The stocky woman sneered. "Well, you are not beautiful to me. You are one of the *mui-mui*—little sisters—and you are one among many others. You will have no other name until you are given one; your only value is in how many cocoons you can gather and how quickly you can fill your baskets."

She mounted the stool again and looked directly at Yik-Munn, whose hands were clasped before him like a man at prayer, his thin lips drawn back in the mask of a smile that showed his teeth in all their glory. "Come forward and sign the *sung-tip*," she said, indicating the contract that would make Li-Xia the property of Ming-Chou for the rest of her life. "Be sure of what you sign, for if it is false she will be back on your doorstep and the name of Yik-Munn will be mud along the river."

She rolled a finely pointed brush on the ink block. "Do you assure me that this girl is a virgin?"

Yik-Munn nodded his head gravely, pressing his folded hands against his heart.

Ah-Jeh scowled uncertainly. "You swear that she is strong as she looks, that she has no illness of any kind, and can carry a load and bend her back? That she has brains enough to care for herself? Do you assure me of these things written in the *sung-tip* and put your name to them . . . or do you lie to me as you lied about her lotus feet?"

Yik-Munn shook his head emphatically. "She has worked my fields as well as any boy, but"—he grabbed his daughter's hands, one in each of his, as he had done in the rice shed—"see, Honorable Sister, she has hummingbird hands." He offered them for her inspection.

Ah-Jeh sniffed with scarcely a glance. "They are the hands of a duck herder. Do not think you can gain another single coin with such trickery."

Yik-Munn dropped her hands, shuffling back with a bowed head.

"Will I also learn to read? Will my great-uncle teach me to read?" Li-Xia was startled by the sound of her own words.

Another vicious prod from Yik-Munn almost caused her to stumble and fall.

"Forgive me. A foolish notion, nothing more," he stammered. "If she should speak of such things again, Honorable Superintendent, I beg that you will punish her."

Again Li spoke without thought of danger. "My mother resides with the moon, and when it is at its brightest, she becomes a white fox and waits for me in the ginger field. She will teach me to read and write. I will be a scholar. No one will stop me."

The willow cane slashed across her shoulders faster than a lick of flame. At first the sound of it was greater than the pain. Li-Xia neither moved nor cried out as it splashed like boiling oil across her back.

Yik-Munn grabbed her arm and shook her violently, his face dark with fury as he spluttered his apologies. "She is a child of wild imagination, but these are foolish fancies. They are easily discouraged."

Superintendent Ah-Jeh seemed unconvinced. "Is it true that a fox has been seen around this girl, that its spirit may have entered her?" she muttered. "I have heard that your elder sister was struck down by the evil in her eye. If this is so and the master finds out, he will send her back to you and demand repayment, plus an amount for the cost of your deception. We want no demons at Ten Willows."

"My sister was old, her heart was weak, it was time for her to join our ancestors," Yik-Munn protested.

Li-Xia spoke out yet again. "Her lotus feet had become rotten as turnips in the frost; you could smell them on the stairs."

Yik-Munn protested with much bowing, assuring the superintendent that the priests had found Li-Xia to be cleared of lost spirits, but he paid Ah-Jeh a sum of money to speak no more of it. The *sung-tip* was hurriedly signed and the money counted out with much care and ceremony. An entry was made in the ledger, and the large chop of Ten Willows sealed the contract with the echoing sound of a stamping foot. The ledger closed with a final thud as Ah-Jeh turned her full attention to the child before her.

"Take off those fine things; you will have no need of them here," she snapped.

Unbuttoning the pretty jacket reluctantly, Li-Xia did as she was told. Again the willow wand cut across the closed ledger.

"Hurry, girl. We do not have all day."

The superintendent gestured impatiently toward Yik-Munn.

"Strip her. Why did you dress her like a New Year's doll? Without the lotus slippers she is just another farm girl—take them off and give them to my assistant."

Yik-Munn ripped the embroidered jacket from her shoulders and the trousers from her legs with nervous haste, until she stood in cotton drawers.

"The rest of them too. She will wear the clothes of the *mui-mui* and nothing more."

For moments, Li-Xia was left to stand naked before the overseer, her hands covering herself uncertainly. For the first time she felt true fear, but with it came greater anger. She asked her heart what she should do, but no answer came.

"Lift your arms and turn around."

When she did not move, her father's hands gripped her shoulders to twist her this way and that.

"I see you have not beaten her. She bears no scars and seems well fed."

Yik-Munn simpered, bowing his appreciation for such a compliment. "She has been treated with great care in readiness for this day."

Ah-Jeh sniffed sharply. "No doubt that is the problem. You have given her airs above her station, this farm girl who would become a scholar."

Ah-Jeh brandished the willow as a gesture to her assistant. "Get her dressed and give her the things she will need."

Instantly, the girl stepped forward with a bundle of clothing: a *mien-larp*, the brown padded jacket and trousers of the field hand, which she helped Li-Xia put on with quick and certain hands. There was another of dark green, with a wide wicker hat for the summer; a cape of flax and a rabbit-skin cap for the winter. There were cotton undervests and pants, two *fan-sarm*—the long shifts for sleeping, one of flannel and one of cotton—canvas gaiters, and two pairs of grass-rope sandals. The bundle also contained a blanket, a wooden headrest, a rice bowl, chopsticks, and a glass jar for drinking tea.

The wicker hat was thrust upon her head and her new belongings as well as the *sam-foo* rolled into the blanket, tied, and slung across her shoulder: Li-Xia, the Beautiful One, became *siu-jeh*, little sister to the *mui-mui*.

The sun was low across the river as Yik-Munn kowtowed his way to the open door, but he did not say good-bye to his daughter or even look her way. She hated him for this, but found strength in his stupidity. *If you will not care for me,* she said in the privacy of her heart, *then I shall take care of myself.*

She watched her father hurry down to the jetty and step into the rocking sampan without once looking back. Tears she could not prevent blurred the sight of him as the sampan, its lanterns already lit, cast off its mooring line and pushed into the current to scull swiftly away.

This is the moment, Li-Xia's heart said, *when I shall live or die. My father has sold me for money he does not need, and he did not even say good-bye. He burned my mother's books and turned her words to ashes.* This, and only this, had made her cry inside, glad that she never wanted to see him again, but angry that he should know so little of her heart and think so little of her mind.

Sudddenly, Ah-Jeh rapped out a name. "Pebble . . . Pebble . . . where are you?"

Instantly, the figure of a girl who had been waiting outside the door stepped into the room. A child from another world, she seemed to Li-Xia—short and squat, wide shouldered and short armed, her legs bowed like a horseshoe, her feet thrust into canvas leggings that reached her knee.

Her hands were small, short fingers curled inward like the claws of a bird, and her wide face was old before its time, but for a constant crooked smile. Her abundant hair was streaked with silver, twisted with strands of colored silk, wound elaborately about her head and pinned like a turban with willow twigs and fish bones. Placed upon it was a crown of morning stars, tiny white flowers freshly picked; beneath this, hardly noticed, protruded two decorative ornaments, dark rings of buffalo horn, one on either side of her head just above each jutting ear.

This small brown creature was wearing a patched *sam-foo* the color of the earth, her careless grin showing nothing of her thoughts. Deep lines around her eyes could not hide the glint behind her crinkled, half-closed lids. They blinked once quickly at the swish and crack of the willow, glanced for a passing second at Li-Xia, then looked briefly at the well-swept floor at her bare feet. Those feet were small and wide and brown, as scarred and cracked as old leather, the toes splayed out and separated.

Hurriedly snatching the tattered straw hat from her head, she took another quick stride into the room and gave an elaborate bow.

"Take this farm girl into your gang if you have need of her, or find someone who does. She is sly and cunning and knows nothing of gratitude. Watch her like a rat in a pantry. Show her the huts of the *mui-mui* and find her a place. If she runs away, it is you I shall flog."

Ah-Jeh turned to Li-Xia, lifting her chin with the tip of the willow switch, looking directly into her eyes and speaking in an almost kindly way.

"Go with Little Pebble. She is mother to the *mui-mui* and will teach you what to do and how to do it. Obey her and keep your place. Let me hear no more about books and reading. You are here to work in the groves. If your hands are quick and your fingers nimble, perhaps you will one day make a spinner . . . even a weaver. First you must earn your place among the *mui-mui*—and remember, you are the youngest and the lowest among your sisters, so do not try to be more than you are."

The cane was flourished at the open door as Ah-Jeh dismissed her with what could have been the suggestion of a smile.

"Go now, before I change my mind and send you back to your white fox mother."

Pebble bowed with hasty backward steps. Li-Xia, her arms filled with new possessions, stepped backward away from the smell of burning joss sticks, into fading sunlight and a breeze off the river. She followed the bowlegged girl with no sense of fear, but the rare excitement of new adventure.

⚹

When they were gone, Ah-Jeh remained upon her stool to reflect upon this purchase. Most *mui-mui* arrived half starved or maimed, brought by stricken parents who could no longer afford to feed them. Occasionally, a girl of exceptional promise appeared, like this one from the spice farm of Yik-Munn, this child her fool of a father called the Beautiful One; already Ah-Jeh had seen a light rarely found in one so young, especially one who had been dealt with so harshly.

Among the amahs of Yik-Munn's house, two were elder sisters of the *sau-hai*. They had sent reports of the child they called the fox fairy and her defiance of his three wives. Nor was it a secret how her mother, a Shanghai tart, had taken her own life believing her infant had been buried alive in the mustard field.

The spice farmer had done well to rid himself of such a burden. Her spirit would be tamed, and perhaps one day she would carry the lantern to the house of Ming-Chou. If not, she could be well suited to become a sister of *sau-hai*. Yes, Ah-Jeh was pleased with her purchase, already anticipating a generous commission. She would watch the Beautiful One with great interest.

⚹

After they were outside and well away from the ears of Superintendent Ah-Jeh, the girl called Pebble spoke in a cheerful, careless way. She led the way with wide, sure-footed strides that rocked her from side to side,

61

turning back at one point to take some of Li-Xia's load. She walked backward, her eyes openly curious and filled with questions.

"Why do they call you Li-Xia? You do not look so beautiful to me." She cocked her head to one side and screwed up her nose. "But your eyelashes are long and curly, so that's something, and your hair is long and shiny for one so little."

"It is a stupid name, one I did not ask for. My father thought it would help to sell me."

The girl called Pebble spoke in haste, as though realizing she might have been unkind. "Look at me, I have eyelashes so short and straight you just can't see them." She snorted back a laugh. "The gods were hiding when I was dropped into this world."

"My mother was *ho, ho-leung*. She was a scholar from the great city of Shanghai. Her name was Pai-Ling and she was *qian-jin*, said to be worth a thousand pieces of gold."

"I have heard of such a thing, but I warn you, do not speak of it to others in this place; the *mui-mui* know little of beauty and nothing of gold." Pebble cupped her hand to cover her mouth in secrecy. "But did I not hear Ah-Jeh say that your mother is a white fox, and that you are a fox fairy?" She did not wait for an answer but grinned, spitting expertly into the dust.

"That is much more interesting. Names and mothers are not important here; anyone with either of these would be looked upon with great suspicion. Few of us know who we are. Our mother is the moon—she brings us rest and shares our dreams."

She shrugged her shoulders and thrust out her chin. "For all I know of my mother, she could have been a three-legged toad or a wolf or perhaps a phoenix who will one day arise from the river to take me away."

Li-Xia felt her heart trip at the mention of the moon mother. Could this be the family she had dreamed of in the darkness of the rice shed? Had Pai-Ling guided her to this place? Pebble wiped a hand across her nose, her lively eyes squinting in the last shreds of golden light as the sun slid slowly into the river. In that moment, Li-Xia thought, she looked like a warrior queen.

"But my bowlegs say she was a Hakka who probably dropped me in a ditch as easily as a buffalo drops its calf, then carried me to the paddy fields upon her hip. These legs serve me well, don't you think?" She held up one of her strangely flattened feet with amazing balance and flexibility. Li-Xia could see that its sole was thick and callused as the knee of a very old goat. She stamped it down, kicking up a cloud of dust. "And these fine feet, they no longer feel pain and are stronger than any boot."

She widened her infectious grin, her rocking gait becoming a skip as her words flowed freely.

"In my heart I was born to be a dancer and an opera star." She struck a theatrical pose and sang a high, quavering note. "But who cares for the dreams of one of the *mui-mui*? Who knows where we come from . . . and who cares where we go? We have no name but that which we give ourselves. I have given myself the name of Little Pebble, because before a diamond is made, it starts out as nothing more than a pebble among many others. It lies buried deep in the earth, waiting to be found and made to shine like the brightest star. It does not need to be large to be of great value."

She laughed, a careless chuckle that matched her mischievous smile. "You see? This is my 'Pebble the dancer' face." In an instant the smile was gone, and in its place was a fierceness that pulled at the corners of her mouth and thrust out her chin, her eyes no longer friendly. "And this is my 'Pebble the warrior' face." She laughed aloud at Li-Xia's confusion. "I like you, Beautiful One. I see into your eyes. You have a good heart and a strong one; already it holds many secrets. But no one has a heart that holds more secrets than the Little Pebble." She thumped her chest with a grubby fist. "I am bursting with secrets. They are all that I have, so I cannot share them, or give them away, or let anyone steal them. Perhaps one day we will do business, one of yours for one of mine, so that our hearts will never be empty."

The overseer made a sudden twisting turn on the toes of one foot, as though it would help her think. "But first we must give you your *mui-mui* name. We will call you Crabapple, which looks good enough to eat but is sour to the taste." They approached a stone water trough where goats were led to drink. "Yes, I like you, Crabapple . . . you are not afraid. I can smell fear as surely as I smell salt fish from the anchored junks when the wind is off the river. Let them think you are a fox fairy, as the black crow says. It will bring respect if they are not sure of your powers."

They passed through an arched gateway hung with sweet honeysuckle, walking away from the mill and its tidy compound toward the oldest and grandest stand of willows stretched along the riverbank. Beneath shimmering curtains of green, a line of four tumbledown huts, roughly made from woven mats lashed to crooked frames of bamboo, leaned comfortably in their shade.

"These willows have withstood many storms. They bend in the wind no matter how wild, but never break. Even when the oak is uprooted and the branches of the tung tree broken and flung to the ground, the willow still stands. It owes its life to the river." She put a protective arm around Li-Xia's shoulder. "You are still a baby, but I think you have already learned to be like the willow."

CHAPTER 5

The Family *Mung-cha-cha*

W*hen they entered the* first of the open-sided huts, Pebble led the way past rows of narrow beds under a roof of ragged thatch. A wicker box stood at the foot of each bed, and above them tattered mosquito nets hung from a rickety crisscross of bamboo beams. She stopped in a back corner where six beds stood side by side, the mat walls hung with shells and bunches of dried flowers and herbs.

"This is where you will sleep." Pebble dumped her share of the bundle onto the cot, extending her foot to tap the box. "And this is where you will keep your things. No one will steal these rags, but if you have something of any value, hide it well." The hut was already dimly lit by the yellow flames of slush lamps—clay pots filled with oil and burning a single wick. Fireflies flickered through the fast-closing shadows. The *mui-mui* were scattered around—squatting, sitting, lying. Some were clothed, some naked and drying their hair still wet from the river, their many voices tangling to be heard. They reminded Li-Xia of ducks chased from the ponds and onto the terraces.

The babble slowed as they turned her way. Li-Xia had never looked into so many pairs of eyes, so many different faces; they showed a passing interest, then turned aside, busy combing and plaiting each other's hair or closely searching for lice.

Pebble whistled softly, and four girls left the others to come to her side. She gestured for them to sit, dropping to her knees to light the lamp.

"We work in gangs of six to a grove, each with its overseer. I am overseer to the *mung-cha-cha* gang and oldest of the *mui-mui*. I have worked the groves longer than any other."

She circled a finger at the side of her head, pulling a silly face. "*Mung-cha-cha* means 'a little bit crazy.' It is sometimes wise to seem stupid when you live among fools." She gave Li-Xia a wide, lopsided grin. "To have spiders in your head gives you power. Everyone is afraid of madness."

She turned to face Li-Xia and placed a welcoming hand on her shoulder. "We do not think of ourselves as a gang, but as a family, and these will be your sisters.

"This one's name is Li-Xia—the Beautiful One, the name of vanity given to her by a greedy father to raise her price. So we will call her Crabapple, sweet to look at but hard to swallow." She grinned at the newest member of her family with approval. "It is yet to be discovered if she is sweet or sour, but already she has felt the cane of Ah-Jeh without flinching, not a sound or the blink of an eye . . . so watch over her until she has learned the ways of the *mui-mui*."

The overseer spoke fondly of the four girls seated cross-legged around her, presenting each in her turn. "This is Turtle, because she hides in her shell. She would rather listen than talk, and this makes her all-seeing. Nothing happens beneath the willows that she does not know about. Call upon her wisdom when you must. She will also teach you to make a needle from a fish bone, to patch your clothes, and to make beautiful things from stolen silk."

Turtle was the smallest of the girls, intent on a bundle of sewing, lost in each minute stitch, smiling her silent welcome as she bobbed her head.

"This is Garlic, because she eats much of it raw and does not smell like a summer rose, but she bows to no one and there is no better friend when trouble comes. She will teach you where to find rare herbs to heal all things, how to make soap from candle wax and flowers, and how to cut and shape a bamboo flute." One slightly taller girl, already half stripped and showing small, dark-pointed breasts, grinned boldly, her teeth shining in a dirty face that hid nothing.

"This is Mugwort, because she is ugly as a sow's behind . . . but inside she is pretty as plum blossom in springtime. Mugwort will teach you to mend your sandals and patch your hat with cane grass and rushes." Mugwort took an elaborate bow, and gave Li-Xia a quick, hard hug.

"And this is Monkey Nut . . . she is truly *mung-cha-cha*, a little bit crazy, but her thoughts are gentle and her spirit is kind, so she is always happy. Monkey Nut will teach you how to laugh when you are sad, which is the greatest gift of all." Monkey Nut stared at the small girl named Crabapple with quiet eyes filled with wondrous things unknown to all but her.

"Mugwort and Monkey Nut are twins and lively as crickets. Together as strong as a bullock, but their hearts are even stronger." The twins were perhaps nine or ten years old, each as sturdy as the other. They moved as one, taking Li-Xia firmly by the hand.

"Little Pebble is mother and father, brother and sister to us all. She will be all these things to you," Mugwort said with great sincerity.

"So we are a family and our mother is the moon," Little Pebble said with a grin. "Now put away your things and lock your box, hide the key, and we shall eat."

Bowls appeared as if by magic. From a lidded bucket, Pebble filled each one with sticky rice, adding a strip of salt fish or fried eel and a shred of cabbage with careful measure.

"Sleep when you are full, Crabapple. We wash in the river before dawn and eat in the chophouse before the sun has touched the willows. To do this we must be first. It is the secret of our survival to be first in all things—first to arise, first to bathe, first to eat, first to reach the groves, first to fill our baskets, first to the chophouse, and first to sleep. Perhaps this is the way of the world outside, but I have not been there so cannot be sure."

For a moment they ate without speaking, hungry for the salty rice, shoveling noisily with busy chopsticks held close to their chins.

"There is another reason for being first to choose our baskets," Pebble said. "We will ride in the donkey cart of our friend Giant Yun, where others must walk. We pretend it is the golden palanquin of the empress and that we are her royal children, carried off to visit the palace gardens to pick lychees and ride the dragon."

Pretending her chopstick was a pipe, puffing imaginary smoke with great relish, she grinned at Li's uncertainty.

"Don't worry, Crabapple, we will be beside you. Giant Yun is strong as a buffalo and almost as ugly, but his heart is light as a silkworm's cocoon and gentle as a mother's kiss." Pebble said this with hushed respect before she swallowed the rest of her rice, licking every grain from her lips.

"Tell her the story of Giant Yun," said Garlic, lying back to listen. The others chorused their agreement. "Yes, yes, the story of Yun."

This must be a very good story, Li Xia said to her heart, *they have heard it many times.*

"It is a true story," Turtle said, nodding with great respect. They formed a circle, sitting, lying, kneeling, as Pebble jumped into its center, wearing her warrior's face.

"Yun-Ying-Chi was once a great temple boxer, some say the greatest in all China. He could fell a charging bull or a galloping horse with a single blow of his iron palm.

"Challengers came from every province, but no one could beat him. Warlords sent their finest warriors with gleaming swords and steel-tipped lances, mounted upon armored warhorses ... but Giant Yun felled them all with ease. One warlord came and offered Yun his weight in precious jade to become champion and teach his martial skills to the imperial guard. But Yun had always been free as a bluecap in tall bamboo, swaying wherever the four winds might take him. He was not born for obeying orders and disappeared to a distant province ... but the soldiers that followed were too many even for him. It is said he killed one hundred men before they could cast the net that trapped him. They cut off his hands so that he could no longer fight for any rival."

She swung her hands high, bringing them down with great force, and looked around her as a storyteller does, while the *mung-cha-cha* nodded, murmuring their agreement.

"So he used the magic of his chi to channel the power into his feet.

68

His toes have become his fingers and there is nothing he cannot do with them. Now he has feet and legs of toughest steel and pulls the donkey cart up and down the hill as lightly as a rickshaw. He is keeper of the trees and never sleeps. No one will raid the groves and steal cocoons while Giant Yun watches over them with his great blunderbuss. He fires it with his toe and it can be heard for a mile along the river."

Pebble waited for the power of her words to be properly heard, eager to continue. "Once, not so long ago, river pirates came in a four-masted junk to raid the mill. They would have taken the silk and the weavers too, but Yun held them off until Ming-Chou's bodyguard came with their guns. The master did not reward him; the captain of the guard did not thank him. He returned to his hut among the groves with no more said of it."

Pebble grinned and spread her hands to complete her story.

"This mattered nothing to him. Since they took away his hands, he says, his wisdom has increased and he has learned to speak with the universe and all things in it. He is a poet and a seer, a teller of fortunes, and he can make beautiful things from shells. . . . Now he pulls his cart to the groves and back again much faster than a buffalo." Pebble bowed to her audience. "The bluecap is very happy in the mulberry tree."

She handed her empty bowl to Li-Xia. "Collect the bowls and wash them in the river; this will be among your duties as the youngest. Then we must sleep. Tomorrow you will ride the royal palanquin of Giant Yun to pick the celestial lychees."

The lamps were soon blown out and fireflies glowed all the brighter, flitting among the drooping swaths of mosquito nets like sparks stirred from a dying fire. The grating of bullfrogs was heard among the rushes as Pebble lay down on the bed next to Li-Xia with comforting words.

"I will sleep beside you until you are truly among us. No one will trouble us. We have secret claws."

Pebble's hands reached into the twisted mass of her hair, a curved hook of sharpened steel suddenly appearing from each of her tightly closed fists. The middle finger of each hand was thrust through the rings of buffalo horn attached to each lethal blade.

"The hair knife," she muttered with secret pride. "I made them my-self from a broken sickle." Even in the fast-growing darkness, Li could see that the steel had been lovingly honed to a razor's edge. "Worn in my hair they are just another clip, a fancy pin, an ornament, just like the willow twigs and my crown of morning stars . . . but once in my hand they are the claws of the black bear and the talons of an eagle, and no one can take them from me unless they chop off my hands." The gleam-ing hooks of steel were again quickly hidden in the nest of her hair.

Night settled over the secret thoughts of the *mui-mui* in a mantle of sounds—their dwindling voices, the breeze sifting through the canopy, crickets singing in the thatch above, the constant rattle of frogs.

"There are both the good and the bad among us. Only the strongest survive without misery. We must always be prepared to defend our-selves and each other. It is the code of the family."

Li-Xia lay in silence, listening to the songs of the river, uncertain of what she might say in return.

"Don't be afraid, little Crabapple. Let the willows sigh in your dreams. Tomorrow you will begin to learn the ways of the *mui-mui* in the noble world of the silkworm."

Early the next morning, Li-Xia was awakened roughly to shouts and murmured curses of those about her. Slow to leave a deep, untroubled sleep, she opened her eyes when her nose was tweaked.

"Wake up, Crabapple. We must bathe before the others and be first to the chophouse while the congee is hot and the steamed bread still soft."

The voices quickly multiplied; bare-skinned girls of every shape and size made their way to the river's edge, giggling as they stepped over those still half asleep.

Mugwort and Monkey Nut grabbed Li-Xia by her hands and feet, lift-ing her bodily from her bed, carrying her down the dozen steps to the water's edge—the cold plunge claiming her with its swirling grip and a silent explosion of bubbles.

This was how Li-Xia's first day of her new life began, beneath the colossal archways of Ten Willows, high and grand in her eyes as the most splendid of temples, on a bend in the backwaters of the great Pearl River. The banks had been built up with blocks of stone to form a shallow pool, sheltered by a screen of trailing greenery, where for a few stolen moments, the children of the moon splashed like otters at play.

Dried and glowing, dressed identically to those around her, Li-Xia became a member of the family. Turtle showed her how to lace the rope-soled sandals, binding them securely around shin pads of stout canvas with strings of twisted reed.

"These will help you climb the mulberry tree and protect you from the snake that hides in the grass."

Pebble stood watching, pleased to see how readily Crabapple was accepted by her sisters. She reached out to check the shin pads with a tug of the thongs that bound them.

"Always tie them well and you will not fall; the bark of the mulberry tree will not take off your skin. From this first day you must do all things for yourself—it is the fastest way to learn. If you fall, ask yourself why and do not fall the same way again."

Pebble's eyes were merry as she placed the wide wicker hat on Li-Xia's head. "The sun can be strong in the groves, just as the rain can wash you away and the wind will try to take you in its arms. You will always need the shelter of this hat; do not lose it or you will have to make another."

She chuckled, pinching Li-Xia lightly on the cheek. "You have the skin of your northern mother; protect it if you hope for more in life than to be mother to a silkworm."

She tied the strip of black gauze that held the hat in place beneath Li's chin, taking a step back, nodding her approval, inviting the others to do the same.

"Well, she certainly looks like one of the *mui-mui*. Now we will see if she can work like one."

The sandals light and secure upon her feet, the plentiful bulk of congee—rich rice porridge—and hot green tea warming her belly, Crabapple followed Pebble and her new family, well ahead of others still swallowing their rice.

"First to arrive and first to leave: This is the way of the *mung-cha-cha*," Pebble said, setting her fast, rocking pace. Moments later, farther along the river's edge, they stopped at a large open shed where a dozen boys were spreading heaps of cocoons with wide wooden rakes. They greeted the *mung-cha-cha* with insulting words and crude gestures. Pebble replied in kind.

"They are the *larn-jai*, Crabapple," she said carelessly when they had passed. "Broken boys with no home but the riverbanks—they sort and clean the cocoons and gather wood to boil them and kill the moth."

"I have seen and heard much worse from those I thought to be my brothers."

"Good, then we shall pay them no mind—words are harmless and they are afraid of me and our protector, Giant Yun."

As if these words had summoned him, a man of enormous size stepped from the shed, his short thick forearms encased in sleeves of leather strapped to his shoulders and capped with hooks where his hands should be. His huge chest was crossed by a leather harness studded with brass, an even wider belt around his girth braced with more buckles and loops of chain. Slung across his back was a huge blunderbuss, its flared muzzle resting against his shoulder, the carved wooden butt below the back of his knee. His mighty legs were clad in loose-fitting brown breeches, leaving massive calf muscles and bare feet brown and scarred as old mahogany. Giant Yun's face was broad and fearsome to look upon, with a wide mouth that showed uneven teeth beneath a flattened nose. His gleaming skull set in shoulders bunched with muscle, his eyes radiated goodwill as he greeted the *mung-cha-cha* with a wicked grin.

"Good morning, young ladies. Yun hopes you slept well and there was *hah-mui* to flavor your congee this beautiful morning."

He bowed low to them, then crossed to the cart and reached for the trace chains that were meant to harness an ox.

"Your palanquin awaits you and your little sister."

"She is Crabapple and said to be a fox fairy—but she is also welcome as part of our family."

"Then she is welcome to ride in the imperial palanquin, and I will be her servant."

Stacks of woven baskets and piles of bamboo carrying poles stood outside the shed. Pebble chose two baskets and a pole, tossing them to Li-Xia.

"Always pick the lightest baskets and the oldest pole, one that bends like willow and is easy on the shoulder. Throw them into the cart and climb after them. The silkworms are hungry today."

The first strong rays of sun gleamed on Giant Yun's wide shoulders as, harnessed to the shafts by leather straps, he trotted along the winding pathway.

It took only a short time to reach the rows of mulberry trees, but to Li-Xia it was a magic journey, climbing higher until she could look down upon the river and the endless world beyond. They entered a grove where bamboo ladders reached into leafy branches, as thick with cocoons as snowflakes on a winter bough.

"Welcome to the gardens of of the silkworm. Follow us and do as we do. Let us begin to fill our baskets. When they are full, we empty them into the cart and Yun takes it down. He will take a dozen loads before he returns to his hut to catch an eel or a catfish for supper."

From this moment—as the *mui-mui* arrived at the hilltop like a flock of chattering birds—as she looked down upon the valley swept clean with early light, baskets swinging from her shoulders—Li-Xia rejoiced in her first piece of pure gold.

⁂

At the entrance to each of the four huts stood a shrine to the Tu-Ti, the earth god that watched over Ten Willows. Each farm had its own earth god, and the Tu-Ti expected nothing less than a small shrine containing an altar upon which the five ritualistic objects must be correctly arranged: two vases for flowers, two candlesticks, and a brazier for burning gold and silver paper. In return, the deity would attend all important events, from births to weddings and funerals, birthdays and festivals.

Made of mud bricks and no bigger than a dog kennel to protect its sanctity from intruders, it housed the clay image of Tu-Ti, who was believed to hear all gossip and to bring down a terrible judgment upon any sign of dissidence. Flowers were changed and a joss stick lit each morning to preserve the prosperity of Ten Willows and its generous master; to bless the cocoons so that they numbered as many as stars in the summer sky, and snowflakes on the winter bough; and to pray for the fattening of the silkworm through the honest work and gratitude of the *mui-mui*.

Behind the huts, the pigs and goats were kept in pens, and a pathway led through rows of cabbage, melon, and white radish. A moment's walk away, a pit had been dug for refuse and sewage—a putrid place of scavenging dogs that only the *larn-jai* would approach.

In the center of this makeshift camp stood a stout post, with an iron triangle bolted to it, and beneath it a pair of rusty leg irons set in stone. It was here, Li-Xia was told, that punishment was carried out. Beside it, a giant gingko tree spread its ancient limbs, its branches throwing a constant shadow; worshipped as the spirit tree, paper prayers fluttered among its branches, spelling out crimes and begging forgiveness and mercy, written by those who had suffered the horror and humiliation of the rings.

✻

Days turned into weeks and weeks into months. With the help and guidance of Little Pebble and her newfound family, Li-Xia had found her place in the ramshackle home of the *mui-mui*. She filled her baskets with cocoons as quickly as any other. And when the work was over, Crabapple joined her sisters in catching eels with twisted strands of silk and a fish-bone hook, then stewing them in a pot with herbs and wild mushrooms. She learned how to fashion a hair comb from the head bone of a catfish, and where to find duck nests in the rushes and frogs along the riverbank ablaze with orange and yellow nasturtiums.

It was here they collected eggs of pale blue and olive green, careful to always leave one or two behind, and to use a leaf to lift the egg so that the scent of a human hand did not cause the mother duck to reject the nest. The eggs were placed into Pebble's hat and carried with great secrecy to the back of Giant Yun's hut. There, while the family *mung-cha-cha* stood guard, she used a bamboo digging stick to uncover a cache of eggs in the soft, damp earth hidden by ferns. They were laid carefully side by side, row after row, one on top of the other beneath thick layers of rotting straw, each one wrapped in a nest of wet brown leaves. Pebble flapped a hand to dispel the strong organic smell, taking one egg from its muddy wrapping and handing it to Li-Xia. "There are more than two hundred salted eggs among these ferns, but only I and Giant Yun know where they are all buried."

Li-Xia rubbed the coating of dirt and crusted salt from the egg, washed it in the river, and peeled off the hard shell.

"To become a true member of our family, you must swear to guard this secret place and eat the egg to seal this oath. But first you must hold it up to the light." Li-Xia found that the white had become transparent amber jelly, through which she could see the dark yolk suspended like a planet in a golden sky. "It is a symbol of our mother the moon. Now you may eat it." It tasted delicious, the yolk soft and salty as the golden heart of a rich man's mooncake. "It is a hundred-year egg, *mung-cha-cha* style," Pebble confided with a chuckle. "We cannot wait for a hundred years, so we bury them in the summer and eat them in the winter when there is nothing to flavor our rice."

The family closed in, to squat in a circle around Li-Xia. Pebble put on her overseer's face. "It is time for your initation." She spat on her hand, rubbing the dirt from the inside of her right ankle to reveal a small tattoo, a simple Chinese character of one unbroken line. Li-Xia knew it was the sacred name for "moon." Mugwort and Monkey Nut, Garlic, and Turtle also showed the moon marks on their ankles.

Garlic handed a needle-sharp sliver of bamboo and the hollowed half of a bean pod containing a dark liquid to Pebble, who spat on Li-Xia's ankle and wiped it clean. "This is a special ink, mixed for us by Giant Yun, who is a master of such things. It is good for the blood and heals quickly." The bamboo needle pricked Li-Xia's skin so many times she ceased to count, until Pebble sat back on her haunches. "There, Crabapple. Now you will always be of the *mung-cha-cha,* and the moon will always be your mother."

From the riverfront, beyond the flat-tiled roof of the mill, the Heavenly House of Ming-Chou sat in splendid isolation. Only distant glimpses of its scarlet roof and walled gardens could be seen from the groves.

The *mui-mui* called it the Roof of Heaven. Even the *mung-cha-cha* spoke of it with awe as they gossiped over *yum-cha* in the shade of the mulberry trees.

"It is a place where diamonds tumble in the waterfalls, where fat fish fill the ponds and have scales of pure gold and tails of finest silk," Mugwort said dreamily, her back against the tree and her eyes closed. "Dewdrops form on the lotus leaves to turn into priceless pearls when touched by the sun. The pathways are set with precious stones of every color."

"The trees blossom all year round, home to nightingales whose eggs have been known to contain precious gems," Monkey Nut piped up. "I have heard that the flowers never die, that it is forever springtime behind those walls . . . and the peacocks that roam among them have feathers plucked from a rainbow, and diamonds crown their heads."

Imagining the gardens of the Heavenly House was a game often played by those who would never see them: Even Turtle took her turn. "There are turtles with shells of jade and ruby eyes."

Pebble stood up suddenly, tossing away the remains of her bowl. "Do not listen to such stupid things, Crabapple. I was among the first to be chosen for the Heavenly House. Many years ago, when I was young and tender as you are today. There are no diamonds in the waterfalls or pearls upon the lotus leaves. The fish are fat and lazy in the ponds, and stink like any other when they are dead. The flowers wither without water and the trees are bare in winter." She snorted her contempt.

"The peacocks and the nightingales are birds like any other; their feathers are not stolen from a rainbow and their eggs are not precious stones." She swished her mouth with tea and spurted it onto the ground, as she did whenever it was time to work. "Now get your stupid tails off the ground and into the trees. One day, Crabapple, I will tell you the truth about the Heavenly House of the great Ming-Chou . . . and of joy behind the crimson moon gate." Li-Xia had never heard such angry words from Little Pebble . . . and never before seen her waste a grain of rice.

❋

As seasons passed—fragrant spring, scorching summer, and perishing winter—Li-Xia found great strength in the closeness of those who called her sister, while tales of the fox fairy led those outside the *mung-cha-cha* to look upon the mysterious Crabapple with a cautious respect.

The hills and the willows had become her home, but Li-Xia often found herself gazing at the domain of the *sau-hai* sisters, so far removed from the bamboo huts, the loathsome presence of the *larn-jai*, and the stench of the animal pens.

The mill stood among shady tulip trees, surrounded by flower beds and a meandering pond spanned by a narrow bridge. On the other side, the weavers' small, neat houses were painted white, with roofs of red clay tile and plots of ground for growing fruit and vegetables.

The weavers could be seen walking the pathways and crossing the bridge, hand in hand, at the beginning and end of each day. They wore the same black *tzou* as the superintendent, with a white handkerchief pinned to the breast, their hair wound into the same tight bun at the back of the neck held by an identical comb. Only brilliantly colored sun-shades distinguished one from the other.

It was rare, Li-Xia learned, for one of the a *mui-mui* to become a weaver. One or two might be chosen in their twelfth year to carry the lantern to the Heavenly House; but only when a sister of *sau-hai* had died or had become too old to work the loom would the comb and the mirror be offered to the chosen one.

The weavers of Ten Willows appeared contented in their work and gracious in their manner. From a distance it could not be seen if they were young or old, but to the eyes of Li-Xia they seemed blessed by the Tu-Ti.

"You should not look so enviously upon the compound of the *sau-hai*,

77

Crabapple. It is not what it appears to be." Pebble's voice was strangely cold.

"But they walk with such dignity and purpose."

"They are no angels," replied Pebble with a note of warning. "Their smiles and gentle ways are for each other, not for us. If you have seen a pack of wild dogs torment a trapped animal before it is devoured, then you have seen the *sau-hai* take revenge."

Pebble had lost her dancer's smile, and it troubled Li-Xia to think she might have been the cause. She was relieved when the overseer squatted in the shade of the willows and motioned her to do the same, as the others joined them. "If you are so interested," Pebble sighed, "I will tell you. It is important that you know the truth.

"The word *sau* in their dialect means 'comb' and *hai* means 'up.' Once the comb and the mirror are accepted, the hair is 'combed up,' plaited into a bun and held with the wooden comb. Then an oath is sworn before the Tu-Ti that binds the *siu-jeh* for the rest of her life. From that moment, she will be safe but she will never be free."

"But neither will we, the *mui-mui*," Li-Xia said, still greatly puzzled. "A family like ours cannot hope for such comfort and prosperity. Yet we are not free. Is it true that they are paid for their work in exchange for their thumbprint? That they are allowed to visit the village at festival time? That they have fans to keep them cool and a stove to keep them warm?"

Pebble spat into the dust, reluctant to answer. "Ming sees nothing but good in the sisterhood of *sau-hai*. He wants no pregnant weavers, so he pays them and provides better conditions. The *larn-jai* dare not go near them. It is the *mui-mui* who must watch for that scum at night."

Pebble jumped to her feet; in a flash the curved hook of steel protruded from her fist. "The *larn-jai* will not touch us either; they know that I will have their balls off before you can say 'bad joss.'" She giggled at Li-Xia's bewilderment, standing erect and raising the bladed fist of defiance. "The credo of our family is this: 'We hide from nothing and run from no one.'" The *mung-cha-cha* clapped and cheered, echoing their leader with fists held high.

Li-Xia thought of the *larn-jai*, who lived like water rats among the

78

livestock and had tamed a pack of mangy yellow dogs to follow them. Some were as young as the *mui-mui*, others gangling youths, vicious and foul-mouthed in their savage energy. Seeing that the *larn-jai* were filthy in their appearance and their ways, she had avoided them, ignoring their taunts when she collected her baskets to begin the day.

"Why are they here," she asked Pebble, "sniffing around the huts like the dogs they fatten and eat?"

Pebble laughed, sliding the sliver of steel into the nest of her hair. "They are mindless brutes, but necessary for the heavy labor. For this they are given enough to eat and a place to sleep among the pigpens and vegetable plots. They seek the favors of the *mui-mui*, offering a fresh vegetable or piece of fruit, and there are some among us who grant them in some dark corner, but only with the mouth or the hand. Virginity is the first rule of the *sau-hai*, so none will run the risk except those already taken and without hope."

Her grin spread wryly. "There is not one among those *mui-mui* fools who does not dream of working the loom." Pebble paused to look around the circle. "Ah-Jeh knows that such things happen, but to separate the *larn-jai* from the *mui-mui* is like hiding the jackfruit from the monkey."

"It is another price to pay for the comb and the mirror, never to know thunder and rain with a man between your legs, or to hold a baby to your breast," grumbled Mugwort.

"There are women who will never be touched by a man and have learned to please each other in that way," Monkey Nut added. "Some say that Ah-Jeh's assistant is under her spell and sometimes shares her bed."

Pebble sniffed with disgust. "Enough of the black crow and and her flock." She threw her hat skimming into the river, running to the edge and looking back. "Never forget, Crabapple, that for all their smiles and purity, the hand of *sau-hai* is merciless to those who disobey them. Their power reaches for a thousand times ten thousand miles. So be wise . . . be very careful what you wish for." With those words she dived into the river after her hat.

CHAPTER 6

The Ghost Tree

Winter *had been long* and raw. The *mui-mui* had patched the roof and lowered the sides of the huts and tied them down. But winds had howled through them and rain poured from the sodden thatch. When the groves were silent, claimed by crackling frost and silent snow, they foraged for firewood and worked inside the sheds. The rabbit-skin hats, padded jackets, and capes of flax grass gave them some small comfort, but hands and feet were frozen, swollen with chilblains.

Three iron braziers were dragged one to each hut and kept stoked with wood and buffalo dung, the glowing embers shoveled into a shallow trench dug between the rows of beds. Li-Xia was certain they would die from cold, or be burned to death by flying sparks. Warmth and comfort were almost forgotten, when the winds were suddenly gone and the chill lifted.

At the beginning of spring, on the third day of the third moon, the festival of Ching-Ming was a day when families all over China paid homage to their ancestors by tending their graves and joining them in a feast of celebration. Generous assortments of fresh flowers were presented, with much burning of joss sticks; gold and silver paper was set alight and sent aloft in honor of the dead, whose spirits were thought to hover while their resting place was restored and their memory properly respected. Most important of all was the gathering of willow catkins, believed to be the symbol of all that is young and promising for a summer of plenty and an abundant harvest. The first of the new season's life adorned the ancient trees of Ten Willows like liquid gold, alive with the drone of bees and a storm of white butterflies.

So auspicious was the day of Ching-Ming that all work ceased, the looms were silent, and the *mui-mui* were allowed to rest.

"Crabapple, today you will see that even that the *mung-cha-cha* have ancestors who bless us with a kindly moon," Pebble said. While others lay on their beds or washed and mended their clothes, the family made crowns of willow catkins and adorned themselves with the golden blossoms. Each carrying a large bunch, they walked the miles of winding river, following the towpath close to the water's edge, picking flowers, mushrooms, and wild strawberries along the way. Junks of every size and shape sailed past. Most were manned by Chinese, but one was of foreign rig. A short mast and patched sail sprouted from its foredeck; the putter of an engine belched black smoke from a tall stack behind its wheelhouse. Inside, gripping the wooden helm, a man unlike anyone Li-Xia had seen, awake or in dreams, steered its rusty hull through the sandbanks with a steady eye. A strip of red cloth trapped his mass of oily black curls, and a ring of gold could be seen hanging from his ear. He wore nothing above the waist, his arms and chest thick with matted hair and shining with sweat. At the sight of the squat vessel and its dark column of smoke, Pebble led them quickly down the slight embankment and away from the river's edge.

"It is a *gwai-lo*—baby-eater—on a Portagee ship from Macao. These dark-skinned foreign devils are worse than the pirates they are supposed to fight. Sometimes they will come ashore and take any girl they see and no one will stop them. Let the stink of him pass."

It was the first time Li-Xia had ever sensed fear in Pebble, but she could not take her eyes off the devil in his red bandana. "I thought the *gwai-lo* was pink and white or red as fire. That is what I was told by Number-Three Wife at Great Pine Farm." Li was afraid but fascinated to look upon such a creature. To her horror, he waved at them and called aloud in words that had no meaning to her. A Chinese crewman, resting on a coil of rope, laughed like a fool and shouted in gutter Cantonese. "My captain will give you good food and wine, perhaps a silver coin if you come aboard to entertain him."

"Tell him he is the son of a sea serpent and we would cut our throats before we would come aboard his stinking ship from hell." Garlic's voice sang out across the water. In reply, the Portuguese captain stepped out of the wheelhouse door and to the rail. There he exposed himself to them, urinating into the river as he passed.

"Are all foreign devils so hideous as this one?" Li-Xia did not realize how foolish her words would sound. The sisters burst into laughter, then quickly assured her that they were. "They are hairy as a goat and smell as bad," Garlic said with disgust. "They do not wash or clean themselves," added Mugwort with a shiver. Turtle spoke with a trace of anger seldom heard from her. "They mock our gods and think that we are less than human, born to work for them and be taken like dogs." Monkey Nut rolled her eyes and shook her head. "Black, brown, red, pink, or white; they are all the same, these foreign devils."

With the riverboat well past, they continued along the towpath to a small house built of limestone close to the river. Its wooden jetty had rotted away and its sampan lay half sunk among the reeds, yet the little house seemed to possess a timeless pride. Countless seasons had stripped its once-fresh paint like dead skin. Some of the tiles of its roof were cracked and needed replacing, and its fence leaned from want of repair, the gate sagging upon rusted hinges. A narrow weir had been channeled into a pond beside the house, where a broken waterwheel had once churned among the water lilies. The walled garden enclosed a dozen mulberry trees and a meager patch of vegetables, overgrown with weeds. A few scrawny hens pecked among the fallen fruit beneath a neglected orchard. The pigsty and goat pen were broken and empty, the rice terrace dry and stony.

An old man sat outside the faded, once-red door, sipping tea and smoking a long-stemmed pipe. Pebble stopped to greet him and warn him of their approach. "Good morning, old lord, how are you today?" His wrinkled face screwed into a show of pleasure at the sound of her voice as he shouted his reply: "Good morning, little sisters. I have been expecting you. It is good to hear your voice again."

"We visit the old lord often to help harvest his cocoons and weed his vegetable plot." Pebble said to Li-Xia. "We will be sad when he is gone and we can no longer listen to the bees in his garden and the doves on his roof or share his ginseng tea. He says that no one will buy his house because it is has too many ghosts, and it is old and needs money and hard work to make it new again. So we have patched the roof and mended the floor and blocked the broken windows and tried to fix the waterwheel. He cannot see very well, but he has the ears of a bat and his chi is still strong."

Pebble continued with words of great respect. "His wife lies buried beside his daughter and two sons under the fig tree. We come on the day of Ching-Ming to help him honor his loved ones. He has no one left on this earth and has lost count of the years. So he has adopted us as his granddaughters, and to us he is Ah-Bart, our esteemed grandfather. He says that his ancestors are our ancestors, and that his house has known much happiness." Pebble looked upon the peaceful little farm with deep affection. "Is it not truly the Heavenly House? It has thick walls and a good roof easily mended, with enough mulberry trees to fill many baskets to sell at the mill. Its garden can provide everything for the table, and when the mill wheel is turning, the water is pure and cold as mountain snow. Our grandfather is truly rich. He is at peace. . . . This is a place of true harmony, filled with a golden feng shui. He will not leave his house on the river until his ancestors demand it."

Pebble opened the squeaky gate, her voice filled with cheer. "We bring the willow blossom, old lord, and flowers and wild strawberries and some mushrooms fresh from the fields. We also have brought a new willow broom to sweep away the cobwebs."

The old man waved, inviting them to cross his gate and share his tea. He had been expecting them and had picked lychees and red apples and fetched a pot of tasty noodles from the kitchen. All of these were gathered together under the fig tree, where the four graves were resting. The *mung-cha-cha* set about clearing the little spot of fallen leaves and weeds, while Pebble whisked away with the willow broom. When the graves were cleaned and swept, the headstones washed and scrubbed so that their names could be clearly read, the wildflowers and bunches of golden catkins were placed upon them, while Pebble fried the fish and braised the eels they had also brought with them. With the lighting of joss sticks and much hammering on an ancient plough shear, the ancestors were invited to share the feast of Ching-Ming.

Time had no meaning as the years passed. Li-Xia filled her baskets as fast and often as any of the *mui-mui*, and when the seasons changed she worked in the sheds, spreading the larvae on the rush mat trays with fast and clever fingers. When the silkworms hatched, she fed them ten times a day from the baskets of mulberry leaves fetched by Giant Yun.

The open air and comradeship of the mulberry groves brought her the most contentment—the chatter of the *mung-cha-cha* among the trees, the scolding of Little Pebble if fingers did not fly and the baskets were not filled fast enough.

A day came when the clear blue of the sky gave way to a towering thunderhead that challenged the sun. It caused a downpour that lasted no more than fifteen minutes but left the trees saturated, every cocoon sparkling like a single diamond. When the sun broke through, warm and fresh as only an afternoon in early autumn can be, the *mui-mui* shook the boughs so that the diamonds fell to earth. Wet cocoons were hard to handle, and it meant half an hour's rest while the sun dried them out.

Pebble led Li-Xia through the sparkling groves to an ancient tree that stood alone on the highest point of the hill, bigger and shadier than all others, its gnarled roots thick with moss. *Like veins on the back of a witch's hand,* Li-Xia thought as they approached.

"It is called the Ghost Tree," Pebble told her, "The first one was planted by Ming-Chou's great-grandfather. There was a girl whose *mui-mui* name was Morning Star, because she was as small and pretty as the tiny flower." Pebble's voice was filled with a sadness Li-Xia had never heard before. "She was not strong enough and could not climb the ladder without fear. I tried to help her, but she grew sick and could not fill her baskets. Ah-Jeh beat her till she bled." Pebble stopped and looked away, trying not to show her tears. "At night she could not sleep and kept her lamp lit . . . she passed the hours plaiting reeds. We did not know she was making a rope. When it was long enough and strong enough, she hung herself from this tree. It is why I wear her flowers in my hair—so that I will not forget her. I was her overseer. I should have seen the rope. I should have saved her."

The overseer tried to smile. "Do you see something strange about this tree?"

Li-Xia gazed into its widespread branches. "It is very old and very beautiful. . . . It seems as old and strong as a rock," she replied, sharing a little of Pebble's sadness.

"There are no cocoons. Since she died, no moth has settled in this tree and no silkworm spun its cocoon." Pebble smiled again, still a little sadly. "Even the finches and squirrels no longer make their home here."

She pinched the tears from her eyes and found her grin. "The *mui-mui* are afraid of this tree. They believe it shelters Morning Star's soul and the souls of those who have died in these hills. It is where I sit to think my thoughts and talk to any god who will listen."

Pebble spoke with deepest sadness as she ran her fingertips across the tree's furrowed bark.

"This tree knows I was meant to be a dancer. Its branches hold the mysteries of time; its leaves are broken dreams, but it still lives, like the heart of a wise old man holding the hand of a lost child. I have shared its magic with no one until now. There can be no secrets between us beneath this tree."

Pebble rubbed away the moss with the palm of her hand to reveal two perfectly carved Chinese characters. "You see, the mark of Little Pebble and Morning Star. I cut it a dozen years ago. Beside it I shall cut the name of Crabapple." She took a knife from her hair and began to carve each stroke and curve with care.

"You can write my name?" Li asked in astonishment.

Pebble put a finger to her lips with exaggerated caution. "I can also read, but tell no one or I shall pay dearly for such a crime." It was as if Li were seeing her friend the overseer for the first time.

Finishing the carving, Pebble brushed aside the shavings and stood back, inviting Li to see her work. "There—Pebble, Morning Star, and Crabapple; no storm will be great enough to part us. This Ghost Tree will never die." She breathed deeply, stretching out her arms to the leafy ceiling above them. "Here we can be whatever we wish to be. Sometimes I am an empress . . . no one knows this but I, so there is no one to say that I am not. On other days, I am the star of the grandest opera on the great stage in Peking with the voice of a goddess . . . no one hears me sing but this tree."

She bowed to Li-Xia with a wide sweep of her hat. "And you, my little Crabapple. What are you in your most secret heart?" Li-Xia answered without hesitation. "I am born to be a scholar, to have a great room filled with scrolls and papers and many books . . . all for me to under- stand and teach to others." Pebble nodded her head and sat down, her back against the tree, her legs outstretched toward the sunlit valley spread before them like a padded quilt with crops of green, yellow, and every shade of brown, the silver sheen of the river winding through it. The earth seemed washed clean, and the smell of farmland reached them from afar.

"We are the same in here." Pebble placed a hand over her heart. "We had no one but our own shadow; now we have each other." She reached for the water gourd and drank deeply, and handed it to Li-Xia with a sigh of contentment. "See how rich we are, Crabapple? The whole of China is at our feet and the great Pearl River is our friend."

That night, Li-Xia showed Little Pebble her precious book. It was the last of her secrets, known only to her heart. All others had been shared with Pebble and she had kept them safe.

"I am the only one who can read in this palace of fools," Pebble whis- pered with a grin of rare delight. "Don't let Ah-Jeh see your book or she will throw it in the pit and take the skin off your back. We are too stupid to read books. That is the law." Little Pebble then grew troubled, speaking without her lopsided grin. "I have learned to read, but I have paid the price. Before I came here, I stayed with an old man who said he was my uncle. I do not know if he was or not, but this does not matter. I swept his room, fetched his tea, and made his soup." Pebble frowned and looked away. "He was not so old that he did not want me in his bed, but he taught me to read. I thought it was good business. But he grew tired of me and sold me to Ming-Chou because he needed opium."

Pebble rolled to one side of her stretcher, lifting the edge of her sleeping mat to show that it was lined with old newspapers. "See? I have read them all a thousand times. There is nothing I don't know about the world. What is your book about?"

Li-Xia hesitated, excited that her friend could read and embarrassed that she could not. "It's about the moon . . . all about the moon."

"What does it tell you about the moon? This is a very big subject—the moon has many faces."

Unexpected tears made Li-Xia blink. "I cannot read the words properly . . . but I think I know what they say."

Pebble did not laugh at her. "Sometimes this is the best way to read—it is called imagination, the silk that weaves our dreams. Because the words are written by another, and do not always say what we want of them, they give you a reason to think," she said wisely. "Let me see this secret book of yours, and perhaps I will teach you to read it as it is written."

These were the words Li-Xia had waited to hear for longer than she could remember. She offered the book to Pebble, who drew the lamp a little closer, turning its pages.

"You are very lucky to have found this book. It is an almanac, the lunar calendar . . . all the magic stories of Heng-O, our Seventh Sister the Moon. Your mother was indeed a scholar; there are many notes on the things that she believed. The images she has made by her own hand are the images of greatness and wisdom."

Pebble looked from the open journal into Li-Xia's anxious face. "You are surely blessed to carry such a mother in your heart wherever you go, and to know that whatever happens, she awaits you in the afterlife."

From that moment Li-Xia began learning to read the words that told the thoughts of Pai-Ling. Every new character she mastered was another step along a promised pathway. Little Pebble was a patient teacher, eager to share the moon stories. One story she never tired of reading while Li traced every word with a careful fingertip was the story of Heng-O and Hou-Yih:

A very long time ago, when magic was everywhere and miracles were as many as there are stars in the sky, there was a Taoist princess, so radiantly beautiful that no ordinary man could look upon her without the risk of blindness, and because of this she flew the skies alone, adorned by nothing but cloud. Her name was Heng-O.

There was a young wizard, possessed from birth with great powers. His name was Hou-Yih, and through his spells and alchemy, eating nothing but the nectar of flowers, he had found immortality. Because of this, he was doomed to walk the side paths of the air carrying an enchanted bow and a single silver arrow. The arrow shot from this golden bow would give the one it struck eternal life, and his loneliness would be over. His search for a companion led him on an endless quest through all the planes of the universe.

One day he came upon an iridescent cloud in the middle of a rainbow and, believing it to be the wings of the immortal phoenix, drew back his bow and released the arrow. From the gossamer cloak of cloud fell Heng-O; the silver arrow had pierced her heart, and he caught her in his arms. The arrow of his great magic was withdrawn and they fell immediately in love. Such happiness had never been known even to those who shared paradise, but a storm came and separated them. Heng-O found sanctuary on the moon, while Hou-Yih was driven to the blazing reaches of the sun.

There they have remained forever as Yin, the Lady of the Moon, and Yang, the Lord of the Sun—immortal rulers of the universe and its cosmic balance. Once each month they come together to make love among the stars. This is why the full moon blooms with such brilliance, never more radiant than in the autumn of the twelfth moon.

"You see?" Pebble said. "Men are children of the sun, blinding, burning, and never still—bursting with their ripening seed. They spill it like a river and do not care where it flows. They do not think it will ever run dry, and when it does they cry tears of stone. But women are children of the moon . . . we are made from soft shadow and pale light—cool, patient, enduring. We are very different, but one is needed to balance the other as the center of the eight trigrams . . . the yin and the yang."

When the story was over, Li-Xia lay still, hoping that the glittering image would not fade too quickly. She took the orange-peel finger jade from its hiding place, to hold against her lips and say a prayer. With her fingers closed tightly around it, she thanked her mother for sending Little Pebble, who was teaching her to read.

The celebration of the Autumn Moon Festival was a special day for the *mui-mui*, but particularly important to Li-Xia, now that she knew it was the birthday of Heng-O, the Moon Lady, who spread her silver mantle to comfort all her sisters in heaven and on earth. It fell on the eighth month, when the harvest moon was at its biggest and brightest, and Heng-O dressed in her fullest glory.

There was no work that day, and each of the *mui-mui* was given mooncakes to eat, joss sticks to burn, and a paper lantern on the end of a bamboo stick, so that the Moon Lady could look down and miss no one in her blessing. The mooncake recipe was unchanged after a thousand years, each cake containing the solid yolk of a salted egg representing the full moon. When lit, each round lantern also resembled a yellow August moon. To Li-Xia, it was a time filled with promise. Heng-O was not blind and deaf and dumb like the wooden gods of the spirit room, who had punished her for seeking her mother. The Moon Lady was gracious and splendid in her robes of gold and silver, driving away all shadows and lighting every path.

Darkness had settled on the river. The *mui-mui* took their paper lanterns into the groves to hang them among the mulberry trees, so that the seasons would be kind, the cocoons plentiful, and the silkworms fat and happy. Li-Xia and Pebble hung theirs in the Ghost Tree, and sat beneath it with a mooncake for the little girl Morning Star. They lit their joss sticks and said their prayers for her, letting them drift into the branches with the curling smoke, looking down on the river valley where the lanterns floated like fireflies.

"This is the time when those who secretly hope to become a wife thread a needle with silk and pray to Heng-O to send them a husband. It is said that on this night each year, a cowherd crosses the sky to find his lost love. Those that thread the needle without difficulty may be looked upon by him with favor." Pebble chuckled at the thought, splitting a ripe pomegranate and handing half to Li-Xia. They sat beneath the Ghost Tree until the last lantern had disappeared among the stars. Pebble did not laugh at Li-Xia's dreams of pursuing her mother's path.

"Who is to say what happens when a spirit resides so close to heaven? That you may speak to your mother and she answers is a great thing. When I was younger I spoke to mine but there was no answer . . . so I became a dancer in my heart, an empress and an opera star, whatever I wished to be. You, my little Crabapple, are different. You are surely meant to be a scholar."

※

The Autumn Moon Festival was also a time for changes at Ten Willows, a time for good news and bad. Those who were no longer useful were told that they must leave, and those who had been noticed were told of their promotion. Ah-Jeh called Li-Xia to her office in the mill. It was the first time she had been inside, to gaze with awe upon the rows of wooden looms, each mounted with brightly colored spindles; the *sau-hai* were busy making rolls of silk as fine as the wing of a dragonfly. No chatter could be heard above the ceaseless clatter and clack of the shuttles.

"You are almost twelve years old, Li-Xia. You have worked well and do not waste time with foolishness, or hide from the overseer or play stupid games among the trees. It is time for you to take your place in the spinning shed. You have grown strong and tall for your age and earned

90

your place in Ten Willows. You will move your bed tomorrow. If you do this work well, you may be chosen to carry the lantern. If not, the next step could be to the weaving mill—you may be offered the comb and the mirror of *sau-hai*." The voice of the superintendent was brisk but not unkind, and her eyes held no threat.

"Thank you, Ah-Jeh. It is an honor to be thought worthy of such great opportunity . . . but . . ." Li-Xia tried to find the words she wanted to say.

"There are no 'buts' in this matter. The new moon has brought you a change in fortune." Ah-Jeh's rage was never far away. "Do you dare to question what the moon and stars bequeath to you?"

"If I am expected to share the master's bed, he will not find me pleasing." As they always were at times of great importance, her words were out before Li-Xia could stop them. She was not even sure where they came from.

The superintendent's face darkened like a cloud crossing the sun. "This is not for you to question. The master will do with you as he pleases. If he does not find you worthy of his attentions, then I will do with you as I please." Ah-Jeh's manner calmed quickly; her scarlet mouth curved into a slow smile. "Perhaps I will offer you the comb and the mirror . . . we shall see."

"I am not sure I deserve the honor of such great blessings."

The smile was slow to fade, but the light in Ah-Jeh's treacly eyes seemed to freeze with its passing as she spoke through clenched teeth. "Do not make the same mistakes that Little Pebble made. It is the greatest good fortune to be of special service to your master or to be considered by the sisterhood of *sau-hai*. You will do best to forget Pebble and her collection of idiots; they cannot help you. Save your trust for those who can."

The superintendent controlled her anger, reaching out to take Li-Xia's hand. "Let me see these hummingbird hands and butterfly fingers." She lifted both hands, circling the palms with her strong thumbs, taking each finger in turn with the lightest touch. "Have you not learned that life in the groves is short?" she asked more reasonably. "That when you can no longer deliver your baskets fast enough and full enough, there is nowhere else to go and nothing else to do but to beg in the streets, or to peddle yourself for a bowl of rice? Even the monasteries are filled with those who would wash the feet of monks before they will choose to die alone. There is no room in the world of Ten Willows for those who can no longer pluck the cocoon and tend the silkworm, and Pebble is soon to be among them."

Ah-Jeh fondled Li-Xia's hands with her short, fat fingers. "You have cared for them well. They are not yet torn and you have no calluses . . . even your fingernails are clean." The superintendent allowed Li to withdraw her hands. "Let there be no further talk. You will move in the morning."

✳

That night, when the evening rice was over, Li-Xia found Little Pebble at the river's edge, watching the moon's bright dazzle dance upon the water. She was fishing for eels. Pebble listened to every word Ah-Jeh had spoken, then said in a voice too tired for anger, "There is nothing you can do. Go with her and do as you are told. It is not so bad to be a weaver. Better than to follow me . . ." She was quiet, stringing the eels on a loop of split bamboo. "I do not have a moon mother to guide me. In truth, I have no voice but that of a moorhen calling her chicks"—she found her dancer's grin—"while you are to be a scholar of great fame and fortune . . . Giant Yun has decreed this."

Suddenly, she embraced Li-Xia and held her close, her cheek hot with tears. "You must forget the Pebble who will never be a diamond. I shall miss you at the Ghost Tree, but I am glad for you. There are better things in life than gathering cocoons. Sometimes pride asks too high a price of us. Look at me and know you make the right choice."

Li-Xia was troubled by Pebble's words, seeking to make her smile again.

"I will never forget you. If I become a scholar, I shall return to Ten Willows and and set you free."

"You are brave and strong enough to make your own way, my little

92

Crabapple, but please, I beg of you, if you are told to carry the lantern to the Heavenly House, you must do it. Forget pride and dignity; these can wait. Ming is old and lazy, his chi is weak and his energy short." She gave a small laugh. "He is a drinker of hot rice wine; see that his cup is always full. Dance for him, sing to him. . . . Use your hands . . . even your mouth if you must. He will be easily spent and soon put to sleep."

She grinned her encouragement. "If that is not enough for him, cry and scream as loud as you can, make such noise that his nerves will not allow him to proceed. Tell him he is too strong for you . . . his ivory staff so big it will split your jade gate in two. If you make him feel that he is young again, and that you fear but admire his manhood, he will be content. . . . If you are lucky he will tire of you in a week." Pebble paused, slowly shaking her head. "But do not run. . . . Do. Not. Run.

"If you are asked to choose the comb and the mirror, think hard about your choices, for they are very few. Whatever awaits you, do not anger Superintendent Ah-Jeh, or you will come to know true evil."

※

Li-Xia left the bamboo huts behind her and entered the honeysuckle gate of the mill compound. She was shown her bed space in a house made of bricks, with doors and shuttered windows that opened and closed. The house was set back from the riverfront, its thick walls distancing the call of frogs, the ripple of eels at night, and the gentle whispering of willows. It was lit with gas lamps that hissed like snakes and glared so white they hurt her eyes.

In moments she found that she missed the breeze off the river and the voices of the *mui-mui*. She missed the wavering yellow flames of the slush lamps and the smell of slow-burning oil; the fireflies flickering among the mosquito nets.

That night, as she prepared to lie down among strangers, Li found something buried in the turban of her hair—a hook of sharpened steel mounted in a fingerhold of polished horn.

CHAPTER 7

The Comb and the Mirror

Li *quickly learned the* art of "tasting the cocoon," telling from its sweet or sour flavor the nectar fed upon by the moth, and grading the endless threads of silk. In less than a month, she graduated to the spinning shed. Five spinners sat at six wheels, and she joined them to perfect the art of "spinning the golden web": teasing out the elusive end and unraveling the softened cocoons—hundreds of yards of single unbroken thread, delicate as the finest strand of a spider's web. She learned how the silkworm wound its cocoon into a ball so tight that only the sharpest eyes and nimblest fingers could find the end of precious thread and wind it onto the spindle without breaking it.

Few could master this skill and few were chosen to try, but Li-Xia learned fast and found each cocoon a challenge of speed and skill. She grew accustomed to twisting the delicate fibers onto the big treadle-operated spools. At first, it demanded a constant focus that suited her, giving her no time to miss Little Pebble or her bed beneath the willows.

The spinning shed also brought her closer to the weavers and gave her a different view of what it meant to be a sister of *sau-hai*. Serenity lay upon them like a drug, their voices never raised, their laughter never heard. They wore the stiff black *tzou* like a uniform, she thought, and their hair would never be washed in the river and dried by the wind. Every day would begin and end at the weaver's loom until they could no longer see or feel to work the shuttles.

Each of them seemed content with this—that there would never be the touch of a man, or children to carry on their name, no hope of anything more than the toleration of Ming-Chou and the favor of Ah-Jeh. Li asked herself in her heart if Pai-Ling would be proud of a daughter who accepted such a life without a voice—and decided she would not.

⁂

The year passed quickly. Food was better in the spinning shed: The congee was hot and plentiful and sprinkled with chopped chives, and there was *mien-bow*—steamed dumpling filled with minced pork—fish of all kinds, and a glass of tea beside her work place kept fresh by an amah. Her bed space was larger and she shared the small house with only five others. The spinning shed overlooked the loading wharf, where trading boats tied up to load the bales of silk.

Li had become increasingly adept at the spinning of silk, learning to grade the cocoons with speed and accuracy, to avoid breaks and joins and eliminate knots until the glistening thread was fine as a spiderweb. The days seemed long without the chatter of the *mung-cha-cha* among the mulberry groves, or the stories of Giant Yun. Most of all, she missed Pebble and the moon stories read by lamplight.

No longer was she the little Crabapple of the *mung-cha-cha*. "There will be no idiotic names in the spinning shed and certainly not in my mill," Ah-Jeh had announced. "You are spinner number five and your name is Li."

Li became so absorbed in the fast unwinding of cocoons that the chopsticks used to separate them in the bowl of hot water seemed to fly between her fingers, and the golden thread so deftly found and perfectly withdrawn gave her the coveted distinction of having hummingbird hands, fast as the flicker of the bird's rainbow wings.

The day of the miracle broke in spectacular glory, a dawn of apple green flushed mauve to burning orange, reaching across the river to creep beneath the willows and steal away the shadows. These were always precious moments for Li, when the light was of softest gold and the day not quite begun. Ducklings paddled bravely from the safety of tall rushes and faced the open water as she lit a joss stick and placed flowers

95

at one of the little shrines beside the huts—then dipped briefly in the cold, brackish waters to wash herself, combing her long hair, the early morning air still cool upon her skin.

There was no one to observe these private moments. She had chosen a spot apart from others, farther downriver, below the spinning shed divided by a buttress of rock. Still farther downstream, the *mui-mui* briefly wallowed and spat, giggled and shoved, churning the shallows to swirling clouds of yellow mud. Here, the surface was smooth, unhurried, undisturbed. In these quiet moments Li was able to see herself as in a pale green mirror.

She looked upon her body and was startled by how much she had grown. The girl she saw was long legged and already well formed; when she stooped to see her face, it was a pleasing one that showed nothing of hardship or unhappiness. Her eyes, she saw, were larger, more round than most. Her nose was small and straight, not the wide, wrinkled nub of Little Pebble; her mouth also small and neatly shaped, showing even white teeth when she smiled at herself.

She slid hip-deep into the river, using a sliver of coarse soap to clean herself, the points of her softly swelling breast stiffening from the sudden cold that gripped her. Once, not long ago, she had seen blood coming from her as she waded in the water. It was as though a hand had reached inside to squeeze her entrails, and she was sure that she would die. Defying the rules, she had sought out Pebble, who had grinned and given her clean rags to stem the flow, and told her the story of becoming a woman and bearing a child.

Li smiled at the recollection, splashing the soap from her breast and shoulders. At this moment, the river was set ablaze with the sun's full strength. She shielded her eyes, conscious that with this sudden burst of golden light came something more—something grand and majestic—something, she felt with a sharp pang of wonderment, from another world. As though a dazzling pathway had been laid before it, a magnificent sailing ship glided into view.

The white tips of its three masts towered high above the tallest willows, long ribbons of pennants unfurling between them—twin dragons of scarlet and yellow, floating like the wings of a phoenix riding the morning air. Swanlike in its gracefulness, the ship sailed slowly past the curtain of trailing leaves, its glossy white hull reflecting shards of light that brushed its sleek bows, cleaving the mirrored surface with scarcely a ripple. It was so close, she could hear coarse Cantonese voices on her decks making ready to dock, and smell the cooking from her galley.

The naked backs of half a dozen deckhands stood ready to cast the mooring ropes ashore, while an unfamiliar and frightening figure stood at the stern rail. It was a white foreign devil—a baby-eater—whose sudden appearance troubled her strangely. He paced like a tiger, stopping to look at the narrowing distance between the ship's side and the dock. She caught her breath, lowering her nakedness into the water with a thumping heart as the ship lowered her jibsails and drifted closer.

As he shouted orders in perfect Cantonese, she shivered to hear riverfront slang coming from the mouth of such a creature. Some of the things she had heard were true, others not, she thought with a curiosity she could not ignore. He was easier to look upon than the black-haired Portagee. She could not properly see the *gwai-lo*'s eyes through gaps in the willow, but they did not seem ablaze with the fires of hell. His strong teeth were not yellow as a dog's and did not appear ready to tear at the raw and bloodied flesh the Western barbarian was said to feast upon. His thick hair was the color of a copper pot freshly scrubbed, tied back to reveal a face that, from a distance, did not threaten injustice or brutality. The color of his skin was fairer than she had imagined.

He held no whip or cudgel, nor wore any weapon that she could see except a silver-hilted knife, sheathed at his hip. The loose white shirt he wore was open at the neck and caught at his waist by a belt studded with silver; tight, fitted breeches the color of cream were strapped into polished brown knee boots. These impressions were formed in a fleeting moment, yet they struck like a stinging slap to awaken her to an unimagined world.

Li had not completed her bathing and had thought herself to be alone. Suddenly aware of her nakedness, her long, thick hair still slung uncombed across her shoulders, she moved to hide herself. In that instant, the *gwai-lo* found her with eyes alert to any movement. She felt his gaze, warm and strong as hands placed upon her body, yet still she could not see him clearly—only glimpses passing slowly through the tracery of green, the distance between the ship's side and the rope fenders of the dock closing fast.

She saw that the ship's towering stern was deeply carved in sun-bright gilt with the same twin dragons that flew proudly on its flag. Between their outstretched claws they held a flowing crest bearing the words GOLDEN SKY IN Chinese characters and below these the word MACAO.

Finding that she could read the name of this great vessel brought a pang of joy. Yet the sudden appearance of this foreign devil, so unlike the vile barbarian she had been taught to fear and hate, unsettled her with many questions. He must have traveled far from the land of the foreign barbarians, descended perhaps from the radiant morning sky.

Goo-Mah and the wives of Yik-Munn had told many legends of these devils:

"They are the foulest of all creatures, more beast than human."

"You can smell them before you can see them; then you must run and hide or they will steal you away aboard their devil ship, eat you, and throw your bones to the fishes."

"They are ghosts and not of our world. The gods will curse those who call them friend. They are sent to do business and this is all they are good for. . . . No money—no talk."

"Soon they will be driven from China forever; the empress has ordained it. We shall defeat them with the righteous fist of the Boxer braves."

She wondered how those warnings applied to the barbarian who had appeared as if by magic with the dazzling sun.

An hour later, from her place in the spinning shed, Li could see the splendid ship tied up at the wharf, its hull longer than two river junks tied end to end. It dwarfed the sampans moored alongside, whose deckhands haggled with the crew over fresh fish, fruit, and vegetables. Watching the barbarian striding down the gangway, she could not deny the strength and dignity in his step.

His dark blue jacket gleamed with golden braid, its cuffs and collar and the peak of his cap also encrusted with gold. His hair extended like the tail of a wild horse between his shoulders, and curled thickly on his cheeks and chin.

Fetched in his magnificent palanquin by uniformed bearers and surrounded by his bodyguard, Ming-Chou himself had come down to meet the *gwai-lo* captain and his phantom ship. Only his robe of orange silk was visible beneath the canopy, the sun already too strong for a nobleman to bear.

A sudden bolt of raw pain sliced across Li's shoulders.

"Do not stop your work to stare at this foreign oaf!" Ah-Jeh hissed. "He is an abomination to eyes such as ours! Have you nothing more important to do? Does the golden thread unwind itself?" Li started in pain and guilt. Nothing had ever taken her mind from her work until this moment. Elder Sister sliced the air with her cane. Li felt as though hot coals had been laid across her back. "Do you think that a sister of *sau-hai* would gawp like a fish at this lumbering brute! Does the sight of him not turn your stomach?"

Li could only nod in hurried agreement, ashamed of her distraction. But she wondered how such grandeur could be so shameful, something so breathtaking of such low esteem.

Ah-Jeh continued to rant. "He is said to be the maddest of all *gwai-los*, to have built his first ship with his bare hands while still a boy. He is called Di-Fo-Lo, because his name is impossible to say in our language. Like all mad foreign devils he is said to have eaten the flesh of Chinese babies . . . he is Di-Fo-Lo, the baby-eater. The mad barbarian of the Macao mudflats."

Ah-Jeh spat her disdain. "He is said to be legendary among his kind, to have faced the black society and survived. They say he gambles like a warlord and is the richest foreign taipan in Macao and Hong Kong, and soon to be in Shanghai. That his ships carry twice the cargo of any junk and sail at three times the speed. That he carries such weapons on board that no pirate junk dares to approach within a mile of him. That is why the great master, Ming-Chou, welcomes this scum of a honey bucket.

Why else would any of us tolerate a moment of his stinking presence? It is business," she snapped. "It is all any *gwai-lo* is good for—only business."

Li tried to stir the depths of such feelings, but could not find them within her. She dared to speak, bowing low, her eyes cast down. "It is the ship that I find of interest. I have never dreamed of such a beautiful ship; where does it come from and where will it go?"

Elder Sister's reply was instant, her pale cheeks flushed with anger. "That is no business of yours—remember your place or be thrashed for your insolence." She was silent, her breath short and paced by her hatred. "It comes from that shit-hole called Macao," she grumbled at length, unable to turn away. "The piece of China the empress has leased to the Portagee for a hundred years, allowing them to trade in return for defeating the pirate king Koxinga. This 'beautiful' ship you find so interesting was built with money taken from poor Chinese and the strength of their backs . . . while Koxinga sails his war junks, raping and plundering where he will."

At last Ah-Jeh turned away. "They are all thieves and cheats, these foreign devils. Barbarians are evil-smelling as the goat and hair grows upon them almost as thickly. Their women paint their faces like the hideous behind of the baboon. They are creatures of foul habit. Many of them do not wash, yet they sweat like a galloping horse." The superintendent flapped her hand before her nose, shaking her head to be rid of the image she had conjured. "Instead of spitting out their snot and being rid of it like any civilized person, they blow it into a piece of cloth and keep it wrapped in their pocket. Can you imagine such a thing? Yet I have seen them do this with my own eyes."

Li was startled by the disgust that contorted Ah-Jeh's face. She had never seen Elder Sister quite so close, and could smell the almond oil in her hair and the cloves she chewed to freshen her breath. "They have the private parts of a donkey that would split a Chinese woman in two. No god can save one who has been mounted by the *gwai-lo*. Only the gutters of Shanghai or the slums of Hong Kong and Macau are home to those infested by their touch."

Aware of Li's confusion, the superintendent suddenly smiled, her bitterness seemingly swallowed. "But come now, let us find the golden thread and forget such things. You are made for much gentler hands than those of the *gwai-lo*." Li felt the superintendent's fingers grip her upper arm, then slip down to take her hand, to spread her fingers gently and rub her palm with a clever thumb. Ah-Jeh's voice had changed to one of stiff persuasion.

"I regret striking you in such a way, but my anger was in your defense against the influence of such a fiend. Even the sight of him can harm you. These fingers should not be red as steamed shrimp. These are precious butterfly fingers, soon to be faster and finer even than the rainbow wings of the hummingbird, the fingers, I believe, of a silk weaver." The pressure of the thumb in the palm of her hand drained all tension from Li. "Soon it will be your fifth year and you are already a woman. Our great lord, Ming-Chou, has asked to see you upon my recommendation. If you please him, you will dwell in the Heavenly House and perhaps be called to his bed. One such as you could rise in his household to take great power, and if this is so, perhaps you will remember the one who chose you." She shrugged her shoulders. "If you fail to please him, then we shall see if you are to be a sister of *sau-hai*."

Ah-Jeh lifted Li's hand, pressing the open palm to her lips; the tip of her tongue wriggled like a worm and was gone. "It would be a pity if he should keep you for himself, leaving you to become an amah when he tires of you."

The words were sympathetic, the pressure of the supervisor's fingers strangely comforting.

"If he finds you as pleasing as I do, you will be lost to the loom forever. Perhaps the choice, my Beautiful One, will be yours."

⁂

The sun had almost set as Li-Xia entered the crimson moon gate escorted by Ah-Jeh. The pale yellow ball of the lantern to light their way scattered shadows all about her. She could not tell if there were diamonds tumbling in the fountains in the secret gardens, if the carp silvered by a rising moon bore scales of pure gold, or if the pathways beneath her slippered feet were set with precious stones. Once inside the Heavenly House, beneath its scarlet roof, such wonders were unfolded that her senses swam and she dared not look to the right or left.

The merchant Ming-Chou was a smaller man than she had imagined, made greater by the gorgeous robes he wore and the splendid divan he reclined upon.

His face was thin and long and his ears large beneath a cap of black silk that displayed a gorgeous peacock feather from a blue glass bead in its crown. It was the hat, Ah-Jeh had told her, of a fourth-class mandarin. He seemed older than Li had expected, and did not look at all dangerous, too old and frail to cause great pain. There were dark pouches beneath his eyes, which were so narrow it was hard to know what he was thinking. She kowtowed three times as she had been told to do, her eyes fixed only on his small slippered feet.

Li remembered Pebble's advice, given with its customary grin: *Use your hands and your mouth. Do this well and pretend you like it; he will soon be fast asleep.*

The merchant beckoned with the raising of a hand, and Ah-Jeh urged her forward. There was a smell about him that instantly stopped her, the sweet, aromatic smell of wine and opium. The smell of her father, Yik-Munn. Ming-Chou's hands were impatient, grasping her arm to draw her to him—feeling, rubbing, squeezing, pinching through the thin silk of her new robe.

"Is this not the disobedient one from the spice farm, who defied her generous father and refused the lotus slipper, attacked his wives, and ran from her home?"

Ah-Jeh bowed. "This is she, Lo-Yeh. Her name is Li-Xia. But she is older now; her work is good and she gives no trouble. She is of age and ready for your service, if you find her pleasing, or perhaps for the weaving mill if she is not worthy."

Ming-Chou replied in a high thin voice. "I think you have your eyes on this little hummingbird." He chortled. "You are certain she has been kept from the *larn-jai*?" Ming-Chou's hands continued to feel her, his

fingers rough and thorough as if he were fumbling the feathers of a fattened duck to guess its weight and value. Li could not stop the shivering
of her limbs or her rising dread; every inch of her shook as though she
were naked in a bitter wind. The sallow face, smug and cruel, was
smooth as carved ivory, the eyes shifting like oiled olives under their
puffy lids. One bony forefinger with its curved golden nail caressed her
forehead, cheek, and nose, teasing her tightly closed mouth. He giggled,
the point of his fingernail tracing her lips, forcing them apart. "Her teeth,
they are sound?"

Ah-Jeh bowed nervously. "As newly opened pearls matched to perfection, Lo-Yeh."

"She is frightened," he tittered, the sharp golden nail crawling to her
eye. "And stubborn too, I have no doubt." Without warning the hand
slid like a viper into her robe and squeezed her naked breast.

Everything that Li had ever learned through Pai-Ling, every warning
Pebble had given her, every word Ah-Jeh had spoken, was suddenly
wrenched from her by a cold hand that squeezed her heart and tried to
take it. Fear turned to fury in a blinding flash as she spat roundly into
his watery eye, swinging her hand with all its force across his horrified
face. Ming recoiled from the blow with a strident squeal, dislodging his
mandarin's hat and kicking his legs like a child. So absurd did he look,
she heard herself howl with laughter. The fox fairy turned and ran for
the door. In the wake of her flight, a great vase crashed to the marble
floor, smashing into a thousand pieces. All Li could see was her father,
and the happiness tile shattered in pieces at his feet. She kicked off the
silken slippers to run like the fox they saw in her, her feet flying upon the
jeweled path, through the moon gate to the packed earth of the towpath
along the river's edge. The only sound was the echo of her own mad
laughter.

All sense of time and place deserted the fox fairy. She felt the pound-
ing of her bare feet, stretched over tufted grass and stony ground, her
heart beating like a temple drum, strong and indestructible within
her . . . while the *larn-jai* with their loping yellow dogs bawled and
yapped with evil joy, in no hurry to end the chase. She led them baying

with their hounds, over fields, through hedgerows, and across streams. There was no thought of how far she ran, for how long or where her feet might take her. Her flying feet felt no pain, only the glory of escape.

The dogs finally brought her down in the bed of a ditch, clawing at her clothes, tearing at her arms and legs, covering her in the slime of their toothless jaws. The *larn-jai* circled her, dancing to the chorus of their savage snarls, encouraged by her kicking feet, as her naked flesh was revealed before they pulled the dogs off. Vicious hands forced her face into the mud and slime of the ditch; a knee rammed into her spine.

When it seemed she must drown in the sludge, her head was wrenched back by the hair, while the *larn-jai* cursed her with vile oaths. She was turned over like a goat about to be slaughtered and skinned.

Their leader was kneeling between her flailing legs, his pants around his knees, the thing protruding red as a sore from his jerking fist, his thighs skinny as a child's. He ordered the others to step aside as he drew back his fist, his narrow chest heaving for breath. Only then did he pause, blinking foolishly at the the hook of steel protruding from the fox fairy's closed fist. She held it close to her chest, bright in the moonlight as the talon of an eagle.

"I am promised to Lo-Yeh. He has chosen me for his bed. If you take me, he will not want the leavings of *larn-jai* scum like you." The face of the boy astride her held its savage leer, but she saw his stupid smile grow thin as her words hung in the cold silver air above the yelping of the dogs. "Ah-Jeh will lose all face. There will be no commission. She will flog you at the triangle until you weep for an early death."

Li gave the *larn-jai* no time for further thought, seeing the hesitation of ignorance in their eyes. "Ming-Chou paid much for my *sung-tip*— more than he has paid for all of you. Think upon his punishment while you can . . . and if you still want more of my blood, it will mix with yours." She raised the blade as Pebble had shown her.

There were seconds of silence as they looked from one to the other, the leader still pinning her down. Finally, he snorted his disgust. "I would not stick this in a stinking fox fairy. I would rather fuck a pig."

An hour later, Li stood upon the threshold of the superintendent's private quarters, the two senior *larn-jai* gripping her arms on either side. Her hands were trussed with grass rope, her ankles bound so that she could stand and walk but not run. Each of the *larn-jai* bore bloodied scratches on face and neck and was streaked with mud. Still, she felt no great fear, only exhaustion from the chase and a ringing sense of triumph at the power of thoughts and words over fools.

The *larn-jai* rapped loudly on Ah-Jeh's door with grimy bloodstained knuckles, taunting Li with whispered details of how they would take revenge when Lo-Yeh had finished with her.

The door was opened to the powdered face and red lips of Elder Sister, the hint of a smile reaching her wary eyes as she stepped back, allowing Li to be shoved inside. She ordered the *larn-jai* to move away. "Have you touched her?" The question was abrupt as a threat. The leader protested their innocence, the difficulty in subduing the demons the fox fairy had summoned to defend her. "They must have been many, if it took five of you and a pack of dogs to bring back one girl. Go now, and if I find you are lying, you will cry for the mothers you do not have."

※

The room was small and crowded. A bed with a quilted cover was partly hidden by a red curtain; papers and record books were scattered on a large table beneath a hanging oil lamp of green glass. Another table and some stools stood on a square of carpet in the room's center. By the door, in a tall china vase, was an assortment of willow canes.

Li-Xia had an uneasy sense of being stared at in her bedraggled state, until she realized one wall was filled with framed portraits surrounding a small shrine lit by dragon candles. The unsmiling faces of Ah-Jeh's ancestors gazed through a drift of sandalwood incense. The superintendent looked her up and down, a smile slowly twisting her mouth.

"You were wise to reject the attentions of the master, but not to do it quite so violently. He is greatly angered and has ordered me to punish you severely. He expects me to flay you within an inch of your life and put you in the rings for a week. But he trusts my judgment and will not

105

wish to see evidence of this. Lo-Yeh does not set foot in the world of the *mui-mui*."

Her eyes glistened in the greenish light, like the ashes of a fire blown upon and rekindled.

Though suddenly struck by fear, Li-Xia was determined to speak bravely. "I have been chased by beasts who are worse than the dogs they run with. They have stripped me and would have used me as a cockerel uses a hen. When I can, I will kill them to restore my dignity and avenge my mother, whom they cursed and insulted."

Ah-Jeh held up a hand, calling for silence. "This is something you brought upon yourself. Did you think that you could run and not be chased? Your freedom has been sold; it belonged to Ming-Chou, but he has no further use for it. Now you belong to me."

She crossed to the corner, returning with a knife, cutting through the grass rope that bound Li's wrists and ankles.

"They are less than the droppings of a syphilitic bat, those *larn-jai*," she muttered. "Only the dregs of hell know what diseases they carry. Are you sure they did not enter you?"

Li-Xia nodded with a glint of pride.

"You were lucky. But I must be sure of this—your future may depend on it. If you are still pure, I will save you. The comb and the mirror shall be yours."

"With great respect, Elder Sister, and with all gratitude, I am not worthy of such an honor. I know now that I can never become a weaver."

The sound of her own voice, so much stronger than she felt inside, encouraged Li to continue.

"Just as I would be worthless in the bed of the old lord, so would I be found unworthy of the sisterhood. My feet are my only freedom; without them there is no path ahead. I could not spend my life at the loom, without the open air and the sky above me. I have a great fear of four walls."

"This is not for you to judge. Nor is it an opportunity to be tossed away so lightly." Ah-Jeh's words seemed more reasonable than angry. "Where do you think this path you speak of can lead you—one of the *mui-mui* without a name, whose ancestors have turned her away and can find no resting place?"

"I have a mother; her name is Pai-Ling and she is a scholar from the great city of Shanghai. I am called to be a scholar, to read and write as she does. Her knowledge lives within me, and together we will follow our path."

Ah-Jeh nodded her understanding, then held aside a curtain to reveal a tub of warm water. She allowed the slightest of smiles, and her voice was lightened with the hint of amusement.

"Well, you are no scholar now, but a spinner of silk, and that is knowledge and skill enough for a child. Your mother cannot be allowed to look upon a daughter so badly used. Take off those rags and wash yourself; I will clean your injuries and find you something to wear, then something to eat and drink. You cannot consider such important things until you are well rested."

She crossed to the vase of canes, selected one, and stood watching as Li shed the muddy garments. She lifted them from the floor with the tip of the cane and flicked them into a corner. Li could see the superintendent eye's examining every inch of her; there seemed little point in modesty and she made no attempt to hide her nakedness. Ah-Jeh clucked her tongue in a show of sympathy.

"You have been punished enough by those sons of pestilent whores." She stepped closer to inspect the scratches and bruises on Li's body. "You are not one who cries easily, I think. But there is nothing serious that I can see. Turn around."

A fingertip crawled like a fly over Li's naked back—down the length of her spine to the cleft of her buttocks. She felt them tighten, but the fingers stopped. Ah-Jeh fetched the kettle from the stove and added hot water to the tub, along with brown drops of disinfectant from a small vial, then produced a large sponge and a cake of soap. She flicked the curtain across its rail to give the pretense of privacy.

"Be sure your hair is free of their filth. Call me when you think you are clean. Your back is lacerated; I will attend to it."

Her voice was almost motherly. The soap smelled of flowers and was like none Li had seen; the sponge slipped over her wet skin like the hand of an angel as she stood in the tub. It was the first time in many grueling hours that she had a moment alone and a chance to think. She realized that she was in the presence of danger, but was this a greater or lesser evil than she had already faced? That Ah-Jeh possessed more power than any of those who had hurt her was certain, yet it seemed that Elder Sister was also capable of pity, and perhaps even sympathy.

Li knew there was no escape from the hands of Elder Sister except to please her, to play her game to its end. How easily the willow cane could have flayed her raw, yet she had been spared. Compared to the loathsome capering of the *larn-jai*, Ah-Jeh was a comfort.

Moments passed and the curtain was flicked back. There was an almost kindly patience in Ah-Jeh's voice.

"Turn around. I will tend your back before it festers."

The sponge was drawn carefully up and down Li's back and across her shoulders, soothing the burning scratches; the water turned rusty with blood and dirt running down her legs and into the tub. Li was grateful for its touch, her uncertainty dissolving with the flood of perfumed water down her back, over her buttocks, and down her legs.

She closed her eyes as Ah-Jeh firmly gripped her narrow waist to turn her around. When she opened them, she realized with a small shock how much taller she had grown since first seeing the superintendent perched like a crow upon her stool. Now she saw the whiteness of Ah-Jeh's scalp, straight as a scar in the parting of her hair.

"Let me see you free of mud and muck."

The sponge was wiped over her chest and along her arms, her stomach, between and down her legs in such an easy way, Li found no urgent reason to resist as exhaustion swept over her till she trembled.

"I see now why your dolt of a father called you Li-Xia. You are almost a woman when most *mui-mui* are still giggling children."

"I do not believe I was ever a child . . . I am incapable of giggling."

"You are also confused, and nervous. Perhaps you find your position too much to clearly contemplate. I can understand this uncertainty. We will drink tea and talk of it."

As though in a trance, Li stood still as Elder Sister reached for the towel, gently blotting her skin, paying close attention to her wounds no matter how slight. From a tray, tinctures and salves were painstakingly applied. Through her sense of gratitude, Li's heart cried out in anger, knowing these were the kindest hands that had ever tended her, the closest she had known to a mother's touch. She cursed the blind gods for cheating her this way; she knew this was a blessing that would soon be snatched away, and the hands that treated her so sweetly would quickly turn to violence.

Allowing the towel to be wrapped around her, Li followed Ah-Jeh to the small table now set with a pewter teapot and two glass cups with pewter lids. Ah-Jeh seated herself at the table, upon a stool of glazed porcelain, indicating a matching stool on the other side. The lilt of amusement was in her voice as Li took a seat on the edge of the stool.

"It took great spirit to avoid the bed of Ming-Chou so dramatically . . . and much good sense. He is like all men when it comes to that, no different from the *larn-jai*, but for his robes and riches—his thoughts and actions just as foul. Men differ only in the clothes they shed when the ivory staff is raised like a spear. But it is I you must now please, so be careful in what you say. Do not try my patience too far with your philosophies. You are too young for such meandering; it is for you to learn, not to teach."

She reached for the teapot, lifting the silver lid of each cup to fill it. Her manner was light and almost friendly. She chuckled in her throaty way, offering Li a cup of the dark green tea with both hands in the proper manner of respect.

"You are not like the others, Li-Xia. Most would do anything to win the master's favor and the benefits it can bring, and think nothing of the risks. This is not wise. The passions of men do not last—they are fleeting as the thunder and rain. You are very young, yet I believe you already know this."

When Li could not find a worthy reply, Ah-Jeh left her seat and came to stand behind her.

"It is good that you find the hands of men distasteful. A woman should not depend upon the needs and whims of any horny goat. You are not a receptacle for unwanted seed, to be filled up and thrown aside—or given a child you cannot feed in return for a moment of bestial pleasure."

As she spoke, the superintendent placed a hand lightly on the top of Li's head. Her other hand lifted Li's newly washed hair to find the hidden nape of her neck.

"If you accept the mirror and the comb and take the oath of *sau-hai*, you need no longer worry about such things. You will have many sisters and a home for life where no harm can come to you. In exchange, you must deny foolish dreams of a scholarly life; there will be no need for you to read and write."

"I have thought fully on this since I was brought to Ten Willows. My respect for the sisterhood and for Elder Sister is great . . . but I could not take the oath required of me if my journey is to end before it has begun."

There was a pause before Ah-Jeh spoke again. Li could see the pulse tripping like the heart of a bird in the vein of her neck.

"You have listened to the prattle of fools who know nothing of *sau-hai*. Your mother is dead. This I know from your father's lips and from the sisters that serve in his household. The voice you hear will fade with time. You are alone. Only I can guide you in this serious matter."

Ah-Jeh's hands were firm upon her shoulders.

"I must first examine you. There is no need for alarm, but your word is not enough. I must be sure of your maidenhood."

Li felt a hand applied to her scalp, the other to her neck, probing, pressing, strong fingers kneading the sinews of her throat; willpower was drawn from her as surely as the golden thread was wound from the cocoon. Li was hardly aware of the pressure applied to a point at the top of her skull and at the base of her throat—only of an engulfing tiredness that robbed her of all energy and drained any thought of resistance. The pressure was increased until she had no wish to move, no voice to question. She felt herself carried bodily and laid upon the bed.

As a rosy cloud settled over her, there was no real thought of protest, only wonderment that she should so easily submit. The towel was opened; the hands of Elder Sister were firm and warm on her skin, applied with sure knowledge of her body—deepening pressure here, then there, the thumbs finding spots that released floods of well-being.

"Your chi is strong, but it is blocked. I will release it so that the channels of your energy flow freely."

Li felt herself become two persons—one who yielded most readily, and another who looked on, deathly afraid. The hands were laid lightly upon the twin swellings of her breasts; she felt their points rise to the touch, then the hands shifted suddenly to her crotch, parting her softness. An unbearable tingling mounted from the roots of her hair to toes that clenched like fists, then a series of shocks passed through her to slowly ebb away, until she was immersed again by the rosy cloud.

Li had no idea how long she slept. For long moments she lay still, piecing together what had happened to her, before opening her eyes to find the room silent and darkened, the lamp turned down. Her perception was fogged, as though she had not taken part in things but had been a bystander. The physical pain that lingered from her encounter with the *larn-jai* was slight, but enough to remind her that this was no illusion.

Slowly, and with strengthening resolve, she recalled everything that had happened. She searched the shadows to find the superintendent seated in a pool of green light, engrossed in paperwork with small round spectacles perched on her nose.

Li left the bed quietly, wrapping herself in the towel. Ah-Jeh looked up, her face bathed in the lamp's sickly pallor. She grinned, showing her dull, uneven teeth, and set aside her pen.

"You are awake and feeling stronger, I hope. You have slept well."

Knowing the danger, Li hesitated for only a moment before speaking the words of her heart. "You betrayed my trust."

Ah-Jeh's eyebrows arched in surprise. She stared at Li, her eyes widened and alert.

Before she could reply, Li spoke again, her voice lowered and her tone even.

"You used your skills to confuse me . . . to take away my spirit. You did not ask for my permission to use me as you did."

Ah-Jeh's eyes narrowed as Li spoke, her mouth set in its grim, unyielding line, her brows drawn into a frown.

"I examined you as I said I would. Did you think that I would take your word as proof of your virginity? Would you admit to taking the cock of one of the *larn-jai* if it was forced upon you?" Elder Sister snatched the spectacles from her nose, tossing them aside.

"You did more than examine me."

Ah-Jeh rose slowly from her seat, then delivered her words slowly, each as deliberate as a slap.

"And you enjoyed every second of it . . . you ate it like cake and would have feasted on more."

She stepped out of the green glare, her eyes caught by sparks of red from the altar.

"I showed you what pleasure can be, when I could as easily have taken you beyond the boundaries of pain. I healed you when it was my duty to skin you alive. You lapped up my generosity like a kitten laps warm milk."

"I am grateful for your kindness, but I ran from the Heavenly House because I am not a duck to be made plump for someone's pot, or a piece of fruit to be eaten while it is ripe—"

Ah-Jeh's brittle voice slashed her words, her round face thrust forward to look closely into Li's eyes.

"How dare you, daughter of a whore? The sisters of *sau-hai* know all and are everywhere. Two of our number have dwelt beneath your father's roof for more years than you have lived. I know the story of the fox fairy and the death of Great-Aunt . . . your defiance of the wives and your refusal of the lotus slippers and your alliance with Number Three, Ah-Su, from the island of Hainan. I even know what happened to your mother."

Li gave a visible start. She no longer feared the short, fat woman before her, and had even found a certain respect for one who had acquired such power with so little beauty. But Elder Sister's words hit her like a kick to the belly.

"What do you know of my mother? They would not even tell me where she rests."

Ah-Jeh lifted the teapot from its wicker warmer, pouring tea in silence. When she had handed Li a cup, she spoke without emotion of any kind.

"It is not a pretty story, but every woman has the right to know her mother's name and of her karma. They say she threw herself from a window to fall upon the tines of a harrow. She thought that you had been buried alive . . . and died for love of you, whom she never saw or held."

Li was not conscious of any change in her face, but felt tears fill her eyes and spill hotly down her cheeks.

"As you know, her name was Pai-Ling and her family, once prosperous, was ruined by the triad tongs. Your father paid cheaply for her as a concubine. She had lotus feet but her spirit, they say, flew high as an eagle. She would be proud of you, I think."

Elder Sister stood and crossed to a drawer, taking out a folded *samfoo* of dark red. She tossed it in Li's lap.

"Put these on and I will fetch you something to eat."

She went to the kitchen corner to fill a bowl with hot and tasty soup, setting it with another bowl piled high with rice and a pair of chopsticks, while Li drew on the trousers and buttoned the tunic.

"Eat this food while I speak of *sau-hai*, so that you can choose your own path. You are very young, yet already what innocence you had has been bought and sold like turnips. This is the lot of a woman who lives long enough to receive her soul but is lost to her ancestors. You cannot change this, and neither can I.

"For more than a thousand years, the sisterhood has taken care of its own as women without men. To be a Ten Willows weaver is to have a secure place for life—to be treated well and to have the love and respect of many friends. To live and eat as comfortably as a woman should, to want for nothing, and to acquire a modest income of your own, that your passage to the afterlife may be a dignified one—our ancestors are your ancestors. For this you sacrifice what—the selfishness of a stupid man?"

Ah-Jeh pulled a face and pretended to spit upon the floor. "The thunder and rain eclipses all else for any man—kindness, loyalty, truth, and let us not speak of *love*. If it is love you are after, you will do better to chase the moon in a water jar. All the pleasure of the ivory staff belongs to him—not to you; if you are lucky, you may catch a few drops. He will ram it into every hole in your body whether you wish it or not—and you will have no voice in this. Your voice will only be heard in the agony of bearing his children and the unhappiness left when he is done with you."

Li watched Elder Sister pause to sip her tea. That she spoke her truth was not in question. Li looked upon her in a clearer light, feeling humbled by the passion of her words.

"Are you one to hope for the love and care of children in your old age . . . for their gratitude?" Ah-Jeh continued, slowly shaking her head with a mockery of sadness. "If you bear sons and do not die raising them—perhaps you will get a crumb from their table. If you bear daughters and they are allowed to live—your heart will weep for them as Pai-Ling's wept for you.

"You cannot change your fortunes—that your father has betrayed you, turning your brave young dreams to ashes. He has sold you, and your future lies in the secret drawer of Ming-Chou's great dragon desk with a hundred others. Nothing will retrieve it but a miracle. So ask these questions of yourself and be truthful: Are the seasons of the mulberry groves all that you will ask of life? To be old before your time, your beauty lost to savage suns and biting winters? Do you prefer to live with fools on a mosquito-ridden riverbank until you are cast out or buried in the Pagoda of Pity at the side of Little Pebble—or do you prefer to be cooled beneath the fans and warmed by the stoves of the mill, to live among flowers and sleep beneath a roof of tile?"

Li listened intently while eating the delicious food put before her. She set the chopsticks aside as Ah-Jeh filled her cup.

"I am unworthy of such valuable advice, and my gratitude is greater than my humble words can express. I beg you to hear my foolish thoughts, as foolish, I think, as the secret of my heart. You have paid me the honor of speaking to me as a woman and not a child. I must try to speak like one, and must beg for your patience. . . . When the man who calls himself my father dressed me as a doll, he showed me the butterfly of hope, then he

114

burned the books I could not read. He brought me to Ten Willows, saying I was to live with a rich uncle. He lied because he was afraid I might run from him again before the money paid for me was safely in his purse.

"He left me here and did not even say good-bye; he took with him my chance of happiness. He will never have my forgiveness, no matter what becomes of me. I do not hate him, as I do not know him—he is nothing to me, as I am nothing to him. Beneath the willows, I soon saw that the world of the *mui-mui* and the world of the sisterhood are greatly different, and like the others, I too dreamed of becoming a weaver.

"But I have watched the weavers come and go, hand in hand across the bridge—from the comfort of their little houses to the safety of the mill. They are beautiful to see beneath their sunshades, like flowers that do not wither and die. Each looks like the other and they are fortunate to be content and happy with the life that they have chosen. But I was kept imprisoned by four small walls for too long. My father tried to take away my feet, to make his purse a little fatter. I was less than a *lup-sup* dog and treated as one.

"I fought to save my feet, which took me into the fields under an endless sky. I suffered much to keep them free and cannot think that they will only cross the bridge and walk the flowered paths of this compound for the rest of my life. In the mulberry groves I can walk or run as I please. If one day I choose to run farther and faster than I should, then let me pay the price of my decision."

Li left her seat to kneel before Elder Sister, kowtowing until her forehead touched the floor. "Ah-Jeh, do not offer me the mirror and the comb . . . I could not accept them. My respect for the sisterhood is too great and I have already found my limitations. Since I could stand, I have chased the butterfly of hope and happiness. Let me seek the miracle you speak of on my own feet . . . I shall never complain of the consequences."

Ah-Jeh listened to Li without showing her thoughts. When she spoke, it was with the voice of Elder Sister, superintendent of Ten Willows.

"Then there is nothing I can do to help you. If you will not accept the mirror and the comb, you must face the punishment your attack on Ming-Chou demands."

The superintendent informed Ming-Chou that the girl who had turned upon him with such savagery had been captured and secured in the rings. The merchant recalled the fox fairy painfully, his annoyance fleeting. This was Ten Willows business and need go no further. He considered himself a fair master: Had he not supplied mosquito nets and built the Pagoda of Pity in a corner of his own land, a place of burial for those whose ancestors had disowned them? He had full confidence that his superintendent would see to it that the demon did nothing more to disturb the serenity of his illustrious domain.

Ah-Jeh did not need to be told that the faster this was put to rest, the better. There were those among the *mui-mui* who nursed grudges of their own, and would need little reason to rebel. Even her small corner of *sau-hai,* a system that kept order and harmony through the strictness of its rules, could be at risk. Li must be silenced as swiftly as possible, an example that would not be forgotten.

The scroll of proclamation was read out and hung upon the gingko tree. Ah-Jeh spread word throughout the huts of the *mui-mui* and the compound of the mill that the girl called Crabapple had been condemned by the laws of *sau-hai* to receive one hundred strokes of the cane across the soles of her feet, followed by one week of confinement in the animal pens—then to be taken to the river in a basket made for the transport of pigs, and there to be drowned at the break of day in the way of all devils and demons who would corrupt the laws of Ten Willows.

Li was taken to the rings of punishment, her ankles thrust into the clamps. When everyone was assembled, Ah-Jeh slashed the soles of the fox fairy's feet until the long, thin cane was too heavy to lift.

As each cutting blow jerked her body, flames of agony licking her precious feet, Li found herself back in the rice shed, waiting for the rattle of the latch and the door to open. She thought only of her mother Pai-Ling descending on a moonbeam to the silver mists of the ginger field. A veil of white wrapped her safely in its gossamer folds, where the flames could not follow.

She was left in the leg irons for a day and a night. Certain that the fiend inside her had turned her raving mad, no one went near her. Even the *larn-jai* muttered their abuse from a distance, while their dogs circled, sniffing for an opportunity. Finally, with daylight gone and a pale moon rising, Giant Yun and Little Pebble led the family *mung-cha-cha* silently from the darkness. They formed a circle of protection around Li, sitting upright on the ground to keep away the *larn-jai* and their dogs.

Taken from the rings, Li's lacerated feet were swollen to twice their size and she could not stand. Armed and uniformed bodyguards of Ming-Chou stood ready as she was dragged to the pigsties and the goat pens, a collar and bell around her neck and tethered by a chain. She was left for a week, to eat what the animals ate and to drink what she could from the trough. The *mui-mui* were ordered to pelt her with refuse, but dared not face the wrath of Little Pebble and the *mung-cha-cha*, or the feet of Giant Yun. Every night, by the light of their mother the moon, her feet were washed with herbs, while Pebble fed her from her own bowl and gave her clean water to drink.

On the seventh day, the *larn-jai* approached Li as they would a helpless goat. They had armed themselves with willow wands to slash her into submission, but could not raise the squeals they hoped for. She resisted them with such frenzy they backed away, giggling as they poked her with sharpened sticks. Only when a vicious blow from behind had stunned her did Li-Xia fall in an explosion of blinding red that slid into instant darkness. It was struck by Ah-Gor, the elder brother of the *larn-jai*, the one who had straddled her in the ditch. She awoke to find that he had tied her hands tightly behind her back with grass rope as another trussed her feet. A filthy hand was shoved brutally between her legs with whoops of laughter as others tore away her clothing.

"We shall see what the beautiful Crabapple is hiding in her hair." Ah-Gor opened a long-bladed knife, hacking at handfuls of her hair. Another gathered them into a bunch and set it alight, tossing the flaming torch onto her half-naked body. It gave off a smell Li knew she would never forget. Even so, it took time and sweat for the *larn-jai* to force her bodily into the long narrow cylinder of the pig basket. The opening of the basket was quickly tied tight, as the gangling Ah-Gor squatted beside her, resting on his bony haunches, lighting the stump of a cigarette.

He flicked the burning match at her and blew strong tobacco smoke into her face with a gust of putrid breath, speaking easily as he would to a friend. "There is no escape from the basket." Ah-Gor grinned, flicking away the stub and climbing to his feet, scooping a dipper of water from the trough, pouring it carefully onto her bound hands and feet. "When the grass rope is wet, it grows tighter and tighter. The more you struggle, the tighter it gets."

Trussed in this coffin of woven reeds, she was carried down to the riverbank and deserted, bound hand and foot, the gag in her mouth. Only the fire of her festering feet told her she still lived. Left there through the freezing night, she retreated again into the moonlit mists of the ginger field—until the first cock crow echoed across the river, dogs barked, and sampans quietly sculled their way to market, the smell of cooking fires from the chophouse strong on the morning air. Lamps were lit among the huts, to the clamor of the triangle. In the rising mists, the bodyguards herded the *mui-mui* to the riverbank in sight of the jetty. They would witness the punishment whether they wished to or not.

Through the weave of the basket, Li saw a procession approaching, headed by two priests and their acolytes in full regalia of red and black, accompanied by the thin keening of trumpets and loud thumping of fish-head drums. The sisters of *sau-hai* followed, their sunshades furled beneath their arms, each with a switch of willow in her hand; and behind them the *larn-jai*, with a great clashing of cymbals and beating of gongs. In moments, the pleasant faces of the weavers surrounded the basket, peering down, looking with bland interest at her muddied face through the open weave, jabbing her with their sticks to see if she still lived.

Looking past them, through eyes almost blind with pain and exhaustion, numbed of all hope, Li blinked her eyes, unsure at first if what she saw was real, or her tortured mind playing tricks: the white-tipped masts and streaming pennants of the foreign ship, twin dragons writhing through the willows like the wings of a phoenix.

CHAPTER 8

Sky House

Captain Benjamin Jean-Paul Devereaux was entering figures into the cargo log when he heard the commotion. It ebbed and flowed like a turning tide underlying the voices of his deck crew as *Golden Sky* made ready to dock at the loading wharf of the Ten Willows silk farm. This was a lucrative new port of call for *Golden Sky*; he had bought his first shipment of raw silk from the merchant Ming-Chou and sold it at a handsome profit to the factories in Shantung.

The silk farm had seemed peaceful enough, almost enchanted, on his first journey, when he had glimpsed the vision of a young girl bathing at the edge of the river. A vision so lovely, he could not be sure he had really seen her; the overhanging willows reflected in the river shadows played many tricks when disturbed by the bow wave of *Golden Sky*. He found that this fleeting image had stayed with him; when he had looked again, there had been nothing but a yellow cloud of settled water and the trickery of dancing sunlight.

Ben Devereaux would not be considered a big man on his forefathers' island of Brittany and the rugged coast of Cornwall, but in Southern China, where a man was tall at five and a half feet, he was seen as a giant. His face was weathered by a lifetime at sea in all seasons and latitudes; his mother's Manchu blood gave his complexion a sallow cast, finely lined as scrimshaw on a whale's tooth. His thick bronze hair, streaked with veins of gold, was tied back with a thong of leather. His beard showed signs of the same sun-bleached gold, kept clipped but far from neat. His eyes, gray as uncertain skies, were changeable as the restless oceans he had made his own.

The babble grew louder and more compelling as he closed the log-book with a sigh: another argument, no doubt, between his crew and the dockers, or with the passing junk crews who hated to see a foreign ship taking their business. Going on deck to stop the trouble, he found his men lining the handrails and hanging from the rigging. They were watching a chaotic gathering on the riverbank. Priests fed a bonfire with bundles of paper, as numerous black-clad women crowded around some object on the ground. They prodded and struck it with sticks, cheered on by a gang of unclean louts with emaciated dogs yelping at their feet.

He had seen such women before, the amahs of his own house and those of his friends, but never in a group of fifty or more like this. They looked, he thought in an instant, like a flock of ravens squabbling over a corpse As the women half dragged the object toward the river's edge just astern of *Golden Sky*, he saw that it was a common pig basket, woven of willow twigs and rushes, known for its strength when restraining the struggles of a full-grown boar. But why would they be trying to drown their own pig? Even to the hardened sensibilities of a lifetime at sea, much of it on China's coast and its far-flung rivers, there was something decidedly sinister in the whole rowdy procession. Ben's partner and sailing master, Indie Da Silva, a native of Macao, was watching from the rail and turned to him, his usual Burmese cheroot jammed between dazzling teeth made mainly of pure gold. "I was about to call you, Skipper. This is a sight not meant for our eyes." Indie was grinning widely beneath a wide-brimmed hat of light sisal hemp.

"Who are they? What in God's teeth are they doing?" Ben asked.

"They are *sau-hai*—women without men." Indie laughed, turning back, not wanting to miss a moment of the eerie spectacle.

"In the basket is one who has disgraced or insulted them in some way. If she has offended the code of *sau-hai*, they will drown her. She is no longer *mui-mui*, little sister, but *hah-dung-gai*—low-class whore. The priests have been brought to contain the demon until it is drowned. That is hell money they are burning, to appease the evil spirits who might interfere on her behalf." Indie shook his head. "They are very un-forgiving, these grim sisters. But I warn you, this is none of our busi-ness." Ben watched in silence as the grotesque bundle was hauled down the muddy riverbank, almost under the swoop of *Golden Sky*'s stern.

No sound came from the pig basket, and he wondered if the victim was already dead. He frowned; he did not share his partner's casual in-terest in the scene before them, nor could he approve of the excitement of his crew . . . but he knew better than to show his disapproval. Indie had spent his life in the China trade and taught Ben all he knew. His fa-ther, so he proudly claimed, was a Chinese pirate and his mother a Por-tuguese barmaid from Macao. The sailing master spoke a half-dozen dialects and was more China Seas than Mediterranean. "Confounded heathens . . . is there no law against this kind of thing?"

Ben knew the emptiness of his question before Indie could answer. "How much justice was there in the ducking stool and the drowning of witches in your own country and half of Europe, not that long ago? None, I think." Indie Da Silva expertly rolled his cheroot from one side of his wide-jawed mouth to the other. "Many a twelve-year-old was set alight because some landlord's prize bull couldn't get it up or his cows ran dry . . . or just for the damned fun of it. Out here in the backwaters they are a little slow in changing such things. If there is no warlord to lay down laws, they are free to make their own. This puffed-up merchant, Ming-Chou, answers to no one but Lu-Hsing, the god of affluence. I don't think such gods have a conscience."

As they came closer to the water's edge, the hissings and mutterings of the *sau-hai* sisters grew quieter, then stopped. In eerie silence, a large rock was fastened to one end of the bundle before it was rolled down the last stretch of riverbank, where it splashed into the shallows with a bil-lowing of yellow mud. It bobbed grotesquely in the whirling current, to slowly sink in a welter of murky bubbles. As if he read his partner's mind, Indie spoke, his tone becoming more urgent.

"Do not think of interfering in this, Ben. The crew will lose face if they see their captain stooping to help one of the *mui-mui* by defying a priest. They will see you as a fool. The ship cursed and themselves with it for serving such a madman." He laughed easily, to make light of it. "Especially a known baby-eater such as Di-Fo-Lo, the mad *gwai-lo* of the mudflats. I know how you feel about injustice and cruelty, Ben, but it's like spitting in the eye of one of their gods. . . . Best go below if it bothers you. We're here to buy silk, not play god, remember?"

Indie's voice took on a note of alarm as Ben stripped off his shirt and kicked off his boots, unsheathing the deck knife from his belt and jamming it between his teeth. "For pity's sake—think, man! If you save the life of one condemned by the *sau-hai*, you pay for her sins as they see them. That life belongs to you and becomes your responsibility for eternity; your ancestors are her ancestors. If you discard her, you are cursed to perdition by the elders and forever hounded by her ghost. Is this what we want?"

Indie would never be sure if Ben heard him before he dived from the stern of *Golden Sky*. He entered the water cleanly, swimming down the slope of the bank, sheering steeply into green depths thick with dense beds of drifting weed. Following the mud trail left by the weighted basket bumping its way to the bottom, he saw the awful bulk of it rolling in the current, a chain of bubbles belching from inside.

The large stone roped to its bottom allowed it to rise and stand upright among clinging blades of leathery weed. His knife ripped away at the binding; the sodden casing came apart in his powerful hands. A howl of fury from the shore greeted him as he surfaced with the girl's inert body in his arms, quickly joined by a babble of protest from the crew. Their nattering voices no longer controlled, the *sau-hai* sisters waded into the water to meet him as he lifted the unconscious figure from the river, falling upon him from all sides as he tried to rise and carry her clear of the shallows. Some clawed at him, while others tried to force him back, to drag the limp body from his arms and into the swiftly moving current. The women backed off only when Ben made wide sweeps with the knife, calling for Indie to bring help.

The ugly spectacle was over but the crew still jabbered angrily at the sight of their captain, legendary dock fighter Di-Fo-Lo, fending off a horde of hysterical women and a pack of skinny yellow dogs. Indie took the companionway in a stride or two, entering the water, cursing the thick yellow mud and his white doeskin breeches, herding the vicious gang of women back up the riverbank and into the mill compound with a string of ferocious threats of his own.

Ben laid the unconscious girl on the bank, pumped the river water from her lungs, and breathed life into her from his own powerful chest. His anger had been made the blacker when he found the body in the pig basket to be that of a child, her feet badly disfigured, her mud-caked body smothered with wheals and cuts, half choked from the sodden rag stuffed in her mouth.

"She's still alive," he said aloud as Indie waded over to help him. "She must have put up one hell of a fight."

"It would have been easier if she hadn't." Indie sighed ruefully. "Better for you, better for me, and a damn sight better for her. Now we need to face old Ming and his hoodlums. The old man won't be too happy about your blasted gallantry, and I don't blame him." Indie spat the soggy stub of his cheroot into the water.

"This is bad joss. Foreigners are not exactly popular at the moment, or haven't you noticed? I mean it, Ben; this is no time for heroics. We may be a long way from Shanghai, but the warlords are already in Canton; we can't hide under the double dragon forever." He retrieved the bedraggled remains of his hat, then helped Ben lift and carry the unconscious girl up the gangway and aboard *Golden Sky*. From the window of her quarters, Ah-Jeh had watched the proceedings with mounting fury, calling down bitter curses upon the head of this interfering foreign devil and all his kind.

Although Ben was no stranger to haggling over the price of anything from a sack of rice to a Ming vase, he was amazed at how little he had to pay for the life of a human being. He guessed the girl to be in her early teens, and she cost him less than he would pay for a good pair of boots. Ming-Chou and his comprador showed little interest in the fate of the girl in the pig basket, being more concerned with the time that was lost in the weaving sheds. Since Ben had chosen to pull her out and to cause much annoyance and great loss of face among his people, the girl was his for the price asked plus additional costs for the trouble caused.

The sum was paid and the *sung-tip* and all her meager belongings handed to Captain Devereaux with a minimum of ceremony. He was told her name—"Lee Sheeah," to his ear—and that she was thought to be thirteen years old. Now that she was his legal property, more dead than alive, reeking of river mud and swathed in weed, it was clear that Ming-Chou and his fat superintendent were anxious to be rid of her.

Beside him, Indie Da Silva tried to keep the impatience from his voice. "Well done, Ben; you are a hero, the owner of a half-dead Chinese chippie, probably riddled with disease. By the look of her, she may never walk normally again. Good for nothing but feeding silkworms and stealing the gold from your back teeth while you are sleeping"—he bowed with a sweep of his panama hat—"yours to do with what you will."

※

The river was still with her as consciousness slowly returned to Li. Aware of movement, a lazy rise and fall to a gently creaking rhythm, she was afraid to open her eyes. Light had been cut off so suddenly, replaced by increasing darkness and cold in a silent world of yellows and greens, columns of rising bubbles, that she had thought the muddy taste of river water would take her final breath—until the foreign devil suddenly appeared before her, a silver-hilted knife between his teeth.

Her eyes flickered open, afraid of what she would see. The searing pain of her feet told her she was alive, but the stink that had been so much a part of her was gone completely. Everything around her was pleasing to the eye and soothing to the heart: a large table covered with maps and papers, a spoke-backed swivel chair, a polished brass lamp, shelves full of books, and pictures of ships. Portholes opened to a warm salty breeze, throwing moving circles of sunlight onto richly colored wooden paneling and showing glimpses of pale blue sky.

She did not know who had bathed her and dressed her feet, only that she was clean and wearing clothes too big for her that smelled fresh as a breeze off the water. There was another fragrance in this strange room; neither incense nor opium, it hung in the air with a mysterious sweetness. She lay in a wonderfully soft bed so large it could hold six others, and her head rested as on thistledown. When her eyes closed, the phantoms of her ordeal returned to mock her, but they were distant and indistinct, her terror cushioned by a sense of comfort and well-being greater than she had ever known.

She knew she must have been taken from the river by the barbarian Ah-Jeh had called Di-Fo-Lo, but could not find fear among her scattered senses. She tried to raise herself but could not move, remembering nothing but the welcome certainty of death, the knife-edged shrieks of the *sau-hai*, and the bellowing of the *gwai-lo* captain as he waded to shore with her held fast by one strong arm, while wielding a blade in the other.

Although she still saw danger, the cloud she floated upon grew softer. This time the gentle voice of Pai-Ling did not come to her. It was as though she had finally embarked on the journey that had begun in the rice shed—an old life for a new. With her eyes still closed, she yielded to the surge and gurgle of a fast ship driving hard through a lively sea.

She woke with a start of alarm as a blunt finger was pressed gently against the pulse of her throat. The foreign devil himself was bending over her. All that she had heard of him and his kind welled within her, but was tempered by a face that said nothing of hate. He did not prod and poke her to guess her weight and value. She was reassured too by the broad, friendly features of a Chinese man leaning closely over his shoulder.

The barbarian's face was serious but not at all menacing. His eyes were not the eyes of a monster; they were kinder and less questioning than she could have hoped for. The hair that curled on his head and chin looked cleaner and neater than she had expected, and did not seem to be alive with vermin as she had been told it would be. Neither was the smell of him as odious as she had been led to believe; he smelled of fresh salt air and something sweet—opium perhaps, of the finest quality. He lightly placed the back of his hand across her forehead. It seemed huge to her, and she shrank from its touch.

"Keep still; I will not hurt you." He shifted his hand to her cheek, first one and then the other, then gently pulled down her lower eyelids and asked her to open her mouth and stick out her tongue. "You have no more fever. How do you feel?" She was stunned to hear his deep voice speaking confidently in her language. At first she could not answer, then whispered, "*Ho, ho,*" indicating she did not feel unwell, but, looking down at her bandaged feet, "*gurk-tong* . . . my feet hurt." He nodded his understanding. "Your feet are badly injured but will soon be strong again." The barbarian allowed a smile to light in his strange gray eyes.

"You are safe now, aboard my ship, *Golden Sky.* You have been here for three days and two nights. There is nothing for you to fear. You need only to eat something, then rest if you can. When you are well enough, you may come on deck to breathe some air." He straightened to what seemed to Li an impossible height. Behind him, the small Chinese man stepped forward with a tray. "This is Wang, my steward; he will look after you until we arrive in Macao. Then we will get you well again and find you something to do. There is nothing to be afraid of; no one can hurt you now."

He was quickly gone, and Wang set a tray of food beside the bed, chattering as he helped her to sit up. "Captain Devereaux is a good master, *siu-jeh.* You need have no fear of him. He does not eat babies like other *gwai-los.* He has paid and signed your *sung-tip.* You belong to him now. . . . You are very lucky." He chuckled happily. "Very, very lucky, *siu-jeh.*"

The hot rice porridge was delicious, smooth as silk and spiced with hundred-year egg. A large mug of orange-colored tea was set on the tray in a special place to keep it from spilling. Wang giggled at her expression. "*Gnow-lie-cha,*" he said proudly. "Cow's-milk tea. Master Ben only drinks *gnow-lie-cha.*" He was delighted to see her sip the hot, sweet tea and give a nod of approval. "I will play healing music for *siu-jeh,*" he said, taking a small bamboo flute from his pocket. It was the first time Li had been properly addressed as "little miss," and it pleased her in the strangest way.

She allowed the gentle movement of the ship to rock her in its arms, and watched the circle of light sweeping the walls and ceiling until her eyes were closed in a peaceful slumber. With no idea of how many hours she had slept, Li was roused for the second time by the looming presence of the barbarian. He filled the doorway as he spoke.

"I think it is time you breathed some fresh air. . . . But first, we shall look again at your feet."

He stepped aside to allow Wang to enter with a bowl of steaming water and a tray of bottles and bandages. She saw that he carried a pipe of polished wood between his teeth, from which sweet smoke whirled about him. It told her that this room was his, that the clothes she wore had known his skin and the bed she lay in was where he slept.

"Wang is the ship's doctor as well as an excellent cook and a clever entertainer, as you have discovered. It was he who cleaned you up and tended your feet. He will change the dressings and attend to you. If you are well enough, I will bring you topside."

A half hour later, her feet soaked and dressed with another herbal poultice, Li was lifted in the captain's arms and carried up a set of brass-bound steps out onto the deck. The midmorning sun hung in a sky of duck-egg blue. Li had never seen the ocean except in her imagination, from the middle of the wooden bridge, when the tide was high and the river was at its widest. The open sea stretched away to the horizon on every side. The wind whipped a thousand white horses from ink-blue waves and filled the booming sails that flew above her like the wings of heaven.

The captain set her in a deck chair and Wang tucked a blanket warmly around her. Breezes sang in the rigging at her side, and a cloud of gulls wheeled and dived upon unseen schools of fish. As the wind drove *Golden Sky* through sheets of sparkling spray, the dark green mountains of southern China came steadily closer. Nestled at their feet, spread like a child's plaything, was the Portuguese enclave of Macao.

Macao did not have the splendid temples and palaces of Hangchow or Peking, the bustle and commerce of Shanghai or Hong Kong, or the picturesque tranquility of the river ports. Macao was said to be like an exciting woman who, deserted by her lover, cast out by her family, and rejected by her friends, had turned thoroughly bad.

Its maze of cobbled streets and alleys were lined with opium dens, fan-tan and other gambling parlors, chophouses, and brothels that never closed. Its people were a mixture of Chinese, Portuguese, Macanese, Indian, a sprinkling of Arabs, and natives of the Cameroons. Among these, connected like the backbone of a snake, a murderous fraternity of renegade Europeans vied with the triad-protected Chinese taipans and their warlords for control of the gambling and vice dens.

There was a seductive beauty in the old Portuguese-styled houses lining the inner harbor, famously known as the Praia Grande—pastel pinks, blues, and yellows of the Mediterranean set against the curling gray tiles of Chinese rooftops. Taoist and Buddhist temples and joss houses stood side by side with the Dominican church, Catholic cathedral, and Christian monastery. Overlooking the bay, the stately buildings of the East India Company dominated the boulevard leading to the governor's palace and other grand villas and mansions of the city's foreign embassies. On the promontory at the mouth of the Pearl and West rivers, overlooking the city and the outer bay, Ben Devereaux had built his mansion. As grand in every way as the ships he built, it dominated the headland with its size and splendor.

Golden Sky sailed into the bay and closed with the dock of the Double Dragon Shipyard and Trading Company. Strangely—but then everything now was strange to her—Li felt no great apprehension as she was carried down the gangway in Ben's arms, the scent of him no longer strange but close and comforting. A young Chinese man in the smart pearl-gray uniform and cap of a driver stood beside a waiting motorcar, the first she had seen, as astonishing as everything would be to her from this moment on. When the driver was ordered to help her into a backseat, he did so instantly, leaning in to make her comfortable. His face remained blank, but the eyes that held hers for a fraction of a second showed resentment. They drove through busy streets, along the wide and crowded boulevard and up the winding coastal road to the promontory. There, great iron gates emblazoned with a pair of golden dragons opened before them, as stone lions glared down from either side.

✵

The head amah of Sky House, Ah-Ho, looked upon the girl before her with obvious distaste. Although she could not say so, she greatly resented a homeless Chinese female being brought into her domain without her knowledge or consent. Ah-Geet, the driver, had carried the girl through the lofty foyer, along a wide hallway to a small, bright room, and laid her down on its clean-smelling bed. The driver's face was passive but his eyes were hostile. Li could not be sure if she heard the whispered word "*cheep-see*"—whore—before he left the room.

Her heart sank on seeing a face that reminded her of Ah-Jeh's looking down at her with evident suspicion. This woman was taller than the superintendent, with the height and girth of a man; the broad muscular face was unpowdered, the wide mouth colorless. Her tightly combed hair was wound into the gleaming bun and fixed by the wooden comb of the *sau-hai*.

Instead of a *tzow*, Ah Ho wore wide-legged black trousers and a starched white jacket with the gilded frogging of her exalted station, jade studs in the lobes of her ears, and a wide leather belt about her ample waist, dangling with a wide assortment of keys. Ben addressed her briskly but with evident tolerance; even, it appeared to Li, with a little respect.

"Ah-Ho, this child has been through bad times; she is crippled and cannot stand. Send for Dr. Yap. She will rest up in this room until she can get about."

The amah's reply was cold and uninviting as her icy stare.

"And when she can walk, Master, where is she to go? Do you wish me to find a place for her as a *mooi-jai*? She may not be worth much, but I know of many who would be pleased to take her."

129

Di-Fo-Lo's reply was equally stiff and unenlightening. "I have purchased her *sung-tip*. She will stay in this room until she is able to walk. Then we shall find her work to do."

Ah-Ho paused, her eyes avoiding his. "But Master, I am not in need of another *mooi-jai*. Who is to care for her? Surely not I . . . or those of my kitchen?"

Ben was thoroughly aware of how little the head amah had to do, as he was of the duties of all the staff of Sky House. He was also aware of the complex hierarchy of Chinese labor and responsibility, of reward and privilege, that governed a stately residence like his. Finding servants who could be trusted to run a house well and with a minimum of theft and intrigue was a foreigner's most advantageous acquisition anywhere in the Far East. Once attained, such service could last for a lifetime and even into future generations. He would do nothing to put this delicate balance at risk, certainly not for an unknown waif whose life he had saved on an impulse born largely of ill-disposed and thoroughly unreasonable anger.

"Let the Fish take care of her. When she is well, I will find her something to do until it is decided what is best for her." He became suddenly irritated by the amah's stubborn face. "By God's teeth woman, have you no compassion? Can't you see she is little more than a child and has been savagely beaten? Fetch the doctor and send me the Fish."

As though she had been waiting for the mention of her name, a sprightly gray-haired woman appeared, bowing energetically as a clockwork toy. Her greeting was as bright as Ah-Ho's had been bleak. "Good morning, Master, how are you?" Age had not conquered the Fish. Her thinning gray hair, loosely held by a clasp carved from pearl shell in the likeness of a leaping carp, framed a face that was brown as dried tobacco. Beneath lids like finely crinkled leaves, her eyes were quick and alive. Her slight, wiry frame was garbed in a loosely fitting *sam-foo*, brightly decorated with the intricate beading of a Tanka elder, fastened by ivory toggles. In the center of her forehead, held by a band of black velvet, was a ring of deep green jade; several bangles of a lighter-colored stone clinked on her thin wrists.

Li was immediately drawn to the impish brightness of this lady called the Fish. Alert and inquisitive, this was a face that had survived many seasons, perhaps fifty, perhaps sixty or even more. Ben received the dignified elder with unconcealed affection. "Ah, Fish, this girl is from a bad place on the Pearl River. She cannot walk and needs attention. I have sent for Dr. Yap. When he has examined her, you will follow his instructions and care for her. Find her something to wear and feed her well. She has had a very bad time." Ah-Ho stood aside in silence as the Fish bowed her clear understanding. With a hostile gleam in her eyes, the head amah of Sky House bowed stiffly, then turned and left without a further word.

The next morning, as the night sky melted into dawn and the kitchen gas lamps still hissed white, Ah-Ho sent for Li, who had no choice but to hobble behind the scullery maid sent to fetch her.

The head amah was seated at a round table set with tea things and a single high-backed chair. Erect as a wooden goddess, she sipped from a large glass of black tea, held in the grip of a silver serpent—its arched coils serving as a handle, its venomous head guarding the lid with open jaws. Li noticed that the marble top of the table was fractured by a web of cracks. *The table is old . . . as unsound and imperfect as she of the arched eyebrows*, she thought to herself, *no longer pleasing to look upon, but deceptively strong*. Ah-Ho savored the tea unhurriedly, watching closely for signs of pain as Li shifted her weight from one foot to the other. "I regret I cannot ask you to sit, but as you see, this kitchen has but one chair."

Li recognized the sullen-faced youth wearing the uniformed trousers and polished boots of a driver. His shirt was off, a singlet hung loosely from a lean muscular frame, his thin face fixed in a complacent smirk. He leaned against the wall behind Ah-Ho, his hands thrust deep into his pockets, a cigarette drooping from his lower lip.

"A night has passed and you are still under this roof. It is time you are told the truth." The amah spoke with slow deliberation. "Master Devereaux has chosen to dump you among honest, hardworking folk like the last skinny shrimp grabbed from the bottom of a slimy barrel. He sees you as helpless and deserving, but I see you as the makings of a slut, or he would not have bothered. He is a *gwai-lo*, sometimes a wise one, but with the heart of a fool; he cannot see what we can see."

Setting the glass down, Ah-Ho thumped her closed fists on either side of it, causing it to spill. "I will know all there is to know of you before you have spent one week beneath this roof. You will not deceive me as you deceived him. Dr. Yap has seen to you at great cost; you can walk now, well enough to stand before me. My advice to you is to leave while the master is away and go where he cannot find you." Ah-Ho fetched a purse from her pocket, counting out crumpled notes, tossing them onto the table. "Here are ten dollars, the wages of a *mooi-jai* for many months. Take it and go where you will . . . there is nothing but bad joss for you here . . . for Di-Fo-Lo too. He has given you your life. Do not make him pay too high a price."

Li found her inner voice. *I have faced your kind before. I learned from her the meaning of injustice but she taught me how to live with pain. . . . One such as you will never make me cry, nor will you throw shadows on my path.* She met the cunning eyes of the chauffeur, squinting narrowly through the plume of cigarette smoke, holding them until he looked away with a sneer of disdain. *And you who wear such a fine uniform, you are no* larn-jai; *there are no yellow dogs to fight for you.*

When she spoke aloud, it was with great humility and downcast eyes. "I am not worthy of such generosity, or of a place in this noble house. I think you must ask your master to send me away. Until then, I will not insult his hospitality, but await his decision." Bowing with great humility, she turned and walked away, showing no sign of her pain and nothing more of her secret thoughts. Ah-Ho came to her feet so violently the glass of tea was overturned, to roll across the table and crash to the floor. Every word she spoke was a threat.

"So be it, little river rat. But do not speak of this conversation; it never happened."

With the guiding hand and ready wit of the Fish at her side, Li grew accustomed to her new surroundings in a few enthralling weeks. Such a world unfolded about her that each new awakening was greeted as a dream that must surely be snatched away.

Thanks to the Chinese doctor, Yap-Lau, and his evil-smelling poultices, she was soon able to walk to the window and tend herself without help. The little balcony of her room looked down upon the curving concourse of the Pria Grande, across the bay with its fleet of anchored junks and busy sampans, out to the wide blue of the sea.

No one had told her to leave the room she found so splendid, with its comfortable bed, a dressing table with a chair, and the wonder of a mirror. It took her many hours alone, with the door bolted on the inside, to explore the miracles of the mirror. It tilted up and down, and with practice Li was able to see herself as never before. At first she had quickly looked away from her still-swollen face, cuts still healing, bruises discoloring her skin. Her hastily cropped hair sprouted in uneven tufts that left her small, neat ears uncovered.

But now each night, in total privacy, she inspected herself more thoroughly, tilting the oval mirror to examine every inch of her body and watch its healing. She would sit before it in the soft light of the orange-shaded flare of gaslight and study herself for hours at a time. As the blemishes faded, so did the horrors of the pig basket, until she was able to see herself anew. She saw the details of her large, almond-shaped eyes and fine brows, the thick curling lashes of her beautiful mother. These were unusual in the south, the Fish informed her, where Cantonese eyes were narrowed with caution, the lashes were sparse and straight, and most brows wore the frown of poverty.

Every day without fail, the Fish brought food she had cooked herself, as well as a pail of hot water to wash her feet and change the dressings. The lively old lady had a habit of looking left and right whenever she wished to speak intimately, which seemed to be much of the time. "The day will come when you will bathe like a princess in the master's snow-white bath." She stretched her arms wide, jangling the jade bracelets. "It is big enough to wash a buffalo and its calf." She lowered her voice.

"I know of the words of Ah-Ho. Nothing occurs in Sky House that I do not know about. When the master is at sea, or visiting Hong Kong, I am his eyes and his ears." She chuckled. "You were wise to speak as you did."

The Fish, she explained with pride, was set apart from the other servants, the only one to be appointed by Ben himself. It was he, she said with pride, who had named her the Fish. "When he was young and building his first *lorcha* on the mudflats, no one would sell him food or fetch him water. All mad *gwai-los* are known to eat Chinese babies when they can, but I was not afraid. I know the eyes and heart of a good person when I look into them, and I know there are fools among our people who know nothing but say much. So I sold him fresh fish every day, got him vegetables straight from the market, and kept his water keg full. My clan name is Kwai-Tzing-Tze, and no matter how many times he tried to say it he could not. So he named me after the fish I caught and cooked for him in my sampan. His favorite was Macao sole, and I knew exactly where to find them on the sand at low tide.

"We shared many fine suppers on the mudflats by the light of a pitch flare. I taught him words of the Tanka and learned words of the barbarian in return. We laughed often and sometimes sang, so no one troubled us. He told me stories of the sea and of the great fortune he would find in the future. I told him stories of the great Tung Ting lake and the dreams I had lost in the past." She gave way to her soundless laugh, tapping the side of her head.

"They thought we were both *mung-cha-cha*. When he could not pay, I kept a tally, and he paid back every copper coin with interest. Then, when he became rich, he came to find me and took me into this fine house." The old woman's face grew calm.

"Devereaux is an honorable man; he is not like other *gwai-los*. He has told me that he saved you from a cruel fate and believes his own gods took a hand in this. You will have nothing to fear from him—you have my word on this. He finds much in you that others cannot see, and says you have great courage."

The Fish was proud of her Tanka stock, still strong enough to carry out her work in spite of her advanced years. Born among the boat peo-ple, who lived and died upon the water, she had grown too old to scull a sampan, but she was still sharp of mind, kept faith in her chosen gods, and was cheerful, honest, and an excellent midwife.

✳

It was almost two months before Li could walk any distance without help. Her feet had known nothing but rope-bottomed sandals and tree-bark leggings. The canvas slippers worn by a *mooi-ja*, little maid, were too tight even in the largest size. Leather sandals and all manner of shoes were impossible to fit, until the Fish took her to a cobbler, who made three pairs of soft leather shoes to fit her feet alone and one special pair decorated with silver flowers to wear when visiting the temple at festival time.

"It is the order of the master himself that you must have shoes to fit your feet, and clothes that are comfortable to wear," the Fish confided with much relish. "Ah-Ho would have you in the rags of a scullery maid, with wooden keks upon your feet, scrubbing floors for her to spit upon, but I am here to care for you and this will never happen."

✳

One day the Fish appeared early with the tray of congee. Li had never seen her looking so resplendent, wearing the festive garb of her Tanka clan: a *sam-foo* ablaze with embroidery of tiny, brilliantly colored glass beads, the same brightly beaded hat coverering her white hair. She proudly announced she had stitched every bead herself "with the eyes of a sea eagle that do not fail me." She continued, "I have come to drink tea with you on this, the birthday of Tien-Hau, the goddess of the sea, the patron saint of my people." She ladled the congee into their bowls. "The Tanka fishing fleet will stream the pennants of their clans, and decorate their junks with great displays off lowers, raise high the flags and ban-ners of their ancestors, and sail to the the temple in Joss House Bay to lay offerings at her feet." The Fish's eyes were filled with pride. "Once, my clan owned seven river junks that sailed the Grand Canal from the

135

Yangtze Valley to Chungking. . . . But all were lost to the water drag-ons."

She sighed, filling their cups with strong black tea. "You are young. Your past does not cover many mountains. I think you have no wish to speak of a journey just begun. So I will speak to you of mine, which will soon be ended." She looked dreamily through the windows, at vessels of every size filling the harbor, each one competing with the next for the extravagance of their finery.

"My family fished the Yangtze River for many generations. I grew up beside the rushing waters, sometimes yellow as a peach, sometimes brown as a yam, sometimes green as a fresh apple. The voice of the river sang me to sleep and I awoke to the chanting of the trackers hauling junks against the rapids, men as strong as oxen, bent to the towrope till their noses touched the ground."

She lifted her head and squared her meager shoulders. "I had a cousin, about my age but perhaps a little older. We were friends and he taught me many things. I could lift a dip net jumping with small silver fish when I was three. I knew the name and hiding place of every frog, and where the white crane made its nest." She paused at the memory. "We grew our own rice and picked pomegranates and pomelos from our own trees. Our life was good, and the river was abundant, our bowls were always overflowing."

Her tone was shaded with sadness. "A great storm came, thundering like ten thousand white horses through the gorges—they say it was the greatest of all storms. The old people on the river had never seen the river gods so angry. The gods let loose their dragons and swept away the fruit trees, our goats and our pigs, and the temple where we prayed in the great flood. Everyone in my family perished, with many thousands of others, except my cousin To-Tze."

She lifted her voice from this passing shadow. "But the gods decided to spare us. We clung to a fallen tree and were swept into the great Tung-Ting Lake, the Place of Peace and Harmony. Reed-cutters took us in and I was raised in the lake's marshes, but To-Tze was given to the Voice of Buddha monastery, named after its great bell that can be heard across the lake. They say he became a great master of White Cane *wu-shu* and left the Voice of Buddha to teach all over China, that he returned to live as a hermit on the wildest slopes of the lake to meditate and become a barefoot doctor." She paused to shake her head and lift her cup. *Her hand is steady,* thought Li, *she is strong of heart and knows so much of life; there is nothing she does not understand.*

"Perhaps he is still there," the Fish concluded. "It is the most beautiful place in all of China. It is my *huang-hah*, the place of my childhood, in the central hills of Hunan. One day, when I can no longer thread the needle, and my hands can no longer find the beads, I will return there perhaps to find To-Tze. There is nowhere else I would rather take my final journey."

✸

Seeing that freedom was so new to her, the Fish delighted in taking Li on her visits to the markets, teaching her to haggle over the price of vegetables, freshly cut or dug that morning, and of fish and crabs still flapping and crawling in butts of seawater.

Each day they discovered another hidden corner of the waterfront and the labyrinth of narrow streets, alleys, and lanes that led to its busy and ever-crowded center. Only a moment's step from the fine residences and fashionable shops of the Praia Grande and the constant breeze off the mudflats, the real Macao began—the Old Quarter, where the first traders had put down roots, many of their families still living above their original shops. The Fish seemed to know every inch of the cobbled streets crammed with narrow shop fronts, streetside vendors, and artists and artisans of every description, threading through the bustling crowds with such energy that Li had to step briskly to keep pace with her.

"They call this the city of sin, and sin can be easily found here. There are many devils—smugglers and pirates, harlots, gamblers, and opium eaters—but it is also a city of angels if you know where to seek them. Many different gods reside here." They passed a street of shuttered houses, large red lanterns hanging from every upstairs window— invitations to sample exotic services from every corner of the Orient

137

scrawled on banners of scarlet silk. "Red Lantern Street, home to whores from every province and beyond. A man can buy an hour in his choice of heaven for a dollar or two."

They passed through crumbling archways into another crowded alley—"Good Luck Street, where fortune is found and life is lost with the turn of a card or the roll of a dice." Pungent cooking smells from every corner of China greeted them on the Street of a Thousand Flavors.

The Fish turned into a lane so narrow and darkened by overhanging balconies that lanterns burned in the middle of the day, and with stalls so close the proprietors could have shaken hands across its shadowy walkway. The air was filled with the mingled scents of joss sticks, the smoke of incense gathering to hang like mist upon a river. "This is Joss Street, where spirits trade with the living in all matters past and future."

Beckoning Li to follow closely, the Fish descended a short flight of stone steps to enter a sparsely lit shrine, the airless space just large enough to house a modest altar.

Upon it stood an effigy of the White Monkey—Great Sage, Equal to Heaven; beside it, a bamboo container marked with many ancient talismans. A coil of joss stick, large as a cartwheel, hung above it, as candles burned on either side. At its feet, folded into a dusty robe of darkest purple, sat the oldest human being Li had ever seen; whether it was a man or woman was impossible to say.

Li's first thought was that the crumpled figure was dead, until it raised its head. The Fish bowed, then squatted before him, waiting until Li was close beside her. "Greetings, Lo-Yeh, I have brought a friend to seek your blessing and to speak with the stars." A long, thin hand emerged from the robe's myriad folds, its fingernails long and curled as the claws of a cat. It seemed without flesh, thin and transparent as rice paper, closing around the copper coins the Fish dropped into the outstretched palm.

"This is Lu-Ssi, once a famous Taoist pope, now the elder of all priests," the Fish whispered reverently. "He is an immortal—some say he is one hundred and sixty years old, but others say this is rubbish, he is only one hundred and forty. He can no longer see or hear and seldom speaks or moves from this spot where he meditates among the stars. It is believed that his spirit can leave his earthly body and return at will. His wisdom is greater than any other's."

The withered claw reappeared, held out toward Li.

"Do not be afraid; give him your hand. He must make contact with your soul."

The claw enclosed Li's outstretched fingers, its grip surprisingly warm, a distinct pulse beating in the center of the palm. His fingers closed tightly over hers, robbing her of the will to withdraw; heat generated by his grip burned its way into the core of her being, draining away her chi like blood from a wound. His sightless eyes told her nothing. Seconds passed and her hand was released, her energy renewed like the gush of water filling an empty gourd.

The priest unrolled a mat marked with mystic symbols, then reached for the bamboo container and shook it with unexpected vigor, spilling slivers of peach wood onto the mat before him. They scattered in a meaningless puzzle, each bearing lines of miniature calligraphy burned into the thin slips of wood. From somewhere above, a small bird fluttered down to settle on the pile of slivers, scratching them aside, pecking first at one and then another, hopping busily from side to side. To Li, it looked like nothing more than a common sparrow pecking for crumbs in the roadside dust.

"It is Lu-Ssu, the heavenly rainbird, said to be the eyes of the Great White Sage."

The Fish had not yet finished speaking when the bird fluttered onto Li's shoulder; she froze, feeling the tiny golden beads of its eyes so intently fixed upon her that she dared not move. Without warning it swooped back to the mat, selecting a single sliver and dropping it into the priest's lap before winging off, swallowed again among blackened rafters. The priest felt the minute inscriptions for several silent moments— sliding delicate fingertips slowly up and down, searching like the hand of a master musician tuning the strings of a fine instrument—then began to murmur in a language Li had never heard. The Fish listened intently, nodding her understanding and asking an occasional question.

His voice rose and fell like wind through the cracks of a window—deep in his belly, then shrill as a frightened child. "It is the voice of the Great White Sage, Equal to Heaven," the Fish muttered close to Li's ear. "There is no higher power in matters of the universe and our place in it." When he was silent, scooping up the fortune-telling sticks, she stood, bowing her thanks, then backed away from the altar with Li at her side. "Let us go to the Street of a Thousand Flavors and drink sugarcane juice among the living. I will tell you then what he sees among the planets."

"Tell me now," Li urged her, more than a little unnerved by the visit.

After a moment's hesitation, the Fish gave her usual grin but failed to meet Li's questioning eyes. "Your future is assured. The path is clear; you will reach the peak of your mountain sooner than you dreamed. You will surely find your thousand pieces of gold." Li was strangely disappointed by the sparseness of the forecast, but the Fish hurried ahead and clearly wished to say no more.

CHAPTER 9

The Shop of a Thousand Poems

For *Li, the visit* to Joss Street soon became a buried memory, the shrine and its ethereal guardian no more than wisps of scented smoke. As though to help her forget, the Fish gave her a silver dollar, large and round and heavy in her hand.

"It is the master's way," she confided. "Only he would pay a bonded servant, and only he would give so generously. Now that you have gained his trust, you too are entitled." It was the first money Li had seen. When told she would receive the same at the end of each month, she could not believe it. "I have done nothing to descrve this. I have taken but given nothing."

"Never take shelter from the winds of fortune when they blow your way." The Fish gave her silent laugh and left Li to contemplate the wonder of the bright silver coin, heavy in her hand. Horizons opened in her mind that seemed to stretch forever. As if this gift was not enough, she could take each Sunday afternoon as her own, to do with as she chose.

On that first Sunday, Li walked the boulevard alone, the coin carefully wrapped deep in the pocket of her *sam-foo*. This was a Mexican dollar, said by the Fish to be of solid silver. She wandered through the crowded lanes off the Praia, keeping the flat blue of the ocean always in sight as she had promised. Acrobats and jugglers, musicians and magicians, all tried to claim her attention, but there was only one thing more wonderful than the silver coin.

She found what she was looking for in a busy lane, close to the market square. Among a row of little shops filled with curios and antiques stood one that sold only books and the fascinating tools of the scholar. It was small and quaint, with a bell on the door, and above it, in faded gold characters, THE SHOP OF A THOUSAND POEMS. Its crowded window was filled with volumes of every shape and size and color. There were glass cases containing brushes, blocks of solid ink, seals, and all kinds of paper, in rolls and bundles tied with tapes of red and gold. It smelled of ink and oil paint, old paper and old books, dust and discovery. Here she spent her first silver dollar. The shopkeeper, whose fine white beard and whiskers were, she told herself, certainly those of a great scholar, was delighted by the interest of one so young. He invited her to explore his treasures more closely, and never tired of answering her endless questions. After many hours, she left the shop with a strong bag containing books both thick and thin, carefully discussed and decided upon, as well as an ink block, a selection of brushes, and a thick wad of fine white paper.

✳

Ben Devereaux had been thinking of the girl from Ten Willows for some time. He had never regretted saving her life, but now he was forced to contemplate her future, with all its uncertainties. The fact that she was legally his property and therefore his responsibility had begun to concern him. Indie had been right; he had acted on impulse.

None of his servants were bonded to him; he had found that fair treatment, due respect, and decent pay commanded far more loyalty and reliable service than a deed of ownership—which was what the *sung-tip* he had signed amounted to. It was more of a personal responsibility than a legally binding contract, a bill of sale, a receipt for goods purchased and delivered with about as much importance as the purchase of a bottle of good brandy.

There were many things Ben admired about China and the Chinese, but its treatment of the less fortunate was not among them. Constantly amazed by its people's capacity for work and their striving for success, he sometimes found himself appalled by the brutality and blind injustice that lurked so close to the simplest encounter. Violence so inde-

142

scribable yet so readily provoked in the saving of face, that he had made it his business not to become involved with anything outside the essential demands of the China trade. This policy had seen him through hazardous times and made him one of the richest foreigners in Macao. If it had made him a few sworn enemies along with an enviable reputation and many Chinese friends, this was an unavoidable part of the life he had chosen.

Li had been a part of his household for almost a year. Even in the little time he spent at Sky House, it had become impossible to ignore her. How quickly her ravaged hair had grown . . . how readily she responded to the simplest word of kindness. Always she had bowed to him, but there was nothing subservient in the gesture. She could meet his eye without looking away; and though the Cantonese dialect often sounded harsh and strident to him, he found her voice almost musical. These things he found enchanting, but above all, he was drawn to the spirit that shone from within her brightly as a flame lights a lamp.

The Fish had given regular reports on Li's progress—how she spent every centavo of her silver dollar on books and brushes, ink and paper; how she could hold her own in the market with any Tanka fishwife or Hakka vendor. "You tell her something, she remembers. You don't tell her something, she asks you why. Her mind is already the mind of a scholar, and her heart is already the heart of a woman. She speaks only the truth and can be trusted in all matters." The Fish had folded her hands and stuck out her chin, a gesture that Ben knew sealed the matter. "This one is no *mooi-jai*."

Li had grown taller and had filled out, her face aglow with health and a natural appeal more attractive to him than any female face he could recall. Beneath her square-cut *sam-foo*, he could not help noticing her energy and grace of movement.

One morning, so early that light had barely touched the gardens still spangled with a heavy dew, he saw her seated on the balcony of her room poring over an open book. A small stack of others stood at her elbow; paper was laid out with ink and brushes. Something more than curiosity drew him closer.

143

"These books," he asked with casual interest, hoping not to startle her. "Where did you get them?" She could not help but spring to her feet and bow, as he picked one at random and examined its cover. "*The History of Sail and Sweep in China*," he read aloud. She would have kowtowed if he had not told her sharply to stand up. "Bowing is not for scholars whose life has purpose and meaning . . . such persons receive the bows of others. Are you interested in such subjects as this?" Only when he had pulled out a chair and seated himself did she do the same.

"I can think of no greater highway than the river on its journey to the sea. It is the passageway of the gods," she said. Ben closed the book and replaced it with care.

"I bought the books in the Old Quarter with the silver dollars you have given me, but I have done nothing to earn them." She picked up a small pocket book, displaying an open page. "I have recorded the Mexican dollar and its value in Macao money, also the purchases I have made from the bookshop and the amount for each item. When I am able, I will repay this sum with whatever interest the Double Dragon Company may require. It is . . . a matter of business."

She spoke with such sincerity, he resisted the urge to smile. "That will not be necessary. I have seen you helping Ah-Kin in the garden and sweeping leaves; a silver dollar is little enough."

"You have never received my thanks, and this has troubled me." She felt suddenly close to this man who had done so much for her. "To save a worthless life so bravely is most honorable. To give that life meaning and purpose is greatness. You took away my pain and gave me shoes to fit my feet so that I may walk among the clouds." She picked up a book and pressed with both hands against her heart. "You have given me books and a fragrant garden to read them in . . . a close companion who watches over me, a heavenly room of my own to sleep in. I have given you nothing in return."

"You have not been well," he said uncertainly. "You almost died from your injuries. You had to learn to walk again, and to heal the terrible wounds in your heart and in your soul. This you did by yourself."

"My gratitude is beyond measure," she persisted, "but I am well now and can walk wherever I wish. I will work for you, to pay for my *sung-tip*."

He cleared his throat awkwardly. "You owe me nothing. To see you well again is reward enough. It is your own courage that has given you the world you speak of. If I have helped, it has cost me little." It seemed to Li that he almost smiled. "Besides," he added, "it is good to have young chi at Sky House." He turned abruptly, as though enough had been said between them, then turned back, offering her his open hand, surprised at the strength of her grip. "I accept and appreciate your words, Miss Li, and I will think carefully about what you have said."

Ben returned to his study deep in thought. He was aware of the jealousy her presence had caused among those who ran his household; Ah-Ho took every opportunity to make him see that her presence was unacceptable from the Chinese point of view. He was not sure what was best to do. The words of Indie Da Silva rang in his ears: *Well done, Ben; you are a hero, the owner of a half-dead Chinese chippie . . . yours to do with what you will.*

After a pipe and a tot or two of rum, Ben sent for Ah-Ho. The head amah remained expressionless when he told her that Li was to become his personal assistant, responsible for the study and his rooms under his supervision and assisted only by the Fish at his discretion. Ah-Ho fixed her narrowed eyes on the wall behind him as he spoke, the grim set of her jaw leaving no doubt of her feelings. When dismissed, she turned and left his presence without a word, her customary bow little more than a jerk of her head.

Ben would have rebuked her insolence, but he knew she was right. Such an appointment was a promotion over the heads of herself and those beneath her, making a mockery of her superiority. It was, he realized, a serious loss of face. That he would raise the eyebrows of his peers as well, and give the acid tongues of their wives something to wag about, was also certain.

Macao was rich in pleasures of the flesh, from the discreetly acceptable to dangerous extremes of depravity. Keeping a mistress or two was routine among Portuguese gentry, whose wives were too busy with the demands of high society to know or care about their husband's pecca-dilloes. Even regular attendance at the city's infamous bordellos was tolerated so long as it remained discreet. But nothing excused the man who allowed himself to be seduced by a servant under his own roof. This, of course, was the only way such a grave mistake could ever take place: The Chinese female was always seen as the scheming seductress, to be beaten and driven from the home, penniless, branded as unem-ployable by the foreign establishment and as the lowest of whores by her own people for sleeping with a hairy barbarian.

Ben had never paid heed to the opinions of others, but easily recalled Indie Da Silva's advice as he dressed for his first night as a member of the Macao Yacht Club.

"Remember, Ben, you are about to become one among many postur-ing hypocrites who would have your throat cut if they could. Because you have European blood they have to admit you—grudgingly, I assure you. Because I am Macanese, the bastard of a Portuguese father and a Chinese mother, I am not worthy to wear such finery or soil the brass handles of their illustrious entrance, although I can outsail and out-navigate the lot of them."

He had grinned without regret. "I would rather seek the company of a good-hearted whore in a leaky sampan than of the hawkish harridans and two-faced fools who call themselves the ladies and gentlemen of Macao society. These so-called gentlemen will see throats cut without a qualm, cheat at the tables, steal from a friend, bed your wife and daugh-ter if they can, and show little shame if caught." Indie had scowled his disgust. "They will buy a twelve-year-old *mooi-jai* for the price of a cheap bottle of wine, casually take her to bed, then have her beaten and thrown into the street while they enjoy a good dinner."

Indie had waited for his words to sink in before making his final point. "But an Englishman never beds his amah, whatever her age and whatever the circumstances. It breaks all the rules. The establishment will shun you for it and the Chinese will see you suffer. As for the girl, she may as well put an end to herself before they do it for her. This is not Edwardian England or even upper-crust Lisbon—this is China, and the foreign clubs are bastions of godliness among the heathens." Indie had lit another of his green cheroots. "In other words, Benjamin, my friend, don't get caught and never, never admit to it, because both sides will cast you out."

⌖

Christmas in Macao was a sad little affair, when expatriate European families made a brave show behind closed shutters with tinsel and fairy lights, bonbons and sugar mice. Devereaux dreaded it with a vengeance. He felt the same about the endless festivals that filled the Chinese calendar, when foreign devils knew they did not belong and retired to the library, the billiard room, or the bar until the streets were safe again.

Ben had no place for superstition in his own life, tolerating it in others as long as it did not affect him too directly or threaten his business. He encouraged ancestral worship in the privacy of the servants' quarters, and the keeping of shrines to the accepted gods. He had found the beliefs of the Tao and of Buddha to be both interesting and benign, and had learned much in the way of common sense in the teachings of Confucius.

As the New Year drew closer, he realized that something must be done about the girl he had fished from the riverbed more dead than alive, who now decorated his well-ordered life with her charm. She was too young and far too vulnerable to be paid off and left to find her own way. Not that he doubted for a moment that she could fend for herself given half a chance. But, even with whatever arrangements he might make through his more reliable contacts, the fact remained she would be in constant danger.

For a wild moment or two he considered sending her to school in England, or even adopting her, but he was too honest not to face the true measure of his interest. As mindful as he was of the rules of both Chinese and Western society, he had never allowed his decisions to be influenced by the opinions of others.

Li was delighted with the new responsibilities that allowed her to spend much of her time in the great room in which Ben sometimes

147

worked. He left early and returned late, but she came to know more of him from the things in the room he called his study: the rack that held his collection of pipes, each of a different wood or clay, which she cleaned to perfection and polished with a yellow cloth to deep amber, russet, and rose; the crystal ashtrays; the tiny, ornate bottles of snuff. She never tired of gazing at the photographs that showed the building and launching of his ships. But to Li, the greatest treasures were the countless rows of books—their covers the colors of old wine, the dark greens of mountain pines, the browns of the earth, and all the blues of the sea—extending from the polished cedar floors to the painted sky of the ceiling, reachable by a ladder that slid at the touch of a finger.

Even more imposing was his desk of Tibetan fir, backed by a huge taipan's chair. Both were decorated with carved dragons surrounded by curlicued ocean crests. In this chair and at this desk, Li allowed herself to dream for stolen moments. She was fascinated by the boats on the rivers of China and by ships on the sea, a world that knew no boundaries, always in search of new horizons.

His adjoining bedroom was larger than the study; its great four-poster bed, the Fish had whispered, was carved from the heart of English oak, as were the giant keels of his ships. A couch and easy chairs of studded leather shone like polished copper on a richly patterned Taiping carpet, before another spacious fireplace with a fender of gleaming brass. A roughly hewn table and chairs stood on the separate balcony, sheltered by the overhanging spread of a lilac tree.

The study opened onto an English garden behind its hedges of box and privet. This was Ben's private garden, shared with no one but Ah-Kin the gardener. According to the Fish, it was where he talked to his gods and made peace with himself.

One area of the estate was out of bounds: the garages. "That is a place you do not need to see," the Fish insisted. "The machinery of the devil himself resides behind those walls." The Fish was unimpressed by the motorcar; she could not understand why the rickshaw, the sedan chair, or the horse-drawn carriage should be replaced by an infernal contraption that assailed the ear and nose, threatening to grind the bones of simple folk beneath its wheels. Li pretended to agree, but was secretly fascinated by the huge, night-blue car that had fetched her from the Devereaux dock in such splendor and comfort.

One day, Li walked past the lodge and into the compound to where the long frontage of the garages stood open. There before her was the Rolls-Royce Silver Phantom, the letters DD on its number plate, with three other cars of similar size covered by white sheets. Beside them, and entirely different, she saw a much smaller car in the deepest of greens—perfectly polished, its trappings and spoked wheels glittering like silver, its yellow leather seats open to the sky.

"It's called a Lagonda; Di-Fo-Lo has the only one in Macao. Only Ah-Geet drives the foreign cars." The voice was that of Ah-Geet the driver, his impudent use of the Di-Fo-Lo name identifying him instantly. Li spun around to find the chauffeur close enough to touch her. He grinned at the alarm he had caused, his thumbs hooked in the suspenders that crossed his thin shoulders, his white shirt carelessly unbuttoned, revealing hairless, pallid skin and a small brown nipple.

Before she could reply, he reached out and opened the passenger door. He patted the seat, stroking the padded leather like the back of a cat. "Very soft. Very smoooth." His tone became persuasive. "Come, sit. No one will know. . . ."

As she turned and walked toward the gates, the driver raised his voice. "Hey, river girl. You forgot something." She turned her head to see his breeches gaping around spindly knees, his angry red shaft gripped in his hand. His mawkish laughter told her he was drunk. He honked the car's horn loudly. "This is why you came to see Ah-Geet. I'll give you a silver dollar like Di-Fo-Lo. . . ."

The rest of his bellowing was lost to her as she swung the gate and walked swiftly to the house.

※

Under the Fish's supervision, Li had been fitted for new clothes. In keeping with her position as personal attendant to the taipan, she wore cheongsams cut from self-patterned silk in muted grays and browns to be worn in the afternoons and evenings when she was cleaning or gardening. With them came matching shoes, soft and light, with slightly higher heels. Her hair had grown abundantly, until it fell softly about her shoulders. Each evening she wound it into plaits on top of her head, held with jade pins loaned to her by the Fish, and selected a fresh gardenia to fix behind her ear, the scent of its creamy petals becoming a part of her.

With the change of dress, she found a change of attitude: She was no longer uncertain of her place in Sky House, and no longer doubtful of her abilities. Her work was easily done, and when it was complete, she washed and changed, took down books, and lost herself in them as hours passed like moments. Few were written in Chinese, and the pages of tightly arranged English text swam meaninglessly before her eyes. But many of them were filled with pictures, both drawn and painted, or photographs beautifully presented.

She had discovered one that was splendidly bound in leather and elaborately stamped in gold leaf. Even the edge of each page was lined in gold, so that when it was closed it shone like the lap of a temple Buddha. Its heavy, gorgeously illustrated pages showed beautiful women proudly entwining their naked bodies with unclothed men. As each hypnotic page was turned, she studied closely the details of every embrace, with deep and increasing curiosity.

In the privacy of her room, Li stripped and examined herself in the mirror, considering her own allure against the superbly painted images. She had become so accustomed to the mirror that her poses were easily found and her eye quick to appraise. How much she had changed in so little time, how well she had healed; no scars remained to spoil the perfection of her skin. She moved her shoulder, allowing the light of the lamp to fall upon its faintly bronzed sheen. She lifted her chin and turned a cheek, lowering her eyes; the lashes Pebble had once admired were indeed longer and more curled than any she had seen. She became bolder; remembering poses from the book, she compared herself to them, curving her back to emphasize the suggestion of her shapeliness, daring to imagine a partner, certain that when the time came she would please and be pleased.

150

The slightest of sounds distracted her, so faint she held her breath. Her attention had immediately flown to the locked door. She waited, the only noise now from the far-off surge of waves meeting the rocky foreshore below the point. In that breathless silence the door handle turned slowly and carefully, first one way, then the other. If it was the Fish, she would knock and certainly speak. No sound came, and after a moment, during which Li heard nothing but the thud of her heart, the movement ceased.

CHAPTER 10

Chinese New Year

The Chinese New Year fell in mid-February by the Western calendar. The three days leading up to this auspicious event were known as "Little New Year," when debts must be settled so that the New Year might begin with a clean slate for rich and poor alike. By ancient custom, comedians and entertainers were obliged to perform free of charge in the village square or the temple courtyard, to draw out bad debtors among the audience, where their creditors could force them to settle accounts or risk the crowd's displeasure by spoiling the show with loud argument. Tailors, hairdressers, beauty shops, florists, and gift shops doubled their prices to cash in on the feverish activities. Old scores were settled, new clothes bought, heads and faces fussed over—trimmed and tonsured, massaged, pummeled, and painted—to emerge bright and shiny as newly minted coins.

Those who had it wore gold, to advertise wealth and success, dressing their children in cinnabar red, the color of good fortune, to be paraded before relatives and friends with their faces painted like precious dolls. Every child was given lucky money by members of their extended families in a sealed packet of red and gold, while gifts were exchanged by adults—silks and ornaments, even jewelry for close and important relatives; fine tea, rare fruits and expensive foods, potted plants, and flowers for distant and less important aunts, uncles, and cousins.

The house, no matter how grand or humble, was carefully swept, metal objects cleaned and polished, carpets beaten and curtains washed.

The house and its occupants must be spotless, so that the feng shui forces of wind and water could flow unhindered, and the dragon at peace in the north would lie down with the tiger of the south. End-of-year bonuses were paid and wages doubled to cover this month of the twelfth moon, while towns and cities were evacuated in favor of the *huang-hah*, the birthplace and spiritual home of the clan.

This, Li now decided, was the time to repay her debt to Ben Devereaux and begin a new page in the book of her life. Accompanied by the Fish, she had mixed with the excited throngs as firecrackers blazed and drums beat, while the lions and dragons pranced their way through houses and streets, driving out the old and welcoming the new.

With Little New Year over, the streets deserted, and all doors opened wide for family reunions, the Fish invited her to visit her Tanka friends. When Li declined with deepest thanks, the old lady offered to stay at Sky House to keep her company. "You will be alone at a time when no one should be alone. It is a time when the master drinks too much rum . . . he will not want you in his house for Chinese New Year."

"But perhaps he drinks rum because he is alone. You have just spoken truthfully . . . no one should be alone when New Year is celebrated. If he wishes, I will be his companion."

"Perhaps you are right," the Fish agreed uncertainly. "Perhaps even a taipan can be lonely at such a time as this."

✣

Ben Devereaux had seen more Chinese New Years than he cared to remember, each lonelier and more frustrating than the one before. With the servants gone and the great house silent, he usually found company in the international clubs, or took a suite at the Palm Garden and visited the bars of Wan Chai on Hong Kong Island . . . to awake a week later in the unlovely bed of a stranger. *Why,* he asked himself each time it came around, *did it have to last for ten days, with the servants gone for the best part of a month?* This time something made him stay. Unsure if it was his conscience or something more, he could not bring himself to leave the girl from Ten Willows alone in the emptiness of Sky House at this time of shared festivities between friends and family.

Ah-Ho had always taken it for granted that, like all foreigners, he had no interest in such rituals, never decorating the house or showing any sign of the ancient ritual that so consumed the population. This year, to his complete surprise, he found his study dressed with all the trappings of the great occasion. Several vases placed around the windows held tall branches of plum and peach blossom, with the characters for health, wealth, and long life painted in gold on red paper. Neatly arranged on every windowsill and along the balcony wall were pots of white jonquils, their tiny white and yellow trumpets filling the air with perfume.

"I hope the peach blossoms will not drop too quickly. I will remove them in the morning."

Li stepped into the room, carrying a miniature kumquat tree in a glazed pot. It was perfectly shaped, with small golden fruits the size of dollar coins smothering its well-trimmed branches. Placed on a round bamboo tray, the pot was clearly heavy.

"It is our custom to give a tree such as this to those of our friends and family we most love and respect. My family is lost to me, and love is a mystery . . . but none could have given me more than your brave heart and generous hand." Before he could take the tray from her, she set it on the balcony table. "Like the opening of new buds, it invites good fortune with its golden fruit. I offer it with my gratitude for all that you have done for me. It is a small, unworthy gift, worthless to such a taipan who holds the world in his hand."

Ben's surprise robbed him of words for a moment, as he tried not to smile at the traditional modesty when giving a gift. Then he spoke hurriedly, to make sure she did not leave as suddenly as she had appeared. He replied as expected, "It is a most splendid tree; it is I who am unworthy of such a gift. Now I must give you something of gold in return. Is that not also the custom?"

He took the gold watch from his waistcoat pocket. Hanging from its heavy chain were several golden sovereigns; he detached one of these, holding it out to her between finger and thumb.

"It is one of the first I ever made in the China trade. It has brought me all the good fortune I shall ever need. Now let it do the same for you."

"But I have already received an extra Mexican dollar for *lai-see*." She held up two fingers, her eyes so wide with astonishment it caused him to laugh aloud.

"Now you have an English guinea. It is worth ten Mexican dollars. What will you do with it?"

Her hesitation was brief. "When I can read the English words, I shall buy many books like these." Li whirled around the library, extending her arms to the shelves so neatly crammed with volumes.

"I have a better idea. Keep it to buy something bright and beautiful. Books are often old and can be dull. They are filled with the thoughts of others, often those who already reside with their ancestors. I am sure you have ideas and thoughts of your own that are young and fresh as your budding jonquils." He paused, as if to make sure that she understood. "Take what interests and knowledge you can from books, but do not let them replace words and thoughts of your own."

"I will remember this," she answered thoughtfully. "But I know so little of the world. To me, there is nothing more wonderful than the words and pictures of scholars and artists."

Ben found it impossible to hide his smile at such grave words from one so achingly young. "If books are what you want, then books you shall have." He waved a hand at the towering collection. "You must explore these books as often as you like and discover all that you can. But when the book is closed, look about you and find stories of your own."

She bowed her thanks, and would have departed had he not suddenly thought how empty this room, which had always through choice been a place of solitude, would seem without her. In his haste to detain her, he spoke before he could think. "Stay; there are other things I wish to talk to you about."

Grasping for an excuse that would not seem too obvious, he seized the first that came to mind: two small changes that had been made to his private domain since she had taken charge of it. "There have always

155

been vases of my favorite English flowers, fresh cut from the garden every day. Did the Fish not tell you?"

"She was careful to instruct me in all such things of importance to you. I beg forgiveness if I have caused you concern, but the flowers can be seen so perfectly through the open doors and windows, I could not bring myself to cut off their heads just to watch them slowly die."

He indicated the tall vases crammed with sprigs of blossom, branches of sesame, fir, and Cyprus pine. "Then what of these—are they not also cut down in their moment of triumph?" At that moment, she no longer felt like a servant before a master, but an equal voice. It pleased her to be knowledgeable of something that he was not. "The blossoms of the peach and plum are not meant to endure. Their life is brief, but they bring new growth and fresh leaves. This is why they are the symbol of Chinese New Year."

He seemed satisfied with her answer to his question and immediately asked another, pointing to the little cage that hung above the balcony, its door open, the bird flown. "There was a rare songbird in this cage, a crested lark found only in the mountains of Hunan. Such a bird is hard to find and costly to buy. For five years it has awakened me with its melody; now it is gone."

"A bird that is caged, no matter how common or how rare, sings because it has to. A bird that is free sings when it wants to. The song of the free bird is always sweeter.

"Do the birds not still wake you from the trees with songs as sweet as any other? In the country where I was born, they say there is no sweeter song than of a sparrow in a field of corn. It sings because the harvest is golden, yet the sparrow has no fine feathers and is given no respect. It has no value among songbirds." Li waited to see if her reply had gone too far, then added, "But these are nothing more than things that seem true to me, and of no other value."

Ben did not ask if the mountain lark owed its freedom to her; he was quite sure that it did, but had no wish to make her admit it. Instead, he moved to open a drawer in his desk and remove a small oblong box beautifully inlaid with ivory and mother-of-pearl. He lifted a fine gold chain from it.

156

"Your opinions on such things are as wise as those of the immortal Sau-Sing-Kung, the eldest of all great sages, and as fresh as those of a child's first thoughts. They are of more value than you know." He held out his hand to her. "Give me your golden guinea."

Had she displeased him after all? Obediently, Li dropped the gold coin into his open palm. "This chain once belonged to my mother. She died when I was born, so I have only my father's word that it was hers, but he too has gone." His large fingers, surprisingly delicate, attached the guinea to the chain. Stepping close, he slipped it over her head. "This is my New Year's gift to you."

As he placed the coin around her neck, her nearness claimed his senses so strongly he knew he must step back. Li felt the quickening rhythm of her heart as she stood for a long moment without moving, her fingertips tracing the fine links of the chain to the solid weight of the precious coin against her skin. She would have looked up at him then, but could not move. "How do you know of the great sage Sau-Sing Kung?" was all she could find to say.

"There are many things I know about your great country that are wise beyond all others, and these have taught me much." He hesitated for a second. "I also know of things that are not at all wise . . . and these I cannot accept. But no more than those of my own people."

In that brief moment of honesty, Li felt closer to him than she could admit. "I have done nothing to deserve such a priceless gift," she said. "The kumquat tree is of no value and will soon wither and die. This is my first piece of gold, as it was once yours. It will stay with me forever."

"The kumquat tree may also remain beautiful forever, if it is cared for. If its roots are strong and it is treated as it should be, it will grow even stronger and more beautiful. With its growth will come new fruit, bigger and more plentiful."

Ben's gentle finger lifted her chin, causing her to look directly into his eyes. "Let us speak just once of giving and taking. You did not ask me to come into your life. You were given no choice in the matter, nor can I be sure what made me bring you here. But it is done, and I am now responsible for your future, which I am both pleased and ready to be. I offer you whatever is needed to allow you to live the life of your own choice. Choice is the greatest of all gifts. It was brutally stolen from you, yet you blamed no one and did not cry for help. You played the cards you were dealt, and this I admire. I ask for nothing in return but your trust."

The touch of his lips on her forehead seemed the sealing of a pledge, the lifting of her chin a simple gesture. Its effect on Li was instant. She would have reached for him, but he stepped away.

"You must sleep now, but before you do, I ask you to consider what it is you wish for your future. Tomorrow we shall breakfast together here on the balcony." He smiled, a light hand upon her arm as he led her to the door. "Can you cook?"

"Only the very simplest of dishes meant for those who work hard in the fields."

"Then we shall eat the simplest of dishes, and perhaps you will tell me more about being a scholar, and we shall speak of faith and choices and questions of gold."

Li was not sure if it was relief or disappointment that accompanied her back to her room. The great house had never been so empty and silent, yet his powerful presence followed her as surely as her own heartbeat. Even the sound of his voice stayed with her. She was glad to close the door to her own small space, to gather her thoughts as she held the golden coin on its glittering chain before her eyes, shining proof that this was not a dream.

✳

The first day of the new year burst brightly through the windows of Sky House. The rooftops of the city lay silent, deserted after the chaos of Little New Year. Even the pigeons that usually circled the cathedral were still at rest in its belfry. There was an air of great promise as, behind closed doors, people rich or poor shared their hopes and planned their futures. It was too early for the visiting of friends and exchanging of lucky money.

Li had prepared a breakfast of steamed dumplings, rice congee spiced with salted shrimp and chopped chives, dragon's eye fruit, and lychees

158

fresh from the garden. The dumplings and porridge were in bamboo steamers to keep them fresh and warm. She had made the English cow's-milk tea, which the Fish had told her was his favorite, and set the pot into its padded raffia basket, beside it the folded *South China Morning Post*. He stepped in from the English garden as soon as she had set the tray down.

Something about him was different. At first she found it startling, so unexpected that she could only stare. His beard was gone; his newly shaved jaw, pale and smooth, showed more evidently the tinge of his Chinese heritage; a thin white scar ran down one cheek and across his chin. When he smiled, he looked much younger than she had thought him to be. *No longer the barbarian*, she said to her heart with a secret smile.

"Good morning, little sister. *Kung Hai Fat Choy.*" From behind his back, he held out a crowded bunch of small purple flowers. "Cornish violets, my favorite of all wildflowers." Li took them with a bow, aware immediately of their exquisite perfume. "Good morning, young lord. *Kung Hai Fat Choy.*"

"Forgive me for picking them on this special occasion." He laughed. "But there are plenty more to be found, and others will grow to replace them." She felt his eyes upon her. He was pleased that he had made her face shine so.

"There are many flowers in heaven's garden," she breathed, "although none but these smell sweet as the breath of angels."

Ben smiled. "They remind me of my boyhood. One sniff of Cornish violets and I am beside a hedgerow of hazelnuts and wild rose after the rain, watching the shadows chase each other across the moor."

Holding out her chair, he insisted she take her seat before he sat down. "The personal assistant to the taipan does not bow and she does not stand while he sits." There was a buoyant humor in his voice that put Li at ease. "This is not a day for business, or of masters and assistants; it is a day of discovery and preparation for the future. Let others gather their families around them and pray for prosperity, while we will do nothing that we do not wish to do."

He passed a hand over the smoothness of his chin. "I have decided to

159

make some changes this New Year. It is a time of good luck and great opportunity, a year for bold decision and bolder action.

"First, I must ask you if you have a god of your own to pray to on this special day. If you must attend the temple, then I will wait for you."

Li shook her head. "I once asked the gods for help, but I was too small for them to see or hear me. They were so many, I did not know which one to bow to, so I bowed to them all. Perhaps the fault was mine, but my prayer was not heard by any of them. I am bigger now, but still do not know which one I should turn to. In things of great importance, I trust my heart."

He seemed pleased by her answer. "I have two gods," he said lightly, "one of my own making, and the other of ancient China and my mother. I pray to them both on the first day of each New Year. They also reside here." He held a hand to his chest. "So we are not so different."

They ate the small steamed dumplings the Fish had taught her to make, filled with fresh crabmeat and shrimp. "We call these dumplings dim sum," she said, placing some on his plate. "It means 'touch the heart,' small pleasures that make us happy and do not cost too much."

When they had finished, he sat back and stretched his arms wide, clasping them behind his head with obvious pleasure. "This is the time and the place for you to tell me of your hopes for the future, and perhaps for me to tell you mine." She needed no further coaxing. From her pocket she slid the orange-peel finger jade, unseen. Its smoothness comforted her fingers, and the chi of Pai-Ling entered her heart.

Li chose her words carefully. "You are a man of business. When you speak of it, you want matters to be clear." Ben nodded his agreement. "With little help, I have learned to read and write Chinese well enough not to be thought a fool. I have become fast and sure enough with the abacus to survive in any marketplace without being cheated."

Li sat forward in her seat. "I want to be of use to you, not merely in matters of tidiness and comfort. I want to develop skills and gain knowledge that can help you in the business of your company. I learn fast, and I wish for nothing more."

He nodded.

"My mother dared to rise above the expectations and limitations of others more fortunate, and for that she was punished. They crippled her for the vanity and pleasure of stupid men, and so that she could not escape those who owned her. They allowed her nothing but the service of the fool who became my father. She killed herself because she thought I had been buried alive in the mustard field. They dumped her like a dog so that her ancestors could not find her."

Ben was silenced by the pain in her eyes.

"I was spared by a white fox and cowardly superstition. Through this, perhaps, I received my mother's spirit, and for that I too have been punished. If I have strength, if I have understanding beyond my years, it is because of her. I will not know happiness until she finds peace. Help me to become the scholar she was meant to be, a person of value, and I will serve you till the day I die."

She ignored the tears that could not be stopped, searching his face for understanding. "I ask only one year to prove to you that I can learn to read and to write in your language, to calculate in your figures, and to understand your business and the ways of your people. You have said that this is a time of great opportunity and success.

"If after one year I do not satisfy your expectations, then I have taken the wrong path and I will leave Sky House, but you will not lose your investment in me. I will one day repay every copper coin that I may cost you one hundred times or more."

"And if you are successful after one year? What would you wish to do?" he asked gently.

"That will be for you to decide. If you and my teachers think me worthy, I will continue to learn until I can be of true value to the Double Dragon wherever I am needed." She closed the finger jade tightly in her fist. He seemed in no hurry to reply, and her heart sank at his silence.

"Tell me what you would you do that is not already done by someone else." He smiled fondly. "How will you earn your pieces of gold?" Li lifted the pot to fill his cup. He tapped the table with his fingertips in the Chinese way of a silent thank-you.

"You have no comprador," she replied confidently. "No Chinese who watches your side of the scales. To the Chinese, your good faith and belief in honesty are virtues too often seen as weakness, even foolishness, especially in one from foreign lands. They will squeeze you in every way they can, and you will never know it without a comprador of your own that you can trust."

Ben frowned thoughtfully. "I have been successful in the China trade for years, trusting only my judgment and experience and that of my partner. We have no faith in compradors; it is well known that they line their own pockets before those of a foreign master. To squeeze and be squeezed is a part of life as old as the first mountain. I have learned to live with this."

"You are wise; 'squeeze' is the way of Chinese business." Li dared to smile openly. "Our ancestors would be displeased if we did not cheat the barbarian or each other as cleverly as we can. It would be an insult to the family and the clan"—she shrugged—"and great loss of face for the comprador."

"How can you be so certain of such things?"

"Because I am Chinese." She lifted her cup to sip the tea. "When you paid Ming-Chou for his raw silk, you paid for highest quality and honest measure. Many spools were inferior, the strands broken and knotted. The wooden spools were larger than they should have been, so held less thread and weighed too much—so slightly this could not be detected, except by a vigilant comprador interested only in your profit and not her own. I can learn to be that comprador."

She took a breath. "I improve my skill with figures every day. The Fish has taught me to bargain in the marketplace, and I can haggle as well as any Hokklo fishwife for saffron worth its weight in gold or a catty of turnips worth a copper coin. I have learned about value for money at the lowest level. Business is business at any time, in any language, and in any place. In China that means every moment of every day and night."

He rubbed his chin, his eyes suggesting she should continue. Li felt a thrill at commanding the full attention of a taipan.

"Already, I have thoughts that may be of value to you. I have not spoken of them because my respect for your venerable partner is great and I would not insult him with my notions without your permission. I am sure he must know how much is bought and sold that does not appear in any tally book."

Ben spread his hands to show that nothing she had said surprised or concerned him. "Indie Da Silva will reward you well if you have thoughts that will save Double Dragon money or lead to higher profits. And so will I."

Li sat straight backed, looking, she hoped, every inch a comprador. "In my studies of the coastal and river trade, it seems to me that much has been lost to the cost of ballast . . . unprofitable cargo. Many chests of tea and bolts of silk have been spoiled by seawater invading the holds in bad weather. Because of this, your schooners take on broken tiles, bags of sand, river stones, and rocks to fill the bilges and stabilize the vessel." He nodded with interest.

"Your principal trade is in tea, silk, and porcelain and sometimes jade, which are carried separately. My thought is this . . . instead of worthless ballast taking up valuable cargo space, porcelain vases could be filled with jadeite and other precious stone, and stowed in the lower holds. The middle holds could carry chests of tea, with the silk in the upper holds. By such layering the vessel would take all weathers, and you would gain a cargo of porcelain and valuable minerals without spoilage."

She bowed her head in appreciation for his patience. "Forgive me if this is a foolish thought. I am sure it must have already been considered."

His eyes had not left her face. Was she indeed a fool to have made such a simple suggestion?

"It is not foolish to speak out; it is good that you are thinking of ways to improve our trade. All that you ask will be arranged. It is not a favor, but a business investment, as you wish it to be."

He reached across the table with an open hand. "But first you must learn what it is to be English. I shall arrange for a tutor to teach you for one year, then we shall set an examination. If you pass, you will be taught the business of a comprador and paid accordingly. Is it agreed?"

She put her hand in his and shook it firmly. "It is agreed."

Miss Winifred Barbara Bramble was a refined and pleasant lady of late middle age from the East Sussex village of Sparrows Green near Wadhurst. She had spent most of her life in senior teaching positions, first in Zurich and then with Hong Kong's most prestigious finishing college for young ladies. Reluctantly retired after fifteen years as its principal, she had returned to England from a life of high activity and social responsibility, to find herself quickly bored by the relaxed pace of her old village.

When Captain Devereaux's Hong Kong lawyer, Angus Grant, offered her a well-paid post to last for at least one year, with the option to renew, she had accepted with genteel enthusiasm. Confirming by telegram that making English princesses of girls from wealthy Chinese families came as naturally to her as grooming promising fillies for the Grand National must come to the consummate trainer, she had sailed from Liverpool on the first available passenger ship.

Of the girl she was supposed to tutor, she had been told only that her Chinese name was Li-Xia and that she was fifteen years of age with a very limited education. This did not concern Miss Bramble; nothing fulfilled her more than molding and refining young ladies, and trying to do so within the very limited space of twelve months only heightened the challenge. When she arrived at Sky House three months later, however, she was surprised to find the young lady in question to be an orphan without inheritance or prospects of any kind—a far cry from the often-spoiled daughters of wealthy families she was accustomed to tutoring.

Winifred had used her Hong Kong connections to verify Captain Devereaux's credentials and found them to be beyond reproach. She did not presume to speculate upon his interest in the beautiful girl, whom she found to be of charming manner. Any misgivings she might have had were soon put to rest by the girl's quick mind, transparent honesty, and beguiling personality. When the captain, in strictest confidence, told her what he knew of Li's frightful background, she found herself eager to help the child achieve her extraordinary ambitions.

Li liked the English teacher from the moment they were introduced over tea in the study. Miss Bramble was smartly dressed in a way Li had never seen before, and was kind enough to explain the philosophy of Harris tweed, silk blouses, knitted twin sets, green pork pie hats, lisle stockings, and stout brogue walking shoes. Her impeccable hair was set in a cluster of silvery waves held in place by tortoiseshell clips; large garnets shivered from her earlobes and spilled across her throat like drops of crystalized blood. Similar stones adorned her wrists and perfectly manicured fingers. A large fan of lavender-scented lace seldom left her hand, a necessity, she claimed, for an Englishwoman in the tropics.

Her face, Li reflected, was nothing like the hideous behind of a baboon, as she had been warned. Free of makeup, her ruddy features were apple cheeked and kindly, her hazel eyes alert but friendly behind highly polished spectacles in their pale lavender frames. Her keen powers of observation and seemingly endless patience made her the perfect teacher.

Miss Bramble intended to inform her pupil of anything she cared to know about the British way of life without in any way diminishing the richness of her Chinese heritage and culture. A sensitive blending of the two, she assured Ben, should produce a young woman of outstanding qualities. "From the aptitude tests I have given her, she possesses quite a remarkable capacity for learning."

Ben had made his study available as Miss Bramble's classroom, confining his own work to the office on the Praia. He also made frequent visits to Hong Kong and Shanghai and several trips at sea extending up to five and six weeks. When he did return to Sky House, it was usually for a short period, accompanied by others who ate and drank late into the night. If he greeted Li at all, it was briefly, although he spent much more time speaking with Miss Bramble behind closed doors.

Li did not admit to herself that she missed Ben's presence, that the sight, sound, and scent of him had become so much a part of Sky House it seemed to lose its luster without him. Her days were too crammed with interest to allow much time to wonder where he was and what he was doing. Even her evenings were spent studying, often late into the night. Miss Bramble was delighted by her appetite for knowledge and the depths of her character.

The Fish considered the appearance of the foreign teacher to be divine intervention in response to her prayers. She did not need to be told of Li's disappointment at Ben's absence; she and the girl had become so close that they sometimes thought as one. "Master Ben has not forgotten you. He will come to see you when he thinks it is time."

No day passed without *yum-cha* in the English garden, drinking tea with the Fish, who kept her informed on the household gossip. There was talk among the servants that the master was overseeing the construction of a villa on the beautiful Repulse Bay in Hong Kong, even more splendid and with gardens more magnificent than those of Sky House.

Concerned about their place in this new residence, Ah-Ho and the other servants kept well clear of Li and the Fish. They bowed deeply on passing Miss Bramble, yet secretly cursed the devil hag from a strange land who would weave silk from straw. The driver, Ah-Geet, had avoided Li since the incident in the compound.

"They are saying that the red-faced Englishwoman cost a chest of silver to teach the farm brat manners." The Fish chuckled slyly. "They are afraid the master will not take them when he moves to Hong Kong— that he will find a new head amah, new maids to do the cleaning and washing, new cooks, and a new driver. There is talk that when he returns he will take you and the *gwai-paw* teacher, and only I and Ah-Kin will be chosen to accompany you. Their suspicion is as bitter as their hearts, but they are sure of nothing, so they will make no move to displease him."

Her chuckle faltered as she glanced nervously at the door. "This does not mean that Ah-Ho and her followers will no longer be our enemies. They will hate us more now that you have become the favored one. They will never believe you are not here to share his bed and turn his head, because that is what they would do if they could."

"I have given Ah-Ho nothing to be afraid of," Li protested, "only that I will be taught to read and write in the language of the English. I am not his *cheep-see* and never will be. How can they think so little of his kindness and so badly of me?"

"They think this is your intention, and that he intends to make you his mistress, even his *tai-tai*—his wife." Li would not let herself think of such a prospect, and nothing the Fish said would convince her that she could ever become Ben Devereaux's *tai-tai*.

The Fish persisted. "They fear you will gain power and take revenge. They will do anything to stop you." There was a note of alarm in the Fish's voice. "They blame their change of fortune on you. Word is spread by the *sau-hai* that you are a fox fairy, that this is why you were condemned to die. They say that the master interfered in this because he is under your spell."

The old lady drew a deep breath, her troubled eyes staring at the closed door. "Ah-Ho is cunning and Master Ben is a good and trusting master—he understands that she must have her squeeze. He is very wise for a *gwai-lo*; he pretends to know only what he is shown of our people and nothing of its dark side."

She shook her head. "He has dealt with the triad tongs and played at their dangerous game and is greatly respected by those who cut throats for a living . . . but he knows little of the *sau-hai* and little of Ah-Ho's true power."

As she lifted her head, Li saw the same hint of fear that had shown itself for an unguarded moment in the smoky shadows of Joss Street.

"He thinks he understands enough—he speaks more of our language than he will say—but he knows nothing. The *sau-hai* are known to consult the black Tao . . . the shaman of evil magic. They are said to raise a curse upon those they fear but cannot reach."

The Fish lowered her voice to a whisper. "You must warn the master of this danger."

Li shook her head. "I will not interfere in things that are his to decide. If he asks me, or if a hand is raised against me without reason, I will tell him. I have faced far greater evils than Ah-Ho and the servants of Sky House, and am not without some cunning of my own. There is nothing that can happen to me that can compare with what I have already suffered. You are dear to me, Ah-Paw, but please do not worry yourself for my safety."

The Fish could not be comforted. "There are kinds of betrayal and treachery that even you cannot imagine." She sighed heavily. "I have heard it said that revenge is a banquet best eaten cold. So perhaps we are safe for now. Ah-Ho dare not be seen to raise a hand against you. She will pay others to take the risks. There are many who will kill for a chicken leg and eat it on the grave, others who will steal a child from under the nose of its parents and send it home piece by piece until the price is paid. This is the way of the black society."

The Fish suddenly reached for Li's hand. "Ah-Geet cannot be trusted. Already two *mooi-jais* from other households have carried his child." She gripped Li's hand tighter. "He is a *sai-lo*, a younger brother of the tong. We must beware of him."

Li had said nothing to the Fish of the silent hand at her door, and decided it could serve no purpose to reveal it now.

CHAPTER 11

The English Garden

U*nder Miss Bramble's amiable* tutelage, Li's life became a fantasyland of learning. The days began with a brisk walk in the grounds and early breakfast in the English garden, followed by mornings spent learning to speak, read, and write in English; lunch served by the Fish under the lilac tree; more lessons; then afternoons or evenings of general conversation, when Li was encouraged to ask all the questions she wished. Sometimes they listened to Western music on the gramophone in the teacher's rooms, or discussed a book and the life of its writer. Every moment was a gift to Li-Xia.

Miss Bramble had acquired two ladies' bicycles fitted with ample baskets in which to carry sandwiches and flasks of tea. This, she explained, was the preferred mode of travel for an English lady in the countryside. The exercise of cycling, which proved the perfect break from intense studying, sometimes took them on tours of the city outskirts or to picnics on the breezy cliffs of the promontory. Even on these welcome excursions, Li would bring her book bag for an hour or so of quiet reading or a lively debate over the complexities of the English language.

Late one evening, six months to the day after Li's schooling had begun, Ben was pleased to receive Winifred Bramble in his study with a half-term report, and to hear nothing but the highest praise for her promising young student. Li had taken readily to the niceties of deportment, showing a natural grace and a promise of elegance. Yet as surely as she had developed manners acceptable in any English drawing room,

she just as convincingly displayed an enthusiasm for the raw propensi-
ties of the China trade perfectly suited to the waterfront godown. She
was, the teacher concluded, a quite exceptional and determined young
woman.

When Ben had confided his intentions to Winifred, she had given
him her heartfelt but guarded congratulations. She had seen enough of
her employer to know that Li could not be placed in safer or stronger
hands than those of Captain Devereaux; and enough of her young pupil
to know that she could not be forced to do anything against her will.
Miss Bramble did not doubt that Li could make Ben a very suitable companion and eventually become an asset to his company. Nevertheless,
the blind stupidity of both East and West when it came to mixed mar-
riages weighed upon Miss Bramble's heart. This could be a difficult and
even a dangerous path. Though she knew that a man of Ben's stature
and courage was unlikely to be deterred by prejudice or superstition, she
wondered how he would respond to the insidious menace that could one
day threaten those he loved. It was a thought she found difficult to cast
aside.

By the end of twelve months, Li spoke enough English to hold a conversation with Winifred Bramble and her small circle of eloquent acquaintances; to speak coherently with Ben on any subject he chose; to write a
passable note in English, Cantonese, Tanka, or her native Hakka; and to
read, slowly but thoroughly, the *South China Morning Post* from front to
back, marking any words she did not fully understand.

Ben visited the house more frequently now, and spoke to her often in
the company of her tutor. He brought small gifts, nothing too large or
obvious—a sandalwood fan from Formosa, a silk shawl from Shantung,
an amber pendant from Hangchow. Li kept these things hidden in her
chest, ever more aware of the vigilant forces at work around her. She had
even taken the golden guinea from around her neck, determined to do
nothing that could inflame the hidden resentment of the other servants.
Under Ben's close protection and in the constant warmth of Miss Bram-

ble's company, Li found it impossible to consider her own vulnerability, but grew increasingly concerned for both the Fish and Ah-Kin, the gardener. Although she knew the time would come when she must speak of these things to Ben, she hesitated, looking forward instead to the training as a comprador that would take her from Sky House to the shipyard's office on the Praia. She did not allow the discontent of others to interfere with her studies or the stiff examination that had been set for her, and passed all tests with the highest of marks and a growing self-confidence that left no room for fear of any kind.

Ben had proposed that Miss Bramble should take a well-deserved holiday at his expense, expressing his hopes that she would return as tutor at large and companion to Li for an indefinite period. She decided to spend Christmas with old friends in Hong Kong and to consider her future in the coming year.

Li became an increasingly familiar presence in the godowns, aboard the company vessels as they loaded and unloaded their holds, and in the tiny office provided for her in the shipyards. She soon learned that Double Dragon clippers never carried the richest and most dangerous cargo of all—chests of raw opium shipped from the poppy fields of India and sold for their weight in silver bullion. When she asked Indie the reason for this, he would only say, "This is something Ben will tell you in good time."

The tall double doors to Ben's office at the shipyards were at the end of a corridor. Their brass handles were polished every day but seldom used. One afternoon, when he had been away for several weeks, Li entered his office to see if it needed dusting. Instantly, his presence seemed to fill the large, high-ceilinged room, which seemed an extension of his Sky House study—the same rich paneling and ornate desk, its surface covered with the same dark green leather as his chair. Curios and antiques stood on shelves around the walls; a vast glass-fronted display cabinet was filled with ancient porcelain and priceless figures of jade in all its many hues.

Almost immediately, her eye was drawn to two photographs in identical frames on the wall directly behind the desk. One showed the genial face of a foreign woman, strong, robust, with a mop of unruly gray hair.

Beside her, as large and dominant but heavily grained from enlargement, was the face of a brutal-looking Chinese man, his heavy jaw thrust forward in a threatening gesture, his eyes glaring menacingly from beneath a high-domed forehead shaved—including his eyebrows—to the top of the skull. She could not see it but somehow knew he wore a queue, the heavy pigtail of a Boxer. The picture seemed so charged with malice, she found herself stepping back.

"Ugly *bastardo*, isn't he?" The voice of Indie Da Silva caused her to start. "I suppose you must be wondering who they are." Indie leaned his knuckles on the desk. "You are looking at the two most important people in my partner's life. He believes, and so do I, that you should always keep your friends close . . . and your enemies too. Neither must be forgotten."

Indie's voice had lost its customary ease. "The lady's name is Aggie Gates, the nearest thing he's ever had to a mother. She is Ben's greatest friend . . . he would die for her and she for him." He paused. "The other one is a Boxer brave, known as Chiang-Wah the Fierce, who is a sworn enemy. Chiang-Wah is a flag bearer for the Yellow Dragon triad, holder of the golden sash. I will say no more of him; Ben will tell you when he must."

⌘

Buying and selling goods, dispatching and receiving cargoes to and from every corner of China and the Far East, became increasingly absorbing to Li as her command of figures and skill with the abacus grew daily. From her small office overlooking the Double Dragon shipyards, she could smell the sawn timber and hot tar mixed with turpentine, paint, and varnish. The sounds of great ships taking shape on the slip rails became more than a noise to her—the hiss of the steaming press, the planing of wood, and the hammering of mallets as familiar as the chatter of the *mui-mui* among the groves.

Quite unexpectedly one day, when she had become accustomed to his absence, Ben filled the doorway of her office with the briefest of knocks and a loud "hello."

"Indie tells me you are born to be a comprador. It seems you have fulfilled your promise in every way." Li had automatically stood up from the ledger she was studying. "Please, do not let me disturb you, but tonight we will put away the tally sheets and manifests to celebrate the success of a prosperous year.

"You will find some new things in your room. The Fish will help you." He was gone before she could speak.

Packages covered Li's bed in a colorful array. The Fish chuckled with delight as she helped unwrap them. There were gorgeous cheongsams in radiant silks, a silver-backed mirror and comb, and smaller things that drifted over Li's body like softly colored mist. These, the Fish whispered archly, were to be worn only in the bedchamber and for his eyes only. Li had learned to overlook such harmless giggling by the old one, and instead caught her breath at the beautiful array of garments before her.

There was a glittering bottle of crystal that filled the air with fragrance.

Li hesitated. "Such splendor is meant for a woman of great standing," she murmured, almost to herself.

"Yes, *siu-jeh*," the Fish replied. "It is meant for you. The master asked me for your size many weeks ago, and also for the shape of your feet."

"I have never seen such things. Will I not look foolish?"

"He is very thoughtful for a *gwai-lo*, and would never allow the woman on his arm to look a fool."

Li selected a cheongsam of shimmering turquoise—the form-fitting full-length dress fastened at the shoulder, leaving her arms bare. Slit at each side to an inch above the knee, the skirt allowed Li to walk freely but with short and feminine steps. The high collar fitted her long, slender neck perfectly, keeping her posture proudly erect, especially in the silver shoes she chose, with heels that made her feel taller. The Fish fetched a mirror and makeup for her lips and cheeks and eyes. Li shook her head. "If my face cannot be seen without such colors painted upon it, then I should not wear such fine clothes."

At the appointed time, Li knocked softly at the door of the study. Ben was seated at his desk, and rose as she entered. He stood staring in silence.

Finally, he said quietly, "I have never seen anyone quite so lovely." He came from behind the desk, leading her by the hand to the mirror over the fireplace, and gently turning her to face it.

"You could not look more delightful ... except perhaps ..." His hands lifted with a sudden flash in the mirror, gently laying a strand of blue sapphires across her throat. "These are from Siam. They are a gift of appreciation for your dedication to the Double Dragon."

Li lifted a hand to touch them, cool and heavy against her fingertips. It was a shock to see herself adorned by jewels so far beyond her station in life and indeed beyond her needs, yet their magnificence lit her eyes and caused her to gasp.

She turned abruptly, dazzled by the moment, to find herself close to him. She would have stepped back, but he bent to kiss her lightly on the forehead. "Their worth is not in their weight or value, but in the life you bring to them." He let them spill through his fingers, his touch so close to her breast, she was sure he would feel her heartbeat.

He lifted her hand, folding it warmly in his. "These are a token of my affection and respect." He put a finger to her lips when she tried to speak, then placed his hands lightly on her shoulders. "At least wear them for tonight, then I shall keep them safely for you, until you are ready to accept them as your own."

He released her. "Now we will go to dinner in the finest restaurant Macao has to offer." As if reading her thoughts, he added, "Miss Bramble will join us as your chaperone, so all will be proper for those who will see us together."

CHAPTER 12

The Bella Vista and the Palace of Fat Crabs

On *the drive to* the Bella Vista, which the Fish had assured her was Macao's oldest and most famous hotel, Li hoped her deep sense of anxiety would be seen as pure excitement. Cushioned between Ben and Miss Bramble on the leather seat of his royal-blue Rolls-Royce, she could scarcely believe this was real.

As if to reinforce her disquiet, the eye of Ah-Geet appeared in the small mirror above his head. She could not see his face, but the eye alone showed his scorn as clearly as though he had spoken aloud. She looked away, but the eye returned to her whenever it could, as menacing as a raised voice or the threat of a physical blow. His hand came up to adjust the mirror so that both his eyes were upon her. For the flash of a second, the mirror framed his mouth as it mimed the unmistakable word "*cheep-see.*"

Ben Devereaux was clearly well known at the Bella Vista. As the car pullled up before the grand entrance, the doors opened and his party was bowed through the elegant lobby and into the instant warmth and glitter of the dining room. Only Li saw the naked malice on the face of the chauffeur as he drove slowly away to park the car. She had met his contempt with a glance of her own, before putting it from her mind in the way she had learned so well. The gloved hands of dark-skinned boys clad in pageboy uniforms of white and gold opened doors of glass to her.

They passed through a great room lit by the sparkling tiers of magnificent chandeliers and a sea of candlelit tables. A string orchestra played softly in the background, as people in rich and fashionable clothes drank wine from crystal goblets and ate from silver plates. Opulence spun about Li in a glittering wheel of purest fantasy. She was silently thankful that Miss Bramble had prepared her for such an occasion, down to the smallest detail.

Ben Devereaux was greeted on all sides; heads turned their way with every step. The exquisite jewels adorning Li's slender neck seemed to burn her skin as she passed between the sparkling tables . . . feeling that every eye and every whisper branded her as one who aimed too far above her station.

They were seated in a sumptuous alcove, sufficiently apart from other tables to allow quiet conversation. Winifred Bramble seemed very much at ease in her surroundings, wearing an evening dress of coffee-colored lace, her garnets replaced by a simple array of jet, a wrap of cream Kashmir wool about her shoulders.

At first, the moments were spent greeting splendidly attired gentlemen who stopped or crossed the floor to speak with Ben. He introduced her as Miss Li, a student of Miss Bramble's. Some were slightly drunk, and squeezed her hand as they raised it to their lips, their eyes meeting hers in the instant it takes to convey true thought.

The Chinese waiters took in her every move, deftly serving the many dishes with looks and whispers, no louder or more obvious than the rustle of their passing, lost in music from the dance floor and sounds of many voices. So slyly were the insults delivered that even she could not be certain of their source or that they were meant for her: *You could only have been brought here in return for your services. How does it feel to be the common slut of a foreign devil? How does it feel to have no shame?* These were insults kept for Red Lantern Street by those who could not afford to cross the Bella Vista's welcoming doors. She did not think of confronting such phantoms, any more than she would satisfy the poisonous tongues of those in Sky House.

Li had no idea what the aromatic dishes were that were placed before her, only that they were wonderful to look upon and a delight to taste: a banquet that included swallow's-nest soup, braised shark's fin, abalone and asparagus, water chestnuts and Chinese cabbage, steamed Macao sole with shallots, fried Shanghai eels in black pepper sauce, chicken and cucumber with mermaid's tresses, Emperor's roast duck and hoysin sauce, lotus leaf porridge, and almond curd with dragon's eye fruit. She was later able to study this list of court cuisine, when Ben presented her with a leather-bound copy of the menu as a memento of their first dinner together. When the tiny bite-size dishes finally stopped arriving and the table was cleared for coffee and wine, Miss Bramble excused herself discreetly.

"Thank you, Captain Devereaux, for a most enjoyable evening. I am sure there are things to be talked about that do not require the observations or opinions of a rather tired old teacher. If you would be so kind as to summon the car, I would be grateful for a moment or two alone with our rather special young lady." Ben rose immediately, excusing himself with a slight bow.

Winifred wasted no time in reaching for Li's hand, which she held with a smile. "I sense, my dear, that there are things for you and Ben to say to each other that no longer need the pretense of a chaperone. In my opinion, Captain Devereaux possesses a quite refreshing sense of honor. Whatever may pass between you, I believe him to be a gentleman incapable of falsehood and that you may trust his word as I hope you would trust my own."

A waiter brought fresh tea, and Winifred waited until he had moved on before continuing even more confidentially, but with a kindly smile of reassurance. "My Cantonese is rather rusty, and I never did understand the language of the local gutters, but I understand enough to know we are not made welcome here. I admire your dignity and your strength; they will always defeat boorishness and crass stupidity."

She released Li's hand and looked closely into her eyes. "I think of you more as a much-loved niece than as merely an exceptional student. Ben Devereaux has built an empire against unimaginable odds, but I perceive his life as a lonely one. I believe, when he considers the time to be well chosen, he intends to ask you to become his wife."

With a wry smile and the slightest nod of her head, she indicated the soft-footed waiters a step or two away. "You, above all, need not be told of the difficulties to be faced by such a marriage, and Ben has lived here long enough to harbor no illusions." In spite of her composure, a single tear escaped.

"I cannot advise you on what the future holds, except that I am certain you have the character and the judgment to make any decisions that may be required of you."

Ben appeared at that moment, to pull back Winifred's chair and offer his arm. Instinctively, Li rose with her, to have Miss Bramble protest quietly.

"There is no need to make a fuss," she said, embracing her pupil briefly. "I am perfectly capable of finding the door."

"Nonsense, I absolutely insist." Ben nodded to the mâitre d'. "If you would kindly have Ah-Geet bring the car . . ."

As soon as Ben was out of earshot, a waiter found reason to remove Miss Bramble's glass, pausing with a small brush and silver tray, efficiently whisking away the smallest crumb. "How much is Di-Fo-Lo paying his whore? Is the baboon's behind his procuress? We do not serve *mooi-jai* sluts in this hotel. *Mooi-jai* scour our pots and pans; they peel our vegetables and scrub our floors." Smartly dressed, his polished spectacles reflecting the candlelight, his hair immaculate, the waiter looked the perfect embodiment of the famous hotel's grand reputation for service. "Are you so stupid that you think we do not know all about you?" His words were hissed at her through clenched teeth. "Ah-Geet drinks tea in our kitchen; he knows his place. Did you not accept a silver dollar for your services to him—the same services you perform for Di-Fo-Lo?"

Li closed her mind to the string of insults, knowing that any attempt to defend or complain would bring only blank denial and embarrassment for Ben in his defense of her. *You and the young lady must be mistaken, sir . . . perhaps a language difficulty?* the restaurant manager would surely respond, as dignified and deceitful as Ah-Ho herself. Li had often overheard laughter from the kitchen: How easy it was to confound a barbarian; every Chinese word had a dozen meanings, each

178

with its own intonation, so slight that even an accomplished linguist could misinterpret subtle nuances that twisted the meaning of a word this way or that. "Oh, no, master," Ah-Ho had mimicked a humble reply, "I would never say such a terrible thing."

The voice kept up its vicious mutterings while she prayed for Ben's return. Suddenly filled with rage, she found herself upon her feet, determined to make the poison stop. She spoke very quietly, in a steady voice. "You can tell the fool Ah-Geet, he with the member of a very small and smelly goat, that I shall remember his lies as I shall record your insults. You have made an important guest of this hotel lose great face." Slowly, Li shook her head from side to side, with a look of false pity. "I think you will not be working here after I have spoken."

As the last word was uttered, Ben appeared. "What's wrong?" Ben asked, surprised to find her standing. "Nothing at all," she replied, calmly resuming her seat. "The *for-gia* was just brushing the table." She purposely used the lowliest term for a waiter, and he was quickly gone.

Ben took his seat and offered Li some wine. She shook her head. "I believe I have enjoyed so much that is new to me already that wine should perhaps be tried at another time."

Sensing her nervousness, if not the cause, Ben smiled reassuringly and reached across the table to take her outstretched fingers in his big hands. Trying to banish all thoughts of hatred, she returned his smile and focused her every sense on him alone.

"Wine can wait," he said, taking a small purse of pink silk from his pocket, opening the simple clasp. A diamond ring tumbled into the palm of his hand, the square-cut stone so large and brilliant it scattered chips of light across the tablecloth. It seemed so ridiculously out of place next to his huge fingers that she wanted to tell him quickly to put it away.

"It is a yellow diamond . . . as rare and remarkable as you are to me. If you accept it, we shall be married three months from today."

As though he realized his words were too direct, he squeezed her hand reassuringly, seeking her eyes with his, lowering his tone in sympathy with her look of bewilderment. "Please, Li—I know this may seem sudden, and perhaps I am clumsy, but I have thought of it for many

months and considered it most carefully, with the kind advice and blessing of our Miss Bramble."

He paused to return the farewells of a group who were leaving, then
continued when they had passed. "I am building a house in Hong Kong . . .
a villa. When I laid the first brick, it was to house a dream, a fantasy I created in the knowledge that my life was incomplete. I hoped one day to
share it with someone I love, and to raise a family there. I have named it
the Villa Formosa, after what to me is the most beautiful place on earth.

"It is where my children will learn the best of both worlds, the mar-
vels of mother China, and her association with my beautiful country of
England—the imperial dragon of the Middle Kingdom and the celestial
dragon of Saint George. Both are legendary and have much to teach
each other."

Aware of his rising enthusiasm, Ben grinned like a boy trying to im-
press a girl—realizing that, as absurd as it might seem, that was exactly
what he was. "I have said too much and this is all too sudden, and of
course there is no hurry . . ."

Li was all too aware of the sneering eyes invading the elegant intimacy he had meant to create. His words seemed as unreal to her as her
surroundings, which she suddenly found unbearable.

"The matter is too great for hurried thoughts and words. May I beg that
we leave this place? Too many eyes are upon us and too many ears would
intrude upon our privacy. I wish my reply to be heard only by you."

His eyes were troubled, uncertain of her meaning as she closed his
hand over the radiant stone, urging him gently to conceal it. She waited
while the ring was dropped back into its silk pouch and returned to his
pocket without another word. She briefly covered his hand with both of
hers. "I am deeply honored, but overwhelmed. May I think quietly for
this night? There are many things to be considered even greater than the
question of our hearts."

He nodded gravely. "I understand," he said, though she knew that he
did not.

✳

Li found it difficult to sleep. She had sat alone among the restless shadows of the garden to watch the passage of the moon in an ocean of stars. Shortly before dawn, she returned to her room and lay down. At first light, the Fish appeared with the tray of tea and a note beneath a single gardenia in a tiny crystal vase:

Please wear this when we meet at the bend in the road beyond the main gate
at seven o'clock this evening. It is best to dress as one of the boat people; I
recommend bare feet. The Fish will advise you. There is no need for
anyone else to know of this.

— *Ben*

What could this mean? Li knew he had been confused by her reaction to his proposal. Had he also been annoyed—could she have insulted him? This last thought gave her an almost physical pain. Why did he want her to wear old clothes, and why bare feet? Was he planning to send her away?

The Fish would hear nothing of such thoughts, grinning secretively as she took from her camphorwood chest a fresh set of neatly folded Tanka finery: the black smock, its shoulders and skirt patterned with tiny beads of pearl shell and coral; the wide, bell-shaped wicker hat of the boat people to shade her face. Li had seen many a junk captain's wife dressed in such a way on occasions of great importance, and always found it pleasing to the eye. "If we are going to dress you as a Tanka, we will dress you as a proud Tanka. I have kept these clothes for a very long time." The Fish sighed. "You look as I once looked as a young girl."

At precisely seven o'clock, Li was at the bend of the road. Ben appeared seated comfortably in a rickshaw, dressed in a rough shirt and cut-off pantaloons, his large feet bare with the look of a man who worked the mudflats for his living. As his face lit up at the sight of Li, she felt a sudden rush of relief.

"The dress of a fisherman's wife suits you well," he said, holding out his hand to help her into the seat beside him. "I don't think you were

181

comfortable at the Bella Vista. I should have known, but wanted you to have the best. Tonight I will take you to a place that I think may be more to your liking. It is perhaps my very favorite place in all Macao."

Li was delighted to take a rickshaw instead of the car and its venomous driver.

"I thought it would be best if we made no great noise about this evening together," Ben said. "It is no one's business but our own, but I know that others watch and listen and play with the truth like dice."

His words surprised and pleased her, as though her concerns were not the great secret she had thought them to be. He seemed to read her thoughts as the *slap, slap* of the runner's feet took them steadily down toward the lights of the Praia. The setting sun had dropped below the horizon, the sky turned deep violet, pricked by early stars, the yellow light of the rickshaw's lamps fluttering on each side of the folded canopy. She felt him smiling at her with quiet approval.

"I have lived a long time in your country, and have discovered that the less you appear to understand, the more you are likely to learn. It is the only way for a barbarian to succeed."

The sway of the rickshaw, open to a clean sea breeze, seemed to Li to be that of a splendid palanquin, briefly recalling the donkey cart of Giant Yun on the homeward run from the mulberry groves. She wanted to tell him so, to speak freely of the mat hut beneath the willows and the little family she had left behind.

When they reached the waterfront, the lights of Sky House could still be seen high on the promontory, a yellow moon balanced on its gabled roof. The rickshaw pulled off the road and onto the rattling boards of an old jetty, stopping beside the vast hulk of a junk made fast to its iron bollards by creaking coir ropes, permanently moored to great plinths of stone.

Well beyond the reach of the Praia's bright lights, the wharf was dimly lit by smoky lanterns salvaged from ships long gone. Pitch torches threw distorted shadows as Ben took her arm to steer her safely up the rickety gangway to the deck.

"Welcome to the Palace of Fat Crabs." Ben spoke its name with the affection of an old and trusted friend as they stepped onto the deck. Glowing candles stood in conch shells on the upturned oyster butts and wine casks that served as tables, occupied by men and women who clearly earned their living from the sea. They were roughly dressed as though they had come straight from a working boat; they cracked big crab claws and snapped spiny legs, sucking out the chunks of succulent flesh with an air of abandon more suited to the *mung-cha-cha* than the Bella Vista. Others were busy over steamed and deep-fried fish taken live from bubbling tanks, spitting bones onto the deck, or swallowing fat oysters, tossing the shells over the side. Ben grinned happily. "I did not think this would be Miss Bramble's cup of tea, although I think she would approve of its ethics."

Playing cards were slapped down and dice rattled over jugs of sangria and beer. Li saw that there were foreigners among the junk captains and Hokklo fisherfolk, some escorting young and pretty Chinese girls. "They have the best and freshest chili crab this side of Singapore. Only people of goodwill eat here—Portuguese, Macanese, Spaniards, even French and English. The Chinese who share their pleasure are old friends. You can speak freely; all eyes are on the feast before them, all ears on tall stories and talk of the sea."

As he led her by the hand through the colorful throng, many of the rowdy company greeted Ben by name, some standing to slap his back or offering bawdy compliments on his choice of companion. When they were seated in a more private spot in the junk's prow, separated by a cordon of fancy rope work, Ben spread his arms wide and breathed in deeply the mild salt air.

"There is no better smell than fat Macao crab fresh from the trap, sizzling in black-bean sauce with just the right mixture of chili and shallots." He sat back, looking about him and beaming with pleasure. "We are among friends here. No tablecloths, no menus, no silverware, no crystal, and no treachery." His merriment briefly subsided, replaced by a quiet sincerity. "Yes, I heard much of what was said last night, but I have learned that to confront such mindless villainy is to create a scene that is so much worse it is unwise to try. Such cowards will always deny their

insult . . . it is always the barbarian who has misunderstood and the female is always to blame." He grinned suddenly. "It is why I never reveal
how much Cantonese I speak and understand. You will be pleased to
know that I am an old friend of the proprietor. I spoke to him when
Winifred was safely in the car, and those who were responsible are no
longer employed at the Bella Vista, nor will they find work in any such
establishment."

He reached across to cover her hand with his, warm and comforting.
"I am sorry to have allowed such a thing . . . but something told me you
could deal with the situation. I had to know, for it will always surround
us." With perfect timing that broke the somber moment, the Portuguese
proprietor descended upon them to greet Ben like a lost brother.

"This is my dear, fat friend Alonzo," Ben said. "I would trust him
with my life but not my woman." Alonzo bowed to Li and kissed her
hand with a gallant flourish, congratulating Ben on his excellent taste in
females, then bustled off to the galley—to return, it seemed to Li, moments later, bearing a vast, sizzling platter of seafood, followed by a boy
carrying a huge wooden bowl of fresh greens and a basket of bread. The
platters were plonked down in front of them without ceremony.

"Macao mudcrab, local shrimp and lobster, mangrove oysters from
Heng Quin Island, Basque salad as they make it in the mountains. Welcome to the Palace of Fat Crabs, all fresh from the sea only moments
ago." The bitter memory of the opulent dining room, with its glittering
chandeliers and vicious undercurrent of resentment and ridicule, was
quickly banished as Ben offered a pile of steaming-hot hand towels.

"Eating crab with your bare hands is one of life's greatest pleasures.
Most of all, it does not allow pretense; even an emperor becomes a fisherman when there is a crab claw in his hand. We have much to talk
about, but first we shall eat. Let me show you—I am an expert at this."

With great gusto, Ben set about the task of destroying crab, lobster,
shrimp, and seafoods of every description—separating the shell, scooping
out the orange roe, cracking the claws, and snapping the legs, extracting
delicious morsels of flesh and placing them before her. His genuine pleasure was all-embracing, and Li felt herself caught up in his enjoyment.

"The best part of eating here is that table manners are unheard of; the more mess we make, the happier our host will be. You may spit unwanted shell upon the deck and belch to your heart's content, and he will bring you more." Ben proceeded to demonstrate this and urged her to do the same. Their hands and mouths were wiped from a pile of damp cloths immediately replaced, remnants of the feast tossed away to be eaten by well-fed cats that prowled beneath the tables or the ever-watchful gulls riding the ebbing tide.

Time passed unnoticed as he spoke freely of his youth. "I wish you to know the truth of Di-Fo-Lo the baby-eater, great taipan of the Double Dragon—who started as an unwanted boy with only the threat of danger and the flame of hope to keep him company. I see in you that same flame.

"I am of mixed blood, the son of a Chinese mother whom I never knew. My father was a Breton master mariner who fled Shanghai after the Boxer Uprising. It was not fear of the Boxers that drove him out, but a blood feud that has left me with dangerous enemies to this day. My father died from the trade that made him rich . . . opium. He fled to save me. I was little more than a newborn. When they killed my mother, burned his house, and took his business, there was little left for him to do." When the table was cleared and a platter of quartered fruits set down with a fresh pot of Bo Lin tea, Ben said, "Forgive me; I have allowed enjoyment to loosen my tongue perhaps too much. It is time for me to listen. There is little you can ask of me that I cannot provide." Li knew that this was the moment to speak of things that had barely left her mind since waking in his cabin aboard *Golden Sky*.

She began cautiously. "I am greatly honored to hear of things so close to a heart as brave as yours. To speak of my childhood would bring sadness over things I would rather forget. But there are also joys to be remembered."

Li gazed steadily at his face. "Do you know the saying: 'Bamboo door face bamboo door. Wooden door face wooden door. Golden door face golden door'?"

He nodded. "It means that we are from very different worlds and may

185

not suit each other. That one may seek what the other may shun. Peasant should marry peasant, merchant should marry merchant, nobleman should marry noblewoman."

"Yes," she said eagerly. "China is not kind to those of mixed blood. Alone, we face its dangers and learn how to survive. Together, we have other lives to care for than our own. . . . This is a different kind of courage. I do not know if I possess it."

She raised her hand as he went to speak. "The world would not be kind to us or our children. Sometimes great mistakes are made in the name of loneliness, choices that once made cannot be undone."

"I have never known this world to be kind," Ben answered slowly, each word crafted for her ears alone. "I am proud to be Eurasian, a *jarp-jung*, as our children will be proud. We will teach them to fight for their heritage if they have to. Our ancestors will rejoice in their courage. Loneliness will never again enter our lives and no one will take away our right to love freely and with all our hearts."

Ben spoke with such depth of feeling that Li did not hestitate to reply. "Then I will ask my questions without misunderstanding." She sat up straight. "How many wives will you have?" She could see he resisted the urge to chuckle, but he answered seriously. "I will have only one wife. My children will have only one mother." She nodded her acceptance. "How many concubines will you have?" Again, he would have smiled, but she looked so solemn that he shook his head with equal gravity. "I will have no concubines. That is not the way of this barbarian." Li's surprise showed in her eyes. "Then will you have the services of a mistress? How can one wife be enough for a man? How can you be sure that you will not grow tired of me?"

Ben's answer was heartfelt as her questions. "If I tire of you, I will tire of living. There will be no mistress. Your health and happiness and that of our children will be all I ask."

He smiled to lighten the solemnity of the moment. "Besides, sometimes I will be away. There will not be time to bore each other, only to count the moments until we are together again."

Li's growing smile was gone in an instant, her tone almost businesslike. Her heart beat faster. These were the words of her future and her fortune. "Forgive me, Seal-Yeh, but I was not born to be a *tai-tai*, to visit the beauty parlor and play mah-jonng. I will be a strong wife and a good mother. But that is not enough. I must earn my place in the noble company as comprador of the Double Dragon. Only this will give me the true happiness we hope to share. I wish to sail with my husband, not wait with my eyes on a horizon I will never reach."

"I would not question your wishes," he said, "because I know they would be honest and considered with great care. . . ."

She did not give him time to finish. "If I do not give you sons but only daughters, what will you do with them?"

The question was so blunt, so much a part of her, he reached over to cover her hands with his. "I will love and protect them as I would my sons. I can imagine nothing more wonderful than the daughters of Lee Sheeah"—he grinned at the thought—"unless it be her sons."

"Will a daughter learn to read and write beside her brothers? Will she be taught, by Miss Bramble perhaps, if the gods are with us?"

He held up his hand, almost afraid of how much this meant to her, again choosing his words as he had once chosen cards. "Both the sons and the daughters of Li Devereaux will be educated in the best schools and taught by the best tutors this world has to offer. This I solemnly pledge. Our daughters will be cherished in the eyes of their father; they will have the pride and dignity of their mother and the opportunities of a scholar."

Li was silent for a moment, determined to leave nothing unspoken. "I do not know what love is," she said at length. "Such a thing has never been shown to me. . . . But if love means giving you pleasure, this I believe I can promise. If it means bearing strong sons and daughters, learning skills that will build the prosperity of your clan, I will do so gladly, if the gods allow it. But love? I must understand love before I can promise it." Her seriousness gave way to the shyest of smiles as he lifted his big hand to touch her cheek as gently as a smile.

"It is something that neither of us is familiar with. Perhaps we can discover it together," Ben said with a tenderness that put her heart at rest.

"I must ask one final thing. If you still want me to be your *tai-tai* after this, I will be honored to cross your door." Ben grinned his relief.

"You know you can ask me anything." He would have left his chair to go to her if she had not raised a hand to stop him.

"You saved me from the river and the sentence of *sau-hai*. Now I must beg you to take me back where you found me." With these words she produced a neatly folded, itemized list of words and figures. His pride in her mounted with every second that she spoke, explaining every line and digit, outlining a business proposition that left him speechless.

CHAPTER 13

The House of the Kindly Moon

The crossing of the ship *Golden Sky* from Macao to the mouth of the Pearl River was swift and smooth, the vessel leaning into the wind as gracefully as a great seabird. As the ship approached the silk mill of Ten Willows, Li's heart quickened. This was a mission she had dreamed of a thousand times. Ben's initial astonishment at her request had quickly turned to approval, giving her new confidence.

From the deck of *Golden Sky*, she could see the tiny figures of the *mui-mui* on the hill, busy as ants among the blue haze of the mulberry trees. In her mind she heard the floating notes of Garlic's flute and the metallic whirring of cicadas, the jokes of Monkey Nut, and the unmistakable laugh of Little Pebble.

With the mooring ropes ashore, Li descended the gangway, stepping, as Miss Bramble had taught her, with the dignity and measured pace of one who could not be hurried. As befitted a person of station, she was wearing the smart uniform of the Double Dragon comprador, which she had designed herself—a fitted *sam-foo* of cherry red, the double-D crest embroidered in gold thread on its breast, her hair held by a comb of ivory and mother-of-pearl. Over her shoulder she carried a splendid sunshade of pale yellow silk, and in her hand a closed sandalwood fan.

Li stepped from the gangway. Wang the steward, smartly dressed in his crisp white uniform, followed a few paces behind, leading two deck boys loaded with an assortment of wrapped packages.

The unmistakable figure of Ah-Jeh appeared at the window of her office. She hurried down to welcome the unexpected arrival, bowing before the young woman in red. The waddling figure, grown even fatter over the past couple of years, led the way, the *swish, swish, swish* of her *tzow* even more pronounced than Li remembered.

In the silk room, the same large room where her father had abandoned her, the packages were stacked upon the table. Li was made comfortable in the silk-lined seat reserved for visitors of importance, while tea was set before her in a silver-mounted cup.

"You do not recognize me?" Li asked when the superintendent showed no sign of it. "Perhaps because my face was bruised and swollen, my hair had been cut off and my body caked with mud and the droppings of swine the last time you saw me; I could not stand because you had crippled me. You saw me dragged from the river more dead than alive. You watched, I believe, from your window, cursing me from a distance because you had not the courage to face me."

Ah-Jeh's thin brows drew down in a moment of confusion; her mouth opened and closed like a fish in a jar. She looked so absurd that Li wondered how this pudding of a woman could have once controlled her life.

"Do not be alarmed; I have returned only on matters of business. First, I come to pay the *sung-tips* of the *mung-cha-cha* family. Let us settle this first." Li found none of the satisfaction she had expected as Elder Sister stood speechless, her eyes, normally so alert, blank with shock and her pallid face flushed as though it had been slapped. Li did not prolong the superintendent's astonishment. Her tone was expressionless, as befitting simple matters of business. She handed Ah-Jeh a sealed red packet. "You will find the sum far greater than their value to Ming-Chou, and of course there is a generous commission for your services in this matter."

At that moment Li saw Ah-Jeh as a fat, overfed frog in a small and hungry pond, no match for the wily taipans of the Praia or the seasoned compradors of the Macao godowns. "If you have the authority to close this matter quickly and quietly, without disturbing the great Ming-Chou, your commission will be doubled." Li shrugged, closing her fan with an air of indifference. "If this cannot be arranged, I shall have to inform Captain Devereaux . . . we will be forced to reconsider our offer and perhaps withdraw."

At the word "we," Ah-Jeh raised an inquiring eyebrow despite the uncertainty of her position. Now that she saw with much amazement who she was dealing with, her eyes narrowed to mask her thoughts.

"I am comprador to the Double Dragon Trading Company," Li went on, "under the authority of Captain Devereaux, to whom I am also personal assistant. I speak on his behalf because you and I are known to each other, but if you wish his presence it can quickly be arranged. I warn you, however, Di-Fo-Lo will not be so generous nor as patient as I; he will demand the presence of your master."

Li found it difficult to suppress a smile at the superintendent's discomfort, but took advantage of it. "Are not the *mung-cha-cha* known to be a little mad, sometimes rebellious and disobedient; did they not show defiance in my defense? Will life at Ten Willows not be easier for you without such bothersome creatures?"

Ah-Jeh opened the fold of the red packet and fingered the thick wad of banknotes with familiar efficiency. Li did not wait for a reply. "Have the *mung-cha-cha* brought here without delay."

There was the slightest hint of mockery in the superintendent's words. "This can be arranged." She affected a sympathetic tone. "But I am sad to tell you that the Little Pebble no longer works in the groves. Her eyes do not see and her fingers cannot find the cocoons. Her basket is empty."

Li felt a growing alarm. What punishment Pebble must have endured at the hands of the *sau-hai* for being her friend! But always there had been the laugh and the dance that reassured her: *I will be here waiting, little Crabapple.* Li summoned the courage to ask one hushed question, her mouth suddenly dry. "Is she gone to the Pagoda of Pity?"

Ah-Jeh sniffed. "She forfeited her rights when she too disobeyed the rules of the *mui-mui*."

Li felt a stab of raw fury at the superintendent's smugness. "Have her brought here, sick or well. Do as I say or I will bring down powers you cannot imagine to investigate her disappearance."

Ah-Jeh was quick to respond, spreading her hands in a show of innocence. "She is no longer the responsibility of Ten Willows or of mine." Again, the shrug of thinly veiled indifference. "Ask the *mung-cha-cha*; perhaps they know what has happened to their Little Pebble."

"Send for them immediately," Li snapped. "We will speak of other business while I wait." She produced a second envelope, sealed with the chop of the Double Dragon and addressed to Ming-Chou in the bold, flowing hand of Ben Devereaux. "This is to be delivered by hand. I do not wish to look upon Ming-Chou's face, so I pass this urgent duty to you. It contains certain requirements if the Double Dragon is to continue doing business with Ten Willows." Ah-Jeh left the envelope untouched as Li raised her hand and Wang handed her a wooden spindle.

"The holds of *Golden Sky* and other Double Dragon ships carry many thousands of these each month, and in half the time of any junk on the coast. Ming-Chou's price has been agreed upon and paid without fail. Yet when delivered, some spindles are found to be imperfect . . . the golden thread broken or knotted, the quality inferior, the weight inconsistent." Li placed the spindle beside the letter. "This is now the standard spindle approved by the factories in Shantung and all the big silk cities. It is the exact size, shape, and weight required. From this day, every cargo will be inspected and all other spindles rejected. The Double Dragon will charge a fee for each rejection."

Ah-Jeh's protestations of innocence were cut short by the appearance of the *mung-cha-cha*, who had run from the groves, breathless and dirty. They stood hesitantly in the doorway, afraid to enter until Li went to them with open arms, calling out their names and repeating her own. Even then, they stepped back, their hats clutched before them, unable to believe this important lady was truly the little Crabapple.

Only one thing tempered Li's joy at this reunion. "Where is Little Pebble?" she asked, half afraid of the answer. Her fears were quickly put to rest. "She is in the care of Giant Yun," Garlic reassured her. "We will take you to her."

"She will be happy to see you, Crabapple," Mugwort said.

"We have missed you," Monkey Nut agreed.

"We thought you had been taken away by the barbarian and sold as a slave," Turtle added. "Pebble has made up many stories. Is it true that you are the only scholar in the harem of an Arabian prince who pays you in diamonds?"

"It is almost true"—Li laughed—"but he is not an Arab and he pays me in sapphires . . . and sometimes diamonds." The *mung-cha-cha* looked at each other wide-eyed.

Li turned to Ah-Jeh. "If our arrangement is acceptable, please have these young ladies bathed in the mill bathhouse and let the masseurs attend to them. Please see that our business is concluded in two hours' time." She indicated the pile of wrapped packages. "Then have them put on these clothes, which are clearly marked with their names. Meanwhile, I would like to inspect the weaving mill."

The sisters of *sau-hai* looked up from their looms as Ah-Jeh opened the door for Li. Accustomed to occasional visitors, they did not pause in the rhythm of their work.

For a few moments, Li walked among them, breathing in the stale air agitated by worthless fans, the clatter and clank of outdated looms, the cheerless concentration and the absence of laughter. From the steps leading to the superintendent's dingy office, she looked down one last time upon the weavers of *sau-hai*, the gentle sisters who would have killed her with a smile. She felt no anger or thoughts of revenge, but only pity as she saw that the sisters of *sau-hai* had empty hearts; they had exchanged their souls for the white handkerchief and the colored parasol. Once outside, with the sun on her face, she said a prayer of thanks to Little Pebble for warning her of the price to be paid for a rice bowl that would never be empty,

Fresh from the delights of the bathhouse, dressed in *sam-foos* of silk, each of a different shining color, with pretty slippers on their feet and their hair brushed and tied with ribbons. the ladies of the *mung-cha-cha* were unrecognizable. Each of them held an open sunshade in pink and blue or green and yellow, as Li led the way along the loading wharf and up the gangway of *Golden Sky*.

Farther upriver at Giant Yun's hut, Little Pebble was carried aboard, and the *mung-cha-cha* helped her to change her tattered *mien-larp* for one of quilted black chased with gold and silver thread. The family was complete.

"I knew you would not forget us, Crabapple. True scholars forget nothing of great importance." Little Pebble grinned up at Li. "I am not as strong as I was. I can't see very well . . . but I am still a dancer deep inside, and my heart is still filled with secrets."

Golden Sky came about, to sail five miles to the jetty of the farm of the old lord, Ah-Bart, who had joined his ancestors at last. As it came into view, the *mung-cha-cha* lined the rail, bewildered by this day of many miracles and amazed by what they saw: The cottage and its out-buildings had been repaired and repainted, with the door now the shade of lucky red. Broken tiles had been replaced, the garden tended, the mulberry trees pruned and heavy with cocoons. The largest of the out-buildings had been converted into a sorting and spinning shed; another contained a new copper boiler and all the necessary tools and equip-ment for making silk. Beside these a mill of brick and tile had been built, fitted with ample fans, combustion stoves, and the very latest in weaving looms.

There were goats in the newly built pen and pigs in the sty. The wa-terwheel was turning again with hardly a creak, while contented ducks paddled among the lilies and fat chickens ran loose in an orchard re-stored to its original glory. Tufts of jade-green rice were already sprout-ing on the rebuilt terrace, and a pair of donkeys grazed in the field, where a buffalo wallowed in a newly dug fishpond. A new iron plow and a four-wheel cart complete with harness stood waiting in the shed. Moored at the rebuilt jetty was a gaily painted sampan with a sky-blue sail and a diesel motor. Most wonderful of all were the rows upon rows of advanced mulberry saplings that had been planted in the empty fields.

Seen from the deck, the perfection of this riverside scene took Li's breath away. When she had entered every item in the ledger and tallied up the total cost, the sum was so great she had wondered if it was indeed possible. Only when Ben assured her that the money amounted to less than he spent on rum and tobacco in a year did she cease to be concerned. Indie Da Silva had arranged the entire operation, delivering materials and a gang of chosen men under the supervision of Wang the steward aboard a Double Dragon workboat.

She looked upon the faces of the *mung-cha-cha*, delighted by their amazement, as she spoke the words that fulfilled a dream she had once thought to be distant as the stars. "This farm is yours. It belongs to the *mung-cha-cha* family." She held up a scroll. "This is a copy of the deed; it is in my name and I will be your agent in Macao and Hong Kong. It has been purchased by the Double Dragon Company, but you are its rightful owners. Our overseer, Little Pebble, will be your superintendent."

She laughed with delight at their astounded faces. "It is proudly named 'the House of the Kindly Moon.'" For a moment there was silence, until Pebble found her feet and began to dance, while her sisters clapped and cheered until they were hoarse.

Li had to raise her voice to be heard over the commotion. "The Double Dragon Company has also purchased the adjoining land and will help you build the House of the Kindly Moon into the most efficient and profitable silk farm on the Pearl River. They will buy all your silk and you will repay the loan over ten years."

She waited for the excitement to settle down. "I have in mind a great friend who can read and write and who is mistress of the abacus. She lives not far from here and will help you in the ways of business as your comprador. She will know where to find me. I am half a day away and we can speak over the telephone."

She turned to Giant Yun, who had stood well back, witnessing these proceedings with the widest of grins. Li bowed to him. "Ah-Yun, you are our father and our brother, our poet and our oracle. We beg you to join us, to be our guardian and to share our fortune for a hundred years." The giant bowed his head, unable to find words as the *mung-cha-cha* surrounded him in their joy.

"There is a gardener's lodge for you by the orchard, comfortably appointed with a room for your precious shells and treasures of the sea. It is there whenever you wish to make it your own." There was immeasurable gratitude in her smile and deepest respect in the tone of her voice. "The donkey in the field is for pulling the cart and the buffalo for the plow. Your great strength will always be needed to protect the House of the Kindly Moon and those who share its harmony. You are also master of the sampan, to transport your produce and see that there are always fish to fry and eels for supper."

Wang and his galley boys carried a roasted pig into the house, along with a feast fit for the family of the comprador of a famous company. Firecrackers were lit in an ear-splitting cascade of good luck and prosperity. Inside, the rooms were fresh and clean, with curtained windows and pictures on the walls. In the kitchen, large enough for many guests, the cooking stove already roared beneath large woks filled with fresh noodles, sizzling vegetables, and flavored rice. A table big enough to serve a banquet had been laid with pretty crockery upon a snow-white cloth, with a red *lai-see* packet waiting to be opened beside each bowl.

When all were seated, Li stood at the head of the table. "The lucky money is enough to take a holiday, to seek your *huang-ha* and perhaps find news of family . . . or just to spend in the village market on whatever may touch the heart. All of this has been made possible by the barbarian you have been warned of, the man called Di-Fo-Lo, whose heart holds all that is best of two great worlds . . . the world of China and the world outside."

There was great applause when Li had finished speaking, then one by one the *mung-cha-cha* responded. Each had found a gift to lay before her. Pebble was the first to speak. "May all gods bless the little Crabapple," she cried, clapping her hands as the other girls stood to join her. "We have little to give, but I have made you a crown of morning stars, each flower a precious gem. And this is the best pebble I could find. It is very old, but the older it gets the stronger it becomes . . . just like me." She placed the crown of flowers on Li's head and a large river stone in her hand. On its polished surface Pebble had etched her *mui-mui* name with the point of her knife.

196

The river stone was immediately followed by Garlic's bamboo flute. "Perhaps you will learn to play it one day . . . and when you do, you will think of me and I will hear its music wherever I am."

Turtle unfolded her finest silk, displaying its brightness as she placed it around Li's neck. "And I will always be a part of your peacefulness. This is a happiness silk; you will never be sad when you wear it."

Mugwort and Monkey Nut presented a pair of sandals, beautifully made from cane grass and stitched with intricate care with stolen strands of silk, with tassels of feathers at the ends of the laces. "Each of us made one, so they may not be exactly the same, but they are true to each other. When you wear them, we will walk with you wherever you go."

Last to approach her was Giant Yun. It was the first time Li had seen him fully clothed, his huge body clad in the simple dress of a river fisherman. With his head bowed and both arms outstretched, he presented a carrying case of closely woven willow twigs, with plaited straps to keep it secure. Its flap was fastened by a slip of willow, which Li opened to reveal a box of such delicate beauty, the *mung-cha-cha* murmured with wonder. Slid from the safety of its case, the box was no larger than the book of tallies that Ah-Jeh had kept upon her tall desk in the silk room—perhaps three hand spans long, two hand spans wide, and one hand span deep. Shells of every size, shape, and color had been fixed into intricate floral garlands on every corner and panel of its pale yellow wood.

Li lifted the lid to find, laid upon a bed of dried petals, the pearly splendor of a large horse-mussel shell, every inch of it exquisitely carved with miniature images of river life: on one side the grand cascade of the willows, ducks among the reeds, junks and sampans on the water; on the other, the mulberry groves on the hill overlooking the valley, the cart beside them, and two *mui-mui* emptying their baskets. Beneath this, in characters almost too tiny to be read, words spelled out the heart of Giant Yun:

> *The bluecap is always happiest in the tall bamboo.*
> *There it will sing forever.*

"Making this box and carving this shell gave me endless pleasure. I did not count the hours or the days or the months or the years before it was finished, because time is slow flowing as the river." These were difficult words for Giant Yun to find, and he hesitated, looking around the ring of faces as though for permission to continue. He saw only the smiles of those who respected him.

"It is made of willow wood and the shells are the gifts of a thousand tides. It is much too pretty for my hut by the river and I have kept it hidden from the *larn-jai* for many years. Now I know that it was meant for you, to hold the things most important to your heart."

Li bowed to him as she would to any lord, placing the river stone, the happiness silk, and the bamboo flute inside. "No empress was ever given such a sacred box. It will hold all things precious to me and always be filled with treasured memories."

Li slipped her feet into the woven sandals. "Thank you for all these gifts, which will remain with me forever. I have one final gift for you." She produced the documents she had purchased from Ah-Jeh. "These are your *sung-tips*. Let us burn them and celebrate your freedom together."

Once the contracts were merrily set ablaze, the blessing of the House of the Kindly Moon continued long into the evening, and joy flowed unabated without the need of wine.

※

With silence settled at last and a moon big and round as a goat cheese smiling upon the little house by the river, Ben Devereaux saw the jib sail carefully hoisted and the moorings quietly slipped. At the helm as the ship pulled away, he turned to Li with inquiring eyes. "It sounds as though this day has been a great success. Everything worked just as you planned." Ben told her that Ming-Chou had been too old and ill to make an appearance, but the terms of the Double Dragon Company had been accepted: The rotting huts of the *mui-mui* would be torn down and replaced by houses of lime-washed brick, with roofs of tile that would not leak in any weather, and with a garden plot for growing vegetables and keeping hens. There would be a bathhouse with hot water, and once each week amahs would come to rub their tired backs; and a doctor from the village would tend them when they were sick. There would be fruit and vegetables to eat; salt fish would no longer need to be stolen, nor eels caught to flavor their rice. A visiting tailor would supply them with changes of clothes, for work and for festivals; they would even have a place to wash them and lines to hang them from. A cobbler would make and mend their footwear.

All of these improvements were long overdue and had been accepted in most silk farms in Kwangtung Province. Ben had said that his threat to do no further business with Ming-Chou, and to send inspectors from Macao, had even secured the reluctant agreement to pay a modest wage and to allow the *mui-mui* to visit the village on festive occasions.

Li-Xia smiled at him with shining eyes. "There are no words to tell you what this means to me. It gives purpose and brings light to those things that seemed forever dark. If I live for a hundred years, I can never thank you enough for giving my family their freedom and their dignity."

Ben nodded his understanding, as *Golden Sky* answered to the helm and a foresail was set to follow the glittering path of the river.

"Go below and get some sleep. Wang will wake you when we approach the Great Pine Farm."

Li was endlessly grateful for Ben's tolerance and tact. When she had asked to revisit her past before moving on to their future, his smile had embraced her without reservation. "If these are things that you must do to help make you whole and show you the beginning of happiness, then they are as necessary to me as they are to you."

Even when she had invited him to be the guest of honor at the opening feast of the House of the Kindly Moon, he had respectfully declined. "The hulking presence of a barbarian, no matter how well meaning, would hamper the freedom of thought and speech that such an occasion deserves." He kissed her gently and held her for a moment, then drew away, determined to wait for the proper time before yielding to the growing need he felt for her. "There will be other adventures for us to share, but these will never come again. You have earned these moments—enjoy them without interference. They mark the beginning of a new life."

With the coming of dawn, as they approached the Great Pine Farm, he turned from the helm admiringly when she presented herself for his inspection. "From what little I know of your business here, they do not deserve such grace and intelligence among them, even for a moment." He sighed with an exaggerated grin. "No comprador of my acquaintance ever looked quite so lovely." He continued less playfully. "I can only imagine what this visit means to you, but I think I know how very difficult it must be. Remember, if things are not as you would wish them, you only have to call my name."

❋

Li waited to face her father with no sense of foreboding, only an impatient resolve to achieve what she had come for and be gone forever from his presence. She looked around the trading room, recalling her fifth birthday and the shattering of the happiness tile. His chair did not seem so high and all-commanding as it had on that unhappy day, now appearing shabby, no longer a throne. She chose not to sit upon one of the merchants' stools assembled around the spice table, determined to make this unpleasant meeting as brief as possible.

She was not kept waiting long before Yik-Munn appeared. He had aged more than she would have imagined: his high-crowned hat, made loose by loss of hair, balanced rather ridiculously upon ears that seemed to have grown larger, their famous Buddha lobes shrunken and no longer godlike. His eyes peered through small round spectacles as if looking for ghosts, with no flicker of his crude energy and pride. Li was curiously untouched by either sympathy or triumph. If anything disturbed her peace of mind, it was her absolute absence of feeling. But it made what she had to say and do much easier.

Like Ah-Jeh, Yik-Munn did not recognize the young woman who stood before him, knowing only that she had been announced as a representative of a Macao trading company wishing to speak to him on urgent business. For a comprador, she was uncommonly young and pleasing to the eye. Taller than most and shapely in an elegant cheongsam of turquoise-blue silk, she carried an ivory fan, and a folded yellow

200

sunshade laid beside her matched the iris in her hair. A surge of pleasure at this lightly perfumed vision made Yik-Munn acutely aware of his advancing years.

Li looked upon her father as a forgotten stranger. "I do not expect you to recognize me. I am your daughter, the one you called Li-Xia, the Beautiful One, the daughter of Pai-Ling Ling." She did not wait for his look of disbelief to be followed by myopic recognition, or the croak in his scraggy throat to form words she had no wish to hear. Only his magnificent teeth remained untouched by the passing of time, but while these had retained their artificial shape and size, his mouth had not. It was hard to tell if his grimace was caused by astonishment or pain.

"I am here to tell you what you must do if you are to save face, or else forever damn the name of Yik-Munn. I bring no hatred or thoughts of revenge, nor do I seek anything that is beyond my right as the daughter of a well-respected man and a member of an honorable family." Yik-Munn could neither smile nor sneer, his watery eyes as fearful as if the spirit of the fox fairy had finally returned to punish him.

"I suggest that you listen and carry out my wishes without delay. You will provide a palanquin to carry me to the ginger field. You will take me to my mother's grave and swear before all gods that this is where she lies. You will have your sons fetch stones for the best artisans to erect a tomb over her resting place without disturbing her remains. You will have them carve this upon its entrance in Hunan marble in both Chinese and English."

She gave him a slip of paper, which he reached for with a trembling hand, fumbling with his spectacles. "I will tell you what it says:

> This is the resting place of the great scholar Pai-Ling. She lives on in the
> heart of her daughter, the scholar Li-Xia, and can be found
> hand in hand with her sister the moon.

"When the tomb is ready, you will summon priests from the temple; they will bring gongs and trumpets, an abundance of offerings and many expensive joss sticks. You will provide a large roast pig, and many dishes of fresh fruit. You will burn a paper mansion, a motorcar, many servants, and a barrow full of paper money. A funeral service will be held at my mother's grave in the ginger field and a rail of iron set in stone to forever protect its sanctuary. You will have her family name engraved upon a tablet of finest ivory and presented to me with all due ceremony."

The cunning of Yik-Munn had not completely deserted him even now. It showed momentarily in his failing eyes, belying his pitiful whimpering. "If I have forgotten the exact spot, and your brothers are not willing—if I am unable to find such artisans, if the priests refuse such a service—what will be your penalty?"

Li ignored his question. "Then you will pay whatever it costs to see this done as speedily as you once honored the great Goo-Mah. When this is done, you will find my mother's family and demand from them her ancestral tablets and what images they may retain. You will give to me any photograph or likeness of her that you still possess and anything that may have once belonged to her."

He clasped his hands, aghast at her demands, afraid of her anger. "This is impossible. The Ling family have left their *huang-ha*, I do not know the name of their new village or its province. I have no knowledge of . . ."

"Then you must find them; those who knew them in Shanghai will tell you." She laughed lightly. "Pretend they owe you money; that will help you find them quickly."

Her manner left no room for barter, and he was suddenly seized by the full extent of his humiliation. He rose so quickly that his taipan's chair almost overturned and his official's hat fell to the floor. His hands extended like claws; a thin lock of hair rose from his head like the plumes of an aging parrot. "Who are you to demand such things of me?" He tried to spit but could not find saliva, only a rasp of hatred leaving his distorted mouth. "You are of my blood; I will have your respect, not your insults." He drew himself up defiantly. "I will call in your brothers to teach you something of filial piety."

Li's reply was cold and immediate. "There are those aboard the ship who would not allow this. I can fetch them now if you threaten me again." Yik-Munn sank back into his seat, staring balefully at his daughter.

"I am no longer a helpless child and now have the protection of someone whose power you cannot begin to imagine. If you are not willing to accept these terms, we will call a meeting of merchants in this room and I will tell them how you treated me as an outcast, how my mother was driven to a hideous death by your hand. I will report the binding of my feet, which is against the law of China, and see that you are ruined." She waved away his further attempts at feeble protest.

"I do not expect this to matter among those who know no better, but I will bring officials of my close acquaintance from Macao who will sentence you to the punishment you deserve. I am also sure of Number-Three Wife's cooperation as your unpaid comprador. I have seen with my own eyes how you cheat those who buy your spices. Your name will be laughed at in every teahouse as the fool who dared defy a fox fairy. Your ancestors will be unforgiving for all eternity and you will be lost forever to the ghosts of shame." She picked up her sunshade in readiness to leave.

"When my mother's place of rest is sanctified and blessed, when her ancestral rights have been honored and fulfilled, you will hear no more from me on this or any other matter. You will owe me nothing . . . not even a word of good-bye."

※

It was with mixed feelings that Li left the mouth of the Pearl River on the following evening. The ceremony had been arranged as she had asked, with no one else present but Number Three. There had never been such a burning of paper offerings—the biggest, brightest, and most expensive the village joss house could provide. A mansion of many rooms, a troop of servants to fulfill her every wish, a gorgeous palanquin with four strong bearers, chests of gold and silver and rolls of banknotes had whirled above the ginger field and into the bluest of skies, to surround the spirit of Pai-Ling and restore her to her rightful place in heaven.

Li thought with pleasure of Little Pebble and the *mung-cha-cha* happily settled in the House of the Kindly Moon. Number Three had willingly agreed to visit them often and to teach them what she could, and would be paid by the Double Dragon for her services. Li had made sure that a room was provided for her use, and hoped the little house by the river would become a welcome haven from the disintegration of the House of Munn.

Despite all these satisfactions, Li was unable to sleep, The feelings that touched her heart when she thought of Ben were far more than gratitude. She went forward to the prow of *Golden Sky*, watching the green fire of phosphorous flaring from the bows, the distant lights of Macao strung like a glittering necklace on the dark horizon, until the bright moon and the soft sea breeze had cleansed her soul of unrest.

"Fire in the water. That's what I thought it was when I first went to sea as a boy." Ben joined her, his bare feet soundless on the deck. The specters of a past he could scarcely imagine, the wrongs she had made right with such dignity, had left him deeply moved. He put his arm around her shoulders, and she leaned against him with a sense of belonging she had never known.

"Does love mean gratitude?" she asked, just loud enough to be heard.

"It can do," he answered as quietly.

"Does it also mean thinking only of one person above all others . . . in the morning when you listen for the first birds, and at night when you close your eyes? And if this person fills the hollow of your heart so completely there is room for no other . . . is this also what is meant by love?"

"What I know of it," Ben whispered. "I believe it is."

She turned to face him, her arms reaching up to him, feeling his embrace tighten about her. "If you still wish me to be your *tai-tai*, Young Lord, I will do so with all my heart and the fullness of my soul—"

He stopped her words with a first kiss. "Yes! I would be a proud and happy man if you will become my *tai-tai*. . . . But only if you will call me Ben."

CHAPTER 14

The Yellow Dragon

Back at *Sky House,* Li fell into a sound sleep. When she awoke the following morning, it was later than usual. A square yellow envelope lay on the floor, slid beneath the door; it bore no name or address. There was something strangely sinister about its appearance that made her hesitate to touch it. She tried to think why it was there and who could have delivered it. It could only be from Ben, she decided with a rush of relief.

She picked up the envelope, to find a wax seal on the underside that bore characters she did not recognize. Breaking it, she withdrew a folded square of the same stiff yellow paper. The center was missing from the front fold; an irregular hole, neither cut nor burned, framed a single Chinese character of the same ancient script as the seal. There was nothing more.

❄

The envelope looked small and unimportant in Ben's large and capable hands. Li watched closely as he examined the slip of yellow paper with the hole in its center. She had taken it directly to the study, and was now seated before him. He stared at it in silence, holding it gingerly by its edges, sniffing it carefully, then placing it on the desk. His expression told her nothing. For a moment he did not speak, looking out to the garden.

The weather had changed overnight; the sky was overcast, and spurts of wind tugged at the trees. A log fire glowed in the iron grate. Li felt as though a great distance had opened up between them. She had a sudden need to go to him, to pledge her support, reassure him . . . but his face did not allow it.

She tried to keep the uncertainty from her voice. "It troubles you. Can you tell me what it means? If we are to become one, we must share all things."

The expression on Ben's face did not change as he turned in his chair to look at her. It was as if he had never smiled at her, she thought.

"You are right. There is something I have not spoken of that I should have." He leaned forward, his voice as guarded as the look in his eyes. "You have heard of the triad . . . the black society?"

She nodded. "I have heard of it."

"There is such a society known as the Yellow Dragon," Ben went on. "Its southern lodge is in Hong Kong, but its brothers are everywhere. It is their mark on the seal." His face was drained of color, his eyes flicking away to search the turbulent sky. But in that fraction of time, she had been startled by the mixture of fear and fury she had glimpsed in them.

He made a physical attempt to throw off the moment. "It is an empty warning, nothing more. From time to time I am reminded by such talismans. The Yellow Dragon overlord and I had dealings in the past, but reached an understanding." He picked up the paper, absently turning it over in his fingers. "This could have been sent by anyone wishing to cause trouble, perhaps someone from inside the house. I will speak to Ah-Ho. If it is someone among us, I will know and it will be dealt with." He had regained something of his composure, straightening in his chair.

"But the warning was sent to me, not to you. I must know its meaning. The hole is not cut by a blade or burned by a flame. How is it made and what does it say?"

He left his chair, led her to the leather couch closer to the fire, and sat beside her. Taking both her hands in his, he kissed them tenderly, holding them to his cheek before he spoke. "What I am about to tell you is known only to one other, Indie Da Silva. If you decide, when I have finished, that you wish to take no further part in my life, I will understand without question and make sure that you are properly provided for and protected."

"If there are things that I should know, then I shall listen and share with you whatever must be faced," Li answered.

For over an hour, Li-Xia listened to the story of the feud between Ben's father and Titan Ching, the Shanghai overlord who had declared a blood oath on the House of Devereaux thirty years ago. Ben had always known that the reason his father had fled Shanghai with him as an infant was not fear of the Boxer Uprising, but the oath that condemned his firstborn son to death.

"There are complex rules governing such vendettas, calling for ritual execution of a boy between the ages of three and ten by any of the Yellow Dragon soldiers throughout the Chinese underworld. If I survived my first ten years, the oath was supposed to be withdrawn and the vendetta at an end. There are exceptions, however; if a boy is thought to show the inclinations of a warrior with the heart for revenge, the Incense Master, the personal advisor to the dragon head, can extend the blood oath a further eight years.

"By the time I returned to Shanghai, both my father and Titan Ching were dead, so I went to the new dragon head, his son, J. T. Ching, and challenged the oath, offering to prove myself in a *ku-ma-tai*, or fight to the death." Ben paused, knowing how dramatic his words must seem.

"To me, a life under constant threat was not worth living. I had become something of a bare-knuckle fighter, a champion in the Western sense, and luck was with me. When I defeated their senior boxer, the holder of the golden sash, it was agreed that honor had been served and the blood oath between the House of Ching and the House of Devereaux was over."

He indicated the vaguely ominous paper. "I do not believe this talisman is from J. T. Ching. Traditional authenticity is important to the triad; they pride themselves on the refinement of their rituals. This is too crude." The steadiness of her gaze, so intensely absorbed she had barely blinked, made him look away.

His hesitation to continue was more ominous to her than his words. "Then from whom? I have a right to know what you suspect."

He took a deep breath, shaking his head as though to clear it of unwanted images. She waited until finally he went on. "My enemies are more than I can count . . . but I think there is only one mad enough to have a hand in such a thing as this. His name is Chiang-Wah, known on the waterfront as Chiang-Wah the Fierce."

Ben could not restrain the twitch of a smile as he described his enemy. "They say he can split the planks of a sampan or crack a stone water jar by charging it like a bull. Perhaps it is this part of his training that makes him such a dangerous maniac. He was the one I defeated in mortal combat."

Ben considered his words carefully before saying more. "Chiang-Wah tried to burn *Golden Sky* before she was launched. Luck was with me again: I caught him before it was too late . . . but the conflict left him seriously burned, hideously maimed by flaming tar.

"I have no doubt that he was acting for one of my many rivals. Double Dragon's Sky Class clippers were proving their greatest competition in the river trade. It was also well known that I am a founding director of the Anti-Opium Smuggling Board, which makes me a threat to those who grow fat on the profits of the opium trade. But J. T. Ching and I had reached a personal understanding that has held firm for over a decade."

"Then why is this thing sent to me?"

"Because Chiang swore revenge upon his honor as a temple boxer. He has lost all face among the tongs, not because of what he tried to do at the Double Dragon shipyards, but because he failed, which brought dishonor upon his brothers. He disappeared, and it was thought that he returned to China. There have been rumors of his death in combat a dozen times.

"This all happened ten years ago, and has not troubled me until this moment. Until now, the only thing Chiang could take from me that could not be replaced was my life, which he knew would not be easy. But now there is you."

He went on, with a careful attempt to make light of the situation that left Li increasingly uneasy. "It is a matter I can quite quickly attend to. Now that I think about it, I greatly doubt that Chiang is behind it, or even that he is alive. It is a foolish attempt to frighten you. I ask you to ignore it and leave things to me."

Li prompted again, almost gently. "The hole in the talisman. What does it mean?" When he hesitated once more, she spoke with quiet deliberation. "At Ten Willows, my family had a credo: 'Hide from nothing and run from no one.' I would not betray that credo now."

"Acid . . . ," he said finally in a voice she did not recognize. "The hole in the talisman is made by a single drip of sulphuric acid." Li left the couch and picked up the talisman in disbelief, sniffing it carefully. It smelled of vinegar and almonds. She tossed it back onto the desk.

"I am not afraid. All my life I have lived with the threat of violence and pain. Perhaps it has followed me here."

She spoke steadily and calmly. "I am aware of the black society; it is everywhere and always has been. No melon can be sold on a street corner, no lantern can be lit in a fan-tan parlor, no pipe can be smoked on a divan, and no building can rise without being touched by the hand of the tong. So please, do not be afraid to tell me." Unable to face her, Ben stood abruptly, his hands clasped behind his back. His words came finally in a voice she hardly recognized.

"The threat of disfigurement through acid is a favorite weapon of the street gang. No secret society worth its name would stoop to such cowardice—but to those who hide like rats it is as cheap and as easy as it is abominable." He turned to the fireplace, reaching for a fire iron, jabbing a smoldering log into a geyser of sparks until the flame caught. "Sometimes the acid is injected into the empty shell of a duck egg, the hole sealed . . . an acid bomb easily tossed into a victim's face." He stopped, his hands on the mantelpiece, staring silently into the gathering flames.

She lifted her voice, dismissing such thoughts with a brighter note. "The house you are building on Hong Kong Island, does it have high walls and a gate? Is it to be made as secure as Sky House?"

Ben nodded, amazed by the coolness of Li's reactions. "Yes," he assured her. "Its walls and entrance will always be well guarded." Ben tried to lift his tone to one of reassurance. "The area of Repulse Bay is home to the wealthy and covered by armed patrols. Every precaution has been taken to assure absolute security."

"And will there be a garden as beautiful as the one here?" she asked. "Will the air bring the scent of jasmine in the evening and gardenias at sunrise, and will the sound of birds greet each day?"

"Even more beautiful; Ah-Kin has designed the grounds after the celestial gardens of Ti-Yuan, in Peking. It is to be our place of peace and contentment; and if it must, it will also be our fortress."

Ben turned to look at her, a slow smile returning to his face. "Your gods and mine placed you safely in my arms . . . and only they can take you away from me."

"Then I am not afraid to live there with you. Already you have given me more of freedom and happiness than I could have hoped for. If our gods continue to smile on us, we will raise sons as brave and strong as their father."

Ben smiled his admiration. "And daughters as brave and beautiful as their mother."

Li smiled back, but knew the discussion must not end there. She picked up the evil yellow square again, inspecting it more closely.

"We must figure out how this was delivered to my room. May I be present when you speak to Ah-Ho? Perhaps we should send for her now."

Again his hesitation was scarcely hidden, but she persisted. "It is under my door that this foul thing has crept. If I am to ease my mind, I beg the right to judge for myself whatever she may say."

Moments later, Ah-Ho stood rigidly before Ben, having bowed to just the right degree. He was seated at his desk, while Li had returned to the couch. The head amah barely glanced at the card upon the desk, nor did her eyes meet his when she was asked how such a thing could be delivered within his house without her knowledge. Her replies to his questions were properly respectful but told him nothing: She could not tell how this could have happened and would make an immediate investigation.

"You have been the head of my household for many years and have always enjoyed my trust." Ben's voice was firm but fair, with no hint of accusation. "I am aware of your squeeze and consider this to be your rightful reward for a large house kept well and without trouble."

He held up the talisman for her to see. "This is bad joss for all in Sky House. If it came from outside, then security is to be blamed. If it came from inside, then you are responsible for harboring a criminal." He tossed the card back onto the desk and stood to face her.

"I expect you to discover who placed this under Miss Li's door. When she is threatened, so am I. You will tell those beneath you that unless this worthless idiot is made known to me, there will be no *lai-see* for the New Year. If this should happen again, I will hold you liable and inform the police. Whoever is responsible will be publicly shamed and locked away. Am I clearly understood?"

Ah-Ho bowed, departing swiftly and silently at Ben's wave of dismissal. Li wondered if he realized that the amah had not once acknowledged her presence.

CHAPTER 15

A Thrush in the Rigging

Li-Xia and Ben Devereaux were married aboard *Golden Sky* moored off Pagoda Anchorage in the Formosa Strait. The ceremony was performed by Captain Da Silva, master mariner, with the sky as their vaulted ceiling and a calm, jade-green sea as their cathedral floor.

Winifred Bramble served as matron of honor, and Wang was present to give the bride to the groom. The only other witness was the Fish, who was then sent ashore with the rest of the skeleton crew for a week's leave. Later that evening, Indie too slipped away in the shore boat, depositing Miss Bramble in the care of an excellent guesthouse in the city of Foochow, which she was eager to explore, while he took himself off to amusements of his own. Only Wang remained discreetly stationed forward to see to their every need, while they occupied the master's cabin and the main saloon, connected by a speaking tube to the galley and the pantry.

It had been the wedding of Li's choice. She could have been married in Hong Kong; Ben had offered to make it the wedding of the year. She could have chosen St. John's Cathedral, with a reception at Government House or the Royal Hong Kong Yacht Club or the grand ballroom of the stately Repulse Bay Hotel. Wearing a lustrous white dress, she could have been presented to the governor and leading dignitaries of the colony; there would have been flowers and jewels of great beauty and a banquet of court cuisine fit for an empress. But Li could not have borne the hidden poison that would make a mockery of their happiness and a fool of her husband.

212

She knew that, in order to please her, he would have used his money and power to force society to at least pretend to accept their marriage. This she could not allow. Neither did she feel comfortable in the company of strangers, even those who claimed to be his friends. The Chinese among his acquaintances would certainly despise her. To them she would never be his *tai-tai*, his legitimate wife; she would always be the scheming *cheep-see* who used her skills in the bedroom to turn his head. The Westerners, with their fashionable ladies, would scorn her and pity him, the lonely half breed who married a girl he found in a pig basket.

In her secret heart, Li vowed that she would do anything to please and to help her husband. He was a great man who believed in the code of loyalty, thinking that through generosity and reason he could command respect, but he did not know the minds of those around him. Because of this, she feared for him. She knew that Ah-Ho and the servants of Sky House were consumed with malice; it was as apparent to her as the large yellow diamond that now sparkled in a band of pure white gold on her finger. She could not tell him of the muttered threats and insults that lurked around every corner. When she was mistress of the Villa Formosa, perhaps she could deal with such matters in her own way.

Meanwhile, she could tell that he was secretly delighted by her request, confessing that a ceremony at sea, with only those who cared about them as witness, suited him admirably. In turn, he proposed they spend the next eight weeks sailing and exploring a dozen ports of call, a time of joy and freedom that he called a "honeymoon," the idea of which pleased her greatly.

The Fish had proudly helped her dress in a simple *sam-foo* of crocus-yellow silk trimmed with gold, crowning her hair with a spray of morning stars. She carried a bunch of gardenias surrounded by Cornish violets. Ben wore the full dress uniform of a master mariner, and Indie that of an officer in the Portuguese navy.

The early morning ceremony was celebrated under an azure sky. A land bird perched in the rigging—a thrush, Ben said, such as could be found in the hedgerows of Cornwall. An omen of great blessing, Wang assured them, as he set a plate of crumbs to encourage its warbling. Certain in his romantic heart that this Chinese girl was born to be his partner's wife, Indie Da Silva pronounced the vows with simplicity and grace. Miss Bramble, in a lavender dress, brought the freshness of an English churchyard to the foredeck of *Golden Sky* by showering them with confetti. Then the good lady produced her Kodak Brownie box camera and took many photographs.

For all of her joy at the occasion, Li found herself anticipating the night to come with a mixture of concern and curiosity: concern that she might not please him, curiosity to experience the thunder and rain she had heard so much about.

Certainly he showed no hurry in taking her to bed. After Indie and Miss Bramble had departed, they spent the first evening on deck, swept by balmy offshore airs, watching the twinkling of lamplight from the Tanka village. Seated beside her on the divan built into the stern, he put his arm around her, encircling her in contentment and comfort.

Her doubts were forgotten as they watched the rising of a spectacular moon. "Did you know," she said, "the Hakka fishermen believe that when the sky is filled with stars, it is Heng-O, the Moon Lady casting her net, and each star is a silver fish? The boat people say that such a starry night as this brings a good catch and assures good fortune."

"Then this should be a gift you will enjoy. It will bring the stars so close, you will want to reach out to touch them. It is the eye of every sea captain, and you are now among them."

He gave her a long, narrow case of polished wood. Inside, cushioned in green velvet, was a leather-bound telescope. He showed her how to focus the lens until the moon and stars fell into her lap.

Wang had brought them a light but delicious meal of shrimp and shellfish steamed in ginger. Now, the sound of his flute drifted aft with the haunting music of Old China.

Ben went below and after a while came back on deck dressed in a robe of light satin, its sheen iridescent as a black pearl. "Wang has prepared a warm bath for you, and you will find a robe like this on the bed."

The small bathroom adjoined the master's cabin, the round bath piled with glistening bubbles. She had taken a glass of sangria and found it calmed the fluttering in her stomach, as she lay in the scented bath almost too tired to stir. Toweled dry, the satin cool and loose against her glowing skin, she lay upon the bed uncertain what to expect, watching the brass-bound steps leading from the deck, waiting for him to appear.

Li remembered nothing more until she awakened beside him in the huge bed. It was morning, the circles of light from the portholes shifting to the lazy heave of a gentle ground swell. He was asleep, his breathing deep and even. Her satin robe was still fastened at the waist. She lay still, recalling the evening, the food and wine, the stars spilling into the sea, the music of Wang's flute, the scented luxury of the bath. . . .

As she rose on an elbow, afraid to wake him, she saw that he wore nothing over his bare arms and chest. The hair that curled thickly on his chest and forearms fascinated her, and she dared to reach out and touch it lightly, gliding the tips of her fingers up and down his arm and across the breadth of his chest. So this was the hair of a barbarian?

She looked closely at his sleeping face, so much younger without the bronze beard, the stubble glinting on his chin and cheeks. With thudding heart and her breath held, she slowly lifted the satin sheet to look beneath it, to find he wore loose-fitting trousers of black silk. She recalled nothing of pain or of pleasure, and felt only well rested, content to gaze at him undisturbed.

She knew that things to be expected had not yet taken place. She thought back over the Fish's advice. "It is a stabbing feeling that may make you want to cry, but you must sigh instead and tell him how strong he is. You may bleed from the wound, but it does not last. It is soon over and if you are lucky, he will go to sleep. Above all you must not cry, but smile and pretend to be floating on a golden cloud. If you want to please him, do not be hasty; have patience and pretend great admiration for his jade stem, treat it like a little god and wonder at its glory. Do this well and he will never seek another . . ."

They took breakfast on deck, where the thrush had appeared in the

215

rigging to sing its loudest. The smiling, silent, soft-footed Wang served her with the flavored rice porridge and steamed dumplings she was accustomed to, and Ben with scrambled eggs. They shared their breakfasts, and she enjoyed the orange jam called marmalade on toasted bread, while he was less than sure about the hundred-year egg that flavored the congee.

He had shaved on deck while she watched from her seat on the hatch, astonished by this ritual she had never seen among the *larn-jai*, who tweaked the hairs one by one from their jaw with dirty fingernails. When this was finished, he dived from the rail and into the blue, unruffled sea, swimming strongly underwater to appear ten yards from the boat's side, calling for her to join him.

Li had taught herself a few scrabbling strokes under the willows but never out of reach from hanging fronds, or too far away from the *mui-mui*, who could swim like frogs. To launch herself unaided into the immensity of the sea was hard for her to contemplate, conjuring up memories of the river's murky slopes and the swaying garden of weed awaiting her with open arms.

Wang suddenly appeared beside her, offering to let down a rope ladder. Ben called to her, "Don't be afraid . . . the water cannot hurt you now. It is deep and clean and gathers sunlight like a looking glass." Ben beckoned, splashing like a boy in a waterhole. "Come and see for yourself. I am here to catch you." His strong voice was filled with reassurance and eager for fun as he swam closer to the side with a dozen plunging strokes. He looked up as though sharing her hesitation, understanding its source—his hair slicked back, his wide brown shoulders gleaming. "I was with you then and I am with you now." He held out his hands to her. "Come, I will teach you to swim like a mermaid."

Li felt her dread of deep water drop away with the shedding of her robe, as she jumped without another thought—plummeting feetfirst into a world of shifting prisms. The light rippled over Ben's naked body as he moved cleanly through them to reach her—the last fragment of her doubt falling away as steady hands encircled her waist, his powerful legs driving them upward to burst through dazzling fragments of crystal-clear sunlight. Within an hour he had taught her to swim the length of *Golden Sky*, first with his support, then with him close beside her, then alone while he lunged ahead, urging her on.

⋇

Over the coming days, Li took to swimming in the ocean with joy and fascination, plunging from the rail and moving through the cool saltwater with growing style and confidence, ever farther away from the safety of the ship and its dangling rope ladder. Wang, a nonswimmer, stood by with a life buoy, certain that it was *gwai-lo* madness to fling oneself into unknown waters filled with sea dragons and monsters of the depths.

One morning, she discovered the delight of floating on her back, to see through bejeweled lashes the vast blue sky with drifts of cloud and gulls skimming down to snatch a glinting fish from the sea. With Ben never far away, she allowed herself to drift alone, afloat on her own confidence and ability to survive. As never before, the trust and gratitude she felt for him created a buoyancy of its own, holding her steady for the world of sea and sky to look upon and admire. This was his world, where nothing dismayed him and nothing stood in judgment. It was a pure uplift of spirit that Li decided must have a name . . . and that name must be love.

Back aboard, the deck warm under her bare feet, Li felt an exhilaration she could never have imagined, throwing her arms wide to the mild blue sky. As though he knew that she had found the true wonder of freedom, and perhaps the meaning of love, Ben closed his arms about her to swing her off her feet.

"Now that you can swim in the ocean like a fish, you must learn to sail upon it; then you will have truly mastered the sea." He held her, laughing aloud, as if he could not let her go. "A comprador and the *tai-tai* of a seafaring man who cannot sail is not worth her rice."

He carried her aft, to where a small boat was slung from the stern davits under a canvas cover. Setting her down and bowing like a magician about to perform his greatest trick, he told her to close her eyes while he stripped the cover away with a dramatic flourish.

217

"It is a wedding present," he said. "Designed and built especially for you." He stood beside her to admire the truly beautiful little craft. Its eight-foot hull was painted a deep blue with white trim and brass fittings; and on its bow and stern, painted in letters of gold, was the name LEE SHEEAH.

"It is your name as I would speak it in English. No one need know its meaning but you and I." His arm tightened about her. "I tell you, my dearest girl, there is no greater earthly joy than that to be found between sea and sky. I will teach you to find it and make it your friend."

After they had breakfasted and Ben had listened to the news on the radio, she climbed in and he and Wang launched the little dinghy; she was delighted to see its sails unfurling a bright canary yellow. He sailed the little boat across calm waters with a skill that left Li breathless with the sense of freedom—skating across patches of wind that teased the surface, bucking lively wavelets in plumes of sparkling spray, playing the wind like an instrument with every pure note of nature's music.

They swept inshore, following sandy shoals as clear as crystal and skirting the swirl of white-water reefs—so close the seabirds left their nests in noisy protest—going ashore on deserted beaches, to eat from the basket Wang had provided. They searched for oysters among the rocks, and haggled for fish straight from the Hokklo nets, combing beach after beach for shells and driftwood.

For three days this was their daily routine, and every hour taught her more beneath his steady hand—how to read the sea, the wind, and the clouds, and master their changing moods. By the end of the fourth day she could sail the dinghy without his help. Swimming and sailing, sharing every second of every moment had liberated Li's heart more and more, yet she knew that this paradise was incomplete.

One evening had followed another with dreamlike perfection—blazing sunsets melting into velvet nights, a delicious dinner served wordlessly and inconspicuously by the smiling, barefoot Wang. She was becoming accustomed to the cool and fruity Portuguese wine. They talked of many things, mostly in English to improve her knowledge of it, sometimes in Cantonese to increase his understanding of many things Chinese that still puzzled him greatly. He listened with rapt interest to her stories of the moon, showing no sign of doubt when she said her mother's spirit sometimes resided beside Heng-O. His eyes never left her face as she told him of the Fourth Moon—a day when the likeness of Buddha, no matter how large and splendid or small and humble, was washed with oils and spices, sandalwood and musk, to see that his image is forever renewed, his health and comfort revived.

She told him of the Sixth Moon, when Lung-Wang, the Dragon Prince, was taken outside and exposed to the sun to ensure abundant rain. As she spoke of such magical things, stars were tipped into the sea like silver lemonade.

On the fifth night, Wang brought a silver bucket, with a bottle packed in ice. Ben popped the cork and allowed its bubbles to subside, half filled two long, thin glasses, and handed one to her.

"To the launching of *Lee Sheeah*, your success upon the water, and the beginning of your new life as a sailor's *tai-tai*."

Her first taste of champagne, Li would later reflect, was like sipping sunshine from a rainbow. He laid his finger beneath her chin, tilting her head to look up and into his eyes. "We spoke of the thing called love, and agreed that it can mean so many different things to different people. . . . So we will speak only of pleasure and trust, which can grow into love. I have waited because love cannot be hurried, and trust is not easily found. Do you trust me, Li, and know that I would do nothing to hurt you?"

The words she sought were bigger than she could yet express in his language, and she knew of no such sentiments in Chinese, for they had never been told to her. She hoped he could see her answer in the light in her eyes and the smile that came from deep within her.

"You must tell me if you are unsure," Ben said. "I will not be angry. We are alone; we have no one to please but each other." She nodded her head. Never had she felt more ready to become a true wife to him.

When they had retired together to the master stateroom, dominated by the great bed where he had slept alone for so long, she was deliciously relaxed. For almost a week Ben had left her untouched in the way she had expected, except to take her hand in his. At first she had felt like a wild bird grounded in a storm, protected and gently tamed, until it found the will to fly.

Now, as he held her in his arms and kissed her softly, she felt her body tense with anticipation. It was the first time she had returned the pressure of his hand, running her fingertips over his scarred knuckles, stroking in silent fascination the hard muscles of his arms. His kisses, light upon her forehead and cheek, her closed eyelids, became more urgent. The warmth of his mouth pressed hard against hers, his chin slightly coarse as his mouth sought her ear, the hollow of her throat, the curve of her naked shoulder.

She felt herself yielding in his arms, breathing in the warmth of his freshly bathed skin, the tang of bay rum so much a part of him, ready to allow anything he wished but unable to let go completely her fear of displeasing him. His lips found her breasts—his mouth and tongue bringing her to a pitch that made her sigh in wonder. His hand left her breast to rest upon her belly, and she could not stop its trembling.

He did not stop, his rough palm grazing the point of her breast. An exquisite shock passed through her, releasing the tension of her body; her legs entwined with his, her arms locked around him, her face buried in the warmth of his neck. All that she felt for him was suddenly released, everything within her inviting his touch, urging him to be bolder, to hold nothing back. Her brave young spirit reached out to him in the pressure of her limbs, in the depths of a passion so long imagined, in the words she breathed so hotly in a voice impossibly thrilled by the wonder of him.

For several days, after greeting a rising sun from the bracing currents of the surrounding sea, they were content to rest in each other's arms upon silken sheets in the spacious cabin—ringing for Wang to provide the lightest of delicacies and fragrant teas. The steward's faultless sense of discretion was surpassed only by his unspoken delight at their happiness. The thrush, he said, had brought its mate, and now invited others.

220

The rigging at dawn was filled with song—an omen, he was certain, of endless joy, many fine sons, and a long and peaceful life.

⌖

On the morning *Golden Sky* was due to leave Pagoda Anchorage, Li left Ben sleeping, her bare feet soundless on the steps. The sun had barely left the sea, balanced still on a soft horizon, a gentle sun that touched their world like the wick of a lamp turned up by a slow hand. The early, peach-colored sky was softly mirrored in a tranquil surface that stretched away forever. It was the first time she had thought of swimming without him. There was nothing she could not do; she pushed away the fear of deep water as she climbed onto the rail, looking down at turquoise depths, lanced with glassy shards of sunlight. She shed the robe and broke the surface cleanly, the sharp grip of cold water embracing her naked limbs as she speared into bottomless blue, unaided and un-afraid.

CHAPTER 16

The Villa Formosa

The first weeks of Li's marriage passed swiftly and idyllically aboard *Golden Sky*, while the Villa Formosa was being completed. The Fish joined them on the ship, protective and attentive as ever. Miss Bramble decided to avail herself of the opportunity to return to England to take care of her affairs, before returning to China to continue her work with Li-Xia and perhaps, someday, with her children.

Ben had arranged her first-class passage on a steamer bound from Shanghai to Southampton. In Winifred's comfortable stateroom, there was a tearful farewell.

"I almost forgot to give you this." The tutor handed Li a framed photograph. "I'm afraid I am not much of a photographer. But this one is wonderful. I am quite proud of it."

To Li's delight, it was a picture of the wedding. On that day she had scarcely noted the small black box Miss Bramble was fiddling with or her requests for stillness as she clicked the shutter. Having no experience with cameras or photography, Li was astounded by the perfect image of herself and Ben beside the rigging, with the flat sea and rugged shoreline as a background. It was the first time she had seen herself as others saw her, and although she did not presume to assess her beauty, she saw at least that her face was happy, and that Ben smiled with her. She traced the filigree of the photograph's silver frame with her thumb. "I think it is wonderful. I shall keep it beside me for the rest of my life."

During the days Li-Xia continued her studies with Ben, becoming ever more confident in the ways of a comprador. But there were also days when they put aside their duties. *Golden Sky* visited the ancient city of Hangchow, as famous for its temples and magnificent gardens as for its exquisite porcelain, and they explored its antiquities together, making private purchases to adorn the rooms of the Villa Formosa.

Ben showed her the suite of rooms high above the Shanghai Bund, in the great House of Sassoon, which had once been occupied by his father. He was in the process of restoring them as offices for the company. He explained his intentions of soon discontinuing the shipbuilding operation in Macao, to concentrate on the Causeway Bay trading business in Hong Kong and Shanghai. It was in these two cities, the British colony of Hong Kong and the treaty port of Shanghai, he said, that future fortunes were to be made.

Golden Sky sailed down the Yangtze River—to the fortress capital of Chungking, through the majestic gorges of the Yangtze Valley. Ben launched the dinghy, and they sailed its narrow tributaries to hidden villages poised upon fertile slopes. He showed her Yung-Po, the city of ghosts, with its old pagodas rising like minarets from the mountain mists; and the great Voice of Buddha Temple with its monolithic bell, heard as far away as the great lake of Tung-Ting. They walked among tea gardens and citrus orchards, visiting the Ming city of Datang, where nothing had changed for a thousand years, and they bartered for priceless watercolor paintings, masterful calligraphy, and the finest wild ginseng.

At night, in the great four-poster bed, they discovered pathways to ecstasy beyond all expectation. By the time *Golden Sky* prepared for the return journey to Hong Kong, Li was astonished by the depth of their intimacy and the dizzying heights of her fulfillment. It made her wish that they could sail forever, with nothing but the sea and sky to follow them. But she knew that life could never be so perfect, and that she was now the mistress of a taipan's house.

The Devereaux estate on Repulse Bay covered a hundred acres of cliff-top land, half of which had been turned into traditional Chinese gardens and the other half planted with the trees and flowers of a grand English manor. In its center, the rambling Villa Formosa was a master-piece of East–West architecture, remarkable even by the standards of those few wealthy merchants and taipans who could afford to reside in the hills overlooking the famous bay.

Towering wrought-iron gates, set in high walls and guarded by two armed and magnificently uniformed Sikhs, opened to a wide carriage-way, leading to the villa's imposing entrance, the celestial dragon of China and the legendary dragon of St. George facing each other across wide marble steps.

During the eight years since Ben had first secured the land, only the finest craftsmen and artisans had worked on building the villa. The holds of Double Dragon vessels had carried back exquisite antiques, furniture, and works of art.

Ah-Kin had shared his magic between Sky House and the Villa Formosa, building the most beautiful tapestry of gardens in the colony. It was, he would say with contentment, also his last. Ben had given him a corner plot of land where he and his family could be buried.

Ben had not yet fetched Ah-Ho and the servants from Sky House, wishing to give Li-Xia time to adjust to the newness and opulence of her surroundings without interference. Li was grateful for this, shar-ing his pleasure in showing her around the large and airy rooms, their lofty ceilings illuminated by chandeliers of Belgian crystal, their walls hung with tapestries from Tibet and Mongolia and paintings by the greatest of Europe's marine artists. The dining room sat twenty around a mammoth table of bird's-eye maple with twenty green leather chairs. Paneled walls opened onto the breathtaking sweep of the ocean terrace.

Ben's study had been reconstructed identically to that of Sky House, the vast fir desk in position, every picture, every item and memento in its proper place. Even the magnificent fireplace had been rebuilt in smallest detail.

"This room and its contents are a monument to my life. Everything of importance to me begins and ends at this desk and among these things." He laughed lightheartedly, holding out his hand to her. "I sometimes thought I had the perfect life, believed my glass to be filled to the brim." He pressed his lips to the palm of her hand and drew her close. "I know now, it has always been half empty." As he led her onto the terrace, its luminous expanse skimmed by salt airs off the bay, Li had never seen him quite so carefree.

Li was already overwhelmed by the magnificence that surrounded her when Ben pretended a second's remorse. "There did not seem to be room enough for your ancestors," he said in a vaguely businesslike manner. "It seemed to me that only farmers and those of little means would share their earthly domain with those who dwell in the afterlife." His grin broke through. "So I have given them a house of their own, which I hope will have your approval and the blessings of the Fish." He led her across the terrace to a wall of aged stone, almost hidden by a living screen of sacred black bamboo. Through its arched entrance stood a Buddhist shrine, its doors covered in shining gold leaf. The light green tiles of its circular roof matched those of the villa itself, sweeping upward like waves on a windy sea, their crest surmounted by a large ball of crystal held in the claws of twin dragons.

"It was designed by a master of feng shui for the earth's energies to gather here." Ben spoke with deep respect. "He said it is a pinnacle of light in the spirit world, and awaits the occupation of your honorable ancestors."

It took Li a moment to absorb what stood before her. "I shall call it the Temple of Pai-Ling," she breathed. "May she find eternal rest here and watch over us forever."

He gave her a silver key, closing her fingers around it. "Hide the key where only you will find it. Not even I need know its secret place. When you have spoken with those you love, I have a guest I would like you to meet. He awaits us in the study."

225

The key turned easily in the lock, the door opening smoothly at her touch. A single shard of light lanced through the crystal dome to throw a pool of radiance upon the figure of Kuan-Yin, the goddess of mercy.

The guest Ben had mentioned came in the quiet, portly person of Sir George Chinnery, the celebrated painter of portraits. There were few dignitaries in the colony, from the governor and his wife to those wealthy enough to afford the artist's outrageous fees, who had not sat for Sir George. Almost every day for a month, Ben and Li posed for several hours on the ocean terrace, she in her favorite cheongsam of crocus yellow, and Ben in the uniform of a master mariner. The completed life-size portrait was magnificently framed and hung in the study behind Ben's desk.

※

For many weeks, Li and Ben were attended only by the Fish and Ah-Kin and his family; the gardener's son was hardworking and trustworthy and his wife a simple but excellent cook. A stone cottage in its own small compound had been built to house the Kin family, with quarters for other servants in a rear wing of the compound. The Fish had a separate room positioned close to the master suites in the eastern wing, adjacent to Li's private rooms and guest quarters that would soon, it was hoped, be occupied by Winifred Bramble.

The Fish pleaded with Li not to let Ah-Ho return. She had learned that Ah-Ho had been using the network of the *sau-hai* sisterhood to probe into Li's past, all too eager to blacken the name of the girl from Ten Willows and to revive the tale of the fox fairy.

"They say that only madness could have caused Di-Fo-Lo to drag you from the riverbed," the Fish whispered. "Fools among them claim that what he fetched from the mud was a monster veiled by comeliness, a ghost to whom he has sold his soul." She clasped her hands together in concern. "Ah-Geet, the driver, has said you went to him at his place of work and took his essence to feed your own. That he was defenseless against your fiendish charms."

The Fish begged Li to inform the master before it was too late. "You

226

are mistress of this great house. This commands absolute respect. Do not show fear or uncertainty in this, or you will be defeated."

The old woman raised a warning finger. "You are protected here; the master has made sure of it. But you will never be safe while she is under your roof. You must tell him that Ah-Ho and her people must be paid a big *lai-see* to be placed with another household. He has many friends who will welcome the head amah of Sky House."

Li reached for her hand reassuringly. "If Ah-Ho is sent away, she will know it is my doing, and hate me even more. There is no escaping the *sau-hai*." Not wanting to exacerbate the Fish's growing fears, Li had decided not to tell her about the warning of the yellow talisman.

"As you say, there is little she can do within these walls. It is better to face a viper in the open than in the bush. I will see that she is given all face, her money increased and her position unquestioned. In time, I will gain her trust and perhaps her respect. It is the best way; I am sure of it."

Seeing that the Fish was not convinced, Li felt less confident than she sounded. The old one did even not seem to hear her. "The immortal," she croaked huskily, "he too saw danger in the sticks. He spoke of betrayal, an assassin who shadows your door. You must tell the truth of Ah-Geet to Master Ben, or the driver will destroy you."

<hr>

Determined not to let the anxieties of the Fish or the musings of an ancient fortune-teller find a place in her mind, Li set about the business of becoming mistress of the Villa Formosa. Ah-Ho and the Sky House servants were brought from Macao to take up their duties, but the Fish alone cared for Li's suite of rooms, adjacent to Ben's in the east wing of the house.

Although instinct told Li that this great adventure could not last, she resolved, for Ben's sake and for her own, to savor every moment that she could. She did request that Ben find another position for the chauffeur, Ah-Geet, saying only that she did not feel comfortable in his presence. To her relief, Ben did not ask for details of Ah-Geet's behavior, paying him off handsomely and finding him a position with an associate.

It was easy to set aside her cares when she stepped onto the ocean terrace to look upon the sheltered bay, with its scattered islands and far horizons of the South China Sea, or walked the grounds that seemed to roam forever. Like the grounds of Sky House, the Ti-Yuan gardens were separated by a series of moon gates placed in such a way that each framed a different vision of perfection—so that one might move from one haven of serenity into another, interlaced by running streams and small cascades, with tinkling fountains feeding ornamental ponds. The trees were rare—shore juniper, dawn redwood, cherry plum, red silk cotton trees, and miniature mountain pine, along with shrubs that were known to attract a gallery of splendid butterflies. An orchard of persimmon, kumquat, and prince of orange served as a haven for a variety of birds, and the heavenly scent of gardenias lay over all. A five-bar gate separated the celestial gardens from a copse of silver birch and spruce trees more than ten feet tall. Daffodils and crocuses grew among them, their shaded spaces thick with bluebell and the elusive scent of Ben's favorite Cornish violets.

Leaving the gates in the early morning, the Sikhs saluting sharply, was a bracing adventure for Li. Ben had taught her to drive before they left Macao; now the rush of the sea wind snatched her breath away and tangled her hair, whipping tears of excitement from her eyes as she steered the Lagonda along the coast road to Causeway Bay. As in Macao, she had an office of her own above the godowns, where she spent hours immersed in the fascinating business of the comprador.

In the early evening, with a brassy sun hanging like a temple gong over the water, Li and Ben would visit the gardens together. They shared this domain with no one, the servants keeping to their own enclosed courtyards and the Fish content to wait until she was called upon. Ah-Kin respected their privacy but welcomed them to take tea in the stone cottage, and discuss flowers and their seasons.

Still, the peace and joy Li had found aboard *Golden Sky*, with nothing more than Wang's flute and the song of a thrush to intrude upon their happiness, was lost. She could not shake the feeling that at least some part of her, perhaps the part that she had left among the mulberry groves, did not belong among such abundance. Enchanting as these riches were, she would have gladly traded them to be alone with Ben and the sea and sky, where nothing was hidden and the changing winds swept all things clean.

⌖

The Fish was the first to know that Li was pregnant. Ben's joy on learning of her condition was so great that it buried her hidden anxieties. An annex of Li-Xia's bedroom was turned into a nursery room, only steps from her bed and left for her to decorate. She prepared for either a boy or girl, with a picture of a boy astride a lion on one wall, facing a girl clinging to the back of a crane in flight on the other.

Ben was more considerate than ever, agreeing reluctantly that she could continue to accompany him to the Causeway Bay office whenever she wished, provided she followed the advice of her doctor. Ben had asked if she preferred a Chinese physician or a Western one, and she had left this choice to him. He enlisted the services of Dr. Hamish McCallum, a dour Scotsman known as "Mac" to his many associates, who had been a close friend and fellow director of the yacht club for more years than they chose to count.

Seeing how much of Li's time was spent outside, Ben resolved to build a *ting*—a garden pavilion or teahouse where she could go to be alone, and even he must be invited as her guest. It would stand on the highest point of the estate, beneath an ancient Bodhi tree, as was chosen by Buddha himself. Li selected the name: the Pavilion of Joyful Moments.

One month later, the *ting* was finished. Great pillars of redwood were placed precisely at the four cardinal points of the compass, each denoting a season of the year. Between these four sentinels were screens of sandalwood carved in designs of peach and plum blossom, enclosing two sides for privacy and leaving open views of the bay and the sea beyond. The floor was of white marble; at its center, the open petals of a lotus flower were set in pale pink jadeite, inlaid with stamens of amber, coral, and blue lazurite. Creepers of wisteria climbed around its entrance, dwarf gardenias lining a pathway intricately patterned with river pebbles.

229

Inside, divans of rosewood scattered with embroidered cushions surrounded the marble table and four porcelain stools brought from the garden in Macao. Li entered its portals for the first time in the middle of the night. Unable to sleep, and careful not to disturb Ben, she found herself drawn to the pavilion at three in the morning. At its zenith, a full moon of honey yellow bathed the sea with its brightness, the stars competing for space and brilliance. She sat until dawn and called for Pai-Ling, but received no answer. Here, in the one place in all the world where she should have felt safe . . . she did not.

***

When Dr. McCallum advised her not to go to the office any longer, Li found peace in the company of Ah-Kin, in quiet contemplation of the restful arts of gardening, or in selecting a book from her own small study. In the Pavilion of Joyful Moments she read of brave deeds, of brave men and even braver women. But each new day began and ended with offerings of fresh fruit and flowers in the Temple of Pai-Ling, where she spoke to her family in private and prayed for advice.

Concerned that she might feel lonely, Ben presented her with a pair of chow puppies, balls of soft, flour-white fur with bright black eyes, round as shoe buttons, and with tongues the color of crushed blueberries. Li named them Yin and Yang, and they quickly became a much-loved part of her life, dashing among the trees after partridges, trotting on red leather leashes along the pathways, sleeping soundly on the cushions of the pavilion or upon her bed.

To the Fish the dogs were a mystery. Her peasant birth had taught her that such creatures were best served up with bamboo shoots and hoisin sauce, with perhaps a dash of chili. But the happiness they gave Li was enough for her to tolerate them.

The bond between Li and the Fish grew in heart and spirit as the old amah dedicated herself to her master's wife and the birth of their son. The Fish twisted a jade bracelet on her thin wrist as she spoke of her childhood as a *mooi-jai*, sold at the age of seven to a family of Parsees. Her cousin was given away to the Voice of Buddha monastery.

Now a seasoned midwife, she was taking every precaution dictated by the Chinese calendar and adding a few of her own to ensure Li's child would be a boy. Li hated to admit it, even to herself, but although there was no question that life would be easier in every way for a son and heir, her heart yearned secretly for a girl. How wonderful her daughter's childhood would be, how different from her own, how blessed by the support of a loving mother. But the Fish's energies were so renewed by the prospect of Ben's son, and her preparations to ensure the child's safe arrival so tireless, that Li willingly complied with even her strangest edicts.

Li had the traditional Chinese respect for her unborn child, believing that its "before sky," or prenatal existence, was as vital as its "after sky," or postnatal future. She accepted the old lady's folk wisdom: Li was permitted no soy sauce, dark soups, or gravies to ensure that the boy would not have a dark complexion, to be looked upon as a peasant who was destined to slave in the fields. She must eat only clear broths and whipped egg whites to guarantee that his skin was smooth and fair. She must not lift her arms above her head or do anything more strenuous than stroll gently through the gardens. Most of the time the Fish urged her to rest in the Pavilion of Joyful Moments and sip an endless procession of herbal brews to boost her energy and strength.

The Fish never even considered the possibility that the child might not be a boy. Every joss stick, every paper prayer, every burnt offering was aimed at the certainty of a son. Even the two scallions or hardboiled eggs left in the chamber pot for use in Li's bedroom were omens tried and true to encourage the forming of testicles. Obediently, Li drank a strong tea of peach leaves to prevent morning sickness. Petals of dried peach blossom were scattered over her bed and a slip of peach wood hidden under her pillow to guard against the hungry ghosts.

"I have been to the temple many times," the Fish told Li, "to ask all gods to give the master the son he longs for. These things I have bought from the priests."

The Fish unwrapped a piece of cloth to reveal a number of talismans: a tiny silver lock to fasten him to life; a silver chicken's foot, so that he might always scratch a good living; a scrap of fur attached to a thread of red silk, so that he would not be attacked by the dogs that scavenged the void between heaven and earth. Most potent of all was a bracelet fashioned from a copper coffin nail to give him courage in the face of ghosts and restless spirits.

Li decided not to share these preparations, made precious by the Fish's heartfelt beliefs, with Ben, who for all his patience and understanding could be forgiven for favoring the advice of Hamish McCallum, whose feet were firmly planted on the ground. There was one thing that the Fish proudly made and gave to her, however, that she showed him with pleasure—a baby sling used by Tanka mothers to carry their infants on their backs while going about their work at sea in all weathers. The sling was strongly made from thin, weatherproof oilskin, and beautifully patterned in tiny colored beads. "You see"—she smiled—"I will go to sea with you, our child upon my back."

Li continued to interest herself in Ben's business and the events affecting its success. Each day, in the Pavilion of Joyful Moments, she studied the English-language newspaper, the *South China Morning Post*, as well as the Chinese daily newspapers. She became increasingly aware of the world around her, at a time of great turmoil that was a warning of things to come.

The colony was crippled by a strike of engineers and seamen that had tied up normal shipping in one of the world's busiest harbors, but left the Double Dragon Company to continue trading under its Macao port of registry. The company had fifteen Double Dragon vessels in China waters, mainly in the silk and tea trades, with others on the Grand Canal carrying jade, porcelain, and artifacts from Peking to the Shanghai godowns on Soochow Creek.

She followed the politics of the civil war that was tearing China in two. It had swiftly spread to Hong Kong, where Communist and Nationalist Kuomintang agitators cooperated with the underground societies to boycott British goods. The Double Dragon took full advantage of the forced trade embargo, and continued to flourish because of it.

Ben encouraged her interest, amazed at how well she understood the conflict and its effect on international trade, without losing sight of the simple principles of haggling—the giving and taking of face, and the age-old principle of "squeeze," the basic belief that while one hand washes the other, all will be well with the world.

She was, Ben insisted, a force to be reckoned with. At this compliment, she scrunched up her nose and frowned quite ferociously, as she did whenever she was solving a new problem—an unconscious habit that he found enchanting. She finally replied, "It is what I think you call 'common sense,' and of course being allowed to read and understand the abacus." Her frown persisted. "It a great pity that Chinese females are not taught these basic necessities as soon as they can talk. We seem to deal with life's conundrums much better than Chinese men."

Ben had given her still another gift—simpler and yet more important than all the others: a diary, neither too large nor too small, its pages stiff and white and waiting to be filled with a lifetime of thoughts and memories. It had a clasp of solid gold and a scarlet leather cover with her name richly embossed in more gold.

Some of her notes were written in Chinese and others in English. She had developed her skills with the calligrapher's brush, and carefully decorated each entry with watercolors as exquisitely detailed as she could make them. In the peace and quiet of the pavilion, with Yin and Yang asleep on the cushions beside her, she chose each thought with the intensity of the confidences she had shared with Pai-Ling beneath the peppercorns and beside the river. Without knowing why, she was certain that these pages would be read by a daughter of her own some day.

On his routine visits, Dr. McCallum found her in excellent health and apparently fine spirits. "It appears to me that if she were any happier and healthier, my dear old chap, you would be hard-pressed to keep up with her." Mac was speaking to Ben on the balcony, where he shared a customary dram before departing. It was agreed that the child would be delivered in the mother's own bed—a great relief to Li.

The more she learned about the world outside the walls of the Villa

Formosa, the more it worried her. She was concerned not for herself, but for the pride and the dignity of the man she had learned to love more than she could find the words to say. She did not need to be told that since their marriage, those he had thought of as friends no longer sought him out. The men among them treated her politely with due respect to Ben, but could scarcely hide the awkwardness in their eyes. Some clearly admired her but for all the wrong reasons. The grand opening of the Villa Formosa, and the dinner parties he had thrown so lavishly to introduce her, had been uncomfortable failures. The Western wives or escorts among the guests could think of nothing to say to her, and the *tai-tais* of his Chinese associates conveyed all they had to say with coldly glittering eyes and either silent distaste or cunning hostility.

The doctor's wife, an overweight lady known for her generous charity work, clearly spoke for them all when she said, "Ben's such a fool. He could have taken her as a concubine, even his mistress, and got away with it. Why on earth did he have to marry the poor little creature? He will regret it, mark my words."

Li overheard these comments and many like them, either because tongues were loosened and voices raised by too many cocktails, or because they did not know or care that the "poor little creature" spoke English remarkably well, and understood all too clearly the meaning of words such as "hypocrisy," "intolerance," "snobbery," and "bigotry." Since her pregnancy, there had been no more dinners and they had not been invited to any social gatherings. Li was thankful for the respite, and Ben did not seem to miss the company. He kept his working days short, returning in time to watch the sun dip beneath the horizon over a drink in the pavilion and dinner in the grand dining room.

If he was aware of her position in the eyes of his friends and important acquaintances, he said nothing of it. Content as he appeared to be, Li recognized that this social isolation could become increasingly difficult for him. Determined to make herself a *tai-tai* to be proud of, she doubled her studies, learning to think and speak as others did. If she could not make them like her, she would make them respect her . . . but they would no longer ignore her.

234

The Pavilion of Joyful Moments had become Li's private sanctuary. Each morning at daybreak she awakened and bathed, a habit from her life beneath the willows that she had no wish to change. She walked with Yin and Yang through the Ti-Yuan gardens to help Ah-Kin feed the fish, where dragonflies were already busy among opening lotus. She passed through moon gates and over scarlet bridges, to the five-bar gate and into the spinney of silver birch, where she waded among patches of bluebells before the dew had fallen from the leaves.

She took her breakfast with Ben on his balcony, or with the Fish if he had left early. Then she rested and read, exchanging letters with Winifred Bramble, who always sent snapshots of her garden and the cottage in the village of Sparrows Green. Seeing Li's pleasure in receiving the photographs, Ben bought her the latest-model Kodak, and soon she was sending pictures of her own to England.

In the little Temple of Pai-Ling, she spoke with her mother and her ancestors, returning each evening to fill the cup with special wine and burn incense with her prayers. She was overjoyed when a package arrived, containing the ivory tablet bearing her mother's family name and a framed photograph in which she could see Pai-Ling's proud but lonely smile. With it were the tablets of her forefathers, faded and dimmed by generations of joss-stick smoke, that now graced the altar at the golden feet of Kuan-Yin, beside the box of shells and its precious contents.

Number-Three Wife had sent the package, along with a letter saying the Ling family had not been hard to find and were not sorry to part with these memories of one who had caused them so much trouble. The letter also bore welcome news from the House of the Kindly Moon. The little house by the river and its gardens continued to be blessed, and the *mung-cha-cha* prospered. Even Little Pebble, who had been fitted with spectacles that gave her back her sight, had grown strong again, singing her songs, filling her basket, and supervising the family's business ventures as briskly and fairly as ever before.

Turtle had needles of steel and spools of silk in every color, and taught local girls to stitch until they had mastered the art of embroidery and supplied several happiness silks every week. Mugwort and Monkey Nut oversaw a small team of older peasants producing several pairs of sandals a day. Garlic made many kinds of bamboo flutes, from small pocket-size ones for playing merry tunes to those as long as her arm that played mellow folk songs. Giant Yun tended his thriving market garden, and had also strung a row of dip nets along the banks, and set up racks for drying fish. He taught a group of eager children how to gather fruit and dig vegetables.

When the donkey cart was full, Ah-Su wrote, he loaded the sampan, and the *mung-cha-cha* puttered upriver to deliver their cocoons to Ten Willows and on to the markets where they had opened a stall to display their wares. Everyone was paid a fair wage and their rice bowls overflowed. *I have taught Little Pebble to use the abacus; no one thinks her a fool anymore and no one cheats her. And every evening when work is done and bellies are full, I teach them all to read and write and understand figures. No one speaks in whispers, and laughter is as constant as the turning of the waterwheel.*

Because of you, the letter concluded, *the House of the Kindly Moon is filled with happiness and harmony, and each day I have shared their joy.*

The package also included a precious bundle of papers tied with a plaited reed. The letters of the *mung-cha-cha* were addressed to Crabapple, difficult but joyful to read, the words scratched as though by hungry hens. Each was signed with the name of the sender and said that Li-Xia was in every prayer.

They also sent a gift that they promised would watch over her forever. It was a fat-bellied, gaudily painted effigy—a laughing Buddha, to be found for sale in every country market, said to keep away all forms of trouble, inviting only merriment and everlasting health.

❄

Li focused her energy on the child that grew stronger every day, allowing only thoughts of perfection and grand plans for the future to occupy her mind. She looked forward to taking her baby aboard *Golden Sky*, to visit her cherished family on the banks of the river. She thought that Number Three might make a splendid amah for her baby now that the *mung-cha-cha* were becoming self-sufficient. And Miss Bramble, of course, would return in time to be the child's governess. Her life seemed perfect, except for a problem as yet unsolved: Ah-Ho. Li chose to take her meals on her own balcony or with Ben on his. With much of her day spent in her sunlit study, in the pavilion, or in strolling the gardens with the chow puppies that grew more delightful with each day, there was little need to encounter the amah. But knowing that this total separation could not continue indefinitely cast a shadow not easily ignored. The closer Li came to her confinement, the more this preyed upon her mind. In avoiding any contact with her, the amah's malice seemed even more pronounced.

Life beneath the willows and the cane of Ah-Jeh had not completely left her. Even the thought of Ah-Ho, or the sound of her voice, recalled the threat of the *sau-hai*. It always began as a small thought, remote until the strident voice of Ah-Ho came clearly from the high-walled courtyard and through the French windows. When Li opened them, the Fish would scold her and close them again, insisting that no breeze must be allowed to chill her.

The Fish sensed Li's fear and did everything she could to drive it from her. She believed that evil spirits were responsible for all misfortune and had carefully hidden protective charms throughout the rooms. When the master found one in Li's pillowcase, a simple slip of peach wood, he was amused at first, and replaced it respectfully.

But a few days later, when he found a similar slip in his shoe and the bedsheets scattered with dried petals of peach blossom, he became impatient and threw the slip into the garden. He had no use for such superstitions, Ben said firmly. He tore down the paper image of Chang-Tien-Shih, the master of heaven, riding a tiger and brandishing his demon-vanquishing sword, and ripped it into pieces.

When he also threw out the scrap of raw ginger that hung beside it and smashed the protective mirror placed above the door to drive off the evil ones with their own hideous image, the Fish dropped to her knees to pray. In a loud voice the master threatened that unless this nonsense was stopped she would be sent back to the scullery. It was he and the Western doctor who would see to it that no harm came to Li and her unborn child, not joss sticks and paper gods.

After he had left, the Fish picked up the pieces of the Chang-Tien-Shih image and burned them with her prayers, begging the eight immortals to spare her mistress from the dangers to come. To both Li-Xia and the Fish, Ben's actions invited the punishment of angry gods. The women purified the room with incense and prayed for forgiveness. They must be doubly cautious now.

Ben soon felt guilty for his intolerance, and showed his regret by bringing home a red-painted shrine to replace the paper one he had destroyed. "Forgive me for the fool that I am. There must be no place for anger between us."

The Fish had never before seen the image of a god destroyed and flung to the ground to be stepped upon. In her mind it spelled disaster, and all her prayers and offerings could not appease Lei-Kung, the god of thunder.

CHAPTER 17

The Ginger Field

Chinese New Year was little more than a week away. As the household staff prepared for their annual holiday, Li decided that the time had come to approach Ah-Ho. She did not want to begin another year with such an impossible situation, which was not only causing the Fish to sometimes take to her bed, but fraying her own nerves. As there seemed no hope that the head amah would come bearing a peace offering, Li would go to her.

Steeling her resolve, Li entered the kitchen to ask for peppermint tea to ease her nausea. Ah-Ho appeared instantly at the sound of her voice. Grim-faced, she neither looked at nor spoke to Li, but addressed the most junior kitchen maid "Where is old dog bones, that her illustrious mistress should soil her silken slippers on the floor of this humble kitchen?" Suddenly, as surely as pointing a blade, she stared directly at Li. "Tell old dog bones to fetch her tea."

Li heard tittering from the scullery and saw the cook smirking over her stove. The *mooi-jai* stood frozen, looking from one to the other. Li stared back at Ah-Ho, wanting to challenge her but acutely conscious that to do so would end badly. "The old one is resting. Please have hot peppermint tea sent to my sitting room."

Ah-Ho let seconds tick by before answering, "I do not believe we have peppermint. I shall send the *mooi-jai* to buy some. It may take some time."

"Then I shall have raspberry," Li replied instantly.

Ah-Ho put a finger to her lips in an insolent manner. "Let me see." She shook her head in mock regret. "I am sorry. Raspberry is never used in this house."

"Very well, I shall have ginger tea. Surely you have ginger in your storeroom. If you do not, I shall have to ask your master to review the ordering of such simple supplies." Li turned and left the kitchen without another word.

When the tea arrived an hour later, it was stone cold. Li lifted the lid from the cup to find a large cockroach floating beneath it, heavy with the pod of its eggs. Li saw it as the test she had always known would come, a reminder of who she really was. Even Ben's care, love, and protection, even carrying his child, could not change the truth: She was a farm girl of no breeding who had been denounced as a fiend by her own people. In daring to rise above her station, she had committed the unforgivable sin of challenging and offending those around her.

The pregnant cockroach, dead in her cup, said all of this. As she stared at it, the fear and humiliation that had followed her for so long froze to an icy core that left no room for hesitation. She returned to the kitchen. Ah-Ho was seated at her special table with the cracked marble top, a jar of green tea halfway to her lips.

"There is a cockroach in my tea. I thought of keeping it until the master returns, so that he may see how filthy his new kitchen has become, and how careless those in his service are from their weeks of idleness in Macao. But I think the cockroach found its own way into my cup without your notice. Could this be so?"

Li's words met with a silence so hostile that only the hens clucking in the courtyard could be heard. All work in the kitchen had stopped dead. Ah-Ho's wide white face showed no response. The big kitchen clock ticked away the long seconds, as two red blotches slowly colored Ah-Ho's cheeks.

When there was no reply, Li spoke again, her words clear and unhurried. "You will stand on your feet when I am speaking to you." She waited for an agonizing moment as the spots of color spread, and slowly, her eyes murderous with hate, Ah-Ho rose to her feet. "I will have a tray of hot peppermint tea with two cups brought to my room by your own hands without delay. You may then take away the cockroach, and nothing more will be said about it. I do not wish to trouble the master with such small matters, but there are things that you and I must speak of before he returns."

Li turned abruptly and left the kitchen, feeling strangely calm. Within moments Ah-Ho appeared with the tray of tea. Setting it down, she straightened up to confront Li with naked hostility in her eyes.

Li was prepared. She indicated a chair, her tone deliberately calm and free of challenge. "Please, Ah-Ho, sit with me and take tea. It is time for us to talk, before—"

Ah-Ho cut Li short with a dismissive wave of her hand, closing her eyes and jutting out her chin as though the one before her were not there. "We have nothing to talk about that is not already known, but I come with a warning that you must heed."

"Then please summon the Fish. I would have a witness to what it is you have to say."

Ah-Ho laughed harshly. "You think she is not already listening, as she does to everything that is said among those of us who earn our silver?" Raising her voice, she called out mockingly, "Old dog bones, do you hear? I know you stand outside this door. Come and join us. We must not keep our mistress waiting."

Ah-Ho pretended to bow as the Fish entered the room to stand to one side of her mistress. Ah-Ho leveled an accusing finger at her. "You will say nothing in my presence; you will do as you always do and listen to things that are not your business."

She turned back to Li, but the Fish stepped between them, her small frame straight and held with dignity. "You may speak to me as a dog without a home, because I do not hear you. You grow fat on the work of others and take from them to fill your pockets, but you will not speak of threats to my mistress—"

Ah-Ho's fury hissed through clenched teeth. "I do not hear the whimpering of an old Tanka bitch—"

Li quickly took the Fish by the arm, urging her to say no more. Ah-Ho

241

turned back to Li. "Do you truly think that because you are taught to speak the words of the *gwai-lo* by the backside of a baboon, you are superior to those who have served Di-Fo-Lo for years?"

The head amah made a show of composing herself, drawing a deep, shuddering breath and folding her arms. "Do you think you are the only one who listens to the witness of others, as you rely on the word of old dog bones—that I do not know that you have humiliated Elder Sister Ah-Jeh, the benevolent superintendent of Ten Willows, and squeezed the merchant Ming-Chou? That you have used your powers and your treachery to enrich those unfit for his service?"

Ah-Ho stepped closer to Li, leaning forward with a snarl of satisfaction. "You would turn upon your own father, leaving him a broken man." She straightened, placing her closed fists upon her hips, her eyes withering in their scorn. "You have turned the head of a contented master and made him blind to your witchcraft. He showers you with gold and jewels, gives you privileges others have worked a lifetime for and will never enjoy, allows you to pick their brains, and gives you power over those who have been faithful to him."

Ah-Ho stopped abruptly, fired by her emotion yet drained by its force. "This grand palace with its emperor's garden, these treasures that surround you, even a shrine to spirits that have no place in it . . ." She spat at Li's feet. "I piss on your shrine; it is nothing but a place for dogs to shit."

Li too found anger burning within. "If you will not hear the truth from me, or give me the respect of your attention as I have given mine, you leave nothing now for me but to ask you to repeat these accusations to the master. We shall let him decide who speaks truth and who listens to the fairy tales of those who would bring trouble to his house."

Ah-Ho's solid body shook with a fury beyond her control. "Now you carry his demon brat, and once it is born he is lost to you forever. Bear him a child and both are doomed." Ah-Ho advanced until her face was close to Li's.

"Leave this place while you can. Return to the house of your father where you belong. Beg his forgiveness and use what you have learned to benefit those who deserve your help." She straightened up with a snort of mockery. "If he will not have you, then return to the gang of idiots you so enjoy and share your gains with them."

Ah-Ho released a long, whistling breath. "You will not do to me what you have done to others. If I leave this house because of you, then you may truly fear me. A curse will come upon you and your whelp that even your lunatic mother could not bring forth. If you truly honor Di-Fo-Lo, it is you who will leave this house, not I. Consider this . . . run to Di-Fo-Lo with your whining and you will pay more dearly than you can begin to imagine. As long as you know where I am, you need fear nothing but your own thoughts. If I am cast out, then you need fear me."

As Ah-Ho turned to leave, Li fought to control her answer. Every wound she thought had healed opened within her; every cut of the willow, every sneer and insult, every filthy hand that had mauled her returned with overwhelming force.

"You disappoint me, Ah-Ho. You are a fool as well as a liar. I have dealt with overfed fools before, so please, do not think I am afraid of you. I will give you one more day and one more night to think upon this. Until then I will say nothing to the master. Look upon me as what you see, not what you have heard. If you cannot see the truth, then you leave me with no choice."

⊁⊰

At dawn the following day, Li rose while Ben still slept, the marble terrace softly touched by the coming of first light. She descended the steps to the temple courtyard, the dank scent of marigolds strong among pockets of garden mist that stirred at her passing. Carrying a small gourd of rice wine, a bundle of incense, and fresh flowers, their petals barely opened, she reached in her pocket for the key to the shrine, her fingers suddenly lifeless as it dropped upon the flagstones. There was blood on the threshold; above it, hung from a string of copper bells, was the freshly severed foot of a fox.

Backing away from the gruesome talisman, Li hastened to awaken Ben, unable to put her horror into words. She led him hurriedly back to the temple, to find the fox paw gone and no trace of blood upon the flagstones.

243

He at first insisted on calling Dr. McCallum, begging her to lie down, clearly concerned for her state of mind. Only the speed with which she regained her composure convinced him that he needed to hear what she had to say.

"If you have ever truly placed your trust in me, I ask for that trust now. Never will it be so greatly tested." They were seated at the round table in the pavilion, where nothing could be overheard. "I have asked the Fish to attend this conversation because she has witnessed all that has been said and done and has advised me many times to inform you."

It took almost three hours to unspool the story of *sau-hai* and its influence on Ah-Ho, the veiled hostility toward Li and the open challenge so recently exchanged. She left much of this to the Fish, certain that Ben would know she was not easily deceived by her own people and had no other interest at heart than her loyalty to them both. As he listened to every threat and insult, the muscles in his jaw tightened and he was forced to look away, staring out to sea while absorbing every word.

※

Hamish McCallum took Li to his surgery in the Central District for tests and then to his club for lunch. When she returned, Ah-Ho and her closest followers were gone.

Ben said little of his parting with Ah-Ho, only that she had spoken strongly and scornfully in her defense. She knew nothing of a fox paw, she claimed, only that the *tai-tai* must be tired. Such visions were not unusual in one so young and heavy with her first child.

"That she lied to my face, thought me such a fool, disgusts me. I dismissed her without New Year considerations and no *lai-see*. She howled over that." He allowed himself a wry grin. "I am afraid my ancestors are in for a rough time.

"I will have the office find replacements; please do not let this disturb you any longer." He took her in his arms. "I am deeply sorry to have been so blind . . . you should have told me sooner."

Li's heart ached for his disillusionment. "Many times the Fish advised me to . . . it was something I thought that I could manage." She searched

244

his face for its carefree smile, dismayed to have brought this trouble to him. "Believe me, I did nothing to provoke such things and tried everything to prevent them." His smile broke through, as it always did.

"Must we hurry in finding others?" she went on. "We have no need of so many servants . . . the Fish is everything to me. The wife of Ah-Kin is an excellent cook and his son a good houseboy. There is only one other I would trust completely. Her name is Ah-Su, Number-Three Wife in my father's house but unhappy there. She showed me kindness when all about me was despair. If you agree, I will write to her, but there is no need to hurry. Let us receive the New Year together, in our own way. If you will allow me, I will choose the time and find those we may need in this new year."

He bent to kiss her forehead, his arms reluctant to let her go. "You are the head of this household, not I. It shall be exactly as you wish. Find what staff you will when you feel they are needed and not a moment before. Until then we shall manage splendidly." He released her, his hands still resting on her shoulders.

"Let us put this unhappiness behind us . . . promise me that now you will rest." His voice was comforting, but Li could see the shadow behind his smile.

For the next week, they settled into simple contentment, only to be startled by a telephone call from Indie Da Silva on New Year's Eve. Some *larn-jai* had started a fire in the Macao shipyard, and Indie had been wounded by a knife thrust. Though Indie made little of this, saying that the injury was slight and that the fire was under control, Ben knew that his partner would make little of it even if faced with certain death. Li urged him to go and see for himself. Leaving her in the care of the Fish, he took the pinnace and headed for Macao at full throttle.

It was a hot night and Li lay unable to sleep after the Fish had gone to bed, her fears renewed by the emergency. Although he had said nothing of it, she knew that Ben had been concerned enough to hire a security guard to patrol the walls at night with a pair of Alsatians. The windows of her bedroom were thrown wide to catch any breeze off the sea. The security grills were kept locked, so there had been no need to check them. A thin moon dusted the gardens but shed little light through shifting veils of gossamer cloud.

She neither saw nor heard the barefoot intruder rising like a shadow beside her bed. A hand clamped hard over her mouth, hard, cruel, and tasting of sour sweat. She could not see the face that loomed over her as the hand put its iron pressure on the points of her jaw, forcing it open and preventing any sound from escaping her.

"*Kung Hai Fat Choy*—Happy New Year, Beautiful One . . . or is it the little Crabapple? Which is it to be, the sweet or the sour?"

Instinctively, Li's hand slid beneath the pillow to raise the hair knife in a flashing arch. She felt the razor sharp tip of its curved blade slice into solid flesh before her wrist was clamped in a grip that robbed it of all strength.

"The claw of the bear . . . I was warned but did not listen," the voice mused with a growl, as her hand was twisted until the hook of steel dropped from her fingers. A thumb wiped away the blood welling from the gash in his flesh. As if in the blackest of dreams, she noticed the nail was thick as horn, rimmed with grime, grown long and uncut.

"But this is not the claw of a black bear . . . it is the scratch of an alley cat." With the ball of his thumb, he smeared blood deliberately, almost playfully, across her forehead and slowly down her cheek, his voice mocking her. "I am not afraid of fox fairies. I have danced with all demons and know their music well." The power shifted to a point in her throat that blocked the flow of her chi, draining all movement yet leaving her fully conscious. A filthy rag was crammed into her mouth, another tied tightly around her jaw to keep it in place. Her wrists and ankles were securely bound.

The bloodied thumb pressed down on a point in the center of her forehead, releasing the inner force that had paralyzed her. The figure straightened, turning its head to reflect the pallid light. Li was jolted into a gasp of horror by the face looking down at her—a hideous melding of scar tissue that stretched from one mangled eye to the grizzled nub of an ear, and down the shining cheekbone to contort half the mouth. Crude surgery had lifted the upper lip in a permanent leer to expose crooked teeth. The puckered skin extended down the thick neck, over one shoulder, and across the naked chest. Blood flowed freely from the flesh wound slashed across his chest. It was the face in the photograph she had seen behind Ben's desk.

She turned away from his burning eyes, but the powerful hand clamped her jaw, forcing her to look at him, his face now inches from hers. "I want you awake and to see me and hear me . . . I will look into the eyes of the famous Lee Sheeah, the Beautiful One, while she is still a pleasure to gaze upon."

He stroked her hair gently from her forehead, strand by strand. "You see me, little *tai-tai*? I am Chiang-Wah. This was once the proud face of a *dai-lo*, high in the ranks of the Yellow Dragon brotherhood, wearer of the golden sash."

The terrible wounds had caused a sibilance in his speech, saliva spitting with each tortured word forced from deep within. "The *gwai-lo* who spreads your legs did this to me. Now I have no face to show and all pride has fallen from me, but I have come as I said I would, to take that which is Di-Fo-Lo's greatest prize. I gave a warning, but he did not believe me. He should have sent you away with the *gwai-paw* teacher, far away where I could not find you."

Chiang-Wah bent ever closer, his mouth twisted in a sneer of triumph. The roughened touch of his thumb continued to trace the contours of her face . . . across the flickering lids of her eyes, the bridge of her nose, to her lips where they lingered, probing their softness. "The dragon head is weak. He does not honor the oath of his father. It is left to me, Chiang-Wah the Fierce, to fulfill the word of the Yellow Dragon and restore the honor of the brotherhood."

He leaned closer, his breath foul to her laboring nostrils. His thumb moved slowly down, over the contours of her throat to her breast, pinching the dormant nipple with such force her head was jerked from the pillow.

"That you chose a foreign devil before a man of your own people . . . You think yourself a *tai-tai* . . . but I see you as farmer's slut, not fit for feeding silkworms."

His hand dived suddenly to her crotch, his fingers ramming inside her with a force that made her body arch with pain. "Well, I will show you how one of your countrymen takes his pleasure, and you may be the judge." Li-Xia fought for oblivion as Chiang-Wah violated her. All sense of time, of place, of feeling seemed transferred to another body than her own. Only when he gave a strangled cry and was quiet for a moment did she return to herself and find him looming over her. She was beyond all fear but for her unborn child.

"Tell Di-Fo-Lo that I have found more pleasure in Red Lantern Street for less than the silver dollar he paid you." He sensed her terror and spoke almost soothingly. "I have been careful not to dig too deep. We must not harm the child: I want it safely born. To take a life before it is begun would be of no value."

Chiang-Wah produced a small porcelain snuff bottle, the kind easily found in the market. It was pretty, delicately painted with tiny chrysan-themums. "Now I will take from him that which he has taken from me . . . my face. I will spare you an eye as I have been spared, so that you may see each day the face that Di-Fo-Lo has given you. So that you can see your child, and the look in its eyes each time it sees its pretty mother. I will take from him your beauty, so that he may live with you in endless agony and ugliness, as I have lived in mine. All his money and his power cannot change things. Let us see if he will bed you then. You will suffer until the day you die, and he will live with the joss that he did this to you."

He held the tiny bottle over her face, tilting it gradually. "If your child is born, I will not harm it, boy or girl . . . until it is three years old and is received into the bosom of its ancestors. Then I will find it, and kill it as I would kill a rat. The blood oath of the Yellow Dragon as sworn in the name of Kuan-Kung by the true dragon head, Titan Ching, will be ended.

"He knows we have unfinished business, the baby-eater and I. Death would be a pleasure to him after he sees what I have done; he will pray for its relief."

※

The Fish would never know what drew her to Li's room that evening. She had felt more than heard sounds that were not part of the night. She always slept lightly; even the swoop of an owl could wake her. She tapped gently on the door, her ear pressed to it. "Are you all right, *siu-jeh*?" she whispered, then heard a sound she could not recognize—faint as the titter of mice. When she opened the door, it struck her like a blow, a smell so strange she could not be sure of it—the elusive stench of rancid vinegar. . . .

Through the heavy curtains of her agony, Li knew that the Fish was at her side; she heard the old woman's stifled cries as the rag was taken from her face and pulled from her mouth. Li turned her face away into shadow as she spoke through the mists of her unspeakable torment. "Do not switch on the light." Her words were barely audible. "You must be strong for me. My child is coming. Do whatever you must to save it; I am beyond suffering."

The Fish was quick to fetch hot water and towels, the mixture of herbs that dulled her senses. Li used the last of her strength to bring about the birth of her child. When the infant was delivered and wrapped, Li reached blindly for the Fish's hand and held it tightly. She did not ask to see her baby, only to know whether it was alive and whole, and if it was a girl.

"It is a beautiful girl, mistress. She is small but perfect in every way. She already has some hair the color of her father's and eyes that shine like pearls." Li's grip tightened, words forced from the failing reserves of her life-force. "You must take her away, far from here. Di-Fo-Lo cannot save her from those sworn to destroy him, and he will die trying. He does not understand the danger I have brought into his life. Take her to your *huang-hah*, to the lake where the gods once delivered you. Find your cousin the barefoot doctor. Take her to his house where she can grow strong in peace."

249

Li was silent for a moment, seized and held on the rack of pain. When she spoke again, her voice was no more than a rattling breath. The Fish bent closer to hear her.

"She must learn to read and write; this is more precious than gold. Promise me this."

The Fish struggled to keep her words steady and sure, but all the strength within her could not hold back her tears.

"I promise this child will learn the ways of a scholar. She will be loved and respected, and I will move heaven and earth to keep her safe."

Li squeezed her hand. "Do not cry for me, dear Auntie. This was written on the talisman of the rainbird; you were told of it but dared not say. I think I always knew that my place on the mountaintop would be brief."

She raised a hand, drawing on the last of her strength. "On the dresser, in the box of shells, there are precious things. Most precious are my diary and the journal of Pai-Ling. In their pages are the thousand pieces of gold as I have found them. It will tell her of my journey and perhaps guide her steps." With a trembling hand, Li removed the golden guinea from her neck.

"Give her this, the first of her thousand pieces. Tell her I shall be with her always; she only has to close her eyes and call my name. There are jewels and other things that are precious to me. Take them and give them to her when she has lived for ten years, and when she is ready, take her to her father's house."

The sedative had dulled the suffering that engulfed her so completely, yet she found a window in her mind still open, a light that led her through all pain toward an August moon. "You must go now, in the sampan at the jetty. Take her before Master Ben returns."

Li entered a domain without pain or fear or sorrow, in which she heard the muffled cry of her child and, moments later, the closing of the door. Gathering the last of her strength, she rose from the bed as in the most mysterious of dreams. A bloodred curtain slowly ascended; in a trance she passed out onto the marble terrace, cool beneath her feet. The moon blazed like a beacon, suddenly draped in a fleece of cloud fringed with silver. She moved toward the balustrade, aware that even at night the scent of chrysanthemums and marigolds lay heavy on the air. The sea winds struck like fire upon the mask that was her face.

A voice broke through her reverie, real and vicious as a lash. "The sea is cold, little Miss Li; it conquers any fire. It opens its arms to welcome you." Beside her, no more than a step away, the dark shape of Ah-Ho loomed against the sky.

The patch of cloud thinned enough to show the glitter of jewels as she slowly trickled a string of sapphires from one hand to the other. "I did not think old dog bones deserved such a rich reward for her treachery." She held up the necklace in front of Li, dangling it for a moment like a plaything. Even through her haze Li could glimpse the unmistakable flash of canary yellow. Then the thin cloud cover drifted like a sail across the beaming face of the moon, and again Ah-Ho was cloaked in shadow.

"Do not worry, dog bones has not been harmed, nor your demon offspring. To take their unworthy lives would see revenge too quickly ended. The fool Di-Fo-Lo you have so enchanted will be allowed to grieve and continue with his tortured life. The box made of shells was too heavy for such hands as hers, so I have lightened her load and taken these . . . to remind me of the slut that was dragged from the riverbed and thought herself a scholar."

From the darkness, Ah-Ho's breath was hot upon Li's face. "Because of you, the New Year will not be a fortunate one for me," she crooned. "Because of you, the great Di-Fo-Lo will never know the joss of his brat; he will spend his life in search of it or the place that hides its bones. Peace will never again walk beside him, nor happiness reside in his broken heart. You alone have brought this curse upon him. Now the choice is yours: Wait for him and let him care for what is left of you for the rest of his miserable life"—the amah chuckled with the mirth of darkest evil—"or give him freedom at least from that."

The layers of cloud drifted apart like silk banners. Beneath them she saw the tall masts and gleaming hull of the *Golden Sky* against the bluest of blue skies. She saw Ben tossing back his hair and blowing like a porpoise as she climbed upon the rail poised above a crystal sea of turquoise. The sound of Wang's flute mingled with the chortling of a thrush, as Ben's voice came to her on an offshore breeze: "Don't be afraid, Lee Sheeah; I am here to catch you. I will teach you to swim like a mermaid."

The cloud passed, the terrace illumined by a flood of brightness. Ah-Ho was gone, or perhaps had never been there. Ben was calling, beckoning her. "Dive, Lee Sheeah—you can do it. I am here beside you."

The waters claimed her and took away her pain. She plunged through dancing halls of moonlight, all movement stopped and all sound forever ceased, as she drifted down on a chain of silver bubbles. Li-Xia was in the ginger field, where butterflies lifted like petals at her passing, wading through white blossoms, to where Pai-Ling waited with wide-open arms to swing her high against a sky of duck-egg blue.

※

Indie Da Silva was half conscious when Ben arrived at the Double Dragon shipyard. The knife wound in his side was not serious, but had bled profusely. A single blow from behind had robbed his limbs of all movement. "The fist that did this knew exactly what it was doing and why." Indie tried to grin, fumbling for a cheroot. "It was the hand of a Boxer." He choked on the rum Ben held to his lips, grimacing through his pain as he lit the chewed nub of a Burmese cheroot, sucking smoke deep into his lungs.

"Someone paid the gang to set this fire. They knifed the gatekeeper and took me by surprise." He winced with pain. "I saw the face of that cocky little bastard Ah-Geet among them. I'm sorry, Ben; I should have dealt with this alone."

Ben drove him to the hospital at a speed that raised curses and horn blasts from those he passed. Sudden fear had sprung within him like a lighted flame.

The fire had been started with a drum of spilled tar, the same thing that had all but burned Chiang-Wah alive. Was it coincidence, or did it have the touch of ritual about it?

The sabotage attempt had been easily contained, with little serious damage and nothing stolen. This was not like them. . . .

252

Kidnap—the word suddenly screamed aloud in his mind. Could this have been a distraction to get him away from Repulse Bay? The word rang in his ears like the echo of a triad gong struck by the Incense Master to seal a prophecy. *Kidnap. Kidnap. Kidnap* . . .

He sped back to the yard to call the Villa Formosa, letting the telephone ring as his thoughts kept racing. It could take two hours to return to Hong Kong. The pinnace was capable of eighteen knots with throttles open. His mind searched frantically for a faster way. There was none.

He leaped aboard and took the wheel as the coxwain cast off the lines. He opened up both engines and kept the throttles wide, the pinnace's bows surging forward with a throaty roar. When the engineer poked his head from the hatchway to warn him of the pressure such high speed was creating, Ben waved him back.

He could not shake his sense of dread. He prayed it would turn out to be a simple robbery; they could empty the house for all he cared, burn it to the ground, so long as Li was safe. *Ransom*: the word was a comfort. He would pay anything to get her back; he'd leave Hong Kong and sail with her around the world on *Golden Sky*.

He had turned on the powerful searchlights that warned other craft to give way. Through the spray-flecked windows of the wheelhouse, the face of Li-Xia seemed to rise from the sheets of spume flung across the bows.

The sun had hauled well clear of the sea when Ben leaped the fast-closing gap from the deck to the jetty and bounded up the steep stone steps that led to the gardens of the Villa Formosa. He prayed he would find her in the Pavilion of Joyful Moments, seated with the Fish over a pot of mimosa tea, with Yin and Yang disturbed from their cushions to growl at the disturbance. His stomach lurched as he found the pavilion empty, its table bare.

It was early, he told himself, vaulting the balustrade, bursting through the French doors of her bedroom; she was sleeping late. It was empty, the bedclothes rumpled. Yin and Yang were nowhere to be seen, the snuffling and yapping that greeted every visitor eerily absent. He rushed from room to room, bellowing for the Fish, his heart thumping as he found her room deserted. The study too was empty, deathly silent but for the steady ticking of the clock. It chimed the hour of six, bringing a fresh wave of horror; the balcony doors were ajar, the security system linked to the gatehouse switched off.

She must be walking. The gardens . . . of course, this was the time for her stroll. He would find her feeding the fantailed fish from the middle of a hidden bridge, the dogs chasing dragonflies. Ah-Kin came running from his cottage as Ben called Li's name, striding from one solitary haven to another to find only fragrant emptiness and the careless chatter of moving waters. Her name echoed in every hidden corner of the grounds, over the five-bar gate and through the birch wood.

"Missy Li has not been to the gardens this morning. I fed the fish without her."

Ah-Kin was frightened by the wild-eyed look on the master's face, the frantic urgency in his voice. The gardener's wife and son appeared at the compound gate, confused by such uncommon disruption of peace and quietude. Ah-Kin assured him they had neither seen nor heard anything to concern them. The Sikh guards heard his calling and arrived quickly with their excited dogs. There was no disturbance during the night, the gatekeeper assured Ben; the walls were patrolled without incident; the dogs had been quiet. Ben dismissed them with orders to search the grounds, and told Ah-Kin and his son to cover every inch of the estate.

A fresh hope jolted his racing mind; he almost cursed himself for allowing his imagination to play such tricks. Of course, of course—the Temple of Pai-Ling. This was the time of prayer; she had walked the gardens and gathered the night's crop of fallen frangipani for the altar. Crossing the ocean terrace, he wanted to call her name, but checked his haste for an instant when he saw the temple doors ajar.

There was something about the little shrine that had always been off-limits to him. Although she had invited him inside to witness the lighting of joss sticks, the burning of paper prayers and offerings at the feet of Kuan-Yin, he had felt himself to be an intruder. He realized there was not enough Chinese in him to share such a sacred place with her.

He approached silently, afraid to speak her name, merely praying to see her kneeling before the goddess, sticks of smoking incense in her hand. He would never leave her side again. A shaft of daylight lay across the prayer mat, bathing the goddess in its beam.

He softly called Li's name, but met only silence. In the strengthening light, Kuan-Yin was ablaze with glory, the bloodied snow-white fur of Yin and Yang hanging before her on their bright red leads. On the floor, in trampled, scattered shards, were the faded faces and forgotten names that Li had treasured, and the broken pieces of a laughing Buddha. The unmistakable stench of human excrement and urine left no air to breathe.

The body of Li-Xia Devereaux was pulled from the waters by Hokklo fishermen returning home at daybreak with their catch. They laid her on the jetty and fled when they saw Di-Fo-Lo taking the narrow steps of rock as though he could fly. They looked at each other in fear; they had no wish to witness the cries of a mad *gwai-lo* who perhaps would blame them for the horror they had dredged from their fishing spot close to the rocks.

⸙

Ben had refused help in carrying Li's body to her room, ordering Ah-Kin and the guards to keep to their places and let no one into the grounds. When he had laid her gently on the rumpled bed, her body still well covered, Ben felt reason slipping from his grasp. The fire in his gut turned to the solid stone of despair, dragging him into a pit of howling darkness that had no bottom and no light. He lurched, on legs that threatened to fail him, into the study to find brandy. In the center of the fir desk, a page of paper was neatly laid before his chair. With a sinking heart, he recognized her writing, though the scrawl was barely readable.

> *Forgive me for what I have to do, but it is written in the moon. Our daughter is in the hands of one we trust before all others. Do not search for her; she has gone to a place where she will grow in peace beyond the evil that stalks our happiness.*
>
> *You could have done nothing to prevent this; it was ordained by powers far greater than ours. When she is grown and the danger passed, she will find you if this is also written.*

255

Thank you, my young lord, for teaching me the meaning of love. To know
it for a golden moment is enough, but you gave me riches beyond my dreams.

—*Lee Sheeah*

Ah-Kin looked anxiously at his wife and son as a bellow of despair came from the house: *"My child. Where is my child?"* The agony of Di-Fo-Lo's cry rent the serenity of the Ti-Yuan gardens, echoing through the moon gates and the empty perfumed screens of the pavilion. It carried out to sea, causing fishermen to shake their heads. Raising a hand to keep his family seated, Ah-Kin quickly stood and left the table.

He returned moments later, his face a study in fear and anguish. "Di-Fo-Lo has been to the Temple of Pai-Ling," he said. "He has torn down the shrine with his bare hands. He has taken the goddess of mercy and flung her far into the sea."

※

Indie Da Silva left the hospital in Macao to be at his partner's side. The only other witnesses were Hamish McCallum and Ben's friend and lawyer, Alistair Pidcock. The tomb was located on the edge of the birch wood, facing the sea and the sunrise; it rose in a gently rounded mound, thickly planted with wild violets and deep-blue periwinkles, to become part of the earth around it. Great bunches of yellow iris surrounded the low arched entrance, sealed with rose-colored quartz. Carved on its face, first in Chinese characters and then in English, were these words:

HERE LIES A SCHOLAR.

HER NAME IS LI-XIA DEVEREAUX.

1906–1924

She ran from no one and hid from nothing.

Ben had insisted on personally dressing the body in the rich red silk and extravagantly embroidered finery of a bride of noble birth. He had

256

forced himself to look upon her mutilated face, then covered it with the bridal veil of spiderweb silk, crowning her hair with a single gardenia. A large and perfect pearl was placed on her tongue to show the gods that she came from a well-respected, wealthy family; a cicada carved in milky jade lay in her closed hand, fastened to the fingers by a ribbon so that it could not be lost or stolen. It was, she had once told him, the most powerful talisman against evil spirits in the afterlife.

In solitude, he had surrounded her with books, carefully choosing each one. By her side he placed a golden statue of Kuei-Hsing, the god of literature. To these he added the photographs retrieved from the temple floor, and the laughing Buddha that Ah-Kin's wife had carefully restored. The maker of heavenly possessions had worked for a day and a night constructing a house like the one by the river in red and gold paper. In it Ben had placed the letters from Ah-Su and the *mung-cha-cha*. In a replica of the Lagonda in shining green paper, he had placed two toy dogs of fluffy white, with collars and leashes of red leather; then added a great deal of paper money. The smoke from these hung low across the sea, as though reluctant to break adrift from the Villa Formosa.

Ben Devereaux stayed alone in the Pavilion of Joyful Moments for a day and a night. Observed but undisturbed by Ah-Kin, he neither ate the food brought to him nor drank the tea. He made no movement and sat as silently as stone. On the third day, Ah-Kin awoke to find him gone.

PART TWO

RED LOTUS

红莲花

CHAPTER 18

Little Star

On an oven-hot November afternoon, the daughter of Ben and Li Devereaux sailed into the vast lake of Tung-Ting in the province of Hunan. Under leaden skies, a great marsh threaded with channels and hidden backwaters stretched along its endless foreshores. At the mouth of the lake, where the Yangtze joined the Yuan River, many of the passengers disembarked—laden with gifts, strings of live crabs, and squealing piglets—to be met with much backslapping, heaving of luggage, yapping dogs, and squalling children.

Those who needed to cross the lake transferred for the last time to a flat-bottomed sampan, stacked high with sheaves of tall reeds. Among them, with the baby quiet in her beaded sling after being fed for a copper coin from the full breast of a Tanka girl, sat the Fish, weary but certain that her gods had not deserted her.

No human hand could steer safe passage through the raging torrents of the Yangtze; through Wind Box Gorge, dodging river dragons through the canyons of Witch's Mountain and Golden Helmet Pass. When they reached the white-water rapids at the mouth of the Yuan, where the aged planks of the sampan threatened to fall apart like a chicken crate, the Fish saw the spirit of Li-Tieh-Kuai, the crippled beggar, who always appeared to those in distress upon the water. She was certain that his iron staff and gourd of comfort would watch over her and the child until they were safe beneath the roof of her cousin, To-Tze.

On the far side of the lake, travelers dropped off along the way until only the old woman and the infant remained. The boatman seemed reluctant to enter the shallows of the marsh, demanding the two remaining coins threaded around the Fish's neck to complete the voyage. Switching the *yulow*, the long sculling oar, for the long punting pole, he nosed the flat boat into a narrow channel banked by a dense jungle of head-high reeds.

"There will be no difficulty in finding the one you are looking for," he said in a voice hushed with caution. "Everyone knows of Old To, the barefoot doctor. The reed-cutters say he talks with ghosts and dances with demons." He allowed the pole to slide effortlessly through his callused hands with a faint but rhythmic sound.

"Is the infant sick? Are you unwell? Old To is said to have saved many children brought to him, and made old people young again . . . even to have given life to the dying." The boatman looked about him, lowering his words to a whisper. "He is one of great mystery and strange powers," he muttered uneasily. "One who is Chinese but has eyes that are blue as the lake on a clear day."

To the Fish, huddled in the stern too tired to speak, he seemed anxious to be rid of her. With his wide brown feet firmly planted on the bleached wood of the stern, the long pole slipping skillfully and more swiftly through his hands, the boatman asked no more about the old woman or the newborn child mewing from the Tanka baby sling upon her back. The infant was white as a maggot, he thought, with eyes as round and pale as pebbles in a pond. No longer comforted by the sound of his own voice, he fell quiet as they approached the shore.

Only the swish of the ferry pole and the croak of a disturbed frog broke the silence as the plank boat glided smoothly through dark green foliage and wandering roots of mangrove trees, where heron and spoonbill waded in the shallows. Goats grazed the gently sloping grasslands where clusters of bamboo climbed the foothills. Above these forests of tung and teak trees, ancient spires of rock rose from the mists like forgotten pagodas.

Ducks flurried from the water as the boatman put them ashore at a roughly cobbled jetty. Naked children squatted patiently over bamboo fishing rods while others searched for oysters among the mangrove roots.

"Follow the goat track and you will find the hut of Old To," the boatman said, glad to be rid of so strange a cargo. Then, emboldened by his departure, he raised his voice.

"This is a place of wizardry and restless spirits," he called across the water when safely out of reach. "And I have carried a witch bearing the spawn of alchemy." The muddy children dropped their fishing lines, the coarse hoot of the boatman's laughter chasing them like rabbits startled by a fox.

The narrow track wound slowly upward through thickets of mimosa heavy with bees. A chorus of cicadas rose in the heat from groves of motionless bamboo, where bluecaps twittered a welcome. The sun was dipping into distant mountains as the Fish reached the hut set in the shade of fruit trees. Chickens pecked undisturbed among the neat furrows of a well-kept vegetable garden, and ducks cleaned their feathers beside a small pond fed by a spring. The energy that had brought her and her precious bundle safely along the China coast and through the gorges of the Yangtze Valley was slipping away, but her destination stood before her like the answer to a prayer.

The hut faced the lake, its doors wide open and rush mats rolled up to catch the last glow of sunset. Bronze light fell upon the figure of a man bent over a large table set out on the rustic veranda, a long-handled brush poised to dip and sweep in the broad and flowing strokes of a master calligrapher. The Fish hesitated, unsure if this could truly be her cousin—the brave, half-naked boy who had pulled her from the churning waters of Tung-Ting so long ago the memory was lost in dreams. He was old enough, but even from the distance of a dozen steps and in half shadow, he was clearly no ordinary man.

He was taller than most, upright as a youth, his movements fluid; he seemed surrounded by a mellow light as golden as the dying sun. He wore a simple ash-gray robe, bound at the waist with the faded saffron sash of a Taoist monk. His white hair was roughly plaited and loosely held with a thong, his long white beard fine as wild cotton and his face brown as a fig. Only when the Fish stepped closer, casting a long shadow across his threshold, did he pause to look up. When the face of serenity turned toward her, with eyes as blue as endless springtime, she knew she had found him.

He did not recognize his distant cousin until she showed him the characters of their clan carved on the inside of the jade bangle that hung from her wrist. His calming presence acted like a soothing balm as he gently took the sling from her shoulders. "I had thought you'd gone to join our ancestors, that I was the last of our blood. Yet it is you, cousin Kwai. The gods that saved us as children have brought us together as the years grow shorter. Surely there must be purpose in such a wondrous thing." His voice was as light and gentle as his smile.

"I have traveled from Hong Kong, cousin, from the house of a good master. There is much that I must tell you. But first, I bring a life for you to save."

Gently, he opened the folds of cloth that surrounded the baby girl, examining her as if she were a wounded bird that had survived a storm. "You have brought her just in time. She would have been taken before another day."

Moments later, liquid he had prepared stood cooling in a clay crock. When it was ready, he fed it patiently into the baby's mouth with a porcelain spoon. "Last night, I saw a sign—a shooting star over the lake. It was closer and brighter than any I have seen, blazing with a purple light." He chuckled. "There is such an aura around this child."

"She was born in terror, many weeks too soon, on New Year's Eve. So already she is one year old, one extra year of life."

Her cousin smiled as a tiny fist closed over his finger. He lifted it to test its strength. "Her before-sky chi is great and her spirit is strong. She clings to life like a warrior. This is no ordinary girl child."

The Fish nodded agreement. "Her mother was a fighter and her father fierce even among the Western barbarians. They found great love for each other . . . strong enough to face a world that sees only the sin of mixed blood. They did not care; they were protected by their pride and their courage. Only treachery could defeat them."

The Fish could no longer fight against exhaustion. Through the long days and sleepless nights of her journey, she had thought only of the baby, clinging to the distant hope that they would find her cousin safely and that he would welcome her. Now, having placed her burden in his gentle hands, stamina deserted her. Old To reached for her arm, placing the tips of his fingers lightly upon her slender wrists, reading the silent pulses that told him of her life-force.

"You have done well, cousin; the chi of our clan still flows strongly within you. I will prepare food and a draught that will bring you comfort and rest. You have nothing more to fear." He massaged her hands briskly. The Fish could feel his energy enter her, bringing new strength.

He busied himself with lighting the lamps and preparing food. "I spoke of a shooting star that blazed across the sky the night before you came, bright as a splinter from the moon." He traced the air with a wide sweep of his fingertip. "In that fragment of time, the lake shone like a beacon. It was a sign this child was meant to cross the lake and enter this house. We will call her Siu-Sing—Little Star. If she lives, she will one day light the heavens."

He placed a bowl of soup on the table. "You are entrusted with her heart and the guidance of her soul; I with her physical being and the ways of the spirit."

The Fish tasted the soup and nodded her approval. When she was finished, she withdrew a tightly wrapped bundle from the beaded sling. "We must find a place of safety for this. It holds the child's future. Many things were stolen from me; an old woman traveling alone on the Yangtze is easy prey. But I have kept this bundle safe at the bottom of the sling."

She pushed aside the soup bowl with a chuckle. "No one would go near such a strange infant except the junk master's daughter, who fed her milk in exchange for cash."

He took the bundle from her, pulled a heavy wooden chest from beneath his bed, and kneeled to slip the three brass pin locks securing its heavy lid. "I made this chest from the keel of a wreck seasoned by a hundred years at the bottom of the lake. It is harder than stone. No hammer could smash it and no axe could split it . . . it is safe as a monastery crypt."

One by one he twisted the pins until they clicked into place and were easily withdrawn. "The locks I made myself and are a puzzle to everyone but me." He lifted the heavy lid to reveal an abundance of scrolls, bundles of papers, and small handmade books tightly packed.

"This box contains the work of my life and the work of sages who have gone before me. It holds the world as it is seen by the immortals, although few would recognize its true value." He laughed with pleasure at a secret shared. "The fools who tell stories in the village believe that the chest is filled with silver from selling the wild mandrake root some call ginseng." He took the bundle from her and found a place for it deep among the papers. "Few come near this place and none dare enter uninvited." He shook his head, smiling. "I think they are afraid of me . . . no reed-cutter would steal from a sorcerer's crucible and no woodsman come too close to a maker of magic. So, I am left in peace and my house is safe."

Old To closed the chest and locked it, then led his cousin to a second cot, in the corner opposite his own. "Another sometimes sleeps here, a herd boy. He is young and strong as a mountain goat; he can spread his blanket in the herb shed." When his cousin laid down, he gently covered her with a quilt made from rabbit pelts.

"Here by the lake, there is no need of clocks. The birds will wake you and the nightingale will sing you to sleep. Have no more fear for the little one. I will go to the camp below to find a milk-mother. Tomorrow I will carve a crib from the heart of a peach tree. It will bring me great joy."

Behind him, through a narrow gap in the mat wall, a human eye watched, unblinking. When Old To had replaced the chest and the old woman was silent, Ah-Keung, the herd boy, withdrew, unable to believe what he had seen and heard. His beloved *si-fu*—his great teacher—had given his place of shelter to a witch and an imp as pink as a piglet. Anger shook him as a dog shakes a rat; then shame and anger. Demons he had thought were gone forever taunted him with a shrillness only he could hear.

※

The Fish awakened to the stirring of birds in the bamboo. As her eyes grew accustomed to the half light, she saw that her cousin's bed was empty, the baby sleeping soundly in a make shift cot. A figure was framed against the open doorway, making no sound as it bent to peer closely at the sleeping child. "Who is there . . . Cousin, is it you?" she asked aloud. When no answer came, she asked again, sitting up and rubbing her eyes from the deepest of sleeps. The figure straightened quickly, revealing itself to be a boy with a wide-brimmed hat of frayed straw in one hand and the long wooden staff of a herdsman in the other.

"Forgive me, Ah-Paw, please do not be afraid. I come to pay my respects to the one who has taken my place in the house of Master To." The voice was that of a boy soon to become a man. He had called her Elder Sister in a tone of cautious respect, but he made her strangely uneasy.

"Do you have my cousin's permission to steal into his house while his guests sleep? Get away from the child. Do not enter again unless he is here."

The boy bowed deeply, as to one of great importance, leaning on the staff with a flourish of his hat. "The milk, Ah-Paw. I have milked the goat as I do each morning. It stands on the table and there are eggs in the bowl, still warm from the nest."

Her eyes now accustomed to the half light, she could see the milk pail and wooden bowl clearly. "Tomorrow you can leave the milk and eggs outside. I will fetch them when they are needed."

"But, Ah-Paw, there are dogs from the reed-cutters' camp, and their thieving children . . ."

The Fish felt her impatience rising. "What is your name?" she asked.

"My name is Ah-Keung. I am the disciple of Master To; he is my beloved *si-fu*." He bowed. "I also find herbs in the far hills and herd goats for the reed-cutters."

"Thank you, Ah-Keung, for the milk and the eggs. Please leave now. I will speak of this to my cousin. Until I have, do not cross this door." He bowed again, then turned and was gone.

※

With the first flush of morning, Old To returned with a cluster of catfish strung from a reed threaded through their gills.. His cousin sat waiting for him, the baby in her arms. She wasted no time in telling him of the herd boy.

He set down the fish on the cleaning board outside the door and began scaling them. "He is not to be blamed," he said thoughtfully. "The boy gathers herbs and cuts firewood, milks the goat and sweeps the pathway to my door. For that he has a place to sleep and food to eat." He seemed hesitant, as though this was difficult to talk about.

"He was to be my last disciple," he said finally, as he sliced the pink flesh into strips. "His family left him on the steps of the temple before he could walk. He was cursed with a twisted foot, so was of no use to them. The monks fed him and as he grew, he swept the courtyard and lit the joss sticks to earn his daily rice. If he left the temple, the children of the village taunted him cruelly, calling him the dog boy, as he dragged his useless foot. He begged to be taught the art of temple boxing, that he might defend his honor, but they would not allow it . . . perhaps because the boy was lame, perhaps because he was seen as unfit to become a warrior."

Crossing to the fireplace to stir the glowing coals, he started the fish sizzling briskly in a pan. "The abbot's heart was not entirely of stone; he agreed to take the dog boy into the temple, but only to work in the kitchen. The boy heard of me while listening to the chatter of novice monks who like to speak of miracles." Crackling from the stove filled the silence, as he turned the fish with chopsticks.

"It was winter; most of the sampans were idle on their moorings and few fishermen ventured out, but the dog boy crossed the lake alone, swam the icy waters, and dragged his crippled leg through miles of freezing mud." To paused as though to gather his thoughts. "I found him in the herb shed. At first I thought he was a wounded bird, a pelican trapped in the mud, but his spirit had defied death and he soon recovered." He broke the catfish into pieces into wooden bowls and mixed it with rice and leaves of dark green spinach. "I did much to straighten his leg, but it is his determination that restored him. I do not even know his true age, but I think he was seven or eight when he came to me. I have trained him for five years. He has taught his twisted foot to obey him."

He set the steaming bowls upon the table. "There is courage and great resolve in his soul . . . but nothing of humility or compassion. It did not take me long to see the seeds of selfishness and impatience. The need for violence grows within him like a sickness. Determination has become blind ambition. These are forces that can never follow the Way of the Tao. This is why I have named him Ah-Keung—the Forceful One."

They ate in silence for a moment, only the calling of birds and the distant voices of reed-cutters drifting from the foreshores. "So you see, I am to blame. I taught him to defend himself, so that he could find his own way. I did not see that this would never be enough for him, or that he would grow to trust me as a son trusts his father . . . or that he would seek no other place but here with me."

Old To shrugged his shoulders. "I chose the wrong disciple. Perhaps with time he will grow brains—learning to become a man is more difficult for some than for others."

CHAPTER 19

Under a Pear Tree

As *soon as she* found the marvel of her own two feet, Siu-Sing began the time of discovery. Every sight and sound and smell seemed to become a part of her—the sky floating on the vastness of the lake, the bump of boats across water, the smell of drying herbs and wood smoke. Birds and small animals became her friends, the marsh a waving jungle of reeds, the groves of bamboo a never-ending pattern of scattered sunlight. Far away, misty mountains touched the sky. The world was filled with wonder, and every day brought new adventures.

One morning by the lake began like any other—the grassy slopes swept by gentle breezes, the cicadas busy in the fruit trees. Siu-sing had washed her face in the water jar, eaten breakfast at the table under the pear tree. Old To had left before dawn and climbed the wooded slopes above the hut, and the Fish was cleaning the congee pot and scouring the fish pan.

Siu-sing's feet led her toward the herb shed. She had been told to stay away from there, but was curious about the secrets that lay inside. Although the bamboo mats in the windows were rolled up, they were too high for her to look through. She could see many strange and shadowy things hanging from racks of bamboo poles.

The herb-shed door was usually closed, and she could not reach the heavy wooden latch. Today it was ajar, with just enough room to squeeze through. Inside was dark and cool, filled with earthy smells and the fidgeting of swallows in the roof. It was a place of great mystery. Hanks of drying plants and flowers hung in rows overhead; pots and urns filled with tree bark, seeds, roots, and mushrooms lined the walls.

Ah-Keung the herd boy rose slowly from his shadowy corner when Siu-Sing stepped through the door. She did not see him until his voice broke the spell of discovery.

"Good morning, Little Sister; welcome to my house." He laughed softly at her jump of surprise as she moved quickly back to the door. He stepped into the flood of light, holding out a clump of seed pods, inviting her to sniff their fragrance. When she bent closer, he stroked her hair and pinched her cheek.

She backed away at the touch of his hand.

"Don't run away so soon. Did you not come to visit me?" He squatted beside her, his eyes blacker and deeper than the darkest corner she had ever looked into. The cicadas seemed to stop singing at the sound of his voice. There was a smell about him that she did not know was the smell of many goats.

She tried again to turn away, but he held his closed hand out to her. "I have a gift for you, here in my hand. Can you guess what it is?" She shook her head; his voice was so friendly that she hesitated.

"Take it . . . it is yours to play with." He held his hand closer, smiling at her.

His teeth are not clean, she thought, *and his hand is dirty*. But slowly, uncertainly, she offered her open hand.

The spider he dropped into it was as big as her palm, fat and hairy, its long legs tickling as it ran quickly up her arm and into her hair. She felt its sticky feet scrambling to escape, rummaging deeper into her hair. Her screams rebounded from every darkened corner of the shed.

He grabbed her arm, anxious to stop her squealing, clawing the spider from her hair. "Don't cry, don't cry." He sniggered. "It will not bite you—see, I have killed it." He opened his closed fist to show her its mangled remains."

Suddenly, the door was thrown wide and the Fish was there beside her, lifting and holding her tightly, her voice shrill with rage. "If you have harmed this child, your master will hear of it."

Ah-Keung raised his hands to fend off her fury. "Forgive me, Ah-Paw, I did not wish to frighten her. When she entered the shed, I was asleep. The light was poor; I thought it was a boy from the reed-cutters' camp, sent to steal ginseng. When I saw it was the Little Star, I tried to warn her. There are things that bite and sting in the herb shed; I have killed scorpions and snakes more than once. A little girl should not be allowed to wander unattended into a place like this."

He reached for his staff and gestured at the shaft of light falling upon the tangle of webs. "This is a breeding ground for spiders, not a playground for little ones." He used the staff to gather webs until they streamed thickly from its tip, black spiders scuttling for cover; then he poked at the bunches of herbs above them. "There are terrible poisons here as well as wonderful medicines. Only my master and I know which will give life and which will bring death."

Ah-Keung shook the clump of sticky fibers from the staff and stamped upon another fat spider before it could escape. "I beg you, Ah-Paw, it was a misunderstanding. Do not speak of this to my *si-fu*."

His voice took on a different tone. "He would not be happy to know that the Little Star was allowed to enter the herb shed unprotected. He will blame us both . . . but it is I who killed the spider, and you who put her in danger."

The Fish saw that he was right; she should not have allowed Siu-Sing to wander alone. "Very well, on this occasion I will say nothing, but if you come near this child again, it is you who will be sent away."

Ah-Keung bowed with a wide sweep of his hat. "It shall be as you say, Ah-Paw, and you will watch over her more carefully." He flopped the hat onto his head. "Nothing must happen to the Little Star." The sarcasm in his words was clearly intended; he had put this bag of bones in her place. The Fish turned away, clucking her tongue and muttering strange and ugly words. From the safety of her shoulder, Siu-Sing watched Ah-Keung set off along the track behind the straggling goats. Only then did she see that his stride was vigorous and his posture straight, but one leg seemed slower than the other, and there was a strangeness in his swinging step.

In the orchard beside the hut, Old To grew fruit and nut trees—plums and apricots, pomegranates, mandarins, walnuts, and almonds—among bushes thick with berries. Most splendid was the old pear tree that grew alone beside the hut, shading its entrance. "This pear tree," he had told his cousin, "is as old as the mountains. All things of great importance are considered in its shade."

A sturdy wooden table and benches had been placed beneath the tree. It was at this table that Sing began to listen and learn, to ask and be answered, to speak and be heard. Though she did not understand everything that was said between Yeh-Yeh and Paw-Paw, the names she had learned for Old To and the Fish, she somehow knew when they talked of her. Today was such a day.

"I have thought well and long about the future of Siu-Sing," said Old To. "If I have your agreement, she will become my disciple, the last of my lifetime. I will teach her the Way of the White Crane."

"I do not possess your great knowledge of such things," answered the Fish, engrossed in needlework, "but I have heard that the White Crane is the art of the Empty Hand created for daughters of noble families who are in danger from kidnappers and bandits. In my eyes, this child is of noble birth, so I would like to know more of it."

Old To nodded, choosing his words as carefully as he would pick fruit for the altar, one perfect piece after another. "Siu-Sing will grow to be a woman in a world of men, who can be cruel and treacherous. What's more, our Little Star is of mixed blood. No matter what she achieves in her life, no matter how pure her heart, how beautiful her mind or courageous her deeds, her journey will not be an easy one."

He looked across the lake a little sadly. "We are no longer young, cousin. Perhaps one of us will be spared to see her safely restored to her father's house . . . or perhaps she must face this journey alone. The secrets of the White Crane can make her strong in body, mind, and spirit. They can protect her against any hand that would be turned against her."

The Fish was torn. "Her mother, whose own life was destroyed by the greed of others, had a heart filled with courage but could not defend herself. Li would welcome such an opportunity for her daughter's survival. But I gave Li my promise that her daughter would be taught to read and write and to understand figures. I will not be prepared to meet my gods until I have fulfilled it."

Old To smiled. "She will learn these things, and to master the brush." He mimed the flourish of an invisible brush describing the liquid flow of calligraphy, then the sawing bow of a stringed instrument. "I will even teach her to play the song of the silver nightingale upon the *er-hu*, as it is taught to a princess. Together we will make her ready for the world beyond the mountains."

"Thank you," the Fish said quietly. "I shall be at her side to help guide her as long as I can. When will this begin?"

"Today," her cousin answered, "on New Year's Eve. This is her third birthday—the most important day of her life, when her soul has entered her body and she is accepted into the house of her ancestors as a human being. It is the perfect time to begin. Her limbs are as flexible as the stems of flowers and her step as light as a bird's."

He chuckled at the prettiness of his own words, then turned to Siu-Sing to cup her face in his warm hands. She felt the affection in his touch, the heat of its power reaching her heart. "It is her spirit that I find most precious, open to all things fresh and new, forever seeking hidden wonders. This is the gift of a true disciple."

"For how many years will she learn; how often and how hard must she practice?" the Fish asked anxiously.

"She will learn to fly as a fledgling bird discovers its wings. First, I will take her to the Rock of Great Strength at the break of each day. With the rising of the sun she will begin to learn the Way of the White Crane . . . and again before the daylight fades.

"For two years the rock will be her playground. She will not heed its hardness or fear its height. It will be the place that she will learn to trust, a center in the pattern of her life. When she reaches the age of five, she will become my disciple and I will no longer be her yeh-yeh but her teacher and her master . . . her *si-fu*. This will be so for eight more years."

The Fish knew there was one important matter left to discuss. "Forgive me, Cousin To, but what of the herd boy who calls you *si-fu*? Has he been told of this decision?"

"I have given much thought to this," Old To assured her. "He is in the hills, but I will talk with him when he returns. We will reach an understanding."

⌗

Two days later, Ah-Keung returned to the herb shed with the long woven basket strapped to his back, filled with wild ginseng. He had set up the scales when Master To spoke from the doorway.

"How long have we trained together, Ah-Keung?"

The herd boy replied instantly. "When winter comes and fishermen must break the ice to cast a net, it will be thirty-two seasons, *si-fu*."

"You have learned well in these eight years. I am proud of you, but now it is time for me to teach another."

Ah-Keung fell to his knees, his forehead pressed to the earth at his master's feet.

"*Si-fu*, you are all things to me . . . you are my master, my teacher, and my father. Without you I am nothing."

To's voice showed no sign of pity. "Stand up, Ah-Keung. You need no longer kneel to any man."

Slowly, Ah-Keung rose to his feet, wiping away his tears with the back of his hand. "*Si-fu*, what shall I do? My life is on the rock; I know no other."

"I have shown you where to find the healing plants of the hedgerow and magic roots of the forest, and taught you their value. Your foot is strong as the iron of your will. The time has come for you to stand alone."

"Will you teach the Little Star . . . is she to become your disciple?"

"Do not question my decisions. I have given you a name and with it your dignity; do not ask for more. There is a demon in you that only you can challenge. Destroy it while you can, or it will surely destroy you."

275

Master To extended the salute of sun and moon, then turned to walk away. "I have said and done all that I can for you. Travel as gently as life will allow, Ah-Keung. When you have found your way, return to share your adventures with me and we will again drink ginseng tea together."

The herd boy stayed for moments longer, gathering the thoughts that whirled around him like wasps about to sting. His pulse did not quicken, but his *chi* ran hot and his heart turned to iron in his chest. The voices, never far away, jeered at the dog boy with the twisted foot. Never had he felt so alone, yet never so strong. And never had he known the flame of hatred to burn so brightly within him.

※

Siu-Sing was kneeling in the warm soil of the garden patch helping Paw-Paw collect sweet yams, when death unfurled in pretty patterns from the vegetable basket beside her. Many times had she seen *yan-jing-shi*, the forest cobra, with Great-Uncle To. They always stopped and waited for it to cross their path, Yeh-Yeh speaking softly as it rustled away across the forest floor. "*Yan-jing-shi* cannot be trusted, so we do not play with him. We must be still and make no noise to let him pass."

"If he will not go away, what do we do?"

"If he will not leave us willingly, we must move slowly away from his place, because we have entered the world in which he is king. If he follows, we do not run; he must not know we are afraid of him. We must never turn our backs and must show respect for his place in the world."

"But if he will not let us pass?"

"Then we must try to kill him before he kills us."

All these warnings raced through Siu-Sing's head, but now *yan-jing-shi* was very close. It slid from the upturned basket in what seemed to her an unending length, its scales whispering over the rough weave. Siu-Sing made no sound as she rose slowly to her feet, her curiosity much greater than her fear. She marveled at its fluid movement, the perfect patterns along its back.

Yan-jing-shi rose with her, so close that she could see into its lidless eyes, pretty as golden beads, looking straight into hers. The belly was white as fresh bean curd, the neck spread wide as a rice bowl, the flickering tongue poised like a spear. It growled like a civet cat, exposing fangs like the claws of bird—and then it was gone in a whirl of black.

The Fish had thrown herself upon the snake. Beneath the folds of patched cotton, the cobra thrashed wildly under her weight, winding from her skirts to flow swiftly away between the furrows of earth. Only then did Siu-Sing cry out. Great-Uncle To was at her side in an instant, but the Fish had risen to her feet, miraculously unharmed.

"We must be more careful, Siu-Sing," she said, brushing the soil from her black skirts. "The next time we gather yams, we must poke the basket with a stick to see if *yan-jing-shi* is hiding inside." She picked Siu-Sing up and held her close.

"Once, when I was no bigger than you, I reached for a yam to peel and found a grasshopper sitting upon it as harmless as a fly. At least it looked like a grasshopper, or perhaps a locust, or even a cricket ready to sing me a song. But it was a scorpion, ready to strike. Things are not always what they seem to be."

Old To looked thoughtful. "I have stopped counting the years that I have lived upon these slopes, and never have I known *yan-jing-shi* to leave the forest for the grasslands. We must be watchful for such things."

CHAPTER 20

Red Lotus

Master To sat with Siu-Sing at the table beneath the pear tree. The Fish had made sweet buns and peeled a plate of lychees, dragon's eyes, and star fruit. Once they had enjoyed this simple feast, Old To lifted Siu-Sing from the bench and held her high, so she could reach the laden branches.

"Today you are five years old. You may choose a lucky pear straight from the tree."

She found one that was perfect to her eye, large and pale yellow with a slightest blush of pink. It was as sweet and juicy as it looked, and while she bit into it, he spoke to her in a way that told her the time for play was over and the time for learning must begin.

"On this day," he said, "we will visit the place where you will learn to become a warrior and the place where you will learn to become a scholar. I have some wonderful things to show you—my gifts for you on your fifth birthday."

Motioning her to follow, he stepped inside the hut and took something contained in a long sleeve of green velvet, tied at the neck with golden tassels, from the shelf high above his bed.

He held her hand, and together they climbed the goat track leading upward to a clearing in the tall bamboo. It was immediately cool. Sunlight flashed through the gently swaying branches, scattering chips of light across a carpet of papery leaves.

From an outcrop of moss-covered rock, a bubbling spring sent cascades of crystal water into a pond edged with blue iris and a patch of lotus. In the center of this hidden glade, a rustic bamboo arbor had been skillfully built, its archway hung with tree orchids in tiers of brilliant color. Beneath it was a table, almost round, with a shining surface of mottled greens and yellows like the tidal fringes of the lake. Around it were three stools carved and shaped from driftwood.

"This is the Place of Clear Water. It is where I come to think and to read and write, and it will be your classroom." He placed his hand upon the table, inviting her to do the same. It was cool and smooth to her touch, its flowing patterns strangely beautiful. "This is the jade table; it is for your studies alone. I carried it here with my two hands years ago. It is polished by time and by wisdom. Here you will learn many things and discover understanding."

From the sleeve of green velvet, he uncovered a musical instrument as reverently as he would reveal the most beautiful of gems.

"I call this precious thing the silver nightingale. It is an *er-hu*, played in the palace gardens of great emperors for a thousand years. This too I fashioned with my own hands, so many years ago they have flown like the swallows in autumn."

The *er-hu* was beautiful in its simplicity—a long, straight shaft of cherrywood curved eloquently at the top and carved into the sleek head and breast of a nightingale, the tuning pegs spread like wings in flight. At the bottom of the shaft, the sound box was no bigger than a rice bowl, covered with the stretched skin of a python.

Siu-Sing watched in silent wonder as he seated himself, nestling the drum of the instrument upon his knee, holding the head of the nightingale close to his ear and drawing the bow across the single string. The sweetest, most mysterious music soared and ebbed through the Place of Clear Water, through its flickering ceiling, and into the open sky.

When the last pure note faded, he smiled with pleasure at her enchantment.

"Music is food for the heart. The silver nightingale belongs to you. I will teach you to make it sing so that your heart may never be empty."

Placing the *er-hu* back in its velvet sleeve, he tied the tassels and slung it over his shoulder.

"Now we shall visit the Rock of Great Strength. You have known it as a playground, but now it is where you will learn to become one with all that surrounds you, so that you will never be lost. You will learn to be strong and straight as the bamboo, to sway with the wind so that you will never fall, and to fly like the great white crane so that you will never be caught."

They walked through a maze of mimosa bush that opened onto a shelf of rock, long and wide, exposed like an altar beneath the endless sky.

He bent to look closely into her eyes, taking both of her hands in his. There was something in his words that she had never heard before. It was no longer the voice of her yeh-yeh but the voice of her master.

"This rock is as old and as strong as the earth itself. It has been here since the beginning of time and cannot be moved by storm or tempest." He sat down in the center of the rock shelf, where it was worn smooth as a temple floor.

"This is no longer a place for a child to play but for a disciple to train. Here, you will discover things that others cannot imagine. On the Rock of Great Strength, you will put down roots that cannot be moved by any force but your own . . . and when you leave this place its chi will go with you.

"From this moment I am your master; you will call me *si-fu*. You are no longer my Little Star, but Red Lotus—disciple of the White Crane. This is your temple name, and you will have no other upon the rock. It is the place where all things are left behind except the will to learn."

So began the training of Red Lotus upon the Rock of Great Strength. Each day she would meet her master in its center an hour before sunrise to begin discovering the art of stillness beneath a waning moon— learning how to drink the air at its cleanest and freshest, like water from a crystal spring, and how to turn it into power through the mastery of breath.

With the first full flare of sunrise came her physical training. There were many different movements in the *chen-tow*—the dance of the crane. With the patient search for perfection, Master To guided her limbs as a painter applies one color to the next or a calligrapher transforms an infinitely fine stroke into a bold one.

When she was tired or stumbled, Master To would say calmly, "There is no gentle way of self-protection. The rock is hard, but so is injustice and cruelty, and these are the things you must be ready for. To be peaceful, we must be strong—each hand a sword and every finger a dagger. The arm is a spear and the elbow a hammer, the foot an ax and the knee a battering ram."

When his disciple looked puzzled, he told her the story of the white crane who wished no harm to anyone. "The crane was content to live quietly in the marsh, to build its nest in the rushes and to dry its wings on the sandbar. But the tiger came seeking the crane in the reed bed and tried to destroy her. She was ready, and defeated her attacker through the power of her wings and the steel of her feet and the blade of her beak. It will always be like this. The crane must be constantly vigilant."

When she fell and drew blood, he would teach her to stand as quickly as she fell. "If you do not like the hardness of the rock, you must learn not to fall. If you must fall, you must learn how to find your feet in the blink of an eye. You must always be faster than the foot or the fist of your opponent. If you do not like the sight and the taste of blood, you must try not to spill any. If you do not like pain, you must learn to overcome it.

"Violence comes in all weathers. It does not wait for comfort or convenience and may give no warning. It strikes from ice or fire, in deluge or drought, in warm sunshine and gentle breeze. We must know all its faces, understand all its moods, and know all its tricks. You must remember the lesson of the brook: The stones are hard and heavy but the water moves them. If it cannot move them with its power, it wears them down with its patience. This lesson never changes. Upon this rock, you are one with the water. Your chi is rooted to the rock; your power is the ever-flowing river of its life-force."

CHAPTER 21

Yan-jing-shi

It was *Siu-Sing's eighth* birthday. Refreshed by her morning exercise upon the rock, she bathed in the Place of Clear Water. Naked beneath the waterfall, she closed her eyes, exhilarated by the shock of cold water on her head and shoulders, then slipped away from the turbulence into the quiet pond, where drifting hyacinth parted as she swam and dragonflies flitted on invisible wings.

She did not see Ah-Keung standing amid the lattice of bamboo at the edge of the clearing. He watched her leave the water, her body glistening, to sit at the jade table where the *er-hu* awaited her fingers. She took the bow and sent the song of the silver nightingale soaring about her, so lost in its sweetness she neither saw nor sensed his presence.

Only when she stopped was she aware of being watched. At first she thought it was a moon bear or a panda that disturbed the shadow, searching the feathery tops of bamboo for mischievous monkeys. A sudden flash of sunlight caused her to blink and shield her eyes. Ah-Keung had not moved, but was lightly clapping his hands.

"I see you have tamed the strings of the old one's homemade fiddle—and have learned the dance of the White Crane. I have watched you on the rock. The *si-fu* has taught you to fly, but has he taught you to fight?"

Ah-Keung stepped into the clearing. She had lost count of the months since she had seen him. A younger boy from the reed-cutters' camp had taken his place behind the goats—a boy who was afraid of her and hurried the goats past the hut. Ah-Keung had grown taller than she remembered. He wore clean trousers of blue cotton, a matching jacket thrown over one shoulder—smart clothes bought in the village market instead of the rags and patches he had once made for himself. A respectable black silk cap had replaced the one of tattered straw, and his calfskin boots looked soft and new.

His naked upper body was lean and muscular, his chest and back adorned with fresh tattoos: on his chest the snarling face of a tiger, on his back a hooded cobra about to strike.

"Do I startle you, Little Star?"

"I am not disturbed by any creature that may come to drink in the Place of Clear Water. It does not belong to me."

"Yes, I have seen you charm the birds from the trees to sit on your finger, and animals feed from your hand. I have lived with them all of my life, but they do not come to me. Have you learned the spells of witchcraft from the old witch, Ah-Paw?" She had been reaching for her clothing, but stopped to look at him. He smiled without showing his crooked teeth. His smile was not as unpleasant as she remembered it, and his unruly hair had been neatly cut, yet stood straight on his head as thick as a brush. His eyes, she saw, no longer looked deep and dark and lost; instead, they seemed amused and inquisitive, livened by self-confidence.

"Do not watch me when I do not know of it. This is called spying, and I do not want to be spied upon."

"If I watch, it is because you are the Little Star. I am no longer angry, nor do I resent your place upon the rock. I have found a *si-fu* outside the village as great as Master To. He teaches wiser things than patience, tolerance, and discipline—he teaches action, expectation, and revenge."

He laughed, thrusting out his chest, raising his arms and flexing his muscles to cause the tiger to snarl. "His name is Black Oath Wu; he teaches me the Way of the Tiger, of stealth and attack with superior strength. Who is to say who is right? Only the *ku-ma-tai*, a fight to the death of one and victory to the other . . . only this will tell."

He turned, the flared muscles of his back causing the hood of the cobra to spread wider. "And I learn the Way of *Yan-Jing-Shi*, the Snake—unseen, unheard, faster than the blink of an eye; so deadly in its poison, it need strike but once." He laughed almost pleasantly. "Honorable rivals to the White Crane, I think. I hope they do not offend you. . . . See, I will cover them up."

He shrugged his arms into the sleeves of the jacket and buttoned it up, then bent forward, parting his bristly hair to reveal three white scars in a triangle on the crown of his head. "He also teaches how to be the master of pain. This is the mark of the triad. Three joss sticks burned their way into the bone. . . . I did not make a sound." He ruffled his hair, covering the scars.

"So you see, Little Star, it is you who has changed my miserable life and led me to my true path. If you had not come, I would still be wasting my time in search of one hand clapping, seeking the mysteries of the Tao. Soon I will travel to Hong Kong, where gold is easily found. For this I will always be in your debt."

Siu-Sing was determined not to show discomfort as she flicked the water from her skin and wrung it from her hair. The Forceful One did not look away. He held out his hand to touch her, stopped by her violet eyes. "You are still a child, Siu-Sing, but already you are *ho-lieng*— beautiful as a red lotus in a lake of pink blossoms."

She ignored his compliment: To be *ho-lieng* was to be lovely as the breast of a bird or the eye of the tiger is beautiful, and she saw herself as neither of these. She pulled on her pants and buttoned her tunic, lacing her sandals without haste. She could feel his impatience rising when she said no more. When he spoke again, his words were harder and had the depth of a man's.

"You show me no face with your silence. If you will not accept the hand of a friend, then I will not offer it again until you are old enough to be worthy of it. I no longer belong in the corner of the herb shed, or need the crumbs that were thrown to me. But I do not hate you, nor do I hate Old To."

Ah-Keung bowed with a short, stiff jerk of his head. "I do not blame you for taking my place in the hut and upon the rock. I salute you as one warrior to another."

Her reply was immediate. "I am proud to be my master's disciple, but

284

I am no warrior. I do not learn the Way of the White Crane to fight, but to survive."

The Forceful One shook his head and laughed unpleasantly. "Believe me, Red Lotus, to survive is to fight; there is no other way."

"No, to survive is to be strong and learn to think . . . to seek knowledge and find peace in your heart. That is a better way."

"Well, we must disagree, but I wish you well. I came to say good-bye before I sail the big river to the world beyond the mountains. I shall not be gone for long and will tell you what I find."

"I wish you good fortune on your journey," Siu-Sing said, as she gathered up her papers and the *er-hu*. She took the goat path with an easy stride, feeling the strange new eyes of Ah-Keung, the Forceful One, following her every step.

CHAPTER 22

The Legacy of Li-Xia

Two *years had passed* since Ah-Keung had gone, and Siu-Sing had almost forgotten him. There was no practice on this special day, only peace at the Place of Clear Water.

Siu-Sing was reading at the jade table, the drone of cicadas as unnoticed as the chirping of a hidden cricket. A sudden streak of rainbow light caused her to look up. A hummingbird, radiant as a forest orchid, hovered over the raft of blue iris, the sound of its wings no louder than those of a bee. The brilliance of its colors enchanted her as it hung motionless, shining like a blue-green jewel. From flower to flower it flitted in sudden, dazzling spurts, its needle beak coated in pollen.

She watched it streak across the clearing and stop, shivering in midair, as though stunned by an invisible blow. The cicadas seemed to stop singing as a spider, big as her hand, bounced greedily down the silken rungs of its invisible web. To her horror, it enclosed the bright jewel with long, furry legs, tumbling it over and over, binding the gleaming wings in sticky, fluid silver. At last the web stopped vibrating, and the spider began to feed.

"See how suddenly innocence is deceived and beauty is destroyed by treachery." The Fish spoke from the dappled shadow of the clearing where she had been standing, a basket in her hand. "The hummingbird was happy; there was no warning of its terrible death. It is a lesson to be learned."

Taking her place beside Siu-Sing, the old woman removed the beaded baby sling from the basket. "This is the sling I made for your mother to carry you on her back through the Ti-Yuan gardens. It brought you here safely, along with other precious things." Reaching into the sling, the Fish withdrew a bundle wrapped in yellow silk.

"Today is your tenth birthday—the age of maturity; you are no longer a child but a young woman of responsibility. I was tempted many times to give you these things sooner, but your mother was sure of her wishes. She wanted you to be old enough to receive them as she did ... not as toys or playthings, but as her greatest treasures. These small things come to you with endless love. They are rightfully yours now."

Unwrapping the yellow silk robe, so fine she could see her fingers through it, Siu-Sing found a small white satin purse, a photograph in a silver frame, two fat books tied in a scarf of embroidered silk, and a leather pouch. The books were almost the same size, one with a cover of scarlet leather closed by a gold clasp, the other much older and carefully made by clever hands. From the silver frame, a Chinese woman with a radiant smile gazed back at her, the man beside her strange beyond any Siu-Sing had seen. "It is your father and mother, Siu-Sing—Master Ben and Li-Xia.

"Your mother was as *lieng* as any flower but strong as the tallest tree. Your father comes from another land far away, but his mother was Chinese. He is known as Di-Fo-Lo to our people and as Devereaux to the Westerners ... Captain Ben Devereaux. He is a brave and successful man who loved your mother greatly."

From the silk purse, Siu-Sing lifted a gold coin threaded upon a fine chain. "Your mother collected a thousand pieces of gold in her lifetime. This is the first of them, the one she treasured above all others. Your father gave it to her; from this coin he built a fortune, beautiful ships and fine houses. For a while they shared the greatest of all dreams ... the dream of happiness."

Also contained in the purse was a finger jade as white as suet that, when held up to the light, was shot with red and orange streaks. "It is called an orange-peel jade, and is very rare. This belonged to your grandmother, Pai-Ling, one with lotus feet from a fine family in Shanghai. It was passed on to your mother, who held it tightly in her hand when she was lonely and afraid. She said it brought her comfort, and the spirit of her mother would always come to her."

The Fish shook her head sadly, as though the recollection were too difficult to contemplate, then quickly found her twinkling smile. She handed Siu-Sing the scarlet book, its leather cover decorated with peony flowers. Siu-Sing's fingertips glided across the letters stamped in gold, soft and smooth to her touch.

"It is your mother's name as spoken by your father . . . he called her Lee Sheeah." Opening the clasp, Siu-Sing was delighted to find its pages filled with the beautiful writing of two worlds, edged with delicate paintings; drawings, tiny yet perfect, some in finest brush, others even finer from the nib of a pen; among them leaves and petals pressed to last forever. "Your mother told me that these are the leaves of the mulberry tree—a special one she called the Ghost Tree. The flowers are called morning stars; she wore them in her hair when she married your father."

The Fish was silent while Siu-Sing turned the pages as though each were a leaf of pure gold. "It is your mother's journal. She said it contained her 'thousand pieces of gold' for you to share. She wrote in it every day in the last months of her life." The Fish took a long and painful breath. "I think she knew her time was short, and wrote this for your eyes alone."

Sing opened the second book. Its yellowed pages were equally beautiful, but in a different hand; the watercolors faded, the stitching broken and pages loose. "This is the journal of your grandmother Pai-Ling. Li-Xia treasured this book when she was your age." The Fish shook off her somber tone. "The scarf was also of great importance to her; she called it her happiness silk, and would tie it in her hair when sadness or worry came."

Sing studied the minute needlework of groves of trees, tiny figures bearing baskets on their backs, and squirrels and finches around its edges. She could find no words for such a moment and closed the books, wrapping them in the happiness silk. The smoothness of the finger jade felt like warm satin in her palm. She looked for a long time at the photograph in its tarnished silver frame.

"There is one more thing I am to give you," the Fish said. "I do not know its purpose or its value, but she said you would discover this for yourself." The object, held in a pouch of soft leather, was heavy in Sing's hand. Inside, she found a gold dragon's claw set with a number of steel pins.

The Fish said gently, "The day will come when we must leave the lake and travel to the Golden Hill on the other side of the mountains. It was your mother's last wish that you be reunited with your father. You are preparing long and hard for this great journey, and I have kept these precious things safe for these ten years."

She embraced Sing, kissing her lightly on the forehead. "I will leave them with you . . . they are not for sharing, even with me. When you are ready, we will replace them in the chest of stone and I will teach you the puzzle of the locks. But now let us drink tea while I tell you everything there is to know about Li-Xia and Master Ben."

※

Training with her beloved *si-fu* continued through blizzard cold, blinding rain, and savage heat. In the Place of Clear Water, Siu-Sing studied at the jade table, often with the Fish at her side. The old lady never interfered, but was always happy to speak when words were needed; always ready with a basket of food—sticky rice wrapped in spinach leaves, steamed bread and green tea in a wicker warming pot—close by.

The Fish seemed seasoned but undiminished by each passing year. On this peaceful afternoon, her grip upon the *yulow*, the long sculling oar that almost seemed part of her, was as firm and strong as ever, as she propelled the flat boat through the marsh to empty the crab pots for the evening meal.

The flat blade of the oar stirred lazy swirls of water; the reed beds whispered with their passing; and sometimes a spoonbill rose suddenly to beat the air with sturdy wings. The first pot yielded two crabs, which soon lay flapping wildly on the bottom boards, their pincers tied with

289

reed. But the Fish found the second pot empty, hauled up and abandoned, its trap wide open.

"The reed-cutters are thieves and liars; they steal from our pots and swear before all gods that they do not." The Fish uttered a string of Tanka curses that could raise the dead, before resetting the wicker pot with fresh bait. "Your *si-fu* gives them herbs they cannot pay for and tends their ills, yet they steal the food from his table. Two crabs and three small fish are not enough." Angrily, she drove the *yulow* deep into the mud and tethered the sampan, sliding her bare feet into the shallows, sending up ochre plumes of silt. From the bottom of the boat, she took two wide-mouthed nets fixed to slender bamboo poles, tossing one to Siu-Sing.

"Let's see if we can catch some shrimp or maybe a flatfish. I will take the deeper shoal; you can try close to the shore." She waded into uncut reeds that closed upon her like a screen. Her words drifted back: "We'll meet back here in no more than half an hour to see what we have caught."

The water was pleasantly cold around Sing's knees, the yellow clouds of silt stirring with every stealthy step. Sunlight had penetrated the marsh on its downward track when she decided it was time to return to the sampan. She was accustomed to measuring the time by the passage of the sun and was seldom mistaken. Her net sagged and wriggled with a lively eel—a favorite when stewed with black beans and peppercorns.

She followed the mud trail to the sampan easily, emptying her catch alive and cleaning the net of weed. Any moment she would hear the Fish's voice returning, grumbling about the reed-cutters frightening the fish and cursing the boatmen for dredging the marsh. Hearing nothing but a distant chorus of herons settling on the sandbars, she called aloud, "Paw-Paw, the tide is turning. It is time to go. *Paw-Pawww.*"

She followed her call with the cry of a marsh hen, a signal they used to locate each other in the reed beds. Once, twice, and a third time more loudly. Never had she known the lake more silent, and never had she not immediately heard the answering call.

At first Siu-Sing was not alarmed. Perhaps Paw-Paw had lost her way, or chased a crab or an eel large enough to lead her into deeper waters. The trail of bent reeds was as easy to follow as a goat track, the mud still settling as Siu-Sing waded strongly into the thicket, her calls louder with every swishing step. Gradually, the water deepened, until it was halfway up her thighs. It was no longer clear and astir with teeming life, but darker and colder where the sun did not reach.

Self-control did not allow for great alarm, but the voice of Master To came to Siu-Sing, first as a whisper, then growing louder as the water deepened: *The crane was content to live quietly in the marsh, to build its nest in the rushes and to dry its wings on the sandbar. But the tiger came seeking the crane in the reed bed and tried to destroy her. . . .*

Her calls remained unanswered. When the sun told her it had been more than an hour since they had left the sampan to go their separate ways, a chill of fear took hold of her heart. Suddenly she saw Paw-Paw's woven hat, sodden so completely it would no longer float, lying still beneath the surface. She lifted it clear of the water, her throat so tight and her mouth suddenly so dry that she could not find the voice to cry out.

She did not need to wade much farther before spotting the wide-legged pants and sleeves of Paw-Paw's loose-fitting *sam-foo*, billowing with so much water that they made her widespread limbs seem no bigger than a child's. The Fish was afloat facedown, blending with the muddy waters, the empty fishnet at her side.

Siu-Sing fell to her knees, gathering up the lifeless weight almost too heavy to lift clear of the water. The Fish's mouth gaped open, a thin swath of hair plastered across her closed eyes. Water cascaded from her clothing as Sing half carried, pushed, and pulled her into the shallows. Beneath her hand the heart was still, her thin wrist lifeless. Shaken by sorrow such as she had never known, Siu-Sing willed the warmth of her own chi to enter the saturated body, begging the gods that had watched over this great lady for so long to bring her back, to help pull the boat from the water, and leave her footprints in the sand.

Siu-Sing did not call for help. She knew Master To was too far away to hear her, and any reed-cutter or boatman within earshot would not heed the cry of a *jarp-jung*. Siu-Sing could only hold the Fish tightly, whispering her good-byes. Pressing lifeless fingers to her lips, through the mist of tears she saw that the jade birth bracelet, so much a part of this brave soul that it was never to be removed even in death, was missing.

⊁⊰

When Master To found them at dawn, Siu-Sing was sitting silently beside the body. She had straightened the old lady's limbs and cleaned her face and hair of weed and silt, arranging her clothing and placing a garland of flowers in her hands. "I did not want the land crabs to find her," she said simply, as he lifted the body of his cousin and carried it up the slope to the Place of Clear Water.

"She will rest here in eternal peace and happiness, and continue to watch over you," he said. "All that you strive to learn she will share, as she has done since you were born." They made a coffin of bamboo, and dug a grave facing the lake. Together he and Siu-Sing carried many large and heavy rocks to cover her resting place, piling them high as protection against wild things. Over these, the rich soil of the glade was planted with flowers that flourished in such shaded corners. Before it, Siu-Sing laid a garden of stones collected from the pond, each selected for its perfect shape and color.

They knelt before the finished tomb and Master To took Siu-Sing's hand. "Your *paw-paw*'s age was great and her spirit even greater. She was not ill, but her heart had carried much . . . perhaps more than it should. Be happy that she is now at rest, yet forever with us." They spoke no more of the Fish's sudden death, and did not question the reed-cutters or the boatmen. Sing continued her studies in the Place of Clear Water, fetching fresh fruit and flowers each day and trying to forget the puzzle of the jade bracelet.

CHAPTER 23

The Last Disciple

Siu-Sing *could tread the* marsh as silently as a blue heron, so that she sometimes saw that which she was not meant to see. She was deep in the reeds late on a hot afternoon, finished with her studies and catching shrimp for the pot, when she heard the pleasant lilt of a girl's soft laughter close by. She traced it quietly, suddenly wondering if she would find the owner of the voice wearing a plain jade bangle on her wrist. Through the curtain of reeds, a young Hakka girl, stripped of her clothes, stood in the center of a small clearing. Her naked body, always well protected from the sun in the custom of her people, shone white as a lily.

A tall stack of reeds tied into bundles served as a makeshift bed, the girl's rough work clothes tossed on top of them. The air was sweet with the scent of rising sap from freshly severed stalks, lending an air of magical secrecy to this place so hidden from the world. The girl bent to wash her arms and neck with clean cold water, tossing wet hair over her strong shoulders.

She seemed to be speaking to someone Sing could not yet see. Her long pigtail starkly black against her pale back, she stood with her face tilted to the sky, beads of water glistening on her breasts. The laughing voice that carried softly, with words that Sing could not quite hear, was answered by the voice of a man. The girl turned toward it, showing a face that was still young, tossing the hair from her eyes and playfully shielding her breasts with her hands.

A man stepped into view, taller and older, his upper body uncovered and browned by the sun. He stepped close to her, her arms eager to reach for him. Siu-Sing found herself unable to look away. What un-folded was not entirely a mystery; she had seen similar things among goats, one mounting the other in just such a way. She watched in silence, strangely affected by the sounds of their pleasure.

⌖

In her bed that night, it was hard to forget what she had seen, and it was not something she would wish to speak of with Master To. He had said that a warrior was neither male nor female, and that upon the rock they were the same, but she would not always be upon the rock. She wondered if one day something like this would happen to her, and could not deny a keen curios-ity. Would she have breasts like those someday? She cupped her own, barely formed but clearly growing. Would she grow hair like the Hakka girl? It did not seem likely as she felt the sprouting tuft, as soft as thistledown, between her legs. She heard the steady breathing of Master To in his corner of the hut, and tried to contain this new wonder without making a sound.

Hours later, after falling into a deep sleep, Sing awakened to discover spots of blood on her hands and in her bed. Only then did she feel fear at what she had done. She should have known such secret pleasure was not possible without punishment. She had wounded herself, and should it heal, she would never again think of the man's brown body so dark against white skin, or listen to the sounds of pleasure.

That Master To knew all things past, present, and future was made clear that morning. When meditation and practice were over and they sat beneath the pear tree to eat the morning congee, he spoke in the voice of her *si-fu*. "You were not as strong or as fast on the rock today. Has something happened to tire you so?"

Sing could find no ready answer. How could she tell him of the injury that cramped her stomach and bled like an open wound? He reached across to cover her hand with his, patting it as he had done when she had hardly left the peach-wood crib.

"I believe last night you became a young woman. . . . I saw the signs. You must not hide such things from me; I am your *si-fu*, but I am also father and mother, brother and sister to you now, and we need hide no

294

secrets. On the rock you are the disciple Red Lotus, but here you are the Little Star, a pretty girl like any other."

"Thank you, *si-fu*, but is this thing a punishment? Have I offended the gods?"

"No, it is their blessing, to prepare you for the pain when you have children of your own." He spoke patiently, unruffled by her curiosity. "The blood you shed may one day create a child, and you may know the pleasures that make it so. These feelings are natural, but you must control them if you are to achieve everything you have worked for."

Relieved to know she would not die of her wounds, Siu-Sing was almost tempted to speak of what she had seen in the reed beds—to ask if it was wrong to be so curious at the sight of a man without his clothes. She decided that as this had been witnessed in concealment and secrecy, it should remain so, and the answer to such questions must be found within her own heart and mind if such a moment ever came.

✴

Sing's faith in Master To's teachings was so complete that she seldom felt the need to question him. When she did, he would answer only if he considered the question worthy of a reply. If not, he would tell her to seek the answer for herself. Sing found her own questions and sought her own answers in all that she could. But one day she found herself asking, "*Si-fu*, I have practiced on the rock for many seasons and begin to understand the Way of the Empty Hand. But when I go from here and we no longer greet the sun together, how will I practice my skills?"

"Life will not always allow you the time or the place." He tapped his forehead with a fingertip and placed the other over his heart. "You must practice in here, and in here; no one can take this from you. No matter where you are, there will always be a new day dawning, always a stillness before the sunrise. In the hour before daylight, the world is yours alone. In your heart and mind you will return to the rock . . . you will see the crane on the sandbar and the tiger in the reed bed. You will watch them in mortal combat and see why the crane is triumphant. You are the crane and you will never fall. It is called spiritual boxing."

295

Master To took an amulet from around his neck, placing it in the palm of her hand. It was a circle of jade carved with the crane and the tiger, its chain minutely woven in links of black, bronze, and silver, as light and glinting as a cord of silk. It felt hot in Sing's hand as she studied it.

"Jade is known by the wise as tears of heaven . . . by the warrior as blood of the dragon. They say its contact with the skin adds to its luster, that it holds the life-force of its wearer, and that the strength of those who have gone before us can be called upon in combat.

"This has been worn by many masters. See how it has become green as moss on a sacred tree through the greatness of their chi. The chain is woven from their hair—eight strands from each master handed down to his disciple. It is protected by the power of their spirits. When I leave you, I will add eight hairs from my own head, and the amulet will be passed to you."

"I would not wish to see the sun rise without you by my side." Sing could not contain her feeling, although she knew she must try.

"The sun will rise just as surely and splendidly when I am not beside you. I do not teach you to become dependent upon me or any other, but to stand alone and follow your own path without fear or hesitation." His words were not spoken angrily but with a hint of warning.

At the entrance to the rock, shaded by mimosa, a fallen log acted as a seat when the time came to rest. Master To sat upon it now, inviting Sing to sit beside him. He filled two cups from a crock of ginseng tea, handing one to her. "In two more years your training as my disciple will be complete, and it will be time for our departure to the world beyond the mountains. I will be beside you if I can, but if this is not to be, then you must travel without me. You must find within yourself the faith to face the world. But you will never be alone; the spirit of the White Crane will always travel with you no matter where you go or whatever lies ahead." He sipped the tea, his eyes intent upon her face.

His smile is gone, thought Sing. His steady blue eyes searched hers for a moment before he spoke. "It is the way of *wu-shu* to prepare the last disciple for all things. The master must decide if that disciple is worthy to learn the deepest of advanced secrets before he passes on.

"It is called *di-muk*—the touch of death." His voice was low and level, his eyes unwavering. "There are nine points of the human body that, when struck by an adept, can cause the instant death or permanent immobilization of your adversary." He waited for Sing to absorb the power of his words, his eyes probing her slightest response. "This can only be taught to the most trusted and skilled disciples. This is why I could no longer teach Ah-Keung. The death touch must never be placed in uncertain hands, or the master must answer to Kuan-Kung, the god of war.

"You have earned my trust and my respect, and for this I will teach you *di-muk*. For two years this will be included in our daily practice . . . one single blow that must be used only if your life is threatened." He paused. "To take another's life is to invite the ghost of the defeated to take revenge. Only you can make this decision in such a circumstance.

"I can tell you, however, that the last disciple of Master To will never lack for help." He reached into his robe, taking from some hidden pocket a slim canister of bamboo. "This contains eight scrolls. It is only eight inches long and eight inches in circumference, yet it contains the answers to all that I and the masters gone before me have asked of the universe. Eight hundred years of wisdom reside in this small space. It is called Pa-Tuan-Tsin—the Precious Set of Eight—which the immortals say holds the secret of longevity." He unscrewed the lid and held it up for her to see. "This was carved by a distant forefather in the Temple of Shoalin from the sacred tree that once shaded the Lord Buddha."

He removed a tightly rolled scroll of parchment, unfolding an inch or two to show that it was covered by the tiniest of calligraphy. "When I was young my eyes were clear as a hawk's, so sharp I could write my name on a grain of rice. I was a novice in the monastery, and time was my closest companion."

He replaced the scroll and the wooden lid, screwing it tightly. "It also contains a letter sealed with my chop. If I am no longer with you and you are in need of guidance, you will take this to Master Xoom-Sai, abbot of Po-Lin, the Temple of the Precious Lotus on Lantau Island, close to the Golden Hill. You will give him your temple name. If the time comes, you must seek his help, and it will be freely given."

"How will I know if the time has come to go to him?"

"You will know, Red Lotus. You will know. Sooner or later, the tiger always comes to the crane."

✳

Crisp breezes played across the slopes as Siu-Sing climbed to the Place of Clear Water with an armful of peach blossoms. She stood for a moment to look back across the lake. The air was clear and sharp; the mountains seemed much closer and there was snow on the peaks. Wood smoke rose from the reed-cutters' fires, driven this way and that by sudden gusts.

She was thirteen years old today, and her training was complete. The time had come at last; in two days they would leave the lake for the Golden Hill, Hong Kong. Master To had given her a bundle of joss sticks and a red candle to take to Paw-Paw's grave. "I traded a rare mushroom for the joss sticks and healed a bunion for the candles. You may go alone to pay your last respects. . . . I have already spoken with my cousin. She is happy in the company of her clan and will watch over you as she watched over your mother."

As she knelt before the grave of the Fish, arranging the blossoms like the fan of a peacock and lighting incense to rise in threads of perfumed smoke, there was a noise that Siu-Sing had heard before—a guttural hiss of warning and a dry slither of scales over loose stones. She raised her eyes warily, knowing she must not move quickly.

The forest cobra had been coiled in sleep, its colors and patterns of earth and stone unnoticed on the small garden of river pebbles in front of the little tomb. The hood was spread wide, the flat, shiny head poised like a blade. Suddenly, the years between were snatched away, and Siu-Sing saw again the eyes of the snake and the perfectly formed sections of its throat and neck, smooth as ivory. Was this the *yan-jing-shi* that the Fish had saved her from, grown now to twice its size? Could it have returned to live in the tomb of the one whose life it had sought?

She had heard the reed-cutters speak of such things. *Yan-jing-shi* was known to find tombs, empty houses, and deserted temples abundant hunting grounds, the perfect place to rear its young. She had seen the

298

great snake coiled in sleep on warm rocks or winding through the cane grass, leaving telltale trails in the snow, and had seen its dead and discarded skin blown across the grasses.

Suddenly, there was a scything of the air above her head, so close it stirred her hair. A sweeping side kick arched over her, delivering a knife-edged foot to the snake's head with such force that it fell. In that same fraction of time, Siu-Sing was thrown aside by Ah-Keung. He had stripped off his shirt, winding it around one hand as he faced the snake, crouching to its level, eye to eye.

He had the stance of the knife-fighters she had seen among the Hokklo fishermen drunk on homemade wine. *Yan-jing-shi* had risen again, swaying back against coils of bunched muscle, its hood strained fully open, its shoelace tongue vibrating like the reed in a bamboo flute. "Ah, *yan-jing-shi*," he sneered, mimicking the sway of the cobra. "Let us dance. We shall see who is faster, you or I." Savagely alert, the cobra struck again and again, its hiss compressed to a growl. Each time Ah-Keung easily evaded the wide yellow mouth, sticking out his tongue in defiance, his hands held wide and ready.

"I give you four chances, *Yan-jing-shi*. This hand? . . . That hand? . . . This foot? . . . That foot? Which is it to be?" He circled the snake, forcing it to move with him, their eyes locked. "See how I wear down my worthy opponent, how much he hates me, how careless and clumsy he becomes. So determined to kill me, he does not see that I am more dangerous than he could ever be; that I am faster than the tongue of a horned toad."

From a boxer's crouch, he snapped out his hand like the fall of a whip to grasp the cobra's head above the spread of its hood, his thumb perfectly centered on its throat an inch below the hinge of its jaws; it dug deep, forcing the mouth wide. He held the thrashing coils at arm's length, then rose fully, with the serpent flinging this way and that from his rigidly outstretched arm.

"You see who is faster?" He grinned. "Yet he is as tall as I am, and as thick as my arm. See how quickly the king of the forest becomes harmless in the hands of his master? There is nothing to fear—I have challenged his threat and defeated it."

With his free hand, Ah-Keung produced a knife from his belt. He tossed it in the air with a juggler's hand, catching it by the polished blade, then offered the bone handle to her. "Could this be the one that tried to kill you and the old one? Perhaps he has returned to try again. Take your vengeance—sever the head. If it was not this snake that hid in the basket, it was one of his clan."

He waggled the gaping jaws before her eyes. "You see, Ah-Keung is back and watching over the Little Star . . . or is your name Red Lotus?" The fangs of the cobra were unsheathed, like the claws of a cat held inches from her face. He worked the thumb that controlled the snake's jaw, until beads of clear venom dripped harmlessly as droplets of dew. When Siu-Sing made no move to take the knife, it was quickly gone, his hand so fast it defied the eye.

"No? Well then, I shall avenge your poor *ah-paw* for you." With the slow precision of a marketplace showman, he turned the cobra's head to face him, bringing it closer to his face, mimicking its open jaws and darting tongue, mocking its helplessness. His thumb shifted upward to close the mouth, clamping it shut.

"So you would bite my friend the Little Star, failed assassin of old hags? We shall see." Without haste he opened his own jaws and stretched them wide, then bit down on the snake's head with a savage grunt, twisting and wrenching it from its body and spitting it at Siu-Sing's feet. A swath of blood streaked his chest like a winner's sash. Ah-Keung held the writhing trunk high and stood looking down at her, his rigid arm jerking as violent spasms rippled through the cobra's length.

"Did I not tell you that *yan-jing-shi* and his kind are not to be trusted? Warriors do not know when it is time to die; they cannot accept defeat. His head is gone, yet still his heart beats. I have tamed the foot well, have I not, Red Lotus?" He spat blood, drawing a forearm across his mouth. "It is faster and more deadly than the king of all snakes. It has saved the life of the disciple of the White Crane. Am I not still your friend?"

His unexpected appearance and the use of her temple name had surprised her, but she looked at him without fear. "You are the victor, Ah-Keung; the honor is yours. We will never know if I would have become the victim of *yan-jing-shi*; we had a score to settle, he and I. I thank you for protecting me, but I did not ask for your help. If your foot had not been fast enough, it would have been my life, not yours, that *yan-jing-shi* would have tried to take."

Ah-Keung seemed not to hear her, his eyes bright with excitement. The tip of his knife ran cleanly down the length of the snake's belly. With finger and thumb he pinched out the gall bladder, carefully emptying the dark green bile into a bean gourd taken from his pocket. "The bile of *yan-jing-shi* is the nectar of the gods. Let us take it to the old master. It will prepare him well for the journey to the great Gum Sarn."

The Forceful One kicked the trembling remains of the cobra onto the garden of stones, crossing to the spring to wash his face and rinse his mouth. He splashed his chest, wiping it clean with the shirt. "We are the same, you and I; we have nothing but our skills to protect us. Let us be friends. I too am traveling to the Golden Hill. I have been there many times since I herded goats and slept with spiders. I have worked aboard the river junks to earn my passage and know the journey well. Perhaps we will travel together, the great *si-fu* and his disciples. Let us see."

⟩❋⟨

Ah-Keung bowed deeply three times, a mark of great respect by a returned disciple to his master. "Master To, as a boy I disappointed you and was not worthy of your teachings. I was a dog with a broken foot who knew nothing of honor. Because of you, I am now a man who walks tall and straight with his head held high." He held out the gourd in both hands. "I beg your forgiveness. The foot you healed so well has killed *yan-jing-shi* and saved the Little Star. I offer you the essence of its life."

Master To returned the Forceful One's bow. "Is this true?" he asked Siu-Sing.

"Yes, *si-fu*. The forest cobra awaited me at the tomb of my *paw-paw*. Ah-Keung was fearless; he destroyed it with courage and great skill."

Master To accepted the gourd, draining the bitter draught in a single swallow. "You have my gratitude, Ah-Keung. I am honored by your respect."

301

The Forceful One bowed. "I ask only to accompany you to the world beyond the mountains. I have recently come from there, and I beg to be your servant and arrange your passage." He grinned. "The boatmen know Ah-Keung well and will not cheat me."

"Perhaps . . ." Master To turned to enter the hut. "Let us sleep and see what morning brings."

※

Siu-Sing slept soundly and later than any morning she could remember. Always Master To was first to rise, lighting the lamp and raking the coals beneath the cooking stove and fetching water from the jar in a comforting start to the day. On this morning the hut remained in darkness, but the first light creeping through the window was slanted higher and brighter than usual. She listened for the sounds of Master To sluicing at the water jar, but nothing disturbed the shrilling of cicadas in the bamboo.

"*Si-fu*, are you awake?" She spoke quietly, her words an empty intrusion that brought no reply. The oil lamp had not been lit, nor the fire beneath the congee pot. There was no sign of movement from his dark corner as she listened for his even breath. "It is time to rise, *si-fu*," she whispered. "*Si-fu*, are you there?"

It was not fear that closed in on Siu-Sing as she reached his side—surely fear could not exist in the master's presence—but why was there no sound or movement from one so readily alert? She reached into the shadows to awaken him and found his hand. It was faintly warm, yet he did not stir at her touch. Even as she spoke his name, her hand grasping his more strongly, he did not move. Her fingertips felt for the silent pulses of his wrists as he had taught her. They beat as faintly as a bird's, and when she pressed her ear to his heart, the steady thump faltered like a weary footstep.

She pulled aside the flannel shirt that was his sleeping garment, feeling for the flow of blood in the hollow of his throat. It too was as faint as a drifting snowflake.

"What is the matter, Little Star; the flatboat is already loading. Is the master unwell?" Ah-Keung was suddenly beside her. He stood looking down, his presence huge against the open door.

302

"Something is wrong—I can't wake him. We must help him; there is an herb he keeps for such an emergency—"

She hurried to the shelf where such things were kept.

"I think it is too late; our *si-fu* has left us." Ah-Keung had lit the bedside lamp. She saw that her master's eyes were open wide, their brilliance dulled and still, the lines of laughter still creased like crumpled silk.

The lamp threw Ah-Keung's shadow against the mat walls until it seemed to fill the hut. He dropped to his knees beside her, quick to seek the old man's pulse as she had done. His words faltered. "He is gone, Little Star. The jade amulet, it is also gone."

"No!" she protested. "No, he lives; his pulse, his heart still beats. He is still with us." Siu-Sing did not recognize her own voice as it whispered such desperate words.

"It is the ginseng, Little Star. . . . the root of heaven." The Forceful One spoke quietly, eager to explain the mystery of this terrible thing. "He drank the ginseng tea every day of his life . . . the finest only he could find. It sustained him to a great longevity. I believe he had lived more than ninety years, perhaps more than one hundred, yet was ever young. It is said the mandrake root contains great magic and can sustain the life-force after the spirit has flown . . . sometimes for many moments, even more than an hour."

"Is there breath? Can you feel or hear his breathing?"

Siu-Sing placed the back of her hand under the master's nose, holding it there for countless moments. There was nothing but stillness and the sobs that shook her soul. Ah-Keung straightened up and waited, allowing the first moments of shock to pass. "The reed-cutters have no respect for such as our *si-fu*; they see only the sorcerer and the alchemist. They were afraid of him, but still they sent their snot-nosed brats to steal herbs from the shed."

Ah-Keung reached out to gently close the *si-fu*'s eyes, covering his face with the bearskin. "There is no way of knowing if they, or some passing trapper, had a hand in this . . . or if his time had come join his ancestors." He shrugged his shoulders sadly. "Perhaps he was not meant to leave this place he loved so much. It is something we will never know."

CHAPTER 24

The World Beyond the Mountains

Dressed in the clothes of a Tanka boat boy, with her hair hidden under a bell-shaped wicker hat, Siu-Sing found herself on the cluttered deck of a junk sailing from Tung-Ting Lake to the mouth of the Yangtze and the port of Macao. She could scarcely believe that so much could change so quickly.

After the death of Master To, Ah-Keung had toiled ceaselessly beside her to build a tomb worthy of so great a man, next to his cousin's grave in the Place of Clear Water. He had wept and fallen to his knees at the tomb, his prayers for forgiveness loud and long. Siu-Sing could find no such tears, only a strange and painful hardening of her senses. A part of her heart closed around his vital memory, sealing all that she had known of him and all that she had learned from him completely and forever. Watching the Forceful One, she did not see the warrior, but the crippled boy who had crossed the lake in search of his salvation. For a few moments they had shared each other's pain.

Siu-Sing did not know what to do. She had dreamed that she and her *si-fu* would find the man in the faded photograph, that they would enter his house together and remain there in peace and happiness. To stay alone in the hut by the lake would end her quest before it had begun; yet to face a world unknown to her without her master by her side was more than she could imagine.

The night had passed without sleep. Siu-Sing visited the Rock of Great Strength alone for the first time. Under a waning moon, she traveled with her *si-fu* on the last great flight of his journey, to see him united with his cousin; then rose to meet the sun. For an hour she performed the ritual dance of the Crane and the Tiger with his bright spirit by her side, while Paw-Paw dozed in the Place of Clear Water. She completed every step, leap, and kick, every sweep, block, and strike with the precision and power of perfection only a decade of training under the greatest of all masters could make possible. This would be the memory she would take with her to the other side of the mountains.

As she concluded with a salute to the sun, the sound of slow clapping made her whirl to meet the intruder. Ah-Keung stepped from the cover of the mimosa bush. "Forgive me if I invade your privacy. I see my master found a true disciple when the goat boy failed him." He bowed, but in the way of challenge, not respect, then changed his tone. "I came to tell you the reed boat will soon be ready to cross the lake, but I could not disturb such an adept."

The humble boy whose tears had been shed so convincingly in the Place of Clear Water had quickly flown. It was Ah-Keung, the Forceful One, who stood before her. "You cannot remain here alone now that they are gone. I can help to fulfill their promise: I have found you a berth aboard the junk that will take us to the port of Macao."

He had tossed a bundle of boy's clothing at her feet. "You must wear these. To be seen as a cherry girl on such a journey is unwise." He laughed unpleasantly. "You should thank me, Little Star; it is not easy to find passage on a junk already crowded. My place has been booked for many days, but the junk master has agreed to take you as a favor to me.

"Macao is only an hour by boat from the Golden Hill. I am known there and have friends who will give us food and shelter. Trust me, together we will find your father's house." He had turned to go back to the hut. "We must take only those things we need; the river has more thieves than fishes."

She followed him across the slope, unable to ignore the strange swing of his step, as though one foot was a little heavier than the other, creating a slight imbalance. For that fraction of time, she realized, she was looking at him with the eye of a warrior seeking a weakness in an opponent.

Inside the hut, Ah-Keung had tapped the chest of stone beneath the master's bed with the toe of his boot. "You have been shown the puzzle of the locks. We must open it and take what silver we can find." When she hesitated, he grinned at her foolishness. "Did you think this journey was a gift, that you did not have to pay the junk master for a week on the river to Shanghai and almost two on the open sea to Macao? You have been cared for for too long, my Little Star; the world beyond the mountains takes everything and gives nothing. You must be prepared."

"There is no silver in the chest, only books and papers of no value to a junk master."

Ah-Keung had shown no anger, but gestured helplessly. "Then I must leave without you and work for my passage. The plank boat waits to cross the lake, and the junk will sail at noon." He had turned to leave.

"Stay here alone and let the reed-cutters take the chest, along with the herbs and everything else they may find. They think this place evil and you a demon. Now that he's gone, they will burn this hut with you inside it."

Having no doubt that he was right, Siu-Sing had pulled the chest from beneath the bed, twisting the metal pins until the lock was released, then lifting the lid and removing the beaded sling. "You see . . . there are some small worthless things belonging to the old one, and the master's words and images."

"And in the pretty bag, what is hidden there?"

She showed him the two books tied in silk. "Small things left to me by my mother, of value only to me."

He rummaged in the bag, finding the bamboo canister and shaking it against his ear. "What is this?"

"Just a case for my brushes and ink blocks."

Ah-Keung had tossed it back into the bag, lifting out the photograph. "And the picture frame? Is it not made of silver?" She had removed the photograph from its silver frame without complaint; if it could help to begin her journey and take his mind from the scrolls, then this was a good thing. If he could read, he might have guessed their true value.

When he had gone, she lifted the canister, wrapped it well, and hidden it carefully in the bottom of the bag.

⊁⊰

Unaccustomed to the closeness of crowds, the unclean habits of too many people in too small a space for too long a time, Siu-Sing sought a place on the deck where curious eyes could not surround her. Among tethered livestock and crates of poultry at the very front of the bow, she made a space large enough to curl up in a coil of mooring rope, and there she stayed, pulling a canvas cover over her head as night closed around her.

At dawn, still hidden as far forward in the bow as she could get, she watched the green and yellow eddies of the passing river with a clean wind upon her face. Orange and cherry orchards reached the water's edge, the neat green tiers of rice terraces sliding by with the steady roll of the junk. From a precarious towpath hacked from the cliff face, strings of trackers shouldered the heavy towrope with echoing chants, hauling loaded sampans through the gorges.

There was little for the crew to do while the junk was under tow. They found entertainments of their own on deck—playing cards, rolling dice, drinking cheap wine, and smoking green tobacco. Ah-Keung had made his place among them; she was glad he seldom bothered her but also glad to be under his protection. She was not afraid of the crew, but saw no sense in wasting her chi on those who could not clean themselves and behaved like monkeys in a breadfruit tree.

The second evening, Ah-Keung was heading a group of men who found him to be lively company. There was the hollow rattle of dice and much beseeching of the gods of fortune, much drinking of wine and many whoops and curses. Siu-Sing could hear the Forceful One commanding those about him with reckless confidence.

She lifted the canvas enough to see the group, squatting in a circle around a pressure lamp, its stark glare lighting the ring of faces. A large wine jar was passed around; tobacco smoke drifted about them. The raised voices were coarse and the language crude, the voice of an older man rising among them like the snarl of a wolf.

307

"You are lucky for a lame dog, good only to lick the feet of monks and follow goats." For a moment, there was no response, but the voice persisted, becoming more belligerent as others fell quiet. "Are you not the dog boy, whose cur of a mother dropped him among unwanted whelps who sniffed the gutters for food?"

When Ah-Keung finally spoke, it was as though he addressed a passing shadow, cocking a hand to his ear.

"I think I hear a voice . . . or was it the fart of a donkey that so befouls the air? Let him stand, that we can see if his balls are as big as his mouth."

"If I stand, dog boy, it will be to teach a yapping pup to know its place. My name is Xiang the tracker; a name you will not forget if you cause me to find my feet." The drunken voice continued. "I hear you also slept outside the hut of Old To with the chickens and the goats, because he found you unworthy to be his disciple." The tracker was goaded further by a ripple of laughter that spread across the lamp-lit deck. "He found more promise in an infant child . . . a *jarp-jung* girl taken from its cradle. It was she and the Tanka hag who shared your place in his house and enjoyed the protection of his ghostly powers."

The ripple broke in a crescendo of raucous laughter. The tracker stood up, a short man with the thick neck and short arms of brute strength, beaming with the victory of clumsy wit. "But Old To is sent to hell like the witch who went before him. Did the hungry dog have a hand in this—did it bite the hand of its master? Is it money from the chest of silver beneath the hermit's bed that brings such good fortune to the hand of a worthless cripple?"

"Old To had passed the time of his power, more than ninety years. He drank too much ginseng tea . . . it stopped his heart." Ah-Keung's reply was calm, its underlying menace lost in the rowdy crowd. Xiang the tracker was not satisfied.

"And the old witch who drowned in the marsh? They say she had no mark upon her, that she was a Tanka elder with the heart of a tiger defending its young. Women of the boat people do not die easily. What do you know of *that*, dog boy?

Again, Ah-Keung answered without a sign of concern. "She was his cousin, perhaps as old as he. She fished the reed beds every day and prayed to all gods with every breath. Perhaps it was her time to meet them. There are worse ways to die than chasing shrimp in shallow water."

It was still not enough for the tracker, who stepped into the circle. "And the demon *jarp-jung*—" He paused to hawk loudly, spitting at Ah-Keung's feet. "The one with the eyes of death that you have brought aboard the junk hiding under a Tanka's hat . . ." He folded his corded forearms across the breadth of his chest. "Did you think we did not know?"

Xiang hitched up his belt in a drunken gesture of bravado, aware of his audience. "I will find the bitch and fuck her before I throw her over the side. We will not have the company of demons aboard this boat."

The deck crew cheered him on. No one saw the foot of the dog boy strike the tracker's chest with a side kick that split his sternum with a meaty click; the big man was lifted from the deck to fly over the wooden taffrail, his legs buckling as he disappeared into darkness.

The splash of his bulk hitting the water was lost in a roar of approval. No one moved to raise the alarm. The tracker was a bully, best left to battle the river alone . . . but they feared Ah-Keung, the Forceful One, even more.

"Donkey-fart was right, the one who travels with me is Red Lotus, disciple of To-Tze, grand master of White Crane *wu-shu*. She is under my protection." He grinned around the ring of faces. "But perhaps I protect *you* from *her* . . . there is not a man aboard that she would not make a fool of."

Ah-Keung's shock of coal-black hair seemed to bristle like the hackles on the neck of a dog aroused to action. "If she is touched, this twisted foot will find you and you will swim to Wuhan with the tracker." He looked around at the silent faces, grinning. "Now, let us throw the dice and see where they fall."

⁂

In the days along the coast and through the Formosa Strait, Siu-Sing pondered the question of Ah-Keung. That night the men had gambled until the first signs of sunrise, and slept where they lay. The junk had left the gorges and their treacherous waters, and hoisted the huge, mud-colored sails. She stood upright in the prow as daylight swept the river with watery sunshine, to see the white dolphins of the Yangtze spearing the bow wave, and breathe the breeze across the choppy yellow waters.

Ah-Keung had spoken convincingly in her defense; he had seen her fed well from the crew's galley, and made sure she was left in peace. He had already found work on the Gum Sarn, he said, and a place to stay. Yes, he knew people who would help her find her father. His manner was sincere, and she had seen how greatly the death of Master To had affected him. But she realized there was much she did not know about the Forceful One, who would forever wear the snarl of the tiger on his chest and the venom of the cobra on his back.

⁂

Amid a colony of sampans and cargo scows so packed you could walk from one to the other, they sailed slowly into Macao's typhoon shelter. Siu-Sing found it best to avoid the eyes of those who turned her way. Some swore, some laughed, others sneered, but none said welcome. She fought her creeping fear in the only way she knew, making it her enemy and raising a wall around her heart, with every rampart guarded. She did not join the loud-voiced people crowding the decks, herding noisy children, hoisting baggage in feverish haste to disembark. Instead, she waited in the bow for the bedlam to pass.

The junk closed slowly with the wharf, rats skittering among barnacle-encrusted pilings, pigeons hovering for spilled grain. Never in the solitude of the lake-lands had Siu-Sing felt so alone or helpless. Ah-Keung shouted to her across the deck: "Why are you hiding up there? Come and see the world beyond the mountains."

Ah-Keung shouldered his bundle, ready to stride down the narrow gangplank. Securing the sling, the *er-hu* slung like a sword across her back, Siu-Sing hastened to join him, jostled and cursed in a sea of hostile humanity beyond anything she had imagined.

310

"This is the wondrous city of Macao, where all things are possible." He turned to her, his eyes shining with a new zeal, as one who had known hunger and was about to enjoy a feast.

"It is called the city of broken promises. It is where the rich *gwai-lo* keeps his mistress, then sails away and leaves her with a broken heart. The place where the taipans come to roll the dice and smoke the pipe. They pay well for pretty girls."

He giggled at the thought, quick to reassure her when she did not speak.

"The Golden Hill lies close across the water. I shall go there to find out what I can and return to take you to your father's door."

"I must come with you . . . ," she began.

"No, I have found a safe place for you here. There is nowhere for us to stay on the Golden Hill. I will go first and return for you."

He left no room for more to be said as the gangplank bounced beneath their feet.

❉

They threaded through the godowns, quickly leaving the noise and stink of the waterfront behind; along cobbled streets and narrow lanes, past sawmills and metal shops, purveyors of meat and fish, coffin makers and joss houses. Curbside vendors peddled their goods and beggars muttered at their passing. They walked for perhaps a half a mile.

Ah-Keung stopped outside a pair of towering iron gates topped with sharpened spikes, The tidal stink of the waterfront had given way to the stench of the slaughterhouse. Dreadful squeals came from behind high walls; bricks so old and scarred that weeds sprouted from every crack were crowned with shards of jagged glass. Above the gates, in a bent and buckled arch of hammered steel, large painted characters spelled the words in red: DOUBLE HAPPINESS.

Ah-Keung tugged hard on an iron ring set into the wall, setting off a grinding of chain somewhere inside and the rusty croak of a bell. "This is the House of Double Happiness, the palace of Fan-Lu-Wei, one who

311

was once a red-button mandarin of the ninth grade," he said with great respect. "A most important and very rich man here in Macao. We are fortunate that he has agreed to help you."

A slot in the gate revealed a reddened eye that swam like a fish in a bowl. A voice, harsh with suspicion, demanded to know their business. Ah-Keung shouted his name, placing a protective arm about Siu-Sing's shoulders as bolts were drawn and one of the gates dragged partway open.

"Don't worry, Little Star," he whispered hurriedly. "You will be given good rice and a place to sleep. Be respectful to Lord Fan; do not forget to bow and you will be treated well."

"He will help to find my father?"

"Yes, yes, Lord Fan is known to all. If your barbarian father exists, he will know of it."

He gestured for her to enter the half-open gate. "Be patient, Little Star. You will be safe here. I will always know where you are, and when your rich father is found, I will claim my reward."

The gate closed with an echoing boom, trapping Siu-Sing inside, with Ah-Keung no longer beside her. She heard his laughter with a flush of shame. How easy it had been to betray her.

CHAPTER 25

The House of Double Happiness

Siu-Sing *took in a* long stretch of cobbled courtyard faced by a row of low-roofed sheds. Pens of mud-caked pigs were crammed against towering walls that echoed with their squeals. Behind a hedge of flowering shrubs that separated it from the rest of the compound, Siu-Sing saw a garden surrounding a great house that reared over the yard with the aging columns and rotting eaves of a forgotten palace.

The man who had opened the gate grabbed her by the arm, peering at her with shortsighted impatience. Under his arm he carried a brass-tipped rod, worn smooth as ivory, mounted by the polished skull of a monkey. On his large ears rested a battered peaked cap bearing a Double Happiness badge. Dangling from the rope around his pinched gut hung a large ring of keys. To Siu-Sing, it seemed the odor of death and decay had found its source in him.

She allowed herself to be marched across the courtyard to a flight of steps where two stone Fu dogs, green with age, guarded the entrance to the house. The gatekeeper's hand twisted hard into her hair, wrenching her head back; her eyes closed tight against the glare of the sun overhead. She heard the sound of doors opening. Then, as unexpected as a kiss, a gentle hand, no more intrusive than the feet of a fly, caressed her chin, her cheek, her throat—turning her face first one way, then the other.

"There is no need to be afraid. Mr. Kwok means you no harm." The words were quietly spoken in a voice that could have been that of a man or woman. The smells of rich sauces on pungent breath and strong body odors were disguised by sickly-sweet perfume.

"Careful, Mr. Kwok. This pretty head is not the rear end of a donkey." The voice rose peevishly, punctuated by a delicate cough. Fan-Lu-Wei, once a mandarin, seemed to fill the entrance of his decaying mansion. His enormous body reclined on a throne of faded splendor; a quilted tunic of finely embroidered silk strained across his massive girth. A long gray gown almost reached his small feet, encased in white cotton stockings and black silk slippers. The mangy tail feather of a peacock was attached to a large bead of red glass set on the crown of his round black hat.

The hand that so lightly caressed her chin, soft and white as a woman's, trembled slightly. Long fingernails, shining with lacquer, grasped a switch of white horsehair attached to a jeweled handle, which he flicked at flies attracted by his perfumed finery. A cream-colored Pekingese sleeve dog grumbled from the security of his lap, shoe-button eyes glistening with malice. There were dark pouches beneath Fan-Lu-Wei's narrow eyes that powder could not hide. *He is ill*, Siu-Sing thought. *His liver is not good.*

He smiled down at her with mild approval, his pudgy cheeks white as lard. Several long black hairs sprouted from a mole on his chin the size of a stranded cockroach, straggling down to lie among the ropes of colored beads on the slope of his chest. Two spindly mustaches drooped on either side of his weak, pink mouth. He looked, Siu-Sing decided, like an ailing Buddha.

Behind him stood two white-jacketed amahs, each wafting a large goose-feather fan. They were short and squat as wrestlers, their round heads sunk into sloping shoulders, graying hair drawn back and wound into a tight bun held in place by identical jade combs. Each wore a jade bangle on the left wrist, a jade ring on the right hand, and a jade talisman on a headband of black silk in the center of the forehead. *They are strong*, Siu-Sing concluded, *but also heavy, too well fed for speed and stamina.*

"You may leave her in my care now, Mr. Kwok," Fan-Lu-Wei wheezed, then turned to Siu-Sing. "There is nothing to fear. Our poor gatekeeper was only earning his rice. Come, the jade amahs will show you your place." The throne began to turn around on wooden wheels that groaned beneath his weight.

"Your brother has told me his sad story and signed the *sung-tip*—you are fortunate to have such a loving brother so concerned for the welfare of his little sister. He has sold you to me as Number-Two *mooi-jai*, to save your family from starvation. Yes, you are most fortunate to have been brought here to the House of Double Happiness."

Siu-Sing backed away from the unsmiling amahs, remembering to bow and show respect as Master To had taught her.

"Forgive me, but the one who brought me here is not my brother; he has deceived you, as he has deceived me."

The piping voice cut her short. "Do not deny the care of an elder brother and question your good fortune. You will obey the jade amahs, or they have my permission to beat you."

"But you can see, my lord, I am not of his blood or his clan. I have white ancestors as well as Chinese. My father is a foreign sea captain, a taipan of the silk and tea trade. He seeks me and will pay many taels of silver for my safe return. He is known as Di-Fo-Lo. Help me to find him, my lord, and he will be most generous."

Fat Fan belched uncomfortably, his thin black brows drawn together in a frown of annoyance. "I know nothing of that. The *sung-tip* is signed and witnessed and the price paid. You belong to me now. If you do your work, do not steal, do not complain, tell no more lies, and cause no trouble, you will be treated well. If you are ungrateful and displease the jade amahs, they will report it to me and you will wish you had never entered the gates of Double Happiness."

He gestured fretfully with the fly switch and the throne continued to turn. "If your *gwai-lo* father comes to find you, we will talk business. Until then, you are Number-Two *mooi-jai*. We will have no more nonsense about rich foreign devils."

As the rumbling wheels trundled into the gloom, Siu-Sing followed the amahs, the steady *squeak, squeak, squeak* of the wheeled throne

315

leading the way through a beaded curtain that opened upon an ante-room made entirely of dingy glass and filled with the twittering, chirp-ing, warbling, and full-throated singing of birds. Cages of every shape and size were suspended among glazed dragon pots filled with flower-ing plants. From their tiny prisons, the birds chattered and trilled in ceaseless disharmony. Siu-Sing was instantly transported to the bam-boo groves high on the slopes of Tung-Ting, and for a moment her heart ached for the Place of Clear Water.

Seated among them in a peacock chair was a woman, thin and gaunt, her hunched shoulders hung with a padded jacket of black silk and a layer of woolen shawls. One hand clutched them close about her throat, while the other dabbed a handkerchief to her mouth. Her voice crackled with anger, forced from her with labored breath. "So, you have found yourself another alley cat."

The heavy pouch of flesh that hung from Fan's dimpled chin trem-bled as he replied feebly, "A *mooi-jai*, a homeless child for the scullery." He held up one hand, its fat fingers glittering with rings. "A bargain, my flower of flowers, only fifty Hong Kong dollars."

"Wasted money, brains of a horny goat." She waved a dismissive hand, snuffling her contempt, then collapsed in a fit of coughing. "See that she does not eat too much and is kept to the kitchen, or she will feel the rod of Ah-Kwok."

※

Siu-Sing was put to work among oily woks and endless baskets of vege-tables in the great echoing kitchen. Sides of bacon, cured hams, and pickled pigs' heads hung from the ceiling, together with ropes of garlic, bunches of dried herbs, and rows of cured ducks. Ah-Soo, the cook, showed Siu-Sing her sleeping place adjoining the storeroom. The wooden stretcher that was her bed was covered with a thin quilt. A cal-endar hung on one wall, the only touch of brightness in a confined and windowless space. A single candlestick threw unsteady light into cor-ners stacked with sacks of rice and baskets of vegetables, shelves crammed with earthen pots and jars of wine, pickles, and preserves.

A smoke-blackened image of Tsao-Wang, the kitchen god beside his heavenly horse, looked down from its grimy niche—the sole witness to the hiding place Siu-Sing found for the Tanka sling. On the first night in this new place so far from all she had known, she held the orange-peel finger jade tightly in the palm of her hand and sought the voice of Master To and the twinkling eye of the Fish. They were instantly with her, reminding her that they had taught her not to let obstacles or treachery stand in her way.

By the light of the candle, she considered her position. Restricted to the kitchen and its small yard, the jade amahs ever watchful, she would not escape easily. The walls of Double Happiness were unassailable, the gates locked and guarded. Ah-Kwok the gatekeeper and his monkey-skull rod would welcome any attempt to evade them. This was a time for observation, for patience and strategy.

One of Siu-Sing's duties as *mooi-jai* was to be Fan Lu-Wei's official food taster. In the small private room where he who was once a mandarin took his meals, he watched impatiently as the array of dishes was laid before her on a side table. Beside them, resting upon an ivory tablet, was a pair of silver chopsticks. Under the watchful eyes of the jade amahs she was ordered to use the chopsticks to taste a single mouthful from each dish. The chopsticks were thin and heavy to her fingers, the food like none she had known but filled with rich and pleasant flavors as she chewed and swallowed each morsel. This done, she was sent back to the kitchen without a further word.

"He is a cautious man," Ah-Soo said when Siu-Sing returned in some confusion. "It was the way of all mandarins to have their food tasted by one whose life was of no importance. Chopsticks of solid silver will turn black if they touch the slightest impurity." The cook laughed secretively. "Don't worry, I will not poison him, and neither will the jade amahs as long as he pays them well. He eats apart from Madam Fan and the rest of his family because he thinks some of them would kill him for his fortune."

Siu-Sing fetched water from the pump, prepared vegetables, cleaned cooking pots, scrubbed tables, and mopped floors. She worked hard and without complaint, learning much from Ah-Soo, who soon recognized a trusted ear and was glad of her company. The cook spoke cautiously of Fat Fan, as though listening for the creak of his wheeled throne, or the soft footfall of the jade amahs.

"He who was once a mandarin is no longer seen as one of noble birth and great power. Now he is a dealer in offal and dead flesh, as bloated as the pigs he fattens. How proud he is to be the greatest of all sausage makers. His secret family recipe makes the great Fan-Lu-Wei one of the richest merchants in Macao.

"Those sacred hairs that sprout from his chin," she whispered, "are his heavenly luck—given him, he believes, by Lu-Hsing, the star god of affluence. He bathes them three times a day in oil of roses; and at festival time, on the birthday of the star god, they are coated in liquid gold." Ah-Soo tossed a sizzling wok on her roaring stove. "Fat Fan lives only to eat, drink brandy, fornicate, and smoke the pig-bone pipe."

They were seated on the kitchen doorstep, drinking tea in a moment of rest. Ah-Soo's voice took on a tone of closest confidence. "I neither believe nor disbelieve your story of the rich taipan you seek. Our past and our future should be our own affair and not the business of others. But even such as we are entitled to our dreams."

Ah-Soo paused for a moment, tossing a handful of grain to the chickens pecking for worms among the cabbages. "Did the one who claimed to be your brother speak the truth . . . that you are untouched?"

Siu-Sing could only nod her head. "I am from Lake Tung-Ting in Hunan. I have lived my life protected by two who loved me. I know nothing of men and before leaving had met none but my master and the one who betrayed me. But it is true; my father is a foreign taipan and I have come to find him on the Golden Hill."

"Then be ready. Fat Fan will send for you; it is his way with all *mooi-jai*. Because he owns your *sung-tip*, he also owns your body and your soul . . . but there is a way to use them in your favor. I have seen a dozen girls no older than you come and go through those iron gates. If they pleased him well, their lives were bearable, but when he tired of them he sold them as I would sell a chicken or a duck."

Ah-Soo looked over her shoulder, to check that they were truly alone. "Listen to me carefully; we cannot speak of this again. Fat Fan is stupid and lazy; he seldom leaves this place. The making of sausages is left to Ah-Kwok, Keeper of the Gate. Business matters are in the hands of Fan-Tai, the first wife, who dies slowly from consumption. He is afraid of her and awaits her death with great impatience. The pipe has taken his courage as surely as the fall of the Ching has taken his dignity, and he is easily beaten. He would not know a jewel's value if it were held in the palm of his greedy hand."

Ah-Soo lowered her voice still further. "There is one in this city of Macao who seeks such jewels in many distant places, and is an expert in their valuation. She has grown rich in gold five times her weight, they say, and to those who matter, she is also widely respected. She is known to them as Tamiko-san, the Golden One, who owns the Tavern of Cascading Jewels. She will pay well for one as rare as you."

"How can this help me to find my father?"

Ah-Soo's reply was mildly impatient. "The Tavern of Cascading Jewels is the most famous opium house in all Macao. Only the richest taipans rest upon its golden divans and enjoy the favors of its precious jewels."

"Are there foreigners—those of Western blood—among these taipans? Would I meet such people; could I speak to them? Could they lead me to my father?"

Ah-Soo thought for a moment, uncertain of the answer. "I am a worthless woman who has known little of the things you seek—the love and care of a family, a home and a future. I have nothing left to search for, but I see in you the light of hope. I cannot tell you who you may find or who you may not. I only know that I have heard in the market that men of power and great wealth seek the treasures of the tavern. Those that live on the Golden Hill of Hong Kong trust Tamiko-san with their secrets."

Ah-Soo stood up to empty her cup among the cabbages and stretch her back. "I am not usually one to give advice." She sighed wearily. "One stove is the same as another, and I am too old and too ugly for anything else. But you are young, and if what you say is true, your future may be one of great fortune. You are *jarp-jung*, different in every way, and I do not envy you the way ahead . . . but I will tell what I know of escape. You must decide what you will."

⚓

According to the kitchen calendar, Siu-Sing had been in the House of Double Happiness for three weeks when, without warning, the jade amahs came to fetch her. It was late, after a sumptuous dinner had been tasted and eaten. She was told to wash herself, given a simple robe of white cotton to wear and nothing more, then led without further word to the private chambers of Fan-Lu-Wei.

The corridor was stuffy with the trapped smells of food and absence of air, dimly lit by gaslights. Siu-Sing was not afraid, but ready to face the test to come.

"It is the new *mooi-jai*, Lo-Yeh." One of the amahs spoke quietly into the shadows, the other silently crossing to the shrine of a reclining Buddha bathed in bloodred light. With great care, a blindfold was tied around its all-seeing eyes. With three deep bows, the amahs left, softly closing the door.

A gas lamp shed patterns of colored light upon the walls of the half-dark room that was heady with opium smoke. "There is no need to be afraid." The thin, feminine voice of he who was once a mandarin reached out to her. "The gods cannot see us. This room is for moments of harmless pleasure. Come, let me see you. I have pickled ginger and plump dates."

The sickly sweetness of the smoke found Siu-Sing's throat. She hesitated, her stomach uneasy, the steady hiss of the gas mantle and the wheeze of his heavy breathing the only sounds.

As her eyes grew accustomed to the dim light, she saw the richly curtained comfort of a divan in the center of the room. Splotches of moving color shivered over the mound of Fat Fan's naked body. Propped on a pile of cushions, the folds of his flesh formed grotesque contours, his wasted legs tucked beneath him and his face in shadow, oily smoke curling from a long-stemmed pipe.

320

"Take off the gown and let me see what treasures I have purchased," he wheedled, setting aside the pipe on an ornate stand. Siu-Sing paused to choose her words carefully.

"May I speak, Lo-Yeh? I have thought much upon this great honor and wish to see that it is to your greatest benefit. . . . I have a warning that must be heard. Your *tai-tai*, sir, what would she do if she was aware of your attentions to one so unworthy as I?"

He seemed not to hear her, his hand reaching for a sticky morsel from a dish at his side. "Troublesome *mooi-jai* are often known to seduce their masters, to gain favor over worn-out wives and tiresome concubines. So I suggest you curb your questions before I tire of them, and take off the gown." He offered her a date, popping it into his mouth when she made no move to take it, the stone slipping from his pursed lips like a maggot.

"My honorable wives would not like it at all if I were disobeyed." He giggled unpleasantly. "They care little who visits my divan so long as it is not them I call upon." He chewed noisily, sucking his fingers. "So we must see that they do not hear of it or you will be flogged by Ah-Kwok. Enough prattle; come closer." His hand closed tightly over her wrist, forcing her hand toward his doughy thighs.

"Wait, Lo-Yeh. I beg you to hear me. I am different from others honored by your interest in the past. I speak the truth. As you can see, I am of mixed blood. . . . I am *jarp-jung*, worthless in the eyes of many, but priceless in the eyes of some as long as I am untouched. If you take my innocence, it will bring you no more than a moment's pleasure." She waited, her words hanging in a tense moment of silence. "But you could sell my *sung-tip* for ten times the price you paid for it."

The grip on her wrist tightened, forcing her closer. "And who will pay such a high price for a *jarp-jung* who claims to be the daughter of a foreign devil?"

His words were impatient as his bulk heaved upon her trapped hand. "The Golden One . . . she will pay. Sell me, Lo-Yeh, to the Tavern of Cascading Jewels."

It was clear he had smoked so much opium that his thinking was unclear, his desires stronger than reason. Yet she persisted. "My services as a *mooi-jai* are of no importance and easily found. Let the Golden One decide my price. If it is not enough or she finds me of no value, I will serve you well and give no further trouble.

"I warn you, Lo-Yeh, these eyes that look upon you are the eyes of death and destruction. The man that takes me will be cursed forever with bad luck." He did not hear her, his hands groping clumsily, his breath escaping like steam.

Siu-Sing reacted swiftly, grasping the straggle of hairs that sprouted from his chin. They came away in her hand as Fat Fan rolled crashing to the floor with a piercing squeal.

✷

Siu-Sing sat straight backed on the edge of a black-wood chair, hands folded in her lap. She had been primped and powdered, stroked and smoothed as though awaiting audience with an empress. The jade amahs had wound her hair in the two circular plaits favored by Macao's concubines of substance. From her ears, two teardrop pearls shivered at her slightest motion. They had dressed her in a rustling gown of emerald-green silk, tinted her lips deep red and her brows and lashes coal black. Scented powder extended to her throat and the swell of her breasts.

Bedecked in the full regalia of the imperial court, he who was once a mandarin fussed about her, perspiring freely under the magnificence of his raiment. "You will sit still and say nothing unless you are told to. She who comes to look at you will have none of your insolence. If you fail to please her, you will be given to Ah-Kwok and nothing will save you."

Tamiko-san, the Golden One, arrived in a splendid palanquin carried by four uniformed footmen. She hurried up the steps with a handkerchief pressed to her nose. A woman of average height, her catlike body was sheathed in a cheongsam of black silk, its high collar emphasizing her long neck and tiny, gold-studded ears, the only break in its severity a single peony flower fashioned in gold high on her breast.

Her hair was piled high in the way of the Japanese *mama-san*, held in place by combs and decorations that were also of gold. More gold adorned her wrists and fingers, the long curved nails sheathed and glittering. Her face told nothing of her age, only the grace of her movement suggesting a feline strength. *She is both yin and yang*, Sing thought. *Both sun and moon, night and day, or good and bad.*

Tamiko-san's eyes were hooded by flat upper lids, as carefully lined with kohl as her perfect brows, as they peered over a large fan of black lacquer ribbed with silver. Siu-Sing felt no fear of her close scrutiny, although the Golden One displayed nothing of the instant approval Fat Fan had clearly hoped for. She stood before Siu-Sing, her head tilted, her eyes the color of frozen honey. Siu-Sing had seen such eyes before, when a river hawk settled on the gunwale of the reed-cutters' boat long enough to swallow a live fish whole. For just that fraction of time, its golden eye had looked into hers, neither afraid nor threatening—*I am here and so are you*. Now such an eye found her again.

"Is she not splendid as the rising phoenix?" Fat Fan twittered eagerly. "Soft as the throat of a turtledove? Firm as a spring peach, white as ginger blossom, and gentle as a fawn?"

The Golden One ignored him, saying to Siu-Sing, "Stand up, if you will." Her voice was not unkind. Siu-Sing did as she was asked.

"Did I not tell you? Am I not correct?" Fat Fan insisted.

The Golden One cast him a withering glance. "You must think me a fool. This girl is of mixed blood." She turned, closing the black fan with a snap as though to leave. "Few men would find her pleasing. She has the hands and feet of a field hand. Her eyes are round as leeches and pale as dishwater. She is not white as ginger blossom—the powder ends at her throat, and she has the skin of a tinker. You have wasted my time."

Siu-Sing held her breath, while a large pearl of sweat escaped from beneath Fat Fan's black silk hat. "Ah, but to an enlightened one who seeks the mysterious, the extraordinary, and the untouched"—his pink mouth quivered—"to a man of taste, she will be priceless as a pink finger jade."

Tamiko-san's eyes fixed unsmilingly on the maker of sausages. "Untouched? Since when have the *mooi-jai* of your house remained untouched?"

Fan raised his hands in feeble protest. "She has only been under this unworthy roof for three weeks. I swear by all gods, this exquisite crea-ture has not been tampered with."

The Golden One's gaze remained fixed upon his perspiring face. "Not once? You should know I am no dealer in secondhand goods, so be sure of what you say to me."

The contempt in her voice brought pink spots to his cheeks. "One light touch, less than a moment of sheer enchantment; I was most care-ful. On the word of my ancestors, she is pure as a lily not yet opened by the morning sun."

"It is true, madam; he has not taken me. He is too fat to try. It was I who tore the threads of fortune from his chin to avoid his sweaty hands." The sound of Siu-Sing's voice was so unexpected, Fat Fan blushed red with fury. He would have struck her if the Golden One had not leaned forward with renewed interest.

"Let her speak. I will hear what she has to say."

"Thank you, madam," Siu-Sing said. "I cannot see you deceived as I have been deceived. I was brought here by treachery, sold to this house as *mooi-jai* for fifty Hong Kong dollars by one who claimed to be my brother. I am no *mooi-jai*; I can read and write and play the *er-hu*. If you take me, madam, I promise to become your brightest jewel."

While Fat Fan searched for words, the Golden One counted out the price of the *sung-tip*. Moments later, Sing left the gates of Double Happi-ness, exactly as she had entered them—the Tanka sling fastened on her back, the *er-hu* in its velvet sleeve across her shoulder. She stepped into the palanquin, to be carried away on a perfumed cloud—contented with the thought that her last act as *mooi-jai* in the House of Double Happiness had been to open the door of every cage in the anteroom and watch the birds spiral through an open fanlight into the clear blue sky.

CHAPTER 26

The Tavern of Cascading Jewels

The crimson moon gates of the Tavern of Cascading Jewels seemed as welcoming to Siu-Sing as the towering walls of Double Happiness had been forbidding. Solid as a fort, the grand old establishment was set among cedar and juniper trees of great age, towering giants that jealously guarded its privacy. The building combined the yellowed stones, stained-glass windows, and arched, heavily carved doors of a Lisbon tavern with the red-tiled roof, upswept eaves, and ornately carved pillars of the Summer Palace.

A cobbled bridge spanned a waterway so filled with lilies and teeming with fish that Sing felt she could have walked upon it. Swans groomed themselves along its banks, while mandarin ducks ruffled their brightly colored feathers on small rocky islands. Peacocks roamed beneath the dark green skirts of the cedars. Through the boughs of the trees, Siu-Sing glimpsed secluded pavilions set in gardens beside ornamental ponds.

A peony tree of great age spread a canopy of bloodred blooms the size of rice bowls above the tavern's entrance, where an elderly gardener was whisking a carpet of fallen petals from the steps with a willow-twig broom.

The reception hall was pleasantly cooled by slow-turning ceiling fans. Stately furniture stood in every well-lit corner, and paintings of great value looked down from their heavily gilded frames. Three doorways led from the vestibule, each heavily draped in burgundy velvet. Above them in a place of honor, Giu-Choy-Fut—the everlastingly jolly god of

325

earthly pleasures—reclined in his scarlet shrine, incense smoldering at his feet.

Curtains parted to admit a dark-skinned woman. A robe of rose-colored silk, so fine it drifted with every graceful movement, was wound around her shapely body and over her shoulder, leaving her small waist and the slight swell of her belly exposed. Through a gossamer veil that covered half of the woman's oval face, Siu-Sing could see dark shining hair and large round eyes of startling gray. Between strong black brows a single jewel, red as a droplet of blood, was suspended by a golden chain. An elusive perfume accompanied her, along with the slightest tinkling from an anklet of tiny silver bells. Her small feet were bare, their toenails tinted the same rose pink as her robe.

"This is Ruby, my head pipe-maker—the best and most gifted of her kind in all Macao," the madam said amiably. "In Hong Kong and Shanghai too, I have no doubt."

The pipe-maker's luminous eyes fell upon Siu-Sing. *She is not Chinese*, Siu-Sing thought, returning her serious, unblinking gaze. *There is something about her that is different from others—as different as I am thought to be.* The notion was strangely pleasing.

"This poor girl comes to us from cruel and stupid people," the Golden One said to Ruby. "Her street name is Siu-Sing. She has no one to care for her. See that she is bathed, fed, and allowed to rest."

Sing felt she must speak at this. "Forgive me, madam, but I have spoken the truth. I am the daughter of a great and famous taipan. His name among the Cantonese is Di-Fo-Lo; to the foreigner he is Devereaux. My father can be found on the Golden Hill. I have his picture and can assure you of a rich reward if he can be found."

Tamiko-san had stepped through the heavy drapes of the center arch, but turned back to glance at Sing. "We have all had a father and a mother somewhere, sometime, whether of this world or the next—but if we are lost to them we are left with nothing but dreams. Dreams are welcome here . . . but it is I who has fetched you from the hands of the sausage-maker, and I who paid well to own your *sung-tip*. This is the only truth."

The black fan spread wide with a flick of her wrist. "You have entered

326

the Tavern of Cascading Jewels through my opinion of your value. You have no past, only the future. This you must understand and never question." The fan fluttered harmlessly as the wings of a butterfly, and her voice was agreeable again. "Be grateful and light joss sticks to whatever god you pray to that it is I who found you in the place of pigs and not a whoremonger from Red Lantern Street, or a slave trader from Ling Nam. Now, go with Ruby. If she finds you worthy of my time, we will talk of such things."

The pipe-maker turned to lead the way, Sing following through paneled hallways softly lit by candelabras, doors on either side, carpet soft and silent underfoot. Ruby's calming voice was punctuated by the hypnotic jingling of her tread. "These are the quarters of the Silver Sisters, those who make the pipes and attend the sleeping dragons. You will meet them when you are rested and prepared."

Ruby's private room was small and simply furnished: a pair of four-poster canopied beds spread with brightly colored quilts, each curtained for privacy; a dressing table crowded with small personal things; two sets of drawers; a tall, hand-painted wardrobe; shelves filled with books and ornaments; and a divan scattered with bright cushions. On a low table of black lacquer stood a wooden bowl laden with fruit, a number of round bamboo food containers, and a pot warmer containing a teapot and two small cups.

In a corner something stood mysteriously apart, veiled in black silk. Sing wondered what it could be. Through the open window came the scent of wisteria, the murmur of doves, and the tinkling of prayer bells.

"You will stay here with me until Ah-Jin decides what your place will be." Ruby noticed Siu-Sing's confusion. "Ah-Jin is our name for Tamiko-san, the Golden One, who is our gracious mother. You will always address her as Mama-san." Siu-Sing knew the Cantonese word for gold was *qian*, and saw that this was a respectful abbreviation: "the Gold."

Ruby indicated the wardrobe with a nod of her head. "If you are to remain here, you will be given clothes and the things you will need. You may keep them in there with mine." She watched as Siu-Sing loosened the buckles and took the beaded sling from her back to place it carefully beside the *er-hu*. "I see you are a musician. This will be a good thing for you. Music is also an important part of pleasure in the eyes of Ah-Jin."

From a drawer, she took a folded cotton nightdress and towel, tossing them onto the bed nearest the window. "The things in this drawer are for you until you are properly received. You may sleep in this bed; I have seen the trees and smelled the blossoms and listened to the mating of doves too often to notice them."

Opening an adjoining door, where a large round bathtub stood on clawed feet, the pipe-maker showed Siu-Sing how to turn the shiny brass taps to fill the bath with clean, fresh water heated to the touch of her hand, and how to sprinkle sweet-smelling oils into the steamy clouds. "To be clean at all times is the first rule. I will leave you to bathe and take some food, then rest. You will not be disturbed."

At the door she paused briefly. "Ah-Jin is the mother of reason unless you anger her—then she is the mother of fury." A smile touched the luster of the pipe-maker's eyes. "But you have nothing to fear. I will guide you gently and fairly; it will not take long to prove your worth. If you are obedient and deserving of her judgment and her trust, she will receive you kindly and your initiation will begin. If you are not"—she gave the slightest shrug—"then that will be a pity. Meanwhile, do not leave this room unless I accompany you."

The smile in her eyes seemed to deepen. "Sleep well; think only pleasant things. It is a great honor to be chosen by the Golden One."

The door was quietly closed, and Siu-Sing ate hungrily from a bowl of tasty noodles and flavored shreds of tender chicken kept warm in the bamboo steamers. She drank deeply from the pot of tea the pipe-maker had said would calm her and help her sleep. Dazed by her sudden change of fortune, she was soon lost among the wonders of her first bathtub, a mound of radiant bubbles at her fingertip's command.

※

She slept soundly until late the following morning. By the afternoon, Siu-Sing was eager to explore this place and learn what was expected of her.

Ruby brought a folded gown of lilac silk, along with two crystal flasks and two tiny, thimble-size cups beside a bamboo whisk on a lacquered tray. With a practiced flourish, she held the first flask high and allowed an exact measure of its golden liquid to half fill each cup. From the second flask, she added to the cups drop by drop, then whisked the contents with greatest care.

"This is the rarest of all tonics," she said, "once brewed only for emperors. . . . We call it Buddha Jumps Over the Fence. It is made from the buds of the wild Lohan tea bush found only in the mountains of Mongolia, sweetened by the nectar of persimmon, mixed with a single tear of the poppy. It is a potion known only to the *mama-san* to set the senses free."

Steadily, cradling one of the fragile cups in the fingertips of both hands, she handed it to Siu-Sing as though it were a droplet of pure gold. "Soon you will be expected to speak with Ah-Jin. Already I see in you many of the qualities required of a Silver Sister, so my judgment will be in your favor; but there are things locked in our hearts that should be freed. This will prepare you."

Ruby drained her cup with a single swallow, watching closely as Siu-Sing did the same. The liquor was sweet to the tongue, soothing her throat, its passage pleasantly warm until it blossomed in her belly, bringing a flush to her cheeks.

The pipe-maker watched closely for seconds more. Satisfied, she set the tray aside and presented the silk gown with both hands. "You are of mixed race, so the silk is from China, the design foreign. It is chosen for the color of your eyes and has only one purpose . . . to make you feel as beautiful as you look."

In a gesture of encouragement, she held up her arms to show the flowing drifts of her own garment. "I am from India; this garment I wear is called a sari, and my chosen gem is the ruby, the symbol of passionate love. Once you are accepted, there will be many splendid things for you to wear. The Silver Sisters are from many lands and wear the clothing of their homelands with pride. There is a seamstress of great skill who will come to fit you for all that you will need, and a doctor to see that you are well and vigorous. The Golden One takes great care of those who belong to her . . . no mother was ever more gracious." She draped the silken gown over Siu-Sing's arm. "Come, you must try it on. I will help you."

At Siu-Sing's slight hesitation, Ruby said gently, "You must never be ashamed to undress before me or any other in this house. It is an insult to the arts of pleasure that are taught and practiced here. To be proud of your body is of first importance. It is my duty to help prepare you." The pipe-maker's tone lifted to one of gentle teasing. "Now, let us see and feel the clay we have to work with in the making of a Silver Sister."

Siu-Sing allowed Ruby to remove the cotton shift; the pipe-maker tossed it aside and stepped back to see her better. The last trace of timidity was discarded with the nightgown.

"I see you are definitely not Chinese," Ruby said, her fingers reaching without warning to lightly touch the tangle of hair beginning to gather between Sing's legs.

"Like me, you are thicker and curlier." Ruby stifled a giggle. "There is only one Chinese among the Sisters. Her name is Jade, and the hair is flat and silky as a mouse's back." Ruby stepped suddenly to the upright object in the corner, stripping away the black silk veil to uncover a full-length oval mirror in a frame of gilded flowers. "I have not looked into the mirror for a long time," Ruby breathed. "Mirrors are meant to present the young and the beautiful, not to record the passing of time or a face forbidden the gift of joy."

Adjusting the polished surface to reflect Sing's full height, the pipe-maker said wistfully, "See how its magic comes alive again because of you." It was the first time Sing had seen herself in this way, and it caused the heat in her to prickle the skin. Backlit by the sun and distorted by ripples, her mirrored image in the shallows of the lake and in the Place of Clear Water had showed nothing of her body and little of her face. There had been no mirrors in the kitchens of the House of Fan. She had wondered what she truly looked like.

Her skin was palest bronze, chestnut hair loose upon her shoulders. Her light eyes were made brighter by thick dark lashes and slender brows. Her neck was long, her shoulders wide and strongly set. She felt the blood warm her cheeks at the sight of her breasts, the nipples tingling as though physically touched under her own gaze. In a trance, she watched Ruby's long, rose-tipped fingers gently stroking the slight flare of her hips, urging her to turn herself to look at the flowing lines of her back, the strong swell of her buttocks. Siu-Sing stood transfixed as Ruby grasped her narrow waist, turning her to again confront the mirror. "See how very beautiful you are." The slender fingers shifted lightly to her breast, the nipple tightening at the touch of a fingernail. Siu-Sing caught her breath as it circled, deliberately teasing. The pleasure was so new to her she gasped in disbelief.

"We can discover the mirror's secrets, you and I. Do you trust me, Siu-Sing, to explore them with you?"

Siu-Sing's nod was shy but eager. Ruby lowered her head, her tongue seeking the tender bud pressed between her fingers. Siu-Sing felt as if her body and her spirit were separated—each watching the other with curiosity and a sweet impatience. "See how ready you are for such adventures? But be patient; passion is a gift worth waiting for, to be given and received in equal measure."

Ruby's face was so close that for the first time Sing was aware of two identical scars, faded but faintly discernible through the gossamer gauze. Finely drawn across her cheeks, they reached from the corner of each eye to the mouth.

The pipe-maker turned quickly aside. "Do not look too closely. I am one without a smile." She lifted the corner of the veil, allowing herself to try, but the skin of her cheeks crinkled like withered fruit. "You see, it has been taken from me, so do not seek my smile. I have found contentment without it."

Siu-Sing felt a moment's sorrow for Ruby. "You do not need to smile to be beautiful. I have seen the heavens reflected on the surface of a great lake. I see the same kind of beauty in your eyes."

Ruby's mouth was wide and generous, her narrow, high-bridged nose finely shaped, her full lips unpainted, parted slightly to reveal her even teeth. She responded in a whisper, her breath sweet and warm. "I think my little sister is wise beyond her years in many things, yet innocent as the youngest child in others."

An inch or two shorter than Siu-Sing, she tilted her head slightly as though on impulse, lightly kissing Sing's brow, the tip of her nose, her cheek, her closed eyelids . . . the warm hollow of her throat. There it lingered before seeking her open mouth with a softly probing tongue.

Siu-Sing's senses reeled, the urge to yield so strong it fascinated her. Suddenly, Ruby turned Sing toward the mirror again as her slim dark hands moved lightly down to her hips and belly. Siu-Sing stood enthralled by the reflections that swam before her as dizzily as in a dream, Ruby's voice no more than a warm breath at her ear.

"I think you have not been touched before by man or woman. This is good; the caresses of a patient woman will prepare you well for the clumsiness and haste of a selfish man." As she spoke, the fingers teased the tuft of curling hair, sliding suddenly deeper to find the slippery bud. Siu-Sing's reaction almost caused her to pull away, her hands grasping Ruby's wrist.

"You are very strong, but do you really want me to stop?" The pipe-maker's whisper was teasing. "We call it the bud of the peony. It is the fountainhead of ecstasy. A word you have not heard before, I think."

The clever fingers increased their gentle friction until Siu-Sing's body began to melt from within. Sensation spread from her burning cheeks to her toes in a surge that made her shudder with a cry of exquisite relief.

She would have fallen if Ruby had not held her close, cooing her contentment. "*Sssshhhhh*, my little one, *sssshhhhh*, how quickly and how sweetly you respond, how ready you are to learn."

Overwhelmed by her reeling senses, Sing turned to Ruby in gratitude and wonder. "May I see you beside me in the mirror?" she asked in a whisper so husky she barely recognized it as her own. "May I not see you as you see me? Is it possible that I may give as well as receive such magic?"

"Perhaps, when we are truly sisters . . . then nothing will be hidden between us. But there are many things that must wait."

Days passed, each night shared with Ruby, the tiny cups of nectar banishing all inhibitions as Siu-Sing's curiosity and desire grew stronger with each new interlude. Ruby came to her in darkness, lithe and strong;

their arms and legs entwined, hands and lips exploring each other in whispered secrecy. Siu-Sing admitted her innocence willingly, eager to satisfy anything that Ruby might ask of her, impatient to know that which still lay hidden. Ruby would not reveal her own nudity, as though to do this would reach a climax best delayed. She did answer one question readily enough, when Sing hesitantly asked if such pleasures were not forbidden to them.

"Oh, no," Ruby replied with great sincerity. "It is my duty to teach you these things. It is for me to decide your readiness for the pleasures of the heart and the body. My report to Gracious Mother will decide your standing in our little world." Her eyes sparkled mischievously. "In my humble opinion, you will become a goddess of love."

She fetched from the painted wardrobe a bottle of wine-colored oil. "Pure oil of roses," she said, bidding Sing to lie down. "Now I must show you the ways of the Indian massage. It is something you must understand well." She giggled, a bubbling little laugh in an unguarded moment. "No tiger roars, no dragon rises that cannot be tamed by rose-petal hands."

※

On the eighth day at midmorning, Ruby escorted Siu-Sing to a shaded pavilion in a secluded part of the grounds. Reached by the graceful curve of a scarlet bridge, it stood in the middle of a splendid water garden arched by miniature willows.

The lilac robe suited her well, reflecting the elusive tints of her eyes, splendidly cool against her freshly bathed skin. She felt poised and confident as Ruby left her framed in the entry to the pavilion, stepping forward to bow before the Golden One. "I have the honor to present the new pipe-maker, Mama-san. She has satisfied all that is expected of her in every way."

Ruby stepped aside, allowing Sing to stand alone. She could see that the pavilion was lined with books and scrolls, tables arranged along its eight sides in the shape of the sacred trigrams of Pa-kua, each holding ink blocks, sheaves of paper, and brushes. Beautiful sculptures of erotic figures stood in each corner.

The Golden One rested on a cushioned seat surrounding a central table. Set upon it was a large and beautifully bound book, and beside it a platter filled with perfect golden persimmons. She wore a kimono of softest orange, the color, Sing instantly reflected, of dawn across the lake. Her hair was dressed in the style of a geisha, combed and curled in wings of gleaming black, held in place by nodding golden trinkets.

"Welcome to the Reading Book Pavilion, Siu-Sing. Ruby tells me you are well rested and at your ease in these new surroundings. I am pleased that she speaks so highly of you. My judgment is rarely misplaced."

"She has been most patient and kind to me, Mama-san."

The Golden One hid a smile behind the fluttering arc of the black lacquered fan. "The robe she has chosen suits you well . . . take it off and let me see you as she has seen you."

The silk slid from Sing's shoulders to puddle at her feet. Since visiting the mirror with Ruby's guiding hands, she had embraced nudity as naturally as she had in the Place of Clear Water.

"You say your age is thirteen years; you look older but in all the right ways. Ruby tells me you do not shrink from the touch of a woman, that the nectar of the persimmon is agreeable to you." She gestured for Siu-Sing to replace the robe and take a seat opposite her at the table. "I am told you are untouched by man or boy . . . yet you are familiar with the masculine anatomy. How is this so?"

"I was taught the ways of hedgerow healing and of the Empty Hand by a master of the Tao. My knowledge is no more than what is shown on ancient charts, but I understand that which will please him and that which will kill him."

The Golden One smiled at the comparison, nodding her approval. "From this day, you will join the Silver Sisters and learn the arts of the courtesan and the skills of an apprentice pipe-maker. I have decided that your name will be Topaz, the jewel sought after by kings and chieftains for its forbidden properties. You will obey my wishes and the wishes of your elder sisters at all times. Punishment is rare in my house, but when it is deserved, then it is severe."

She poured pale amber tea into small translucent cups. "I have paid a high price for you, Topaz, because I wish to please a taipan of great importance to me. He has an eye for the rarest of gems, yet has rejected each of those I have placed before him. You are like no other; perhaps he will choose you at the end of your year of apprenticeship. If he does, I will be handsomely rewarded, and your future could be one of great wealth and prospects of power. But this will be up to you. I can teach you the secrets of your body, even some secrets of the mind. Only you can command your heart, and only your heart can decide your destiny."

She paused, her honeyed eyes intent upon Siu-Sing as she lifted her cup. "You will eat well but carefully. If a doctor is needed, I will provide one. I can see you are no stranger to exercise and you may pursue this at your leisure. All I ask is that you listen and learn. Always remember that I have purchased you; you belong to me and to this house until your future is decided. Do you understand this?"

Siu-Sing replied instantly, bowing her appreciation. "I am most fortunate to be chosen, Gracious Mother. I will do all I can to earn your trust and deserve your kindness." In her heart, Sing knew this was the beginning of deception. From this moment she would be two separate people: Topaz, who would become the perfect Silver Sister, and Siu-Sing, the warrior, daughter of a brave and noble Chinese mother, who would one day stand before her famous father.

Tamiko-san carefully selected a ripe persimmon. The golden orb rested lightly in the palm of her hand, her glittering fingernails forming a cage around its perfection. "See how luscious it is," she murmured thoughtfully. "I import them from Japan. Did you know that the Chinese persimmon is slightly inferior to that of the Japanese? And that those grown in America ripen too quickly and are too soft?" She tossed the fruit lightly, as though judging its weight. "It is hand picked and properly packed for me by an expert who knows just how well and how far the fruit will travel, just how long the flesh will remain firm, fresh, and sweet." She laughed. "Of course, such perfection takes the most careful of handling by the finest of experts to command the highest prices."

Suddenly, she tossed the fruit high in the air, flicking wide the black fan in a graceful swoop with the sound of a striking snake. The persimmon fell to the floor, sliced neatly in two, its syrupy nectar seeping slowly across polished flagstones. "See how in the blink of an eye this gorgeous, carefully nurtured fruit is worthless, its long journey wasted, of no more value to me than a withered flower. It will be cast aside, trodden underfoot, and left to rot untasted."

Tamiko-san's golden eyes were steady as a cat's, the gold-tipped fingers reaching to caress Sing's forearm lightly as a crawling insect. "One thing above all others: While you are beneath this roof you will know no man but the one you are chosen to attend. You will not leave this house unescorted or without my permission. Everything you need is here."

She gestured to the crowded bookshelves. "All of this has been collected over many lifetimes, and is the work of wise and adventurous minds and of gifted artists, both good and evil. Yet they deal only with lust. You will find little in these thousand times ten thousand pages about love."

Tamiko-san rose to leave the pavilion, the golden ornaments in her hair shivering with the slightest turn of her head. "Love is a luxury few can afford, Topaz; it will not put rice in your belly or clothes on your back. Lust, though, is legal currency in all languages, in all places, and at all times. It will feed and clothe you like an empress, and I will teach you to spend it wisely."

The *mama-san* walked across the bridge, opening a parasol of the same softly glowing silk as her kimono. "But first, I will introduce you to someone you will find of great interest . . ." She smiled mysteriously, beckoning with the closed fan for Siu-Sing to follow. "One man you may become acquainted with and will never forget.

"Men are often very stupid in matters of the bedroom. They believe that a woman is no more than a plaything, an expensive toy to be enjoyed whenever the fancy takes them. Most of those that come here have wives and concubines of their own . . . often too many, yet never enough. They will take a mistress and find her a fine home, buy her whatever she asks him for . . . then throw her out to make room for one that is younger and prettier. Such is the way of the taipan if we allow it." She laughed, a little ruefully, it seemed to Sing. "It is such stupidity that has made me rich and given me power. If you are as clever and as careful as I believe you to be, such a man will also make you rich and give you power."

Siu-Sing wanted to cry out, *I have no interest in the wealth and fame of such a man. I have been taught by the wisest of all teachers to choose my own mountain and to climb it alone if I must. From him, from the spirit of my mother and the father that awaits me, I have learned what it is to be alone but not lonely . . . to face great danger yet be unafraid.* Those were the thoughts and beliefs of Siu-Sing, disciple of the White Crane, but the words she spoke were those of Topaz, the Silver Sister. "I will do all that I can to earn such confidence."

They walked across the bridge to another small pavilion. It too was lined with shelves of scrolls and books, along with many pieces of sculpture in precious stone. A raised bench stood in its center, covered by a sheet of exquisitely embroidered silk. The Golden One pulled the sheet away. "Behold, the perfect man," she said dramatically. "The Grand Duke of the Sacred Persimmon. He was carved three thousand years ago by Chen-Lao, the finest sculptor China has ever produced, from the rarest, most precious of woods . . . ebony, the sacred heart of the persimmon tree."

The naked figure she revealed was the perfect life-size effigy of a splendidly handsome young man, its glossy hue like no other Siu-Sing had seen—in places purplish black as a ripe plum, in others the deep sheen of burnished bronze, seamed with veins of palest yellow. He lay on his back in a posture of complete relaxation, his eyes closed, his hands by his sides, as though deep in meditation. In his left hand he held the glowing orb of a succulent persimmon that seemed to be made from solid gold.

"You may touch him," said the Golden One. Siu-Sing reached out to place her fingertips upon the smooth chest. Its patina felt so real she withdrew her hand quickly. Tamiko-san laughed. "Don't be afraid. You will come to know every inch of him before we part." She took Siu-Sing's hand and placed it firmly on his shapely thigh, guiding it gently downward over the contours of well-defined muscle, to his knee and back again.

"Explore him. Feel his beauty." She chuckled wickedly, pleased and

337

amused by her student's caution. "He will not awaken. But does he not cast a spell?"

She watched Siu-Sing's small hand trace the lines of the duke's noble face, gliding over the planes and hollows of chest and shoulders, arms and hands, abdomen and back to thighs, calves, and feet. The figure had the touch of cool marble and was slippery as silk. Tamiko-san's amusement increased as Siu-Sing's fingers delicately skirted the empty socket above the scrotum modeled in minute detail.

"Our duke hides many secrets." The Golden One smiled. "Take his hand." Siu-Sing did so. "Now spread his fingers." Each joint moved as though the hand were alive. When she looked closely, Siu-Sing saw that the knuckles and joints were intricately tooled to move independently.

"Now bend his elbow, raise his arm." The Golden One stepped across to demonstrate, lifting first one leg, then the other, letting them fall back into a natural position. "Open his eyes that he may see his new mistress." Gingerly, Sing laid her fingertips on the duke's eyelids. At her slightest touch they rolled smoothly upward to reveal eyes so real they caused her to step back.

The Golden One laughed aloud. "He cannot see you. His eyes are of finest onyx, set in ivory. But look closely. He speaks to us." She pointed to his finely sculpted ear. When Sing bent closer, tiny Chinese characters became apparent, meticulously inscribed over every fold and turn of the ear.

"And here, and here and here," said Tamiko-san, pointing with the tip of her long fingernail. Sing realized that every inch of the model was covered in tiny pinholes bearing inscriptions so finely drawn they were almost indiscernible. "They tell us all his innermost secrets." A small frown of concentration creased Sing's brow as she tried to read them.

"They are in a tongue long buried," said the Golden One. "I will teach them to you in time."

She slid open a shallow drawer beneath the reclining figure, to withdraw a long flat box, its lid inlaid with characters and symbols in the same ancient hand. "Now we will make him whole." Inside the box, carved from the same exquisite wood, were two rows of lifelike phal-

338

luses of different sizes and shapes. "We will begin modestly." Tamiko-san surveyed the arrangement as critically as a duelist choosing a weapon. "But not too modestly," she concluded, selecting one of medium size and slotting it into the socket. "See. It also moves." The penis, its plum-shaped head gleaming, moved smoothly back and forth between Tamiko-san's fingers.

"This," Tamiko-san said with playful reverence, "is the erect penis . . . the jade stem . . . the ivory staff . . . the golden rod; call it what you will. To tired wives and mothers, it is no more than a ridiculous appendage, far more trouble than it is worth. This is why their husbands come to us."

❋

One evening each week, the Golden One descended among them in the glittering pavilion they called the Palace of Lights. It was the place of entertainment for those who were guests of the tavern and served by the Silver Sisters. Its domed ceiling was inlaid with thousands of tiny convex mirrors, with a chandelier of five hundred candles that filled the space with cascades of shimmering light. Beneath it, a central fountain fed a pool of green marble. The Silver Sisters swam naked, playing like children in its emerald waters. Around its edge, tables were spread with tempting foods and flasks of the golden nectar. Beyond them were divans of great splendor and comfort where the sleeping dragons could rest and smoke a pipe.

The Golden One reclined on the most elaborate divan, clad in the scarlet robes of a geisha with an obi of gold silk, smoking from the golden bowl of a pipe fashioned in the shape of a peony. Her face was chalk white, her honeyed eyes thickly lined with kohl, her mouth red as blood on virgin snow. She invited each of the Sisters to take the stage and entertain. Some sang, danced, or played music; others told stories or recited poetry. Some displayed secrets of sensuality practiced only by their people, alone or with a chosen partner. As the evening wore on and the flasks were emptied, most of the Sisters reached a languorous state of abandon.

From shadowed balconies set around the circular walls, the richest and most important of Tamiko-san's guests could observe at their leisure in curtained privacy.

"They may watch," explained Ruby when Siu-Sing asked, "but they may not touch. This is where they may choose a pipe-maker. If she pleases him sufficiently, he will pay much so that she is kept only for him." She placed a butterfly kiss on the tip of Siu-Sing's nose. "I must dance now." A flashing red gem set in her navel, a string of silver bells around her waist, Ruby performed an exotic dance that commanded attention, her hips and belly gyrating to the fevered music of the bazaar and the rhythmic clapping of the Silver Sisters.

When Siu-Sing was called to the stage, she played the songs of the silver nightingale on the *er-hu*. There was silence as the music of the mountains filled the glittering hall; for those moments, Siu-Sing felt as if she sat alone at the jade table in the Place of Clear Water.

In the private balcony reserved for a taipan of great power and wealth, the lone occupant sat back, his fingers idly twisting the stem of the brandy balloon on the table before him. His eyes were closed, enchanted by the pure notes of unknown music that seemed written only for him. It was played by a girl no more than a child, with hair thick and glossy as the mane of a thoroughbred from his stables, and a body that moved with grace and hidden strength. Through small mother-of-pearl opera glasses, he had studied her for an hour, seen the wild beauty of her face, the deep copper lights in her hair, and the rare coloring of her large eyes.

※

The entertainment in the Palace of Lights continued until dawn, and the following day was one of rest. Ruby took Siu-Sing's hand, holding it closely to her cheek for a moment. "You belong here now, and to her. She thinks you are her property, as this house and all things within it are her property. When it pleases her, you will be sold to the great taipan, J. T. Ching, but that will not be soon. We have time to plan, but you must heed her warning . . . her punishment is permanent."

The pipe-maker's fingertips traced the faint white line across her own cheek. "If you escape her, she will find you. She will take away your happiness forever, so simply, so finally, as she has taken mine . . . with the flick of a fan."

Ruby unwound the silken sari from around her body. Stepping into the candlelight, she stood naked before Siu-Sing for the first time. Her limbs were scarred by the same puckered lines that crossed her cheeks . . . as thin and deliberate as though made with the point of a rapier.

Ruby lifted her arms above her head and turned slowly. The white scars were everywhere—on her back, her buttocks, her legs, marking every part of her body. Quickly, she picked up the silk as though to cover her shame.

"My father was a wealthy Parsee merchant in Bombay, my mother a French tutor who schooled his younger children. He made her pregnant, and his memsahib had her beaten and driven from her house. I was born in the gutters of Bombay. So you see, I am also of mixed blood. In India, I am a *chi-chi* . . . a half-caste, an untouchable.

"I loved a boy once," Ruby whispered. "He worked here in the garden. At first we loved at a distance, more with looks and thoughts than with words. He would come to my window at night. For the first time some-one cared for me without condition, and I tasted happiness. We left through the gardener's gate and took the ferry to Hong Kong. I worked in a bar and he sold newspapers not far away. We found a rented sleep-ing place and shared it together. I carried his child, and the bar would not let me stay. We were often hungry.

"I had his son in our bed. It was a fine boy, but when he cried they told us we had to leave. I was caught and taken back to the Golden One. She marked me so that no man would desire me, to be sure that I would not leave again, or if I did, I would be easier to find. They took the boy and my baby away and I have never seen or heard of them again. I thought many times of ending my life, but she had use for me and I have stayed."

Siu-Sing looked with deep compassion at the little pipe-maker who had so willingly become her friend. Delicately, she pulled the drift of silk away to touch the scars on Ruby's shoulders with infinite tenderness.

"She spared my arms and belly," said Ruby bitterly. "You cannot hide the arms when making a pipe, or the belly when dancing. Such scars are unsightly for those she entertains."

"She is a monster, but you are wrong," Siu-Sing said firmly. "She could not spoil your loveliness."

Ruby smiled sadly. "That is as may be. My life within these walls has been bearable but without hope . . . until now. But you are different— you do not belong here, and I will help you to escape."

Ruby shed no tears, looking into Siu-Sing's eyes with the spark of a spirit that had once been strong. "I have acquaintances in the district of Wan Chai on Hong Kong Island, people who would pay you well and ask no questions. They know much about the *gwai-lo* soldiers and sailors who spend their money there. Also the rich foreigners who seek the company of women. When we are ready, we will find them."

They began to plot their escape. "It must not be hurried," Siu-Sing said. "Ah-Jin is teaching me the language of my father and other things I must know. I will take all the knowledge that I can from her and from those that teach me their special skills. But I will not become the whore of any taipan."

⁂

When she was not being taught to speak English, to move and dance like a courtesan, and to observe all the finer points of both Chinese and English etiquette, Sing was learning the refinements of eroticism from each of the Silver Sisters. The pipe-makers were all virgins, girls of around her own age, spectacularly beautiful and highly skilled in the arts of pleasing men and each other. Originally from many nations, each was given the name of a jewel, with Ruby the head pipe-maker overseeing them all. Each Sister had her own small room, decorated in the way of her culture and with a shrine of her own making to worship the gods of her people.

According to the custom for apprentice pipe-makers, Sing shared a room for a month with each of the Sisters: Amber from Japan, famous for her magic feet, tiny as a child's but with toes of steel, who taught Sing to massage the body of a man with feet more soothing than the most experienced hands. Sing learned to step lightly as a bird upon a dragon's back—to find and isolate the muscle and sinew, to tell from each breath the delicate boundaries of pleasure and pain.

Sapphire, from Siam, taught her the secrets of blending fragrant oils to stimulate or subdue the senses. Emerald, from Africa, was a teller of fortunes and a weaver of spells, able to divine a man's needs and expectations at a glance.

Jade was the only pure Chinese among them. Hers were the arts of hidden energy, the ancient techniques of acupressure. Pearl, from Arabia, had perfected the pleasures of the bath; Coral, from the Philippines, could use her mouth and tongue with astonishing skill. Crystal, a white Russian, was mistress of the erotic arts that were taught to the women of the tsars; and Turquoise, from Tibet, studied the dark stars and could see into a man's soul.

The Sisters welcomed Topaz and shared their most intimate secrets, but Siu-Sing was more interested in their stories of distant lands, eager to learn all she could about the wide world that awaited her.

Siu-Sing enjoyed the lessons in pipe-making, relishing the challenge of its need for precision. She learned to combine just the right amount of hemp and the root of the grass-cloth plant with tiny beads of opium no bigger than the eggs of a fat salmon. She would chop the mixture finely with a knife of tiger bone, then heat it in a small copper pan and add it to tobacco. Her knowledge of herbal medicine made such formulations second nature.

At the Tavern of Cascading Jewels, each dragon, or client, had his own water pipe that was left in the pipe-maker's care, some studded with gems, others chased with gold and silver or carved from ivory, while some preferred the simple pig-bone pipe of the workingman. The Sister would sit by the side of the sleeping dragon, ready with black Swatow tea and cool towels to clear his head when the passage to paradise was completed.

CHAPTER 27

The Taipan

T*he years of apprenticeship* were nearing their end when Siu-Sing was summoned alone to the Golden One's lavish apartment.

Tamiko-san was seated at a dressing table, closely inspecting her face in the mirror. She turned as Siu-Sing entered, returning her bow with a brief nod of the head. The *mama-san*, whom Siu-Sing had never seen without the intricate mask of her makeup or one of her magnificent wigs, was shorter and thinner than she had guessed.

The Golden One turned from the mirror with an approving smile. "You have been chosen, as I had hoped, by the one I wish you to please. He has watched you in the Palace of Lights and found you interesting beyond all others. That you are a virgin was his only remaining concern, and that he has been assured of. He has honored you as his chosen pipe-maker, but I have told him you are not yet ready to become more than this to him. You will be available as soon as I consider your training to be complete, perhaps in a month or two. Meanwhile, he will grow impatient, which is my intention. During that time you will make his pipe and ensure his dreams are only accompanied by you."

Siu-Sing was not invited to reply, but listened dutifully to every word. To be traded without her consent strengthened her resolve to escape.

"There is a private lodge within the grounds that was designed as my personal retreat, but he has paid me well to use it. You will take up residence there and await his pleasure.

"There are simple rules you must remember. Never question him.

What he wishes you to know, he will tell you. Your duties as his pipe-maker do not include his bed. Do whatever is in your power to make him desire you—charm him, enchant him—but resist his embrace until you belong to him. Do you understand?"

Siu-Sing bowed, then asked, "And what, Gracious Mother, will I be when he holds my *sung-tip*? His servant? Will I be mistress, concubine, or *tai-tai*? Am I to bear his children, and if I do, where will I stand in his household?"

The Golden One looked at her gravely. "This will be for him to decide and will depend upon your skills. If you use all you have learned here wisely, you can be everything to him. He is no longer young, and should not be difficult to entice. You are not like the others, Topaz; your spirit resides on a different and I think a higher plane to theirs. I see in you all the signs of an adept. I also am an adept, and have shown you due respect by not questioning you. So I will break the rule of confidentiality to tell you this. He is one of Hong Kong's richest and most feared taipans, born of a famous Hakka clan of landowners. Their fortunes were made in the distant hills of Yunan from the humble tea bush; from this he has built a legitimate international empire."

The Golden One reached for a gold box on the small table beside her, lifting its lid to select a thin black cigarette with a gold tip, tapping it on the lid. "He owns much of the Golden Hill and a great deal of land in the New Territories, including the garrison lines at Fanling, which he leases to the British Defense Forces. This gives him great powers of negotiation between the British rulers of Hong Kong and the Chinese government in Peking."

She sat back in the chair, fitting the cigarette into a long slim holder of white jade with studied attention. "Such a man has many secrets, important friends in the highest of places, and this brings the most dangerous of enemies. His name is Jack 'Teagarden' Ching, known to the business society as J. T. He does not choose pleasures lightly, nor is he easily pleased. If you are all that he hopes for, my time will not have been wasted and your future will know no bounds. If you disappoint him, he will return you to me. If you dare to betray him, you also betray me. . . .

I must warn you. He is neither a patient man nor a particularly gentle one, but he is honorable and fair . . . until his face is questioned or his trust betrayed." Tamiko-san said more with a shake of her head than words could have done.

The cigarette was lit from a heavy gold table lighter, its curling smoke seductively perfumed. Tamiko-san allowed a trickle of smoke to escape her nostrils. "Balkan Sobranie, a rare blend of Russian and Turkish tobacco . . . his favorite. The box and the lighter are of solid gold, one of his many gifts of appreciation. He is most generous to those who please him. His tastes in all things are rare and exotic; this is why he has chosen you. If you make yourself indispensable to him at all times—make him feel like the master of the universe he believes himself to be—you will be richly rewarded by his gratitude."

The jade holder balanced perfectly between her fingers, the Golden One ended the conversation with a final word. "The Silver Sisters are prone to two dangerous habits that I cannot cure them of: the evil of gossip and little green devil of envy. It may be said that the taipan Ching is dragon head of the Yellow Dragon triad. You must know this as a falsehood owed to idle chatter from empty heads he found no interest in. You must never raise this subject anywhere, anytime, under any circumstances whatsoever. If you do . . . I cannot save you."

Jack Teagarden Ching enjoyed the boundless privileges of great power and immense wealth. While he was widely acknowledged as a pillar of Hong Kong society, only three trusted lieutenants knew that he had inherited the title and responsibilities of overlord to the Yellow Dragon triad. The affairs of the society were largely left to the Incense Master, responsible for ritual and ceremony; the White Paper Fan, in charge of secretarial affairs; and the Red Pole, the most senior general in charge of the Yellow Dragon army—an underground force several thousand strong deployed throughout the world.

His success had not been entirely without its price. He did not consider himself addicted to opium, telling himself that his regular indulgence was only one of the many benefits of his good fortune. His Hong Kong mansion took up half a hillside overlooking Big Wave Bay, housing two of his wives, numerous children, and countless servants . . . yet his visits to the tavern in Macao were becoming more and more frequent. The excellent attentions arranged by the Golden One left nothing to be desired, even for a man of his extravagant expectations.

That she would procure for him a suitable concubine or a satisfactory mistress was only a matter of time. From the moment Topaz had first attended him, he had known, with the instinct of a collector, that here was a rare find. Since then, he had spent many of his most pleasant hours in this room and in her hands, enjoying the pleasures of the bath and the divan. His visits to the Japanese-style lodge Tamiko-san usually reserved for her own use had increased from once a month to once a fortnight, to once a week, and now he sometimes stayed for days on end.

Honor prevented him from taking Topaz before Tamiko-san considered her ready and the *sung-tip* properly exchanged. Until then, he was content to know that she would attend no other man.

As he watched her making the pipe, he thought how well they had named her. The topaz had been the favorite gem of monarchs since ancient times, of immeasurable value but only to the most discerning eye. He prided himself that he chose his women with the same care and disregard of cost.

Following Tamiko-san's strict adherence to custom was the closest he had ever come to doing as he was told, but he respected the concept of tradition. He believed that a little discipline, like everything under the tavern roof, was good for a man used to taking any woman he wanted. With Topaz he would follow the rules. The girl would remain untouched until all the formalities had been observed and she was properly bought and paid for.

※

To Siu-Sing, J. T. Ching was an ugly man, of an age impossible to guess, perhaps almost sixty, perhaps seventy or even older. She saw greed, power, and cruelty in his flat, round features, his pockmarked skin paler than most through constant pampering. Behind heavy horn-rimmed spectacles, the upper lids of his narrowed eyes were as puffed from good living as the dark pouches beneath them. The lower lip of his wide, slack mouth showed uneven bottom teeth flecked with gold.

His thinning black hair was flattened with pomade. He was not tall, but his body was large and heavy, his muscles running to flab. He had not been unkind to her, even showing consideration as a generous uncle might show to a favorite niece, and it had not been difficult to deal with him. She had been sure to give him no reason for complaint.

Manipulating his body through massage could influence his energy levels, and she used this to her advantage, increasing or blocking the flow of his chi to influence the vigor or languor of his senses to suit her best. Seeing that the intimate pleasures of the bath were followed by the perfect pipe, she treated the body and mind of J. T. Ching as an opportunity to experiment; observing his reactions and responses with clinical interest while pretending the shy fascination of innocence.

As he drew the first thick plume of smoke deep into his lungs, the mind of Jack Teagarden Ching would open upon vistas of which he never tired. Siu-Sing would wait until his breathing was settled, then put the pipe aside and take out brushes and ink blocks, or a book to read. Some two hours later, when he opened his eyes, she was ready with small towels dampened by rosewater, cool ones for his first awakening, then warm. There would be an hour more of drowsiness and many cups, no bigger than seashells, of bracing tea.

When he was thoroughly refreshed, she called for his favorite dish of baby abalone—the tiny, mother-of-pearl ear shells, their delicate morsels steamed with lotus roots and ginger. When he had finished eating and she had bathed him in the mineral spring bath, he would enjoy a large brandy and she would administer a relaxing massage that would soon see him asleep for whatever length of time she chose.

This had been the unhurried routine for several weeks, when he placed a small box of purple velvet before her. "A gift for your services," he said, turning to the mirror and reaching for a comb to begin the precise arrangement of his hair. The topaz lay in the palm of Siu-Sing's hand so softly she hardly felt its weight, about the size of one of the pebbles she had once collected from the Place of Clear Water.

"Such a stone is very rare," he said. "It means that I have chosen you. Tomorrow I will pay a very large sum for your *sung-tip*. You are to become a special companion to me. Your Gracious Mother will inform you of my decision and what is to be expected of you."

Siu-Sing bowed to show her great humility. "I am honored, sir, and glad that I have pleased you."

"Tonight I will receive visitors of great importance to me. You will entertain us with your music. The Indian *chi-chi* will accompany you and dance for them." As she helped him dress, bowing him to the door of his huge black car, she knew the time for escape had come.

⋇

Under Tamiko-san's supervision, the tavern's wardrobe mistress chose the finest gowns for Siu-Sing and Ruby, and the hairdresser took great pains with every detail of their elaborate coiffures. Coral, who was expert in the care of finger- and toenails, saw that each was trimmed, shaped, painted, and polished to perfection. Pearl applied long, intensely black lashes and painted their mouths a vivid crimson against their white powdered faces and delicately rouged cheeks. The *mama-san* personally approved their jewelry, then stood back to inspect them.

Topaz wore a robe of lilac satin, trimmed with silver, the jewel given to her by the taipan glowing from a silver chain at her throat. Her dark bronze hair was set in gleaming coils, held with silver combs. Ruby was elegantly draped in a sari of spiderweb silk in deepest magenta edged with gold, and richly adorned with anklets, bracelets, and necklaces of tiny golden bells, her waist-length hair a glossy cape loose about her shoulders. Her midriff was bare; a ruby matching the one upon her forehead flashed in her navel.

"The celebrated guests are foreigners of highest station . . . Colonel Justin Pelham, commanding officer of the British Defense Force, garrisoned on the border at Fanling, and his adjutant, Captain Toby Hyde-Wilkins, who is also military attaché to the Hong Kong government.

349

"What you may be privileged to see or hear during this evening must never be discussed or repeated by either of you. It is a very great honor to be chosen to attend this banquet, but you will eat or drink nothing unless invited by the taipan. Do not speak unless you are asked to do so. You are in attendance to obey and to entertain when called upon; otherwise, you are invisible. Remember, you have my reputation and the reputation of this house in your hands. Do not disappoint me."

The Golden One herself was exquisitely dressed and in a traditional obi of shimmering gold. The plain black fan had been replaced by one of scarlet, patterned with seed pearls. "You will wait in the annex until you are called for. Do not speak to each other or make any sound until it is time for you to entertain or attend the table."

It was the first time Siu-Sing had seen the tavern's banqueting hall, its splendid table set with silver candelabra. The small annex was separated from the main hall by a curtain of crystal beads, which enabled Siu-Sing and Ruby to observe the room without being seen by those at the table.

Tamiko-san graciously led the party to a table for five, summoning the head chef with a clap of her hands. "It is a court tradition for the chef to read and explain the menu before the dishes are served," Ruby whispered. "This could be a long affair before we are called upon."

Siu-Sing was hardly aware of Ruby's words as she watched the taipan and his guests take their seats. He wore the dark blue robe of a high-ranking Chinese dignitary, with a single medal pinned to his chest. Siu-Sing had never seen anything like the two foreign men that preceded him. The first, silver-haired and more thickset than his companion, was immaculately dressed in a scarlet tunic resplendent with gold braid and decorated with rainbow-colored ribbons. His complexion was ruddy; his manner formal and his eyes alert.

The other, a much younger man identically uniformed, was fair-skinned, his neatly trimmed hair the color of ripe corn, glittering like the braid upon his wide, straight shoulders. Even through the beaded screen, Siu-Sing could see that his eyes were as blue as indigo ink.

Another Chinese man entered, standing behind the chair of Taipan Ching, his back against the wall, his hands folded before him. He was dressed in a black suit and black polo-necked shirt. Jet-black hair stood almost upright on his head, thick and wiry as a brush.

Siu-Sing's pulse began to race in disbelief. Ah-Keung had not changed much since the iron gates of Double Happiness had clanged shut behind her; he was unmistakable. His sloping shoulders were more heavily built, his face not much different but for a thickening of his brows and perhaps a slight squaring of the jaw. His mouth remained the same—thin, straight, cruel.

Siu-Sing hid her initial shock so quickly that even Ruby did not notice. There was nothing to be done but to let events take their course. Mama-san had insisted on such heavy theatrical makeup that there was a chance he might not recognize her, and if he did that he might not choose to make it known. Fiercely subduing her racing thoughts, Siu-Sing focused on the man with golden hair as they awaited the summons to perform.

True to Ruby's prediction, the head chef presented dish after dish. As protocol demanded, Ching apologized for the inferior quality of such humble offerings: the heart of a tiger, wild swan, the paw of the Himalayan black bear struck from the living beast, among countless other delicacies enjoyed for a thousand years in the banquet halls of emperors.

"You will note that our chopsticks are made of solid silver. Any impurity will turn the tips instantly black . . . It is nothing more than a precaution." He spread his hands, the diamond on his finger catching the light. "Is it not the price of those in power to be forever at risk of the assassin?"

Ching laughed loudly at his own joke. "Indulge me, gentlemen—or, of course, if you prefer more civilized utensils, you will find knives, forks, and spoons set before you, also of solid silver and made, I am proud to tell you, in your famous foundries of Sheffield."

Their discomfort evident, the guests tasted small portions of each dish. Ching wasted no opportunity to highlight the gulf between their different cultures, in preparation for the business yet to be discussed. The final dish was a rich soup ladled by the chef himself from a huge tureen in the center of the table. The taipan slurped noisily, encouraging his guests to do the same. "It is made from the testicles of the civet cat." He grinned, delighted to educate the barbarian taste. "They have four, you know; how fortunate they are. This soup will give you the benefit of such a gift." He leered unpleasantly, crudely indicating an instant erection by clenching his fist and jerking his forearm abruptly.

Hours seemed to pass before Tamiko-san clapped her hands, commanding Ruby to dance. She did so exquisitely, to the music of two Indian musicians, before returning to the annex to the polite applause of the guests.

The moment had come for Siu-Sing's performance. She parted the curtain of beads to seat herself on the stool that had been set for her, grateful that her face was fixed in a downward position, her cheek cradled into the neck of the *er-hu*. She was thankful too when the lights were dimmed to enhance the magic of her music.

Not knowing what this evening would hold for her, Siu-Sing lost herself in the melodies of childhood happiness, playing without thought of time or place. The one with hair the color of ripe corn and eyes of indigo blue never took his eyes off her and held each note like a gift, as if she played her music just for him.

It was Ching who broke the spell. He had been drinking heavily, first the hot wine he claimed boosted virility, then the brandy that showed in the flush of his face. He ended her playing with evident impatience. "Is she not a delight to the eye and to the ear? Or is the scraping of a Chinese fiddle an abomination to the superior Western sensibilities?"

He did not wait for a response, but called even louder as Siu-Sing lowered the instrument, rising from the stool. "Join us, Topaz—bring the *chi-chi* with you. I have entertainment of my own to amuse our honorable guests."

Siu-Sing and Ruby were quick to obey, taking the chairs left vacant for them. Although Siu-Sing knew that she was now fully exposed, there was no sign of recognition from the silent figure of Ah-Keung. And even the shock of his sudden appearance seemed to fade in the presence of the man with sunlit hair.

"With respect, Mr. Ching, we have been sumptuously fed and enchantingly entertained . . . could we perhaps move on to the business at hand?" Colonel Pelham studied a gold fob watch as he spoke.

"This will take but a moment . . . a small display of our futile and pathetic powers."

At the snap of Ching's fingers, Ah-Keung stepped forward, striking a stance on widespread feet, knees bent, clenched fists drawn into his sides. He faced the six half-burned candles in their silver holder in the center of the table. Without warning, his fist struck out with whiplash speed to stop inches from the first candle, instantly extinguishing the flame; then repeated the feat so rapidly the six candles stood smoking faster than the eye could follow.

"The power of chi, gentlemen. Intrinsic energy developed beyond all accepted boundaries of physical potential." The taipan chuckled. "Each punch was pulled four inches from the candle, yet its velocity put out the flame. If such a blow connected, it would deliver the force of one thousand pounds per square inch from a distance of six inches and at a speed undetectable to the eye."

Ching clearly enjoyed the brief silence amid the wavering threads of smoke from the blackened wick and the acrid whiff of hot wax. "Ah-Keung is a man who says little but sees much. He is my driver and my—" he paused for a second, "personal assistant. He takes excellent care of both my car and my person."

Ah-Keung had instantly stepped back to his position behind the taipan's chair, his hands folded, his face an impenetrable mask, his eyes revealing nothing of thought or intention. Siu-Sing sat obediently, her eyes downcast, conscious only of the young British officer. It was as though the room were empty but for him.

"You are right, of course, Colonel—enough of entertainment. With the Japanese in Manchuria and now in Shanghai, there is little to stop them pushing south." J. T. Ching held up his brandy balloon to be replenished. "We must be ready." As he spoke, a large covered salver was placed in the center of the cleared table. The chef lifted the silver lid with a flourish, revealing a mound of golden confectionary neatly cut into squares.

"No banquet is complete without the rarest of all desserts." Ching selected a piece with his silver chopsticks, chewing it with noisy relish, urging them to join him. "Such important proceedings must begin or be completed with the sharing of *mu-nai-yi*. You will have noted, gentlemen, that we poor Chinese have little taste for sweets . . . jam roly-poly, bread-and-butter pudding, or spotted dick, delights that I am sure you enjoy in the comfort of the officers' mess."

His guests each selected a square of what appeared to be a rich toffee or perhaps a fudge. He watched attentively as they consumed the morsels, nodding in appreciation of its taste and texture. Visibly delighted by their approval, Ching turned to Siu-Sing and Ruby.

"Help yourselves, ladies. It is unlikely that you will ever enjoy such delights again."

"It is quite delicious," Colonel Pelham remarked politely, "but perhaps a little too rich for a man more accustomed to jam roly-poly." The stiffness of his retort showed clearly that he found Ching's words offensive.

Captain Hyde-Wilkins, who had remained noticeably silent throughout the proceedings, nodded his agreement. "May one ask what it contains? It has a flavor unlike any I have tasted . . . certainly not in the class of spotted dick."

Ching beamed his satisfaction, his face blotched from too much brandy. He offered a piece to Siu-Sing with great ceremony, giving her little alternative but to accept. She found it pleasantly sweet . . . like caramel, with a strange aftertaste she could not define. When chewed, it slowly disintegrated on her tongue and was easily swallowed.

"*Mu-nai-yi* is otherwise known as 'mellified man.' In certain distant villages where poverty rules necessity, when a man dies of natural causes, preferably of great age and possessing an accumulation of wisdom, his family may sell the corpse to the local physician. If he so chooses, however, the man may pledge his cadaver at any age, or sell it from his deathbed, so that he can greet his ancestors knowing that he has benefited those left behind." Hugely satisfied that he had the attention of his audience, Jack Teagarden Ching reached for another morsel, holding it in his chopsticks as a rare gem might be held up to the light and scrutinized.

"It is a fascinating process," he continued as though unaware of his guests' discomfort. "The corpse is cleaned and then steeped in a stone casket filled with wild honey. The name and date are marked upon the sealed casket and it is stored in a cave, mysteriously selected for the purpose, and left untouched for no less than one hundred years." Ching's flushed face showed his mounting enjoyment of the moment. "The casket is then opened and *mu-nai-yi*—mellified man—is the result."

He popped the portion into his mouth with an exaggerated display of appreciation. "You will be pleased to know, ladies and gentlemen, that the cadaver you now enjoy was in life an ancient sage of great renown."

Before he had finished speaking, Siu-Sing felt herself choke on the half-eaten confection. The taipan seemed more amused than concerned. Captain Hyde-Wilkins was instantly on his feet with a clean napkin held to Siu-Sing's mouth. Ah-Keung had moved to prevent him, but a flick of Ching's head caused him to step back.

"I see our precious Topaz is more *gwai-lo* than Chinese . . . ," Ching said with contempt and impatience. "There is no need for such attention, Captain; please do not concern yourself."

In a sharper tone of voice, he addressed Tamiko-san, who had rushed to the table. "Get this slut out of here before she spews all over the table . . . and take the *chi-chi* with her. We have business to attend to." Tamiko-san apologized profusely, hastening the girls from the banquet hall at the point of her fan.

Before Ching could say more, Captain Hyde-Wilkins tossed the napkin onto the table. "With your permission, Colonel," he said flatly, "may I strongly advise that while we are appreciative of our host's hospitality and tolerant of his sense of humor, the serious matter of extending our border patrols and strengthening our defense would be better discussed at another time and place? Perhaps with more attention paid to the enemy advance and less to an excess of food and drink."

Ah-Keung's folded hands parted and his stance grew alert. He took one small step closer to the adjutant, his eyes returning the cold blue stare.

Ching dropped his patronizing manner. "You may leave us, Ah-Keung. I apologize, gentlemen. You are right—let us discuss our business." Ching led the British officers to the comfort of divans, his manner suddenly businesslike.

"For many years, gentlemen, my company has traded with the Japanese. I have many friends in Tokyo, and they have made me a proposition, which I now put to you. As you know, Japanese forces under General Jiro Toshido are advancing on Hong Kong."

He smirked. "They are in no hurry . . . Hong Kong will not go anywhere. My associates in Tokyo have proved that to stand against them is futile. Many thousands of Chinese are dead because they resisted the Imperial Japanese shock troops."

"Correction, Mr. Ching," said the captain. "They were defenseless Tanka boat people and Hakka peasants trying to protect their homes and families. The Japanese slaughtered them."

Ching lifted his hands in a gesture of acceptance. "My apologies. As you know, I am a great believer in British diplomacy; I wear this medal with pride." The officers were well aware that J. T. Ching had been awarded the Order of the British Empire for his philanthropic services to the colony. He was not the only rich Chinese to "buy" his OBE.

"I am also a realist, gentlemen," Ching went on. "We do not want such a tragedy to take place on our soil."

"What are you proposing, sir?" Colonel Pelham demanded. "Let us get to the point of this meeting."

Ching poured himself another brandy. "Very well, Colonel." He rolled the liquor in its glass, lifting it to sniff the bouquet. "General Toshido, I understand, is an honorable man. He has given his word that there will be no bloodshed if his troops are allowed to cross the border without resistance, to march through the New Territories into Kowloon, and occupy Hong Kong Island."

Colonel Pelham and Captain Hyde-Wilkins were quickly on their feet. "You are asking me to have my forces lay down their arms . . . to surrender Hong Kong without resistance?" the colonel said in disbelief. "You are a traitor, sir, as well as a bore. I shall see that you are treated as such."

Ching remained seated, his florid face quivering with suppressed fury. "No, Colonel, I am Chinese, and do not wish my people to be slaughtered to save a British colony." He raised his glass in a mock toast. "Die at the border if you must, gentlemen, but the Chinese are not interested in your stuttering king or his mealy-mouthed *tai-tai.*" He ripped the medal from his chest and flung it at their feet.

Colonel Pelham nodded his head curtly. "We thank you for a most interesting evening and apologize for an early departure. You will hear from Government House in the morning. Good night, Mister Ching."

"As you wish, Colonel." The taipan lifted his glass in mock salute. "The Imperial Japanese Army is on its way, with nothing to stop them but the rabble gathered around the traitor Chiang-Kai-Shek, or the starving Communists who die like flies around an empty pot." He rose unsteadily to his feet, the brandy balloon held high. "Long live the British Empire."

Back at the Japanese-style lodge, Siu-Sing moved quickly. Tamiko-san had turned on Siu-Sing in fury as soon as the taipan's guests had departed. "That you should puke on such a priceless delicacy has taken all face from this establishment. Could you not have swallowed it and smiled? Instead, you have made a fool of him before his honored guests. That the *gwai-lo* soldier has laid his paws on you may cause him to reject you."

"I am sorry, Gracious Mother; I had not eaten human remains before."

The Golden One waved aside any excuses with contempt. "When he retires, see to it that you show him all respect; say that you were unwell and beg his forgiveness. Do whatever he requires . . . or I will personally return you to Fan-Lu-Wei and the pigs of Double Happiness."

Siu-Sing had watched the staff car drive off, the pennants of the colonial government and the regiment fluttering as it disappeared through the wide-open moon gates. The shock of Ching's association with Ah-Keung confirmed the necessity of leaving at once. That Ah-Keung had shown no sign of recognition meant nothing; he was disciplined enough not to show his hand or make a move until it suited him.

The taipan's limousine remained in the garage, suggesting that the Forceful One would be quartered in the servants' wing for the night, and his master would soon be escorted to the lodge.

When the taipan appeared an hour later, Siu-Sing was ready, a bath drawn and the accoutrements of comfort and the ultimate escape at hand. Too much brandy had taken the sting from Ching's humor and much of the sense from his speech. He mumbled curses against the British imperialists and spoke of the Japanese as conquering heroes.

He said nothing of the evening's events, and under her ministrations was soon asleep. She had been careful to see that his pipe was a strong one, that he would not return from the Emperor's Garden for many hours into the following day.

Siu-Sing changed into the simplest of *sam-foos*. Careful not to attract attention to herself, she scrubbed her face clean of makeup and plaited her hair into a single braid like any *mooi-jai*.

The Tanka sling fastened about her, the *er-hu* slung across her shoulder, she placed the topaz on the night table beside his bedside, and silently left the lodge, keeping to the moon-etched shadows until she reached the window of Ruby's room.

CHAPTER 28

Nine Dragons

The *Nine Dragons Teahouse* and Ballroom was the biggest and grandest of its kind in downtown Hong Kong. Buried in the neon jungle of Wan-Chai, the infamous red-light district, it lured its customers with a gigantic pink and blue sign on which nine cavorting dragons chased each other up one side of the building and down the other in a crackling blaze of electricity.

Occupying the tallest and most elaborate building on Lockhart Road, it was a restaurant, ballroom, brothel, and casino under one roof. The lower floor was the traditional teahouse, patronized by those who walked their caged songbirds each morning to take exercise in Victoria Park, then met for *yum-cha*. At midday, dim sum girls with trays and trolleys of steaming delicacies in bamboo containers roamed among the tables, calling out their wares in loud, singsong voices.

Above this, on a different level of sophistication, was the gaudy and extravagant Nine Dragons restaurant, where Hong Kong's finest chefs provided a sumptuous meal to those who could afford it. On the third floor, from nine o'clock each evening until four in the morning, the Nine Dragons Ballroom offered Wan-Chai's most luxurious nightclub, where the cream of local male society could drink, dance, and enjoy the expert attentions of a Nine Dragons hostess.

On its central stage, beneath a turning ball of crystal mirrors that scattered light among candlelit tables, an orchestra alternated the Wan-Chai version of the latest Western music with the popular songs of China.

An endless progression of entertainers, singers, magicians, acrobats, and after-midnight striptease artists crossed every licentious boundary to entertain the guests.

For those who looked for more, there was an elevator to the floor above, where prior arrangements with a chosen hostess could be carried out in absolute comfort and privacy. The rules were strict and rigidly enforced by bodyguards dressed as waiters. If an amicable agreement was reached, the client could accompany the hostess to her room upon payment of the negotiated sum.

The owner of the Nine Dragons, Three-thumbs Poon, prided himself that there was nothing a man could ask for that could not be provided by taking the elevator from the ballroom to the floor above. It was why his hostesses were carefully chosen for their looks and style, and above all for their expertise in extracting the maximum amount of money from his regular patrons while leaving them impatient to return for more.

※

The yellow-shaded light above Three-thumbs Poon's desk hung so low that it illuminated the account books and row of soapstone chops, but left his face in shadow. His hands, however, could easily be seen, the sleeves of his shirt rolled back as if spotlighted to exhibit the deformity that had given him his name. On his left hand, some mischievous god had bestowed a second thumb, almost perfectly formed, growing outward from the lower joint of his normal digit as though stuck on as nature's last-minute joke. To emphasize this distinction, he wore a ring set with many diamonds on the extra thumb. A well-chewed cigar butt smoldered between his tobacco-stained fingers as they beckoned Ruby forward.

"I remember you, Ruby the *chi-chi*, though you have grown older and your face bears the mark of the Japanese whore Tamiko-san. There is no longer a place for you in the ballroom. In the kitchen, perhaps, or to serve dim sum in the teahouse." He leaned forward into the circle of light to look more closely into Ruby's face, leering at her with more amusement than kindness. "The last time I filled your bowl, you were nothing but trouble. Why should I fill it now?"

360

"It is my companion I bring to you; I am no more than a shadow compared to her. Her name is Siu-Sing, number-one pipe-maker for the Golden One. I am here to attend her; you will get the work of two at the cost of one because we share in everything. Together, we will bring you much business."

Ruby moved back as Siu-Sing stepped forward to take her place. Three-thumbs Poon tilted the lamp to look at the tallish girl with bronze hair, his bulging eyes peering through his rimless spectacles, reminding her of a frog on a lotus leaf. "Does the *chi-chi* speak the truth . . . were you pipe-maker to Ah-Jin?"

Ruby had prepared Siu-Sing on the two-hour ferry ride from Macao to Hong Kong. "They are rivals, those two. It would please him greatly to take a pipe-maker from Macao's most famous opium house."

"Yes, but Ruby was my teacher. She tells me the Nine Dragons Teahouse and Ballroom is the most famous establishment in Wan-Chai and, its owner is a rich and successful man who is called the Emperor of Pleasure. His fame is such that there is nothing he does not know, and nothing he cannot do on the island of Hong Kong."

The frog eyes looked her up and down suspiciously. "How do I know you are not sent by Ah-Jin to spy upon my business?"

Siu-Sing hurried on. "I speak English, Cantonese, and several dialects. I am a dancer and mistress of the *er-hu*. I know folk medicine and can cure a headache and bring relief of pain. . . . I can make a man happy and put him to sleep in moments. I am an expert pipe-maker if this is required of me. I am also a virgin, but this is not for sale."

Siu-Sing played her final card. "It is the great importance of your esteemed position that also brings me to you. I am the daughter of an English taipan, known among our people as Di-Fo-Lo and to the British as Devereaux . . . Captain Ben Devereaux. If your incomparable connections could find news of him, his gratitude would know no bounds. On this you have my word."

"*Gwai-los* are not welcome here. If they come, they soon leave and do not return. I can do nothing to help you in this fantasy." There was a moment of silence while the cigar butt was drawn into glowing life. "But if you are all that you say you are, what do you ask for these great skills of yours?"

"I ask only what is given to any Nine Dragons hostess—a place to sleep, to eat as they eat, be dressed as they are dressed, and paid as they are paid."

After the briefest of pauses, he nodded. "Your room is number twelve and that will be your name. I know no one called Siu-Sing, only Number Twelve and her *chi-chi* attendant." His thumbs disengaged long enough to take a key from its hook on a crowded board behind him. "But I warn you. I know nothing of foreign devils, rich or poor. If this is what you seek, then go to the bars to be fucked for a dollar by a drunken *gwai-lo*. If you are to be a Nine Dragons hostess, you will forget such grand illusions and say no more of it."

Sliding the key across the desk, he dismissed them with a flick of his sparkling thumb. "Number Five is the *mama-san*. If you break the rules, if you hide money or lie about your business, she will know it and report to me."

⌖

Siu-Sing found the bar district of Wan-Chai strangely exciting. When walking its bustling streets or riding, wonder of wonders, in a taxi, she dressed in perfectly fitted cheongsams made by the ballroom's resident tailor in different hues of violet, from the palest wisteria to the rich purple of the iris; it was, she had decided, her lucky color.

Her training at the Tavern of Cascading Jewels served her well: The tired clients who were eager to escape their *tai-tais* for an hour or two seemed easily pleased, and she quickly learned how to separate such men from their money with the least possible effort.

The hostesses received a small commission on every drink that a client bought. A "lucky drink," which was nothing but Coca-Cola or cold tea, cost as much as five-star brandy or twelve-year-old whisky. Very soon, Siu-Sing was handing in more drink receipts and receiving more requests for the pleasure of her company than any other hostess. After scarcely a month, seeing how popular she was among his most impor-

362

tant customers, Three-thumbs gave Siu-Sing and Ruby a small suite of their own in which to entertain her clients. High above the chaos of the streets below, the view from its tiny balcony reached across the spread of Victoria Harbor to the high rise of Kowloon. From that suite, she attended to the needs of a procession of customers who interested her no more than the Duke of the Golden Persimmon.

Those that required her private ministrations paid dearly for the experience. So skillful were her techniques that she could part a man from every cent in his pocket and often in his checkbook for a few moments of indescribable bliss. No man was allowed to touch Number Twelve, and yet there were no complaints, and those who could afford it became her regular clients. She did not go to sleep as soon as her shift had ended, but sought out a place on the roof, where she would recall the words of her *si-fu*: "No matter where you are, there will always be a new day dawning, always a stillness before the sunrise. In the hour before daylight, the world is yours alone. In your heart and mind you will return to the rock . . . you will see the crane on the sandbar and the tiger in the reed bed. You will watch them in mortal combat and see why the crane is triumphant. You are the crane and you will never fall. It is called spiritual boxing."

High above the never-sleeping streets, she and Ruby would watch the harbor come to life at dawn. With the happiness silk in her hair and the finger jade warm in her palm, Siu-Sing would look at the ships from every corner of the world and wonder if her father could be on one of them, or perhaps not far away.

Every day she read both Chinese and English newspapers from cover to cover, thankful for the English lessons she had attended to so diligently. As long as she possessed the photograph and the few other relics of her parents, safe in the bottom of the Tanka sling, there was hope. For now, the little balcony and the view from the rooftops were as close as she wished to come to the world outside, and Ruby the only companion she needed.

Recognizing the Eurasian beauty as a gold mine, Three-thumbs Poon made no attempt to discover more about Number Twelve's past. His philosophy was simple and direct: If a girl made him money, he would pay and treat her well. The moment she failed to do so, he would see her back on the streets without a moment's thought.

Even if he had wanted to inquire about the foreigner Number Twelve claimed as her father, only a fool would call attention to an establishment such as his. Prostitution and gambling were forbidden under colonial law—which made little difference to the massage parlors, casinos, and vice dens that prospered under the garish lights of Wan-Chai, or to the members of the Royal Hong Kong Police Force who fortified their meager earnings by accepting lucky money at the end of each month, unconcerned with the ridiculous laws of a distant king. Their British officers seldom ventured into the area, except during the propitious days of Chinese New Year, when they were wined and dined in their chosen venues with a fat packet discreetly folded into the menu.

Beneath this level of authority, the local triad gangs controlled their territory with brutal enforcement, demanding protection money from every business that opened its doors. The Nine Dragons was visited regularly by the younger brothers of the black society, who answered only to the rules of violence—collecting the squeeze, eating and drinking, and taking women without payment whenever they wished.

Number Twelve seated herself before Three-thumbs as he began counting out banknotes with a practiced hand. "You have done well, Number Twelve. You are entitled to your commission of five percent."

He was taken aback when Siu-Sing replied, "I thank you for your generosity, sir, but I believe the other hostesses receive ten percent, and I wish to be paid the same. I would also ask that this become fifteen percent if I am asked for special services."

Three-thumbs paused in his counting, his frog face thrust into the lamplight. "You ask too much. You are new here. If those that have been here longer knew of such demands, there would be great trouble."

"Then we will not tell them. I am contented here and do not wish to seek employment elsewhere. I make no further inquiry of my father, as I am sure you have done your best to seek word of him."

The glare behind the rimless spectacles grew less belligerent, the hands once more busy counting money, his voice bearing a hint of admiration. "Agreed. While you continue to make money, you will share in the profit." He handed her a wad of notes. "But do not let Number Five find out."

"There is one more thing I would ask. Can you find me a trusted messenger to deliver a package to the Tavern of Cascading Jewels? I have a small matter of business to take care of."

Siu-Sing dispatched a fat envelope with a letter to Ah-Jin, The Golden One:

Dear Gracious Mother:

It is not in me to run or to hide. I ask your forgiveness, but no man will own me, and I will not let a woman rule my life. I am also honorable, as you are in your way. You taught me things that make money, things I might not have learned without your help. You saw in me what others could not. You taught me the difference between love and lust, and I owe you much for that.

Enclosed is three times the figure you paid for my sung-tip, *and more for the* sung-tip *of my sister, Ruby. Do not seek us in anger, but forget us both. You cannot be forgiven for taking Ruby's happiness, but I have made her smile again, so leave us to find our way without you, and to take love wherever we may find it.*

I know I must one day face the man who would own me, and I will accept the consequences. I am the new woman and you are the old; our worlds are different. We are each possessed of a warrior spirit, and if we fought, one of us would conquer the other. Or one of us would die.

Let us respect each other and go our separate ways, so that we shall never know.

Siu-Sing

Siu-Sing had worked in the Nine Dragons Ballroom for six months when the Englishman appeared. He was the first foreigner she had seen there; she might not have even noticed the shadowy figure sitting alone unless she had overheard others buzzing about the *gwai-lo*.

With every eye upon her, she moved between the tables toward him. He wore a blazer of dark navy blue over an open-necked white shirt. The shaded candle in the center of the table threw a dim light upon the gold braid of a regimental badge embroidered on the breast pocket. As he lit a cigarette, the flare of a match showed briefly the glitter of golden hair and the unmistakable deep blue eyes of Captain Toby Hyde-Wilkins.

He flicked the matchstick into an ashtray, rising from his chair at her approach. At that moment Number Five appeared close behind Siu-Sing, hissing a warning in barroom Cantonese. For a second, Hyde-Wilkins stared into Siu-Sing's eyes. Then he produced a card from an inside pocket and offered it to the *mama-san* without taking his eyes from Siu-Sing.

"I beg your pardon, but I am not a banana-eating ape, and this lady is not my whore. I am Captain Hyde-Wilkins, adjutant to the officer commanding the Eighth Royal Rajput Rifles and military attaché to His Majesty's Government. This young lady is a friend of mine, and you will kindly apologize."

He crossed quickly to hold a chair for Siu-Sing, sitting down with a slight smile as Number Five stared in stunned amazement. Meeting a foreign devil who could speak her language so fluently reduced her to the customary denial. "You must have misunderstood me, sir," she stuttered.

In reply, he took out his wallet, handing her a red one-hundred-dollar note. "Perhaps I did, in which case I need not complain to Mister Poon of your rudeness . . ."

He selected a second hundred-dollar note. "Unless I misunderstand you again?"

At a loss for the words normally at the tip of her tongue, Number Five accepted the money with a stunned bow. "Any possible misunderstanding is most regrettable, sir," she stammered. "May I bring you a drink with compliments of the Nine Dragons?"

"Thank you." He ordered a cold Tsingtao beer and turned to Siu-Sing. "Perhaps you would care for something a little more interesting than Coca-Cola or cold tea?" She shook her head as Number Five hurried away.

"Forgive my poor Cantonese," he went on. "I have learned enough to know that foreign devils such as I are not very popular, especially in places like this. May I also beg to be forgiven for not recognizing you immediately? I thought I must be dreaming . . ."

Siu-Sing had thought of him many times since the banquet: so clean and young—she guessed perhaps twenty-five or thirty years old—and altogether different from the flabby jowls, stale perspiration, and sickly pomades she had become accustomed to. His thick hair was the color of bamboo leaves that had fallen and been bleached by the sun, she decided. His skin was not white, but a light honey brown like her own; his nose quite large and strongly shaped. The shaded candle flickered in his remarkable eyes.

"I was unable to thank you for your kindness to me on that evening at the tavern of Tamiko-san," she replied, delighted by the astonishment it caused him.

"You speak English!" He laughed, reaching across the table to offer his open hand. His warm, strong fingers closed firmly around her own. "We were never properly introduced. . . . My name is Toby—Toby Hyde-Wilkins. I hope sitting with me will not cause trouble for you. Chaps like me are not entirely welcome here."

"You must forgive her; she would not dream that you might understand her. Such insults were for my ears alone . . . they do not bother me."

He had already forgotten about Number Five. "That night I wanted nothing more than to speak with you, to know more about you, but that was impossible. I could not believe that someone like you could be part of J. T. Ching's world. How fortunate that I decided to see for myself what the famous Nine Dragons has to offer."

He took a small leather wallet from his breast pocket and held it open. "I am here partially in an official capacity; it is part of my job to make sure our chaps are not losing their pay in places like this." He put it away with an encouraging smile. "Now you know who I am. Will you tell me about yourself?"

"My father is British, my mother was Chinese," she said, trying to keep the excitement from her voice. "You are the first Englishman I have ever seen. Please forgive me if I stare."

"You are forgiven. We shall stare at each other. . . . May I ask your name?"

He looked at her with such friendly interest that she blurted out, "My father's name is Devereaux, Captain Benjamin Devereaux. My Chinese mother was called Li-Xia, a southern name. I am called Siu-Sing."

His smile returned comfortingly. "Little Star," he mused. "You are no longer little, so, if I may, I will call you Sing . . . a star. It is clear that you were born to shine like one."

Releasing the strength of his hand was like letting go of a lifeline in a gathering storm. She lowered her voice to lean closer, aware of the many eyes upon them. Words tumbled from her lips. "I need help, but we cannot speak of it here. My room is on the next floor, with the number twelve on the door. Come up in a few minutes."

The music seemed to fade and the chattering voices to drop away as he stood to draw back her chair with a slight bow. It was the smallest of gestures, yet it helped her to walk tall and straight as she mounted the stairs with every eye upon her.

Moments seemed like hours before she heard his gentle knock. She opened the door in an instant; he slipped into the room as she fastened the chain. "I don't believe I was seen."

She shrugged, smiling up at him. "It matters little now—we have committed the unforgivable." She did not want to lose his closeness, drawn to him in a way that went beyond the pleasures to be found in the arms of the Silver Sisters.

In that moment, the need for him to hold her was stronger than the need for words. Toby seemed to sense her yearning, yet held back.

"I am here to help you if I can. I am not one of those who would use you."

Every man she had met except Master To had tried to use her. But from the moment she had seen Toby, there had been no question in her mind. "I believe you," she said.

In the privacy of the apartment, Sing spoke of her background and the search not yet begun. She showed him the photograph of the man in a master mariner's uniform beside his Chinese wife.

"I think it is fate that had us meet not once, but twice in so short a time. As it happens, it is part of my job to investigate the difficulties of British subjects in China." He studied the photograph closely. "From what you have told me, your father is a man of importance. Men like him do not disappear easily. A name of such prominence should be easily traced."

Placing the photograph in his wallet, Toby took out two calling cards and handed them to her. The first was embossed with the official crest of his regiment; below it were his name, rank, and a Kowloon telephone number. The second bore the official crest of Government House and his private number.

"Keep these safe; one number or the other should reach me at any time. If it does not, I can be quickly found. I will see that the photograph is copied and safely returned." His manner became briskly confident. "But first, we must get you out of here for a while. You need to get some fresh air and to see something of this place you call the Golden Hill."

Ruby appeared at the door of the adjoining room with a look of concern. Sing smiled reassuringly at her friend. "You remember Ruby, my companion—"

"How could I possibly forget such dancing?" He held out his hand to Ruby. "Don't worry. I will bring her back safely."

Sing was almost surprised when the elevator took them to the ground floor and no one stopped them from leaving the Nine Dragons. Toby flagged a taxi, and under the canopy of neon signs they left the crowded streets of Wan-Chai behind them.

Toby took her to the Army and Navy Club, where the dignified dining room was filled with soft-spoken Westerners. If they glanced her way, it was with only passing interest as he patiently explained the menu. It was the first time Sing had tasted such food as mulligatawny soup and a dish he introduced, with obvious pleasure, as steak and kidney pie.

Afterward, he took her into the heart of the Central District, where brightly lit shop windows were filled with gold, sparkling gems, and beautiful clothes. Most magic of all to Sing was the cinema, where they sat in the dark, transported to a world filled with happy people doing strange and wonderful things; where children played on perfect lawns with white picket fences. She watched a beautiful woman who sang like an angel and whose eyes were as clear as a summer sky and whose hair was as bright as Toby's. Surely this must be a vision of the Westerners' heaven.

⁑

Sing watched the three lucky thumbs slowly circling each other under the glare of the desk lamp. "It is not good for you to see this foreign *bing*. He can cause only trouble." Three-thumbs Poon had used the term of contempt for a common soldier. "He belongs in the bars with drunken sailors, buying drinks for low-class whores. You must not see him again."

"He is no barroom soldier. He is an important officer sent in search of me. While he is here, his money is as good as any other. If he pays to take me out, I will go with him. He says that if you do not agree with this, he will report you for keeping me locked up."

Three-thumbs Poon was a greedy man but not a cruel one. She reached into the pool of light to lay a gentle hand on his nervous thumbs. "He pays well and is a gentleman. He asks nothing of me but my company. Please, you cannot stop him without great fuss. You lose nothing by this and can only gain. If he is satisfied he will make no trouble. I will speak only well of you."

Over the following days, Sing began to see why the city of Hong Kong was called the Golden Hill: They lunched in the old hotel in Repulse Bay; dined overlooking the harbor; and visited the outlying islands

370

aboard the steam ferry. Sing felt a new kind of happiness, as though a part of her that had been sleeping was now wide awake. When a dangerous shadow suddenly fell across her path, she was unprepared.

᛭

A few days later Number Twelve was sitting at a corner table waiting for Toby to arrive. He had promised to take her to the cinema to watch the film again, this time with Ruby. She could not think of a time in her life when she had longed so much to see someone, and she eagerly watched every man who stepped from the elevator or mounted the red-carpeted stairs from the restaurant.

She was still looking for Toby when a tall figure dressed in black pushed his way through the dance floor and walked toward her. There was a momentary lull in the chatter as the dancers instinctively drew aside to let him pass.

The reflections of the revolving ball made it difficult to see his face, but she felt a flash of warning in the slight rise and fall of his walk. Without asking permission, Ah-Keung sat down in the chair opposite her, his face gaunt but well groomed, his hair neatly trimmed yet as unruly as ever, standing straight as though charged with electricity. Along with a well-tailored black suit, he wore an extravagant wristwatch and a heavy gold ring with a large stone of pale green jade on the small finger of his left hand. He twisted the ring as he regarded her with mild curiosity.

"I have heard of the new *jarp-jung* hostess who has so quickly become queen of the Nine Dragons Ballroom," Ah-Keung said. "I hear she has turned her back on her Chinese heritage to seek the ghost of a mysterious *gwai-lo* who does not exist." His voice was calm, as though he were speaking to an old and trusted friend about an unsavory acquaintance. "A *jarp-jung* slut who chases an impossible dream. They say she is possessed by a demon . . . born of a fox fairy that hides among the bones of her bastard ancestors." Only a slight rhythmic motion of his outstretched foot gave away his inner tension.

Sing replied with equal calm. "The boy who herded goats and searched the hills for herbs has done well . . . chosen by the taipan Ching

371

to protect his person. It makes me wonder why such as you would be seen in the streets of Wan-Chai."

He showed no irritation at her insolence, clearly pleased by her perception of him. "There is nothing in these streets that is not known to the Yellow Dragon. The fat fool with the lucky thumbs has to report on those he employs. It seemed a strange coincidence; I thought I would see Number Twelve for myself. No one but the Little Star has the eyes of a ghost."

His eyes crawled slowly over her, the same unblinking stare as *yan-jing-shi*. His unpleasant grin bared uneven teeth, cleaner now than she remembered them.

The expression on Sing's face did not change, though she could suddenly taste bile in her throat.

Ah-Keung flashed the signet ring and wristwatch as he signaled the bar. Number Five came at once. "Brandy . . . the best old moneybags has hidden under the bar. This is no ordinary bar girl; a prized jewel such as she does not drink cold tea or Coca-Cola."

Number Five looked at Sing with frightened eyes. "Ginger tea, please. I will not take brandy."

"We have so much to say to each other, you and I. Did you not think I recognized the Little Star at the banquet for the foreign *bing*? Did you think me fool enough to make our secret known?" He laughed harshly, his outstretched foot slightly increasing its pace. He waited while Number Five set down the brandy and the tea.

"Do not hate me, Little Star. Did I not find you a roof to sleep under as I said I would?" He gave a snort of laughter. "Is it my fault that you did not please the Emperor of Sausages?"

"You sold me as a bond servant when I trusted you."

He shrugged. "It was business. I filled your rice bowl; I had to fill my own. Could you have found a place to take you in if I had not? Far worse could have befallen you on the streets of Macao than the feeble flesh of Fat Fan."

He reached across the table to cover her hand with his. "Besides, I knew you would find a way out. I have faith in the Red Lotus."

The grin faded from his face as she drew her hand away from his touch. He swallowed his anger, reaching over to fill her cup, then sat back, swirling the brandy under his nose.

"I did not fear for the last disciple of Grand Master To-Tze. Surely Fan-Lu-Wei and his fat amahs could be easily dealt with by a warrior such as you? Did you not go on to be a pipe-maker in the Tavern of Cascading Jewels, favorite to the Golden One herself? And did you not learn things of great value from the Japanese *mama-san*?"

He lifted his glass in an exaggerated toast. "You were the chosen one of J. T. Ching, one of the richest men on the Golden Hill . . . you, the Red Lotus from the Rock of Great Strength.

"Let us drink to the Place of Clear Water, where the old ones are at peace." He smirked as he swallowed the brandy and stood up, offering his hand. "But come—this is not the place to speak of such things. Let us go upstairs, where we can talk privately."

Sing looked past his hand. "I will not go upstairs with you. I choose those I wish to speak with; they do not choose me."

His face darkened visibly. "You will welcome me, if you do not want me to report you to a very angry taipan who is eager to find you."

He withdrew his hand and looked her contemptuously up and down. "Master To chose the wrong disciple; you are obviously not a warrior but a whore. It is time that I prove this to be true."

The cup of tea flung into Ah-Keung's face caused heads to turn and Number Five to press the emergency button in her cubicle behind the bar. A sudden flush turned the Forceful One's sallow face burning red.

"So the spirit of the Little Star has not been dimmed by squealing pigs or sleeping dragons." The hand that shot out to grasp her wrist was swift as a lash. His other hand would have swept across her face and back in a double slap, but Sing blocked it and broke his grip with ease.

The elevator doors slid open. Three-thumbs Poon emerged with a bodyguard on each side. When they saw Ah-Keung, the guards stopped short, leaving Three-thumbs to proceed alone. Sing could smell his fear.

"Please, Ah-Gor." Poon used the respectful title of "Elder Brother." "I want no trouble. Tell me what has happened to displease you?"

Ah-Keung picked up a napkin to wipe his dripping face. "You can teach your whores some respect," he hissed. "But I will deal with this one myself."

The voice of Three-thumbs Poon was shrill with alarm. "Please, I beg of you. She is young and inexperienced. She has not yet learned. She will be punished for her disrespect."

The orchestra had stopped playing, the voice of the singer trailing away with the sound of discordant strings. Ah-Keung's fury seemed to slip away in the silence. "No. Do not punish her. We are old friends, Number Twelve and I. We have much to talk about. Perhaps the surprise was too much for her."

He winked at Three-thumbs Poon. "I will be here tomorrow at this time. See that she is ready to receive me in your finest rooms as your most important guest . . . and that she shows me respect, or I will blame you for her bad manners."

A new voice interrupted him. "It is you, my friend, who will learn some manners." Toby Hyde-Wilkins stood two paces away. He had come from the stairs without being noticed. Sing's heart clenched with fear for him.

Ah-Keung ignored him, addressing Three-thumbs directly. "What is this *gwai-lo* doing in the Nine Dragons?"

Toby flicked open his official wallet and held it up. "Government authority," he snapped sharply. "This young lady is a British national and the subject of an official inquiry."

The Forceful One stood in the almost-careless manner of one who welcomed violence. "Tell this tin soldier to get out while he can."

Before Toby could react, Sing stepped in front of him. "Ah-Gor is right. You do not belong here. You belong in the *gwai-lo* bars where the beer is cheap and so are the girls. Do as he says. Get out while you can. You can cause only trouble for me here." Sing slapped Toby hard across the face.

He stood motionless as she thrust her face close to his, trying to warn him through the look in her eyes of the danger he was in. Silence among the tables and from the dance floor was broken by a murmur here, a titter there, until it swelled into laughter, whistles, and shouts of approval:

The *gwai-lo* should go, he was not welcome here. Someone began to clap his hands, which quickly became a rising tide of applause.

After breathless seconds, Toby turned and descended the stairs without a word.

When he had gone, Ah-Keung straightened, running his hands through his brittle hair, smoothing his lapels with a grin of approval as the applause became scattered and dropped away. "I am most impressed, Little Star. Perhaps there is more Chinese blood in your *jarp-jung* veins than I suspected." His mood changed as he turned to Three-thumbs Poon, who was sweating freely, a grin of fright fixed on his face.

"You should know better than to serve *gwai-los*, old moneybags. Do you want the police here?" he said icily. "I expect you to pay for this embarrassment." He glanced at the gold watch. "See that Number Twelve awaits me in her room at this time tomorrow."

He straightened his jacket to look about him. The music had begun again and dancing had resumed as the buzz of excitement ebbed away. "Tell her who I am and what this means here in Wan-Chai. Let her not misunderstand me again, or I shall hold you responsible."

After Ah-Keung had left, Three-thumbs Poon warned Number Twelve that there was nothing he could do to help her, that her only protection would be in the deference and quality of her service to the Forceful One when he returned—or if she were just to disappear without delay. . . . He was almost in tears. "I will pay you well to leave my place of business. I have done nothing to deserve this terrible thing; have I not treated you well?"

"I have been insulted enough this evening," Sing replied. "Let us rest upon it." She felt almost sick at the thought that she might have lost Toby forever.

Early the following morning, after a sleepless night in which she and Ruby reviewed possible courses of action, each more dangerous than the last, Sing was summoned to the darkened office of Three-thumbs Poon. To her joy and relief, Toby was sitting opposite the desk, with Poon in the shadows, his unsteady hands holding a letter beneath the glare of the lamp.

Toby stood the moment she entered, giving her his hand with a smile that told her all was understood. "Good morning, Miss Devereaux. I have been discussing my business here with our friend, Mr. Poon. We have found your name in the files at the Missing Persons Bureau. I have asked Mr. Poon to release you from his employment into my custody while we make further inquiries. He has kindly agreed."

He looked down at the uneasy face of Three-thumbs Poon. "Unless, of course, Mr. Poon would prefer to lodge a complaint against the removal of one of his employees? This would mean accompanying us to the department's offices and revealing his methods of employment, details of his operation, a roster of his entire staff, and of course his taxation files over the past seven years . . . an ordeal I am quite sure he considers unnecessary."

Sing restrained her delight, almost sorry for the man with lucky thumbs. "Mr. Poon has been a generous and just employer. If he will kindly pay me the amount owed for my services, Ruby and I will leave him in peace."

✳

An hour later, they had taken a taxi to the Star Ferry and were halfway across Victoria Harbor to Kowloon. Ruby watched the bags in the crowded saloon while Sing took Toby by the hand, leading him out onto the open deck and forward into the bow.

"Please forgive me for last night's unpleasantness. I do not know how to thank you for helping us in this way." She looked up at him, his blond hair tugged by the crosswinds. "You have not asked me who he is or why he threatens me."

"You will tell me when you are ready." He looked away across the choppy, olive-green waters churned by the harbor traffic and the midstream blow. "Meanwhile, it is my great pleasure to be of service. I am taking you to a place where you will be safe for a few days while we follow our inquiries."

The ferry pitched in the churning wake of a faster vessel, throwing her against him, and for a moment Sing was held tightly in his arms. It passed much too quickly.

376

"His kind is not unknown to me," he said, "nor is Jack Teagarden Ching. They are extortionists and enforcers, feared by their own people but not by mine. They do not welcome trouble with the British government. J. T. Ching is too clever to risk intervention over an issue as personal as this appears to be. He is a cunning operator; we suspect he has connections with organized crime in Japan. Believe me, J. T. Ching has been under close surveillance for a long time."

The wind freshened in sudden blasts. He placed his jacket over her shoulders. "Wouldn't you rather join Ruby inside where it is warmer?"

Sing shook her head. "I have learned how to find space on a boat that carries too many people. You just go as far into the bow as you can, and all the noise and scramble are left behind. From here you can feel the wind on your face, and if you are lucky, you might see dolphins. Everything unfolds before you; nothing lies hidden. It is always the best place to be."

They stood side by side, holding on to the pitching rail, the wind ripping at their hair. "I think I love rivers and boats, ships and the sea more than anything, perhaps because my father is a sea captain and my mother was a comprador. I spent my first days of life on a wondrous voyage up the Yangtze River. I owe my life to that voyage, and to the courage of the Tanka woman who was my father's friend and my mother's devoted servant. She told me many stories of my father and the beautiful ships he built . . . how he took my mother away on the grandest of these, with a name so wonderful that it holds a special place in my heart: *Golden Sky*."

As she spoke, his clear eyes were watching her mouth in a way that secretly thrilled her. She felt her cheeks burn under his gaze, telling herself that it was the freshness of wind over water.

"One day," he said, his arm tightening around her, "you must tell me of these amazing adventures of yours. Nothing you could say would surprise me." He drew the jacket closer around her throat. "You are quite the most unusual young woman I have ever met." Once again they were thrown together by the pitch and roll of the ferry. His arm tightened, and this time held her fast with no thought of letting go.

CHAPTER 29

The Happy Butterfly

On *the Kowloon side,* they joined the swarm of passengers disembarking on the wharf beside the Ocean Terminal. Sing trusted Toby so completely she did not even ask where they were going until they were settled in a taxi.

"I am taking you and Ruby to a quiet hotel for tonight; it is better that you are on this side of the harbor and away from Wan-Chai. I have been making inquiries about your father, and his business seems to have vanished. There is an acquaintance of mine, however, who once owned a small restaurant in Macao. She knows everyone and everything in this part of the world. We will meet with her tomorrow morning, but not too early; she does not receive visitors before eleven."

A wave of exhaustion washed over Sing, and she was grateful to sink into oblivion in the comfortable room he had found for her and Ruby on an obscure side street.

In the morning, she awoke much refreshed, to find that Ruby was up before her, clearly relishing her regained freedom. "I never expected to leave the Nine Dragons again," she said to Sing and Toby. "Thank you for taking me with you."

The ladies were amused by Toby's apparent nervousness about introducing them to his old friend. "She may be a surprise to you, as she always is to those who do not know her. Her name is Lily Chu-Tin, known in Kowloon as Firecracker Lily, because everything about her seems to go off with a bang, although some say it is because of her explosive temper."

He turned to Sing with a quick grin of devilry. "Others say she earned it in bed when she was younger. Whatever the truth, she makes a wonderful friend but also a powerful enemy. Lily owns a dozen bars on the Kowloon side. No madam holds more power or is paid more respect. Even the *sai-lo* are careful in their dealings with her."

They were riding in a taxi along Nathan Road, a wide thoroughfare parallel to the waterfront flanked by massive buildings. The most imposing of these, Toby pointed out, was the famed Peninsula Hotel, the spectacular fountains at its entrance as splendid in their changing colors as a morning sky above the lake. He pointed out the military barracks a few blocks north, a high-walled enclosure entered by huge iron gates bearing the royal coat of arms.

"I use an office there, from time to time. We sometimes visit the local bars for a beer or two, so I am quite well known in certain places."

Shortly beyond the Peninsula Hotel was a teeming side street with a sign over its entry reading HANKOW ROAD. Even before noon, they could see the neon signs ready to flicker to garish life: PINK PUSSYCAT, BOTTOMS UP, SEVEN SEAS, CAVE BAR, FIREHOUSE, YELLOW BRICK ROAD, WELCOME SAILOR, COLD BEER AND A FREE MASSAGE. Most spectacular of all was a gigantic butterfly that stretched its rainbow wings from one side of the road to the other.

"Welcome to Hankow Road and the Happy Butterfly . . . the center of the universe," he said.

Firecracker Lily was indeed formidable. Built like a wrestler and standing only five feet tall in absurdly high-heeled shoes, she wore a wig that climbed in tier after tier of ringlets until it resembled an immense beehive. She greeted Toby like a loving mother. "Where have you been for so long? Why haven't you come to see your Lily?"

When she saw Sing and Ruby, she pushed him away in playful rebuke. "Why do you bring girls from the Hong Kong side? There are plenty of girls here waiting for you." Instantly, a dozen girls smiled and called out greetings from the bar's shadowy cubicles, where they read, knitted, sewed, or dressed each other's hair in readiness for the evening trade.

Toby was suitably embarrassed by the boisterous welcome, but embraced Lily with equal gusto. Sing smiled within, seeing enough in this gaudy little barroom to tell her more about Captain Toby Hyde-Wilkins than he could ever attempt to explain. A few minutes later, Lily led them upstairs to her private apartment overlooking the bedlam of Hankow Road. Seating them in her best armchairs and producing the inevitable pot of tea, she listened as Toby explained the purpose of their visit. When she inspected the photograph of Ben Devereaux and his wife, she nodded her head.

"Yes, I remember Di-Fo-Lo. When he was a young man, he and his partner, Indie, came many times to my restaurant in Macao. I haven't seen either of them in a long time, though."

She sat thinking, then said suddenly, "I know who might be able to help you. He was once a big doctor on the Shanghai side, and was a friend of your father's; they used to go to the racetrack together." She lowered her voice. "He once said Di-Fo-Lo sold guns to the Kuomintang to fight *yut-boon-jai* . . . very big business."

Sing knew "*yut-boon-jai*" meant "the Japanese boy"—the hated soldiers of the rising sun that were China's oldest enemy. Sing leaned forward and asked Lily, "Where can we find this friend of my father's—what is his name?"

"Nobody knows his real name; he's an American, but the girls call him Shanghai Smith. He drinks a little too much, but he's a good doctor and he takes care of the girls. I give him free meals or a drink or two."

She smiled happily. "You were right to come to the Happy Butterfly. It's eleven o'clock; he's probably sitting down to breakfast in the bar right now."

⁂

When Lily introduced Shanghai Smith, Sing's first thought was that he must have been truly handsome as a young man. His angular jaw was close shaven, his graying hair carefully trimmed and combed, his long-fingered hands well manicured. He was dressed in a baggy suit of crumpled white linen, a cream shirt brightened by a colorful hand-painted necktie, his two-tone shoes buffed to a high polish. He rose politely and

380

kissed Ruby's and Sing's hands with the air of a man who had known many attractive women and never lost his respect for them.

This gallant gesture was accompanied by a strong blend of fragrances that contrasted with the bar smells of stale beer, tobacco smoke, and burning joss sticks. When Sing commented on this, the doctor gave a slight bow of acknowledgment, speaking with a broad American accent. "Florida water for the skin . . . Californian Poppy for the hair, and lashings of Lifebuoy soap." He rubbed his hands together vigorously. "I trust you do not find it too overpowering; one is often tempted to be a little heavy-handed in matters of hygiene when reduced to practicing on Hankow Road."

Sing returned his friendly manner with a smile. *I like him*, she thought. *He smells nice and has good manners and makes me feel important. I think he will help me if he can.*

"It is an honor to meet you, sir. We are grateful for your precious time."

He invited them to join him in his corner booth, bearing a brass plaque elaborately engraved with SHANGHAI SMITH, MD. He made sure that the ladies were seated before sliding into the seat facing them. "I can recommend the full English breakfast," he said, shaking out a napkin. "There are few establishments on the Kowloon side that serve a better one than our Lily. But," he turned to Sing and Ruby, "if you would prefer, Lily also serves an excellent rice congee."

He exchanged business cards with Toby. "Now, what can I do for you and these lovely young ladies, Captain?"

The doctor's face lit up when Toby explained their mission. "I was privileged to know Ben Devereaux very well indeed." He paused as Lily bore down on them with a tray loaded with tea things.

"*Gnow-lie-cha*—cow's-milk tea for you, and *ching-cha*, green tea for the ladies," she said. "One Bombay oyster for our good doctor." She set before him a tall glass, a bottle of ice-cold beer, and two eggs, then bustled away to the kitchen.

Smith poured the beer into the tilted glass with the precision of a pharmacist dispensing a critical potion, cracked the raw eggs into its foaming head and drank the concoction with relish. "A hair of the proverbial dog. I find it an indispensable start to the day." He signaled to Lily for his first gin and tonic, then turned to them seriously. "Now, what is it you wish to know about Ben Devereaux?" He inspected the photograph, listening carefully to Sing's account of her circumstances. After a moment or so, he reached across the table to lay his hand on hers.

"We could talk for hours about your father, and I would be delighted to do so in time to come. But you are wondering where to find him now. Sadly, it has been many years since he and I last shared a drink in the long bar of the Shanghai Club, or placed a bet at the Happy Valley racetrack."

He finished the drink, which was immediately replaced by another. "You should seek out Indie Da Silva, who used to be Ben's partner in the Double Dragon Trading Company. They were like father and son." He toyed with the swizzle stick mounted by a glass butterfly. "Indie took your father aboard his trader when Ben arrived in Shanghai as a boy, and I was a bright-eyed student at the American College of Tropical Medicine. I became a surgeon, while they sailed the rivers of China together for a few years before Ben decided to command a vessel of his own. . . . Several years later they became partners in the double-D shipyard."

Smith took a long pull at his drink, the ice clinking in his glass as he set it down, glancing at Toby to see if he should continue.

"It is said he destroyed a statue of Kuan-Yun, goddess of mercy, when he found your mother . . ." The American doctor hesitated. "They say that he searched for you in every way he could, through the corridors of colonial power and the underbelly of the triad. He got help from neither." Again, Shanghai Smith reached across to cover Sing's hand. "The only certainty is that he turned his back on Hong Kong and those who had turned their backs on his terrible grief. He swore never to return, and he never did." He twisted his glass, tracing beads of condensation down the glass. "But Indie can tell you more of these things than I can."

Sing bowed her head to him. "I am very grateful for your help. Can you direct me to this man?"

"The last I heard of Indie Da Silva, he was said to be living among the Tanka boat people in Silvermine Bay on Lantau Island. He had gambled every cent in his pocket and run out of credit in the bars on both sides of the harbor."

"Lantau is an hour or so by launch," said Toby. "I know the sampan village in Silvermine Bay. If he is there, we will find him."

He looked at Sing, who could feel his concern for her as surely as his touch, then turned to Shanghai Smith. "How can we repay you, sir?"

The doctor held up his empty glass. "My dear fellow, you have repaid me with such delightful company. Another of these and we'll consider it quits." He stood as they made to leave. "If you find Indie, come back and tell me what you learn about him and my old friend Ben."

Toby obtained the use of a Maritime Services launch, which cut cleanly through the dark green water at a steady fifteen knots. The morning was almost windless, the occasional cat's-paw of light winds ruffling the surface. They had left at 6:00 A.M., the perfect, bright orange orb of the sun hardly lifted from the China Sea. Toby had given the coxswain an unexpected day off duty, and sat at the wheel with Sing beside him. Ruby had accepted Lily's invitation to stay at the Happy Butterfly; she said she wished to enjoy her newfound freedom, but Sing recognized her friend's tact in sending her and Toby on the journey alone.

The huge mass of Lantau Island, its highest peak still shrouded in mist, loomed a little larger with each moment. Junks near and far drifted beneath batwing sails. To Sing it was one of the most important mornings of her life.

With Toby beside her, the sunlight in his hair lighting his face with its glow, she again felt the thrill of his closeness. He wore white shorts and a white shirt, its sleeves rolled up to reveal sunburned forearms. She found herself fascinated by the light gold hair that glistened from the back of his hands to his elbows. She reached out and touched it lightly, causing him to turn and smile at her.

"The hairy barbarian." He laughed, lifting his leg to show the same vigorous growth on his shins. "I'm afraid chaps like me are covered in it." He grinned easily.

She shook her head, returning his smile. Toby eased the throttle, slowing the constant throb of the powerful motors, coasting through the moored and anchored village of the boat people. For Sing there was a fleeting sense of coming home; the wooden hulls, fishnets hoisted up to dry, the unmistakable tang of salted fish, voices calling across the water. They were like the foreshores of the lake, it filled her with a moment's longing for a time and place she would never know again.

Most of the Tanka barely looked up from cleaning nets, splicing ropes, and squatting over their rice bowls, though a few watched them pass with idle suspicion. "I doubt they have seen too many government boats, but they are used to foreigners commuting on the ferry. This is a favorite spot for fine seafood at half the price of Hong Kong."

"I have learned to speak the language of the boat people," Sing said eagerly. "If he is here, he should not be hard to find." She looked up at the master of the largest junk, the long pennants of his clan unfurled at the masthead proclaiming him an elder of his people. When she greeted him respectfully in his native dialect, he gave her a gap-toothed grin, answering in a loud, cheerful voice accustomed to bawling orders above the wind. They had an animated conversation for several minutes.

At last, with all words of respect, greetings, directions, and farewells complete, Toby pushed off in the direction the junk master had indicated. Sing said, "The man we seek is known to them as 'Eagle Beak,' because of the size and shape of his nose. He is to be found around the point."

She smiled at Toby's expression. "I know it seems a lot of talk for so simple a question, but it is the way of the Tanka to discuss small things before giving an answer. It is not polite to show impatience."

The launch rounded an outcrop of jagged rock and headed into a small inlet. "He says that Eagle Beak is a strange one of many secrets. They think he is a ghost, neither Chinese nor *gwai-lo*, and that his junk is a phantom ship from the past. But he is kind to their children and makes no trouble."

Sing could not suppress a giggle. "He also says Eagle Beak lives here because he has too many women, too many children, and too many bar bills on the Golden Hill."

A lone vessel was anchored off a curve of sandy beach littered with driftwood. "Good God!" Toby exclaimed. "It's a bloody *lorcha*, designed by the Portuguese to chase pirates. They stopped building them thirty years ago. Your junk captain was right; it *is* like a ghost from the past."

As the launch drew closer, Sing saw that eyes had been painted on the bows of the *lorcha* in the way of all junks on the lookout for sea-monsters. Above them, in faded letters, she read the name: CHINA SKY. MACAO.

The man looking down was different and solitary-looking as the craft that was obviously his home. Some sparse items of washing flapped from a line stretched between the masts, the unexpected smell of brewed coffee drifted from the stern, and a large tortoiseshell cat stretched itself upon the hatch. Tall and upright despite his years, Indie Da Silva stood at the rail stripped to the waist, his brown skin scarred and pitted as old timber. Faded tattoos roamed the long, wiry arms folded across his chest. The *lorcha*'s freeboard put him a good five feet above the white bleached deck of the launch. A mane of tangled hair the color of gunmetal fell below his shoulders, hard to distinguish from an uncombed beard that reached his chest. Thick rings of gold pierced the lobes of both ears.

To Sing he seemed almost a giant from another world. She remembered the words of the Fish: "Gossip among the fish-cleaners says he was once a pirate in the Caribbean Sea. Perhaps he was, but he was a father to Di-Fo-Lo and respectful to your mother."

Sing knew that the man looking down at them might be the only person who could tell her the truths she had to hear. She called up to him, "I am the daughter of Ben Devereaux and Li-Xia. If you are the one who was once his partner and his dearest friend, then I beg to speak with you. I offer these things as proof of my words."

She held out the photograph and the golden guinea from around her neck. "These were given me by the Tanka woman he called the Fish, who took me from my mother's arms to safety and watched over me as her own. I have traveled from the province of Hunan to the Golden Hill to find him, if he lives, or where he lies if he is gone."

Indie Da Silva made no move to reach for the photograph, looking down for a long moment before replying, "A scrap of paper with a likeness on it is easy to come by; so is a gold guinea." He took the launch's heaving line, making it fast to a cleat. The cat uncurled itself, padding tigerlike along the deck, observing them with round yellow eyes.

"But no person would be fool enough to find me to tell such a lie. Only a Devereaux would have come this far." He threw his head back and laughed so loud, the cormorants left the shallows to circle the crescent of sand. He sent a rope ladder over the side of the *lorcha*.

"Come aboard, Ben Devereaux's daughter and whoever you've got with you."

Fingers strong and hard as iron closed around her hand as he helped her over the gunwale and onto the deck. "This is a good friend, Toby Hyde-Wilkins," Sing told him quickly. "Without him I could not have found you."

Indie nodded, shaking Toby's hand. "Well then, I'll take your word for it." He motioned them both to follow him. "You've got this far, you might as well come below and see if it was worth the passage."

The saloon of *China Sky* was lined with the rich sheen of Burma teak. A mess table of the same mellow wood was slung on brass gimbals, a polished copper lamp hanging above it. Indie quickly sent a scattering of eating utensils into the sink of the adjoining galley space. "I don't get many visitors," he said, emerging with a battered coffeepot, three chipped enamel mugs, and a board bearing a chunk of bread and a lump of white cheese.

He sloshed scalding coffee into the mugs and gestured for them to be seated on the bench that ran the length of the table, then turned his attention to Sing. "There's a whole lot at stake for the daughter of Ben Devereaux. I've got no way of knowing for certain who you are. As I say, you could have come upon the picture any number of ways—the gold coin too."

He watched Sing closely over the steaming rim of the mug, his face forming its easy grin. "But there's no way in all seven of God's great seas you could beg, borrow, or steal his eyes." He thumped the table at his own words, leaning over to cup her face in his huge hands and give her a kiss on the nose.

Indie sat back, lowering his voice as he reached back to another time, another world. "You could tell the weather by your dad's eyes . . . see a storm coming and know ahead of time when to shorten sail or ride it out." He smiled. "But when the skies were clear, you never saw a brighter light or a calmer sea. I see the same deep waters and God-given light when I look into yours."

The cat appeared suddenly at his side, leaping lightly onto the table, its golden eyes wide. Indie ran a caring hand down the length of its back, scratching the scruff of its neck, causing it to arch, its tail erect with ecstatic expectation. "She's damn near as old as I am and she's careful about talking to strangers." His words were affectionate."Looks like she's about ready to give you a chance, which is something she doesn't do easy."

With the unblinking eyes of the cat fixed upon her, Sing sought the right words for this moment. "I have dreamed about finding my father for a long time. But all I know is what the Fish told me of his life before I was born . . ."

She would have said more, but Indie Da Silva held up his hand. "I'll tell you what I think you must be told. . . . Then, if it isn't enough, I'll answer any questions that I can. That way we'll not be wasting each other's time.

"First thing for you to know is Ben and Li-Xia were properly married under God's great sky, which is as good as any church there is. I know because I married them according to the law of marriage at sea by a master mariner . . . so you're no bastard and don't let anyone say you are."

He reached for a flat, half-empty bottle in a rack by his side. "The last time I saw Ben was more years back than I care to tally. He was at the helm of *Golden Sky* with a cargo of guns and ammunition, and a crew of reprobates we scratched up from Aggie Gate's mission."

Sing's heart beat faster as she watched him, hungry for every word. "There wasn't a clipper afloat on the China coast that could come close

387

to *Golden Sky* with the wind behind her, and no master worthy of the name could handle a ship the way Ben Devereaux could handle his." He paused for a second, his mind elsewhere. "But no sailing vessel can out-run a Japanese gunboat with a full head of steam. They blew us out of the water."

Indie stopped, twisting the cork from the rum bottle, adding a generous glug to the remains of his coffee. "Truth of it is, I never saw him again, dead or alive. I woke up in a Japanese prison camp and stayed there till they got tired of waiting for what was left of me to die. As soon as I had the strength, I took the only thing left of the Double Dragon Company, and that was *China Sky*." He grinned. "Nobody wanted her, see? They had her tied up at the wrecker's yard. I just jumped aboard and sailed away."

Indie paused to gesture at the saloon of seasoned wood and polished brass so lovingly preserved. "Your father built this *lorcha* from a derelict hulk he dragged from the Macao typhoon shelter. It took him two years and the work of ten strong men to restore her. She was his first command, and together we built twenty more, each one finer and faster than the one before. A Sky Class ship could leave even an opium clipper wallowing in her wake. We lost them all in the Pearl River blockade . . . all except *China Sky*."

Sing's eyes were bright with tears as she reached across the table to offer her hand to him. He continued, "This boat was carved from your old man's heart. It's all I have left of him, except for this." As if by magic, a heavy silver coin appeared between his fingers. He flipped it spinning in the air, catching it neatly, holding it up between thumb and forefinger for her inspection. "The famous Double Dragon dollar . . . There was a time when this was safer currency than any coin of any realm . . . valued more than Mexican silver or Spanish doubloons."

Sing felt a depth of gratitude for this man who an hour ago had been no more than a name that cost a drink or two. She wanted to tell him so, give him something in return. "Was there nothing more for you? You were my father's partner. . . ." He was clearly ill at ease with sentiment, cutting her short before she could say more.

"We started out like father and son . . . we grew to be partners, but we saw the world in different ways. I taught him all he knew of the river trade, but he never shared my bearings on how to set a course in life. I spent what was mine the way I wanted, while he saved his and built for the future." Again, he tossed the silver coin high and caught it. "Where did it get him?

"Anyway, he didn't do everything right. He made some big mistakes, but big mistakes go with big ambitions." The deep-set seams around Indie's eyes crinkled at some long-forgotten thought. "He gambled too much, drank too much . . . but it was his fortune at stake and his body at risk." Indie took a swig from the mug, looking Sing in the eye. "The only thing your old man didn't do was womanize. Seems he had a notion that there was only one woman for him—the right one or none at all. I think he found her in Li-Xia."

Indie Da Silva seemed suddenly uncomfortable, as though he had said too much. He continued more quietly. "When your mother was taken from him, it changed everything. He searched like a man demented—which, when I think about it, he probably was. He had built his world around her and the child she carried . . . to him, you were the future." Indie rolled the coin from knuckle to knuckle with practiced ease. "I can't tell you exactly how Li-Xia was taken; too many stories have been told by too many people, and I was in Macao with a hole in my gut and a fire to put out. I know your father tried everything to find you. When there was nothing left for him in Hong Kong, he just closed everything down and went to Shanghai.

"He left the Macao shipyard to me, but the Double Dragon was finished. We never said so or put it in writing, but we knew it was over." There was a sadness in Indie's eyes that made Sing want to comfort him. "I heard that Ben went about his Shanghai business in a way that should have seen him dead a dozen times over. So far as I know, the risks he took paid off and he was richer than ever . . . until he ran out of luck. It took a Japanese deck gun to get Ben and *Golden Sky*."

The coin transferred from one fist to another, its momentum hardly changed. "I played some high stakes for a year or two, but never really needed anything more than a deck beneath my feet and a good spread of canvas above me. There was a time when these would give you anything worth the taking. Those days are long gone, and Ben and I went with them, except for the trip from Soochow Creek to Formosa . . . the big voyage. He sent for me and I joined him. I think we both knew it could be our last trip together, and I guess he hoped it would be."

Indie Da Silva fell quiet for a moment, then went on in a softened tone that reached out to her with infinite care. "They say Chinese women don't know love the way a *gwai-lo* looks at it, but your mother loved Ben Devereaux as truly as any man could hope for. And he loved her the best way a man can . . . he saw past her good looks and showed her respect. She didn't need anyone to teach her about pride; she already had a following sea on that. I don't know the Chinese word for dignity, but she had a fair wind on that too. The same goes for courage . . . she was brave as any man alive and said less about it."

He spun the coin one last time and handed it to her. "I wish you well in your search for him. The Japanese kept no records . . . what they couldn't use, they burned. Take this coin; it may bring you luck. If you find Ben, show it to him and he'll know I gave it to you. I'd help you if I could, but I washed up on this beach ten years ago and don't expect to leave it alive." He grinned ruefully. "I have an understanding with the boat people . . . when I'm gone, they'll tow me out to sea and put a torch to *China Sky*. The Tanka are people of their word."

He stood up in a way that said the talk was over. "But I think you know that from the old woman he called the Fish. Ben put a lot of faith in her, and I think what hope he had went with her when she took you. It's a good thing she lived to see you grown; Ben would be happy about that."

He cast off the launch's bowline, watching as Toby put the throttle in reverse to pull slowly away from *China Sky*.

"One more thing you should know," he called after them. "There was a witness to that wedding . . . a teacher. She taught Li-Xia how to be a lady. Her name, I think, was Bramble . . . Winifred Bramble. Englishwoman . . ."

Indie Da Silva raised a hand, calling loudly as the launch gathered speed and the gap between them widened. "You find what you're looking for, you let me know. *China Sky* is so full of holes, I won't be going anywhere. . . . And you, Toby Whateveryournameis, you take good care of Ben's girl, or I'll come looking for you."

�֎

The taxi had hardly stopped outside the Happy Butterfly before Ruby was at the door. She was pale with terror, her words so wild that Sing had to hold her close before she was calm enough to be understood. "The taipan's bodyguard, the one who came to Nine Dragons, he came in search of you." The front door of the bar was locked, the windows boarded up. They entered from the back to find nothing but wreckage— mirrors smashed, chairs and tables overturned, broken bottles and glasses littering the floor.

"He brought *sai-lo*, the younger brothers, with him; they did this. The Forceful One beat Lily. He choked her . . . but she told him nothing. I hid among the other girls. They have gone now; the bar is closed. I think the Shanghai doctor is trying to help Miss Lily."

Firecracker Lily lay on the bed in her private room upstairs, which looked even worse than the bar below. Shanghai Smith was mixing a potion, his medical bag open on the bed. Her face was swollen, an eye half closed, the bruises fresh upon her neck.

Lily tried to speak, her words difficult to hear as Toby leaned close. Filled with anger and fear, she pointed at Sing as though she were a ghost. "The Forceful One came looking for this girl. He said her *sung-tip* belonged to the big boss Ching, and anyone who tried to hide her would pay for it. If he returns and finds her here—"

Trembling, Firecracker Lily tried to sit up, but cried out in pain and agitation as Shanghai Smith pushed a needle into her fleshy arm. "Please, take this one and her *chi-chi* girl away. She brings very bad joss to the Happy Butterfly."

391

CHAPTER 30

The Valley

The old walled village of Lok-Choy-Lam was set in a valley at Fanling, on the border between Hong Kong's New Territories of the Kowloon Peninsula and mainland China. Duck farms and fishponds were scattered among terraces of rice and market gardens as far as the eye could see. An air of tranquility settled over the valley, as though Kowloon and Hong Kong were worlds away instead of an hour by car. Rows of black-clad Hakka women bent over curving furrows, wielding hoes and carrying wooden buckets of water on springy bamboo poles, their wide-brimmed hats fringed with a valance of black gauze to shield them from the sun. Images from a separate world, unchanged by the passing of time, the women plodded serenely behind straining buffalo and wooden plows, chattering like sparrows.

Sing felt a comforting sense of homecoming as the army vehicle bumped along tracks of yellow clay churned by ox carts and working buffalo, with geese scattering from under the lurch of their wheels and dogs barking at the grinding of gears. She was seated in the back with Ruby, while Toby sat beside the smartly turned-out Rajput driver steering skillfully through ruts of yellow mud. The driver's wide mustache was neatly brushed and clipped, its pointed ends twirled with wax. At every opportunity, Sing noted, his deep-set dark eyes reflected in the rearview mirror seemed to seek those of Ruby, who sat quietly watching the passing countryside.

Hardly anyone had spoken since they had left Kowloon behind.

Finally, Sing felt forced to speak. "I am sorry to have caused such great trouble to your friend Lily."

Toby turned in his seat with a grin. "Firecracker Lily is no stranger to the ways of the triad enforcer," he reassured her. "She has protection of her own, and I have taken steps to see there is no further trouble. The Yellow Dragon may terrorize the Chinese, but they avoid any confrontation with British authority that could lead to an investigation." He paused warily. "This Ah-Keung, however, seems to have a mind and purpose of his own. For a man like that to be chosen as Ching's personal bodyguard means that he is respected by his kind—and suggests he is also highly dangerous."

The vehicle pulled to a slithering halt beside a narrow bridge stretched across an irrigation ditch. "This is the farm of Po-Lok and his family, who supply the garrison with fresh produce. These Hakka people have cut themselves off from all but the Tolo Market a few miles farther on. I would trust Po-Lok with my life. You will be safe here for as long as necessary."

The driver left his place behind the wheel, and with a stiff salute opened the rear door, his dark eyes fixed ahead. "We must walk to the house," said Toby. "As I'm sure you know, the Hakka rely on the buffalo and the ox cart for transport."

They had left Hankow Road so hurriedly that there was little to carry; Toby had promised to collect their belongings from the hotel and keep them safely. He had not asked why Sing wore the beaded sling so securely buckled.

He led them across the bridge and onto a well-trodden pathway, among endless rows of cabbage, white radish, and sweet potato. Nearer to the farmhouse and its outbuildings was a field of ripening barley, the lower slopes terraced with flooded rice paddies glittering in bright sunshine.

"Welcome," Toby said, "to the Residence of Eternal Peace." The first to greet them were the dogs, quickly silenced by Toby calling them by name. Po-Lok's youngest wife, Kam-Yang, a robust woman of indeterminable age, hurried from the main house and bowed to Toby, who delighted her by bowing even lower as he introduced his companions.

In the large, cool room kept for special occasions, they were received as honored guests. There were no telephones in the little valley and no other way of announcing their arrival but barking dogs, yet Po-Lok quickly presented himself, dressed in his best shirt and jacket of a Western style long forgotten. Tea and mooncakes were fetched for Sing and her companion, with bottles of cold Tsingtao beer for Toby. The host offered his deepest apologies for such miserable fare in such unworthy surroundings. The *siu-jeh*, his "younger sister," and her worthy companion were welcome for as long as they cared to suffer the inferior hospitality of Po-Lok.

There was a mill house, half hidden in a grove of citrus trees, well apart from the main buildings. Used as a store for winter rice, it could soon be cleared out and made comfortable. If the *siu-jeh* could suffer such humble accommodations, she and Ruby would be assured of their privacy. In return, Sing protested their unworthiness of such generosity in this place clearly blessed by heaven itself. With everyone's honor satisfied and all face intact, Toby thanked Po-Lok and Kam-Yang and took his leave.

"I wish I could stay longer," he told Sing quietly, "but there is too much work to be done in these uncertain times. I think you will find it pleasant here. Meanwhile, I will follow up on our inquiries with my contacts in Shanghai and see if the teacher Da Silva mentioned is registered with the Ministry of Education. I will be back as often as I can."

As Toby started back along the pathway to the road, Sing had to stop herself from running after him.

✠

The small, two-story mill house was very old and a little tumbledown, but had a sound roof and thick walls. Downstairs, an old table and four stools had been hurriedly placed under a window looking out to the millpond. The room above held two small wooden beds and clean bedding, cooking pots, and candles, delivered by Kam-Yang and her giggling granddaughters.

In contrast to the island of blue water hyacinth that bloomed in the

394

pond, the walls and roof were overgrown with a tangle of wild honey-suckle. Tiny, heavily scented flowers framed the windows and door with a creamy, luster, drawing hosts of pale yellow butterflies. The tangy perfume of citrus blossom seemed trapped in the stillness of this quiet corner of the valley. So exquisite was this secret haven that it brought tears to Ruby's eyes.

Sing and Ruby were each given field hats and the short, wide-legged pants and jacket of waterproofed cotton worn by the Hakka. Invited to join the family for meals or to make their own in the makeshift kitchen of the mill, they preferred solitude to endless exchanges with their attentive hosts. There was little Sing could talk or think about but Toby and the discovery of her father's fate.

In her quietly contented manner, Ruby turned the little stone house into a home, sweeping the flagstone floors and shining the windows. She picked sprigs of orange blossom, placing them in jars on the window-sills. She made sure there was always a pot of tea at hand.

As she went about her tasks, Ruby sang songs from the land she was born in, soft and melodic, in her own language. In the evenings, by the light of an oil lamp, she worked with scraps of cloth in many colors and designs collected from the kindly Kam-Yang, stitching them with great skill and patience to make a *mien-toi*, a patchwork quilt for Sing's bed.

Nights in the Residence of Eternal Peace passed in the deep sleep that comes with the finding of sanctuary. Hard work, plain and plentiful food, and the absence of malice had brought a kind of comfort Sing had almost forgotten. If she and Ruby both knew this could only be temporary, they did not speak of it.

On their third night, after a long walk exploring the slopes, they washed naked in the millpond, and enjoyed a supper of chicken dumpling soup. It was still early as they lay in their separate beds. Pleasantly tired but unable to sleep, Sing watched the rising moon through the open window; an owl hooted in the orchard and the far-off yap of a fox was lost in the distance. Sensing that Ruby too was awake, Sing said at last, "I am sorry that I have placed you in danger. Ah-Keung has hated me since I was two years old, even in my crib. I believe it is written somewhere that we are destined to face each other . . . I do not know when."

Ruby answered without hesitation. "I have spent my life in danger. But I am no longer afraid to see myself in the mirror, or ashamed to smile—and you have given me freedom. For that I will always love you."

Sing was thankful for her words, yet unable to shed the creeping burden of guilt. "So much has happened so suddenly, there has not been time for us to talk as we once did. . . . Is there room for me beside you?"

A pause made her wonder if Ruby had fallen asleep, or had not heard the quiet words in the dark. This time when she answered it was not without an edge of sadness. "We shared a bed because that was the way to survive . . . it was expected of us. If we discovered pleasure and kept loneliness away, it was because we had no one else to turn to and nowhere else to go."

Before Sing could reply, Ruby spoke again, the sadness gone. "Things are different now. I think you have no need of me nor I of you. The young lord looks at you with tenderness; there is love in his eyes and a place for you in his heart. He longs for you to lie beside him. I think you long for this too." She sighed playfully. "He will teach you more of love than I ever could."

Sing could not argue with Ruby's words, but felt their loneliness. "The driver looked at you in such a way," she said with a touch of laughter. "Did you not feel it?"

"I have had my chance at such a wonderful thing, but it was taken from me. It will never come again." There was a long moment of silence as the owl's shadow crossed the window. "I think of love as the rarest, most beautiful bird . . . wonderful to see and sweet to listen to, but always out of reach. From the time we are born, if we are allowed to live, our only value is our virtue. It is traded and bargained for like a yard of silk or a jar of wine. While we are untouched, they will not leave us alone until a man old and unpleasant but rich enough to pay takes us painfully and without thought, to give him strength . . . and then we are forgotten."

She turned over in her bed, then spoke with no trace of bitterness.

"Lie with the young lord, Siu-Sing; he is clean and kind, and I believe he truly loves you." She yawned. "Soon you will find your father. I am content to see your happiness."

⋈

On her fifth day in the valley, the barking dogs caused Sing to look out the window. The whine of the army vehicle's engine carried across the fields as it drew away, leaving Toby to follow the path through the barley field.

It was a day of celebration, the Festival of Hungry Ghosts. Po-Lok and his family had left early for the fishing village of Tai-Po, a two-mile journey by ox cart laden with market produce and excited grandchildren in their festive finery. Ruby had gone with them, as if she had known that this was the day Toby would come.

Sing found herself running to meet him. He walked with a long, easy stride, a large brown paper parcel under one arm, a short leather swagger cane swinging from the other.

His voice reached out to her. "Is it me that you are so pleased to see . . . or the news I may bring?"

"Both, of course," she answered breathlessly.

He paused for a moment beside the millpond, observing a family of water hens dipping among the hyacinth. "Can there be anywhere more idyllic than this peaceful valley?" he asked, ducking his head to follow her into the house. Tossing the package on the table by the window, he dragged a wooden chair across the flagstones, looking around the little space with its bright window, well-swept floors, and pots of freshly gathered orange blossom.

"By the color in your cheeks and the light in your eyes, this little place agrees with you."

"We call it the Honeysuckle House," she said, bringing a stone jug of fresh, cool orange juice to the table by the window. "Ruby squeezed this straight from the tree before she left this morning."

He sprawled comfortably in the chair, tossing the cane onto the table beside the parcel. "I have news of our inquiries. . . . Some of it you will be pleased to hear."

397

Sing filled the cups with juice. "Whatever it is, I thank you for it, as I thank you for all you have done. I have burned joss sticks to the earth gods for your safety and good health."

He pretended to bow while seated. There was a moment of hesitation, as though he looked for a place to begin.

"Unfortunately, our Shanghai contacts confirm everything we learned from your father's partner." Toby reached across the table to take Sing's hand in his. "I regret to say it seems that . . . Captain Devereaux was lost with his ship."

Sing sat straight, but turned her face to the window.

"There is, I am pleased to say, one promising discovery. Da Silva was right—your mother was tutored by an Englishwoman, Miss Winifred Barbara Bramble, a highly distinguished lady long retired but still living in Hong Kong. She is elderly but still very active socially and prominent in affairs of community welfare."

He waited as she turned to look at him, smiling at her look of anticipation. "The lady was astonished but delighted when I explained the reason for my call. She is eager to meet you, and we are invited to tea this weekend at her home on Stonecutters Island, a minute or two from Kowloon. She told me it was she who 'snapped' the photograph you carry. She was matron of honor at your parents' wedding."

He pushed the package across the table. "It appears that Miss Bramble is a lady of considerable style and taste. I have brought you something to wear."

In the parcel, carefully wrapped in layers of paper, was a pink and white dress of the finest cotton. She dared not lift it from the bed of tissue, running her fingertips over the softness of the material. "It's a summer frock, the kind an English girl would wear to a garden party or a fete. Colonel Pelham's wife, Margaret, was kind enough to choose it. She insists pure cotton is cooler than silk. . . . I hope it fits; she had to guess, but has a daughter about your age.

"She said you would need other things, so you will find them in the package too—gloves, shoes, a hat . . ."

"I have never seen anything so beautiful," Sing whispered.

He stood up. "You can try it on later. What is it the Chinese say—'pleasure before business'? It's a beautiful day. Perhaps we should go for a walk."

She agreed eagerly. "Let me show you what I have found . . . a special place that will be our secret."

They walked the pathways through the fields, over the bridge across the paddies, and up the slopes to the thick jungle of head-high tiger grass that crowned the hilltops. The well-worn track wound past patches recently cut, leaving swaths of short yellow stubble. "We have been taught to cut and tie the tiger grass . . . it feeds the cattle and burns well when bound with ox dung. It reminds me of the reed-cutters I knew as a child."

Halfway up the hill, almost hidden by sheltering trees, stood a ruined temple, its roof collapsing with age. "It is the Temple of Tien-Hau, shrine to the Last Tiger. Po-Lok says it has been here for many centuries." She led the way through its overgrown courtyard and into the dark inner chamber. A group of wooden images, once brightly painted, stood in faded glory, surrounding the central figure raised on an open lotus flower.

"She is the goddess Tien-Hau, protector of fishermen and farmers, sister to the earth gods." On the wall above an altar was the skin of a tiger. "It is the last tiger to be found on this side of the border. Now its spirit stands behind the goddess, guarding the valley and those who live here."

Sing reached into a darkened corner. "Kam-Yang has given me fresh joss sticks. We will light three sticks and each say a silent prayer. If Tien-Hau hears us, she will grant any wish."

It was midafternoon when they returned to the mill. The sun had lost much of its heat, throwing lengthening shadows among the orange trees. They were alone in the Residence of Eternal Peace, and she knew that there might never be another moment such as this. Even the beautiful things he had brought her must wait. Forbidden thoughts whirled in her head: the white skin of the Tanka girl in the marsh; the rose-petal hands and butterfly kisses of Ruby; the clean scent and honey-colored skin of Toby, the golden hairs on the back of his hands. . . .

Her heart beat faster as she kicked off her sandals at the door and held out her hand. "You have not seen the room upstairs . . . let me show you where I sleep."

She led him up the narrow stairs—to find the little room filled with flowers. The beds had been pulled together, Ruby's padded quilt smoothly spread and strewn with petals. There was little need of words as she began to loosen the ties that fastened her jacket, letting it slide from her shoulders.

Toby stood for a moment, unable to speak, then whispered gently, "Are you sure?"

"With you I am sure," she answered in a breath. "You will be the first, and I am honored by it. I do not understand the love of a man, but with you I am happy." Stepping close to him, she began to unbutton his shirt.

"Wait . . . ," he said. Tenderly, he brushed her soft lips with his, her chin, her cheeks, her temples, her eyelids, the warm hollow of her throat. For Sing it was as though a captive bird had at last escaped, soaring into endless space. She found her mouth responding, returning his kisses with an ardor she had never felt before.

She could smell the warmth of his body as he leaned so close she could detect the sap of barley grass he had chewed as they walked through the field. She wondered again at the fairness of his hair, her hand reaching up to touch it, feeling its texture, fine to her as spun silk.

The feeling that welled inside made her suddenly bolder as she pushed her hand through his hair more strongly, letting the weight of it fall through her fingers again and again. She felt his hands close lightly on her waist and then hold her more firmly, their warmth reaching through the thin cotton of her vest.

Toby stepped backward, drawing her with him until the back of his legs touched the bed. Carefully, he lowered his body until he sat on its edge, leaving her standing before him, her hands still buried in his hair. His hands slipped to her hips as he pulled her to him, resting his head against her breasts. She could hear the thud of her heartbeat as his hands moved cautiously over the swell of her buttocks and down her legs to the backs of her knees, feeling the smoothness of her skin sliding under the coarse weave of cotton.

Quickly, almost roughly, his hands found her breasts, his palms brushing their growing hardness through the vest, its fabric so fine that the darker rings around her jutting nipples were clearly visible. Breathlessly, Toby slid his hands over her shoulders, holding her firmly, his mouth gently teasing through the tight skin of material.

His hands went still as her legs began to tremble, as though he was afraid she would break away from him. She made no move except to draw his cheek closer to her breast. They stayed for moments unmoving but for her fingers stroking his hair.

"Don't be afraid," he whispered softly. Standing slowly, carefully, he lifted her chin with a gentle finger. "You must never be afraid of me."

The thrill of his touch seemed to weaken her limbs, filling her with sweetest wonder. How would it feel if there was nothing between them? Reluctant to detach herself from him, Sing quickly stripped the vest upward and over her head, allowing the eager warmth of his mouth to engulf her completely.

His fingers reached for the drawstring that secured her loose cotton pants. She felt them slip away; a second's pause, then, more slowly, the silken fabric of her undergarment was removed. She gasped at the heat of his breath upon her skin, then fumbled for the fastenings of his clothes, eager to feel his nakedness against hers, stroking his muscular body in wonder.

He brought her close to the thunder and rain, but drew back until she gasped with longing. Finally, he entered her so carefully that she craved all of him, delighting them both with the passion that uncoiled with such urgency as she drowned in the blueness of his dazzling eyes.

Sing awoke to the voices of Po-Lok and his family returning from the village. The bed beside her showed the hollow of his body in the goose-feather mattress; his scent still lingered.

He had left a sprig of blossom on the pillow with a note:

My darling,

This would not have happened if we had not found love so quickly and so surely. Neither of us would have allowed it.

I will do all that I can to help you fulfil your dream, and if your father's resting place is to be found, we will find it together. Whatever lies in store for us, we have found each other, and that is miracle enough for me.

I will come for you early on Saturday, about 8 A.M.

Toby

Sing pressed the fleshy buds between her palms, breathing their tangy fragrance and knowing at last what it meant to love and be loved. She stretched languidly, then glanced at the box Ben had given her with the beautiful dress. She would try it on now and show it to Ruby, but she could scarcely wait for Saturday.

CHAPTER 31

The Storm

When *the storm came* on the following day, Sing and Ruby were high on the hillside, cutting the tiger grass to weave weatherproof capes for the coming winter. In just one more day, she would see Toby again and meet Miss Winifred Bramble, who would tell her about her parents and who might know where her father was buried. Meanwhile, Sing looked back over the cluster of square, whitewashed houses, the circular remains of the walled village, the perfect green lines of cultivation.

The scene, usually so serene to look upon, was suddenly bathed by an early twilight, a brassy glare that made everything unreal. From far below, the distant voice of Po-Lok's son drifted up, urging mud-caked buffalo through the terraces to the shelter of the barn. She could see the ducks heading for the ponds as though it were the end of the day.

The first gust of wind snatched at Sing's hat, flattening the grass around her like the sweep of a scythe. At first the change seemed welcome, as the day had begun still and humid. But Po-Lok had warned them that they should not go far up the hillside and must return quickly if the weather changed. Word had reached him that the observatory on the island of Hong Kong had hoisted a storm warning. This was the season of *dai-fong*—the big wind that the Westerner called "typhoon."

Sing had known such signs before, when the lake looked like beaten copper under a sky of steel, when sampans sailed for the safety of the typhoon shelter and the reed-cutters closed their shutters and barred their doors. Sing had seen dragon winds scouring the surface of the

403

lake, sending the yellow waters in rolling waves to swamp the reed beds, but passing them over like a beast in search of larger prey. Now she had only to look at the sulturous hue of the sky, to see more birds soundlessly filling the trees, to know it was time to find shelter.

As abruptly as if a switch had been thrown, thunderheads piled up like molten rock to hide the sun. The valley seemed scorched by an eerie light. A flock of egrets, usually content to prowl the furrows, whirled upward to circle the highest trees.

Often the *dai-fong* passed them by, Po-Lok had informed them, or lashed its tail across the island and left the valley in peace. But this was coming directly for them, rearing over the valley like a rising bear. The gusts increased in sudden blasts heavy with the chill of rain.

Sing had become separated from Ruby; she heard her slashing the cane grass nearby but could not see her. Sing called her name, telling her to start down the slope. Before she could shoulder the bundle of grass, the first deluge arrived, fat drops thudding on the brim of her hat and smacking her shoulders with stinging force.

She had taken no more than a dozen steps before hail sliced across the slopes in icy sheets. Again she told herself she had seen such storms sweep the lake before moving on, but she could remember nothing that felt like this. From where she stood, the gray expanse of Tolo Harbor was lost in a blanket of rain driving in from the sea. There was no time to descend the slopes and reach the safety of the mill house. Leaving the bundle of grass on the path and calling out to Ruby again, urging her to take shelter, she waded into the thickest growth on hands and knees, burrowing into the densely packed roots until they protected her like a cage. She wormed herself farther into the dense jungle of stalks, still calling Ruby's name, as winds slammed frozen sleet into the hillside with the impact of bullets.

She entwined her hands and feet into the mesh of roots, clinging to the earth. Flattened by the gale, the grass formed a thatch, deflecting the wind, absorbing the onslaught, holding off the full impact of the slashing rains that followed in wave after drenching wave.

She lost all sense of time as the storm swamped the hillside, penetrating the matted tiger grass and beginning its steep downward run. What started as a trickle quickly became a gushing torrent, finding its way from the higher slopes through the tangled roots in a flash flood, loosening the earth beneath her.

The harder she clung to the grass for safety, the more its roots came away, the cascade of mud and stones growing stronger with each moment. Chilled to the marrow, Sing fought against the downward rush, grasping for an anchor, feeling it torn away from her icy fingers. As one handhold was lost, she grabbed another, dragged from her hiding place by the gathering mudslide. The high, stony ground above the grassline began to crumble with the rush of yellow mud.

Boulders came free—first the smaller ones, bouncing ahead of the landslide, somersaulting high and wide as the hillside began its rapid collapse with the sound of a steam train torn from its rails. Trees that had stood for a hundred years were ripped from the peaks and flung into the valley below.

Over the shriek of wind, she heard her name called, uncertain at first, then definite and closer. Ruby's mud-caked body rolled toward her from above, blood streaking her face. Sing snatched her arm and clung to it with all of her strength, but felt it slipping slowly from her grasp. Ruby was below her now, her grip feeble and her hand slick with mud. Sing called for her to hold on.

Ruby looked straight up into her face, as though she knew her weight was dragging them both down, her lips moving with words Sing would never hear. Her grip suddenly released, Ruby slipped away and disappeared into the cataract that yawned beneath them. Sing cried her name, as wind roared in her ears and she hurtled downward to the flooded valley and into darkness.

The blackness stayed with Sing, wrapping her in a clammy tomb. In place of howling wind and battering rain there was a deathly silence, broken only by the slow drip of water and faint sounds like those of a fast-beating heart. When she moved, pain shot through her like a white-hot blade. The sound persisted—the *tick-tick-tick* of a fast-running clock, rising and falling, coming closer and then receding.

She thought she heard a voice carried over a great distance, calling her name. She tried to answer, her lips numb. She fought against the darkness closing in, forcing it back like a deadly presence. Slowly it circled her, like a stealthy opponent looking for an opening in her defense. Then came an unearthly light and a glimpse of Ah-Keung staring down at her. She closed her eyes to rid the blackness of this apparition; when she looked again, it was the gentle face of the goddess Tien-Hau.

꿏

Toby had hardly slept in the twenty-four hours since the typhoon. Standing at the tiller of the naval cutter he had commandeered the moment he had come off duty, he could see the roofs of buildings on Po-Lok's farm. The farmer and his family had reached safe ground moments before the storm had struck, but Kam-Yang said that Sing and Ruby had not come down in time from the hillside.

The boat glided through scenes of devastation that filled him with fear for Sing's safety. The dense, steamy heat that had preceded the typhoon had settled over the desolation in a vaporous mist. Clouds of insects gathered in the suffocating stench that lay trapped across the valley floor. He could see no signs of life on the flat roofs that showed above the floodwaters. The trees, he saw through his field glasses, were still filled with birds, who shared the branches with the rotting carcasses of livestock.

He searched the floating debris of planks and lengths of broken fence. Complete wooden outbuildings drifted by, and waterlogged bales of cattle fodder had formed islands for ducks and small farm animals. There was no sign or sound of survivors; her name merely echoed in the eerie stillness when he called out to her.

The farm of Po-Lok was several miles from Tai-Po village, where the wall of water had rolled up the channel and followed the course of the river as far as a neighboring village before it had spent its full force. Hundreds of junks, sampans, and vessels had washed up as far as two kilometers inland. He had seen a junk high on a hill, rotting fish still hanging from its nets. More than ten thousand people had been reported drowned.

Toby fought against despair as he scanned the deserted buildings, the silent trees still half submerged. The floodwaters had raged through the valley, breaking over the rice terraces before being stopped by the surrounding hills.

Circling the deserted mill house, he called Sing's name many times with no answer. He swept the devastated hillsides with the field glasses, hoping for a sign she had made for higher ground. He leaned on the tiller, steering the cutter in a wide arc, its bow headed toward the nearest dry ground.

He searched the lower slopes for an hour, calling her name, picking his way over the tides of drying mud and shale. The whole side of the valley seemed to have shifted. The clump of oaks that had sheltered the Temple of Tien-Hau had disappeared, leaving only broken ground, jagged stumps, ancient roots exposed like the rotting bones of a dinosaur. His last hope was that she might have somehow reached the middle ground safely and found shelter there. . . .

In the first terrible moment of finding Sing half submerged in the bed of silt on the temple floor, Toby thought she was dead. There was no sign of blood, but the mud had claimed her body like a grave, settling around her until only her face and hands showed above its silken surface.

She was unconscious, but he felt a definite, if sluggish, pulse. Frantically, he scooped away the compacted mud to reveal extensive bruising and a broken leg. He fashioned a splint from broken branches, binding it tightly with strips torn from his shirt, talking to her softly, unceasingly, certain she could hear him. Her flesh was ice cold; he cursed himself for not bringing blankets.

As though by magic, the ceiling of cloud over the valley peeled away, allowing a burst of brilliant sunshine to chase across the floodwater and brush the ravaged slopes. A single shaft of pure light penetrated the broken roof, illuminating the figure of Tien-Hau and, for fleeting seconds, the skin of the Last Tiger stretched upon the wall. He reached for it, to find it miraculously dry. It had been well cured and was reasonably soft. As he rolled her in it and carried her down to the boat, his heart thumped painfully with the thought of losing her.

⚙

The Royal Military Hospital was a rarefied enclave reserved for those who lived in the foreign embassies or the grand homes of British government officials and giants of Hong Kong commerce and industry. It was shrouded in mist when Toby pulled up outside the emergency entrance.

As he carried Sing up its wide tiled steps two at a time, a male orderly came from behind the reception desk with one of the wheelchairs lined against the wall. When he saw that the patient was a woman in the mud-caked tunic and trousers of a Chinese peasant, wrapped in the skin of a tiger, he stopped dead.

"It's a woman, sir," he said. "A Chinese woman . . . in a tiger's skin." He shook his head emphatically. "We can't admit a Chinese civilian, not wrapped up in a tiger skin, sir."

Toby ignored his protest, pushing past him through the door.

"Get me the matron," he snapped, lifting Sing gently onto an examination bench.

"But, sir—," the orderly stuttered. "It's against the rules, sir . . ."

"The matron. Now!" Toby's bark sent him scurrying away.

Sing was admitted under the name of Devereaux, signed in by Captain Hyde-Wilkins, remaining in intensive care for several days for a fractured shinbone, which was healing well due to immediate and expert attention, and for extensive bruising and abrasions, with a risk of minor organ damage and signs of fluid on the lungs.

On the fifth day, when she had been moved to a small room of her own through Toby's machinations, he arrived bearing a huge bunch of pink, white, and red roses, along with the excellent news that Miss Winifred Bramble would be honored if the daughter of Mr. and Mrs. Benjamin Devereaux would complete her recuperation at her residence on Stonecutters Island, as soon as she was released.

"Or," he offered with a grin, "you could marry me and I could take care of you. Or is it too soon to think of that?"

Her heart was too full to answer for a moment, but then she looked at her bandages ruefully. "I think it is not quite the right time."

Toby nodded and kissed her gently on the top of her head. "I understand. And I'm afraid there is something else I must tell you." He held her hand as he gave her the news that could not be avoided: Ruby's body had not been found, but there was still a chance that she would be identified among the casualties. Sing had been right: The Indian driver, Raj, had been so taken with the little pipe-maker that he was heading the search party with the thoroughness of a military exercise.

If there were tears, he did not see them. She was clearly tired, though; he left quietly, thankful that she was in the best of care.

When he had gone, Sing allowed herself to think of the little pipe-maker with the passionate heart that had been so badly broken. For many sleepless hours she told herself that Ruby's grip had weakened and she simply slipped away; that for all her training and the hidden powers she possessed, there was nothing she could have done to save her. Master To had said nothing on how to fight the storm . . . only that it would come.

Sing could have wept like a child, but knew that Ruby would not wish her to.

⌖

When Sing Devereaux was released from the hospital three weeks later, she insisted on being taken directly to Tai-Po village to see for herself.

She spent two days in the hastily erected depot where families gathered in hope of news of their lost ones, wailing in terrible grief as their corpses were revealed. She wanted to join the search, but Toby gently pointed out that she would only slow down the efforts. At her request, they went to the Tai-Po temple, to light joss sticks and beg Kuan-Yin for Ruby's safe return . . . or for her safe journey to the afterlife. After going without sleep for two days and nights as she looked into a thousand faces, alive and dead, Sing accepted the truth and began to bury her grief.

409

CHAPTER 32

Return to the Villa Formosa

No *more than a* few acres in any direction, Stonecutters Island was a tiny bastion of Englishness in the bustling Chinese mass of Hong Kong, ceded to the British in 1860 along with the Kowloon Peninsula. The granite quarry that gave the island its name had been used to build a prison in 1866. Later it became an isolation hospital for smallpox and cholera victims.

Apart from this grim reminder of the past, the island had been transformed into a sanctuary of verdant woods, loud with missel thrushes and blackbirds, bred by homesick English expatriates a hundred years before.

At the base of a high hill someone had named Wuthering Heights lived an elite community mainly made up of high-ranking British officers and their families. Cut off from the rest of Hong Kong, except for water taxis that operated day and night and the official Stonecutters ferry that ran to a schedule, the island's two landing jetties were closely guarded by a platoon of Sikh policemen.

Sing was both excited and curiously nervous at the prospect of meeting the English lady who had known her parents so well. Having rested well for a day and a night in a small, comfortable hotel owned by a friend of Toby's, she had taken the cotton frock from its box. Beneath it, in separate tissue, were two sets of filmy white underwear, as beautiful to touch and look upon as the cream-colored frock printed with palest pink roses. The wide red belt emphasized her tiny waist, and the shoes were a perfect fit, making her two inches taller and adding the slightest swing to her hips. She had washed and combed her deep auburn hair to lie in long, soft curls over her shoulders. The hat of light straw she tied loosely beneath her chin.

Toby was drinking coffee in the lobby when she appeared. The look in his eyes made her blush with pleasure. "I have truly never seen anything more lovely in my life," he breathed.

⁜

They took the same motor launch that had carried them in search of Indie Da Silva, this time with the uniformed coxswain at the helm. Toby looked dashing to her in cream slacks, a cream polo shirt, and his regimental blazer. He handed Sing the Tanka sling that he had been keeping for her. "I thought you might want to show some of your things to Miss Bramble."

Toby was smartly saluted as they disembarked at the landing wharf and entered the car, a vintage burgundy Bentley, sent to fetch them.

Winifred Bramble's bungalow, the Elms, was large and spacious, built around the turn of the century by someone who wanted to bring a breath of rural England into the midst of an alien land. Its wide gated entrance was flanked by two towering elms, its rambling gardens thick with rhododendrons and the neat flower beds of an English estate.

The door was opened by a white-jacketed amah, who showed them into a sitting room crammed with comfortable furniture covered in floral uphostery, its window seat scattered with books and magazines, and vases of carefully arranged flowers everywhere.

The lady who stood awaiting them was smiling and gracious, slightly stout but straight backed and surrounded, Sing saw immediately, by an energy far younger than her years. She was smartly and simply dressed in a skirt of homespun Scottish tweed and a coffee-colored silk blouse, unadorned but for a single string of matched pearls and one of equal luster in the lobe of each ear. Her silver hair was perfectly groomed and waved, the hazel eyes keenly alert behind lightly tinted glasses.

She held out her hands to Sing at once, her eyes bright with the threat of tears. "Welcome, my dear . . . what an absolute joy this is." She embraced her visitor warmly. "For more years than I care to count, I have prayed for this moment."

Sing bowed her head. "I too have dreamed of such a moment. I thank you with all my heart for allowing it to come true."

Miss Bramble beamed with pleasure, then turned to Toby, taking his outstretched hand. "Lady Margaret Pelham, the wife of your commanding officer, is a dear friend of mine, Captain Hyde-Wilkins. She speaks most highly of you, as of course does the colonel."

She waved them to the comfortable armchairs. Sing reached for the beaded bag and took out the photograph of her parents. "This has been close to my heart since the treasures in this bag were given to me on my tenth birthday."

Using both hands, in the way in which all things of great value are exchanged, Sing proffered the photograph.

Winfred Bramble was unable to suppress a single tear. "This was taken by my own hand so many years ago. I still have the Brownie box camera I used on the deck of *Golden Sky* to capture the moment they became man and wife.

"I believe our meeting was decreed by a destiny greater than we can begin to imagine, and there are important things to discuss. However, I propose some light refreshment before we proceed." She paused, while the amah wheeled in a trolley holding a silver tea service, an array of delicate sandwiches, and an assortment of extravagant pastries.

Miss Bramble effortlessly served them both. "Afternoon tea, Miss Devereaux, an old English habit I simply refuse to abandon: Darjeeling, and pastries from Gaddi's restaurant in the Peninsula Hotel, greatly enjoyed by your dear mother." She filled dainty, hand-painted cups, passing them around and offering milk and sugar, while she chatted breezily of her garden and life back in East Sussex.

Finally, with pleasantries completed, Miss Bramble's manner became brisk and businesslike. "There can be no doubt that this delightful and courageous young lady is the child of Li-Xia and her husband, Ben; it is as though they stand before me. You have been blessed with the best of

412

both of them." Crossing to a Victorian rolltop desk, she returned with two sealed envelopes and turned to Sing. "I have something rather momentous to tell you, my dear."

She looked at Toby. "As you no have no doubt discovered, for many years Captain Devereaux's trusted Hong Kong solicitor and friend was a gentleman named Alistair Pidcock. Sadly, he has passed away, leaving me as the sole executor of the Devereaux Hong Kong Trust. The instructions were to invest the fund in the name of Captain Devereaux's missing daughter for ninety-nine years. If during the course of that time the daughter was found and identified upon the basis of my judgment, she would become the legal heiress to his entire fortune, which I am able to tell you is very considerable indeed. It includes the deed to the Devereaux estate at Repulse Bay known as the Villa Formosa."

She turned the warmth of her smile upon Sing. "It is a most beautiful place, though I believe the house is in need of restoration. You must see it as soon as you recover your strength.

"You see, my dear, your father did not leave Hong Kong before investigating every possible clue to your disappearance. He apparently tracked down the amah, Ah-Ho, learning from her that your mother's personal servant, fondly known as the Fish, was believed to have taken you with her into the hinterlands of Central China . . . a challenge that even a man of your father's caliber and connections would find most daunting. Nevertheless, he tried. For two years he sailed his flagship, *Golden Sky*, for thousands of miles in search of word that might lead him to you."

Again Miss Bramble paused, this time with a frown of disapproval. "I am ashamed to say that the officials in Hong Kong had little interest in your mother's death and your apparent kidnapping. Had this terrible event involved a British or European family, or even that of a high-ranking Chinese, there would have been a full-scale investigation."

Setting down her cup, Miss Bramble shook her head. "Your father was forced to abandon all hope of discovering your whereabouts . . . but not before he had posted a vast reward for any information from any source, including, I understand, the secret societies known as the triads." She picked up the pair of envelopes, squaring them efficiently on the table's polished surface, before handing one of them to Sing. "This is a letter to Mr. Adrian Lau, chairman of the Hong Kong–Shanghai Bank, who was also well known to your father. It will give you immediate access to everything you are likely to require in further assessments. And this," she added, handing her the second envelope, "is to the most trustworthy man I know, Angus Grant, who was a very close friend of your father's and may know something of his activities in Shanghai. He is the solicitor who took over Alistair's practice, and as such I have appointed him coexecutor of the trust."

She held out her hand, clasping Sing's firmly. "Congratulations, my dear, and welcome home."

⌖

The lovely old bungalow was the perfect place for Sing's recovery. Miss Bramble tended her like a doting mother. She was surprised and pleased at the speed of her improvement, her color returning steadily, her remarkable eyes clear and possessed of a calm that made it a pleasure to be in her company.

They had, as Miss Bramble had foretold, many things to talk about. Sing brought forth the books from her beaded bag. "This," she said of the red and gold volume, "is the private journal of my mother, Li-Xia." Sing reached for the second book with its faded cover of peach-colored silk. "This is also the chronicle of a difficult life, written by one who fought hard to find her voice as a woman. I am told it is the work of my grandmother."

"It will be my great privilege and joy to read them, my dear," said Miss Bramble. In return, Miss Bramble never tired of telling stories of Sing's mother Li-Xia, and of her father's legendary adventures,

Winifred was often out for the day on her social engagements and community rounds, but always returned with some thoughtful gift—a piece of fresh fruit or pastry or the quite wonderful thing she called chocolate. "For the healing," she said emphatically, "of the heart and the mind."

414

Sing set up a table in the garden, where she practiced the art of calligraphy. Winifred looked on admiringly. "There are certain things, my dear, that I was privileged to teach your mother. She was an avid student, with a capacity for learning the ways of her husband's people that society requires. I would be delighted to share the same basic requirements with you whilst you are here."

She paused to watch the tip of Sing's brush dip and swirl from strokes bold and full to the finest of lines no thicker than a hair. "And perhaps," Winifred added, "you might show me how to create such magic. It has always struck me as good for the soul."

Miss Bramble's cheerful kindness enclosed Sing in a cocoon of generosity. As her strength returned, Sing enjoyed her lessons in the refinements of English behavior, and began rebuilding her physical and spiritual well-being in the ways she had been taught. Winifred, who had never seen the practice of Chinese folk medicine or the astounding grace and agility of *wu-shu*, was fascinated by the burning of moxa sticks and the insertion of hair-fine acupuncture needles in the most extraordinary parts of the body. She never complained of the strange odors from the brewing herbs. Pleased by her genuine interest, Sing explained her procedures with patience and care.

Colonel Pelham's married quarters were no more than a stroll away. The colonel returned to Stonecutters Island each weekend, bringing his adjutant with him. Toby spent every hour he could at the Elms, and he and Sing were frequent dinner guests of Sir Justin and Lady Margaret, who sometimes joined them for an evening of whist or gin rummy, which Sing learned to play with alacrity. When they were alone, she and Toby sometimes spoke of marriage, but it was clear she still had too many unanswered questions about her past to be fully ready to embrace her future.

⁂

Nearly a month after Sing had learned of her inheritance, she and Toby were on their way to the Villa Formosa. Fewer and fewer buildings dotted the open green of the countryside, where the blue-green waters of

415

Repulse Bay swept away from rising cliffs. Sea air reached through the car's open window to ruffle Sing's hair as the car traveled smoothly up the winding coastal road toward the house.

They had spent the morning in the office of the bank manager, Adrian Lau, who had given them his undivided attention upon reading Winifred's letter of introduction. They were joined by Angus Grant, the amiable Scottish lawyer who listened well and spoke only when he had something of value to say, his brown eyes frank and engaging. "I knew your father very well," he told Sing. "He was one of the most interesting men it has been my privilege to call a friend. I am at your disposal at any time."

Mr. Lau was so intrigued by the unexpected appearance of a claimant to the Devereaux estate after more than a decade that he offered to accompany them to the Villa Formosa. A limousine was at the steps of the bank in record time for the half-hour journey to Repulse Bay.

Seated beside the chauffeur, Mr. Lau turned to address her. "When Captain Devereaux left Hong Kong at that terrible time, he gave his trusted gardener, Ah-Kin, the deed to his own cottage on the estate, plus an endowment to maintain the grounds in their original splendor. Ah-Kin has been notified, and awaits the mistress's arrival with much burning of joss sticks to Ho-Sen-Yi, the god of lost travelers."

The iron gates of the Villa Formosa swung silently open. Ah-Kin, his white hair and beard framing a face that still appeared young, bowed low as the car crunched slowly up the wide gravel drive toward the deserted villa. Typhoon shutters barred its many windows, and drifts of leaves had gathered in the bold scoop of its eaves. In contrast, the gardens that fell away on either side of the house were all the more grand and exquisite.

A wide flight of hastily swept marble steps led to the imposing entrance. Mr. Lau produced a ring of keys, talking as he sorted through them. "I understand the main structure remains in good repair, but if it is decided to reopen the property, may I suggest engaging the right tradesmen to undertake a thorough inspection and restoration? The original furnishings and furniture are stored in the company godowns at Causeway Bay."

When the doors were thrown open, Sing hesitated on the threshold, then turned to Toby and Mr. Lau. "Forgive me. May I beg, with great respect, that you enjoy the view of the bay for a few moments? This is a place I must enter alone. If there are voices here, only I can hear them . . ."

She faltered, concerned that her request might be misunderstood. Mr. Lau seemed momentarily surprised, but Toby smiled, releasing her hand. "You have waited all your life for this moment. Don't let it pass too quickly."

Sing stood alone in the domed entrance hall, light through panels of colored glass casting patterns onto the dusty marble floor like the windows of a church. The long-dead vibrations of those who had come and gone through these doors resounded in her mind.

She expected to feel an invitation to enter, but it was not there. A vast emptiness enclosed her, her footsteps echoing in a void as she passed from one large and musty room to another, entering every forgotten space until she stood in the empty chamber that had once been her father's private domain.

Drawing the bolts of the shutters, she threw them wide to the sounds and smells of distant oceans, an undeniable presence brought to life.

Time passed as she sat in the window seat, a sea air blowing through the empty room, chasing a stray leaf that had somehow found its way inside. Many voices spoke to her: Master To, the sunrise in his eyes; the Fish, lifting a crab from the shallows; Ah-Soo, tossing her flaming wok; Tamiko-san, in her golden robes; Ruby, with her crinkled smile. They all seemed to tell her that there was something left to see.

She had put it from her mind—the only place she was afraid to find, the room where she was born and Li-Xia had suffered so. The Fish had told her about that terrible night.

Sing knew without asking where it was to be found: The door to the master suite was closed, while all other rooms had been open.

Sing entered to a chill that closed around her like a shroud; there was no welcome here. She felt the hand of evil heavy on her shoulder, urging her to leave this unholy place and not return.

Instead, she unbolted the shutters with trembling hands, throwing them open to the Ti-Yuan gardens and beyond—windswept spaces drenched with light. She stood her ground, sending down her chi till it was rooted on the Rock of Great Strength. Demons danced about her, but the wind gusts swept them out, until the hand on her shoulder slowly slipped away. Here, in this dark room, so suddenly invaded by the energies of life, only the fragrance of the gardens and the sound of birds remained.

✠

Miss Bramble was delighted to welcome Sing back to her bungalow while the Villa Formosa was being restored. But the dogs of war were gathering beyond the peaceful oasis of Stonecutters Island in those early months of 1941.

Toby brought the daily newspapers, and Sing had discovered the magic of radio, finding that the world outside her own was filled with the threat of invasion. As she learned of the Japanese Imperial Army swarming down from the north and read of the dreadful massacres of Nanking and Canton, she began to understand the terror that was eating its way into China's heart.

Sing's personal wars had been fought without knowledge of such things; only now did she realize the size of her country, or begin to understand its history. She learned of the warlord Sun-Yat-Sen; the young Mao-Tze-Tung and his rebel hordes; and his enemy Chiang-Kai-Shek, leader of the Kuomintang. The Japanese had occupied Manchuria and Shanghai for years, and were pressing farther south with every passing day.

That the man who had shown her the meaning of love might himself be in danger made her moments with him more precious. Toby's visits grew less frequent as the buildup of Hong Kong's defenses increased with the Japanese push south. The news that was once so alien to Sing seemed more personal to her every day. Miss Bramble redoubled her philanthropic efforts, and Sing joined her as much as she could, grateful for the chance to do more than bask in a luxury that still felt strange to her.

418

The restoration of the Villa Formosa was complete by the time she considered herself fully recovered. Angus Grant had supervised the work, using photographs and memory to replace all the furnishings as they had been for Li-Xia and Ben.

A separate vehicle had carried countless bottles of rare wines, wrapped in sleeves of straw—vintage champagne, scotch, Napoleon brandy, and kegs of Navy rum. Angus had volunteered to check the inventory and organize the restocking of the cellars, but Sing had insisted he take what he wished of both the liquor and the sealed containers of pipe tobacco and crates of Havana cigars.

The Scottish lawyer had politely refused. "It all belongs here, lassie; for all we know he'll be back to claim it." He had selected a bottle of Glenfiddich. "But if you care to have a bottle of this upstairs for when I drop in, I'll not say no."

Angus turned more serious. "There's one thing I ask of you."

Sing had become extremely fond of him. "Anything, Angus, whatever you wish."

"Don't go past the five-bar gate and into the birch wood until I take you myself. That garden is out of bounds to Ah-Kin and has been let grow wild, in keeping with Ben's wishes. It'll be riddled with snakes. I'll have it cleared, perhaps in a month or two, when you've got your sea legs."

Her first week beneath her father's roof was one of sound, untroubled sleep. From the Pavilion of Joyful Moments, she found peace before the altar of a dawn sky. And as the new day bloomed around her, she drank the air and called upon the White Crane, sending down her chi to find its roots, until an apricot sun was balanced on the rim of the world.

Angus had been concerned at leaving her alone in the vast old house, and Toby had assured her that Winifred Bramble would be delighted to keep her company until things were settled. She had thanked them all, but asked to be allowed to make her peace with the Villa Formosa, and whatever ghosts remained, alone. She was more than happy, she said convincingly, with the attentions of Ah-Kin and his family.

Sing's favorite room in these new and sumptuous surroundings was her father's study. She spent hours examining his books and paintings, the scale model ships made by his own hand, the collection of meerschaum pipes, the aroma of his tobacco jar. Even his monogrammed notepaper, with the Double Dragon chop in scarlet and gold on every sheet, had been replaced in the drawers of his gigantic desk, the original inkwells, cigar box, and crystal decanter displayed on its green leather top. The most personal items she found were placed in a top drawer: a bottle half filled with a delightful cologne labeled BAY RUM, and beside it a flat silver flask of brandy, his name embossed on its leather case. Next to these lay a little ivory container of silver toothpicks, a bunch of keys to the desk drawers, a cigar cutter, fingernail clippers, a solid-gold snuff bottle, and a pair of Double Dragon cuff links.

Her father's desk seemed the perfect place to keep the contents of the Tanka sling she had carried so far. From it, she took the precious journals, the finger jade, the happiness silk, and the Double Dragon dollar, placing them neatly in the drawer beside his personal items. Last, she removed the dragon claw from its worn leather pouch.

She had never looked at it thoroughly, but now realized it was of the same scale, design, and metals as the inlay that covered the desk so lavishly. "I know nothing of its purpose or its value," the Fish had told her, "but Li-Xia said that it was precious."

The desk, Angus had explained, had been made to Ben's strict specifications. Sing examined the claw carefully. Could it be some kind of key?

At first she found nothing to suggest a locking device hidden in the desk. Patiently, she inspected every separate panel, deeply carved and inlaid with ivory, turquoise, and coral, until she found one that included the crest of the Double Dragon, cleverly concealed in the rich extravagance of its elaborate scrollwork—the imperial dragon of China entwined with the legendary dragon of Saint George.

420

Looking even more closely at the tracery, she saw that the claws of each outstretched talon were missing, leaving minute spaces where they should have been. Carefully, she fitted the dragon claw into the recessed spaces. The pins lined up, and she pushed them into place, but sprang no hidden lock. She was about to put away the pouch when a slip of paper fell to the floor, bearing a drawing of the Pa-kua, with its eight sacred trigrams of three broken and unbroken lines, and the words *The Double Dragon Has Eight Eyes*.

The panel was placed low in the back of the desk, and Sing needed to kneel in order to study it. She found that the Double Dragon crest was repeated by a replica below, the bulging eyes of each creature inset with beads of turquoise. Again, although each moved easily when she pressed it with a fingertip, no hiding place emerged. Studying the tiny symbol, she remembered Master To's instructions in Pa-kua: *We must always face the trigram correctly, or chaos will reign.*

Sing tried again, using the sequences of broken and unbroken lines as a guide to press the dragons' eyes in new combinations, until, with a series of eight definite clicks, a wide, shallow drawer sprang smoothly open. Inside lay a collection of files tied with tape, several ledgers, and numerous sealed envelopes. The top one of these was addressed with two words: *My Child*.

Trembling, Sing broke the wax seal, to find a folded vellum sheet embossed with her father's chop. She moved to the window, where sunlight fell on the boldly written lines:

My precious child,

I pray to what gods there may be of both East and West that you will one day read these words. Know above all things that your mother gave her life so that you might live, placing you in the hands she trusted most in this world. Know that your father was a decent man who loved her as deeply as one can love another.

We cared nothing of race or the conventions of a savage society. We breathed the same sea air, were warmed by the same bright sun and cooled by the same ocean breezes. We were together beneath the same miraculous sky, the same kindly moon, and the same brilliant stars. These things I had lived with for a lifetime . . . but it was your mother who showed them to me.

I can only hope with all my heart that life has not been too cruel and that you may one day find such a love. The world is a lonely place without someone to share both joy and sadness.

That you are reading this letter means those I trusted have carried out my wishes. This house was a dream of mine. It was meant to shield the people I loved from those who could not see true beauty or understand the concept of innocence. That the dear one who was your mother should have these taken from her so cruelly and unjustly has left me with nothing but despair.

May the Villa Formosa and its gardens give you shelter and make some small recompense for any injustices you may have suffered from being of my blood and carrying my name in a world so violently thrust upon you.

Seek no further, my dear child; your true journey begins here, where Li-Xia's ended.

Your loving father,
Benjamin Devereaux

Among the papers, she found a collection of files labeled YELLOW DRAGON, but she turned her attention first to her father's personal diaries. It was early the following morning by the time she finished reading Ben Devereaux's account of his life. The diaries ended abruptly on the date of her mother's death—the page as blank as the life that had ended except for a single name scrawled across the page as though by another hand: *Chiang-wah.*

❖

One morning, as she stepped from Ben's study onto the terrace, Ah-Kin turned from tending the urns of marigolds to bow to her politely. "Forgive me, mistress. May I beg a moment of your time? There are things I must show you that are for your eyes alone."

Sing returned his bow. "It will be my honor to follow wherever you may lead in these blessed gardens." She followed the gardener to an old stone wall behind a screen of black bamboo, down a short flight of steps to the little shrine of Pai-Ling. Opening its scarlet doors, he stepped aside to reveal a golden statue of Kuan-Yun, bathed in a blaze of rainbow light. "The heavens have forgiven my master Di-Fo-Lo. In his grief, he flung the goddess from the cliff. For years she lay at the bottom of the sea, until fishermen raised her in their nets. They were afraid that the ghost of Di-Fo-Lo would haunt them if they did not return it to the shrine."

He beamed with pleasure as Sing bowed before the statue. "When Kuan-Yun was returned, I knew that you would soon follow. I have kept her safely in my home with other things that were precious to your mother."

At the feet of the goddess, among fresh flowers and ripe fruit, lay a box encrusted with seashells, a child's bamboo flute, a sheaf of letters bound with a golden ribbon, and a pair of sandals splendidly woven from flax grass.

From the Yellow Dragon files in her father's office, Sing learned the true nature of the triad threat against the House of Devereaux. Under a plain black cover, the first journal outlined the history of the Yellow Dragon secret society—from its centuries-old origins as an underground resistance army pitched against tyranny and corruption, to one of Shanghai's most notorious tongs—and named the controlling family dating back several generations as the House of Ho-Ching, whose eldest sons served as supreme overlords, or dragon heads. Focusing on the years from 1880 to 1900 and the dragon head Ho-Tzu "Titan" Ching, it detailed crimes from extortion, torture, and murder to kidnapping, arson, and blackmail against prominent government officials of the day. It was signed "Jean-Paul Devereaux."

Angus had told Sing of the empire her grandfather had built with the staggering profits of dealing in opium. It had been taken from him, and his properties burned to the ground with the Boxer Uprising of 1900. The second journal was similarly laid out, but in the more flourishing hand of her father. It covered major Yellow Dragon activities in Hong Kong and Macao—under the dragon head J. T. Ching.

When she had read each page twice and digested every word, she called Angus Grant and told him of her find.

"Have you told anyone else, anyone at all?" he asked immediately. Sing assured him she had not.

"Good lass," he said. "Put them away under lock and key until I get there."

He arrived in less than forty-five minutes, and insisted she fetch the file to him so that he would not see the secret drawer. "If Ben had wanted me to know, he'd have told me." Sing had never seen the usually easygoing lawyer look so tense.

He poured himself a Glenfiddich from the bottle she had set aside for him. "I want you to bring me the file on J. T. Ching; I'll copy it and bring it back. Tell no one of this, not even Toby or Miss Bramble. If it is what I think it is, it might as well be a case of dynamite on a short fuse."

CHAPTER 33

The Cloud Garden

W*inifred Bramble announced a* Flood Relief Ball to be held in the Peninsula Hotel, with the proceeds to be used to help rebuild the ruined village of Tai-Po. On Winifred's advice, Sing attended the ball in Western
dress, an evening gown of oyster-colored silk and a string of black pearls.
Her hair was dressed in gleaming coils high upon her head, showing the
length of her neck and the matching pearls in her ears.

She knew that people wondered and whispered about her. Being in
the company of foreigners had taught her to look and act as they did, to
use the English language and avoid the subject of her heritage. If any
Chinese she encountered muttered against her, she pretended not to
hear or understand. She was well aware that the English ladies looked
down at her; for all of Winifred's efforts to introduce her into society as
"a young friend from Macao," Sing knew she was dismissed as "Captain
Hyde-Wilkins's Eurasian bit of fluff."

She had quickly learned that to observe much and say little was her
best defense. She would not allow herself to be intimidated into staying
home, especially when the cause was so close to her heart.

On this evening, Sir Justin Pelham's party was second in importance
only to the governor and his entourage, so she expected little in the way
of confrontation. Every prominent Hong Kong family or enterprise was
represented, including the foreign consulates and the wealthiest members of Chinese society.

Sing stepped from the Rolls-Royce on Toby's arm, to follow Sir Justin

425

and Lady Pelham past the gushing fountain and up the wide marble steps to the famous foyer of the hotel. Both Colonel Pelham and Captain Hyde-Wilkins were resplendent in their dress uniforms, with miniature medals and decorations on scarlet cutaway jackets and golden cummerbunds to match the braided trappings of rank.

Elegant in a velvet evening dress and her beloved garnets, Winifred Bramble was escorted by Angus Gordon in the dark blue uniform of a major in the Hong Kong Volunteers. But it was the stunning girl on the arm of Captain Hyde-Wilkins who turned heads as they entered the grand ballroom.

The colonel's table was in pride of place, close to the raised stage but enough to one side to suggest exclusivity. Sing listened to the speeches, enjoyed the music of the string orchestra, and played her part in the proceedings when called upon to do so, but in truth she was uncomfortable and would welcome the evening's end. With the speeches over, Toby led her to the dance floor. She held her head high, looking neither right nor left.

As if he read her thoughts, Toby held her close and whispered in her ear, "They stare because you are the most breathtaking woman in the room. It is called good old-fashioned jealousy."

She felt safe in his arms, her love for him growing stronger with each day, but she was not yet free to show it. When they returned to the table, a man stood with his back to them, talking with Lady Pelham—a short, stocky man dressed in an expensive American tuxedo, the jacket stretched across once-powerful wide shoulders. When he turned to face them, Sing found herself looking into the flushed face of J. T. Ching.

It was as shocking as if she had been suddenly disrobed. The sounds of the ballroom seemed to melt away as Lady Pelham introduced her.

"Ah, there you are my dear. This is Mr. Ching, one of our most important guests. And a most generous one, I might add, when it comes to helping those less fortunate." She gestured gracefully. "Mr. Ching, may I present Miss Devereaux, a new friend of ours from Macao."

Sing's heartbeat quickened as the taipan offered his hand. She saw the dawning of surprise become a smile that spread across his broad face but did not reach his eyes. Only deep-rooted discipline stopped her from snatching her hand away. Instead, she smiled politely as he lifted it slowly to his loose lips to plant a lingering kiss.

"Miss Devereaux was of great help in the aftermath of the typhoon," Lady Pelham went on, "even though she was herself quite badly injured at Tai-Po."

Ching's expression did not waver. Only the light of triumph in his eyes told her that a change of fortune could not hide the truth of who she was.

He bowed with exaggerated elegance. "It is always an honor and a great pleasure to meet those who show concern for our underprivileged people." His hot hand let go of hers reluctantly. "I too am always happy to help in my humble way . . ."

"Mr. Ching is too modest," Margaret Pelham broke in. "It was he who founded the floating clinic in Shatin and the tuberculosis wing of Queen Mary Hospital, not to mention the civic center that bears his name." She laughed melodiously. "I could go on, but I fear I might embarrass the poor man."

Sing took her seat beside Toby, while Ching remained standing, smiling down at her. "Surely we have met before," he said, his tone communicating clearly to Sing that he would enjoy this game immensely.

"I do not think so, sir," she said quietly.

Ching persisted, the smile twisting his mouth unpleasantly. "How could I not remember such a charming young lady?"

"I think you must be mistaken, Mr. Ching," Toby said briskly. "You and I have met, but Miss Devereaux is quite new to the colony."

Toby was so convincing that Sing could almost believe he had not witnessed her humiliation at the Tavern of Cascading Jewels. Taking heart from his steadfast gaze, Sing recognized there was nothing to do but play Ching's game and see where it led.

Ching had been drinking, brandy fumes strong on his breath. He did not seem to hear Toby's remark. Taking a wallet from his breast pocket, he selected a card of compressed gold leaf that he presented to Sing with a smirk.

"Hong Kong streets are not always as gentle as those of old Macao. Allow me to put my office at your disposal. I hope you will find time to visit me. . . . I am sure there must be something we can assist you with while you are here. If you call this number at any time, I will send a car to pick you up."

⌖

The roof gardens of the Ho-Ching Asia complex in the North Point district of Hong Kong Island had been designed to J. T. Ching's precise requirements. The place he called the Cloud Garden was a private retreat that few had been privileged to see.

In a city where extravagance was the hallmark of success, the three HCA towers dominated all other landmarks. Rising from the docklands like mammoth blades of steel and glass, the angles of its shadow were designed to cast *shar-chi*—the arrows of darkness—upon surrounding competitors. The superstitious called its creeping menace the "sundial of destruction," some believing that the colossal foundations were laid in the configuration of the triad symbol.

Several days after the Flood Relief Ball, Sing had telephoned the number on J. T. Ching's business card. Toby had been hastily called back to his regiment, and though he had begged her not to do anything rash, Sing thought that the time had come when the most dangerous course was inaction. She had no illusions about the ruthlessness of the man who believed he owned her. By presenting his card without revealing their past connection, he had issued both a warning and a summons.

Wearing an austere Western-style business costume of charcoal gray, her hair severely dressed, Sing wore no makeup or adornment of any kind. She had left the Villa Formosa satisfied that she bore as little resemblance as possible to the apprentice pipe-maker from Macao.

As the limousine sent to fetch her sped smoothly along, Sing did not notice the sweep of open water that had always beguiled her. Her mind was on the challenge she was about to face, and the contents of the slim aluminum briefcase she held in her lap.

A uniformed security guard escorted her from the car into the opulent foyer of the Executive Tower, across a wide expanse of marble to a private elevator. A young woman, smartly dressed in a white cheongsam, accompanied her silently on the smooth ride up to the penthouse. She led the way through a whisper-quiet anteroom to the base of a wide staircase lined with priceless artwork, then bowed and departed.

At the top of the stairs stood a pair of gigantic doors of burnished steel, guarded by two standing Buddhas on the same enormous scale, resplendent in a coating of gold leaf. More gold leaf, in delicate, postage-stamp squares, stood in a crystal bowl on a gold plinth in front of each statue. She did not need to be told that to be admitted, she must first pay homage to Siddhartha Guatama, the Most High. She took a square from each bowl, adding them to the thin crust of pure gold that gave the Buddhas their shining glory. The doors parted with barely a whisper, revealing the astonishing vista of the Cloud Garden.

It was as if she had stepped onto a different planet. Cool, iridescent mists from sprinklers drifted across pockets of verdant lawn, giving the air a mountain freshness; the chuckle of moving water subdued a distant clamor from the waterfront far below.

Seeming to float in the midst of these spectacular gardens was a teahouse belonging to the age of the Han. Dazzled by her surroundings, she followed a pebbled pathway through banks of white chrysanthemums, to where ancient statuary guarded the entrance.

J. T. Ching waited there in a black silk robe that gave him a priestly appearance. "Welcome to my garden in the clouds. I did not think you would come so soon," he said, waving her to a comfortable seat.

"I do not need to sit for what I have to say."

"Nonsense," he said, "even an occasion such as this requires good manners." He gave a sharp clap of his hands, and a young Chinese boy appeared, bowing, to sit in the lotus position behind a small table set with many tiny cups, bowls, and teapots. A row of gleaming samovars were arranged on a sideboard within his reach.

"You may know that I have an interest in fine teas, as did our fathers and their fathers before them. It is a passion I once shared with your father. Is what you have to say so important that it cannot wait for the drinking of tea?"

Sing was almost disarmed by his engaging manner. "Forgive me if I appear less than cordial, but if our conversation is to be a civilized one, then I accept gladly."

He nodded agreeably. "This boy can neither hear nor speak, but he has a nose for blending tea. May I suggest he choose a blend according to his perception of you? He is rather good at it."

The boy looked at Sing with large, intrusive eyes, then began the intricacies of the ancient tea ceremony.

"I admire the great ones of the past, both Chinese and Japanese." He turned to a narrow altar stand of black lacquer, backed by a latticed screen of great beauty that housed a magnificent samurai sword.

"For many generations the House of Ching has imported fine tea and lacquerware from Suruga Bay on the island of Honshu." He was speaking as though to himself. "It is the home of the last shogunate, the family that ruled Japan for three hundred years through the knights of Bushido—the way of the warrior."

Ching removed the sword with great reverence, admiring its double-handed hilt of gold and ivory, its scarlet scabbard exquisitely inlaid with gold. When he slowly drew the blade from its sheath, it made no sound but seemed to slice the air. "This sword was given to me by General Hideki Tojo, the finest military mind in the world, who is soon to be the greatest leader under the Rising Sun." He ran a finger lovingly along the back of the blade, which suddenly flashed in an arc so close to Sing's head that she could feel her hair move from its force.

"A little demonstration in case you think me old and slow." He sheathed the sword with practiced ease, bowing to her. "You did not blink an eye. I am impressed."

The tea was served in tiny thimble-size cups from a black lacquered tray. The boy's eyes looked directly into hers for the second it took to offer it; she could not be sure if it was with impertinence or warning.

"This is a tea so rare it must be served in cups of pure gold," Ching boasted. "Battles were fought over the mountain where this bush is grown." The aroma alone threatened Sing's resolve. She remembered the nectar of the golden persimmon. It hastened the words she had come to say.

"We both know that I am here because you have found me. I expected this to happen, but had no way of knowing where or when. Hearing you speak of my father makes my purpose easier. It means that you know who I am."

"Devereaux is a name of greatness," he replied with absolute sincerity. "Respected in many parts of China open to the river trade, and feared in some." He bowed with an exaggerated sweep. "It pleases me to know that Topaz, my choice of jewel, was born to one of such great taste in all things rare and pleasing to the senses."

When Sing ignored his clumsy flattery, he went on. "You are the only person to have taken tea in the Cloud Palace other than my sons, certainly the only woman. But then, you are a member of my family, are you not?"

"You know that I am not. You had no right to possess me. I do not believe that money and power can buy a human life."

"Sadly, it can. This was a business transaction. In good faith, I entered into a contract with a procuress of the highest esteem. No law has been broken. It is you who dishonored this agreement, not I."

Sing fought to keep anger from her voice. *The warrior's greatest enemy is rage . . . the crane sees the tiger's rage but she remains calm.*

"My family name is as respected as the name of Ching—I am no one's slave. You judged my value by the services I rendered for your comfort and pleasure, an accompaniment to your borrowed dreams. I withdrew those services. I am here as the only child of a great taipan, to repay my debt to you and to end the blood feud between our two families."

Sing placed the briefcase on the table before him and sprang the twin locks with her thumbs, revealing neatly arranged documents bound in place with red tapes. She removed several packs of new banknotes and stacked them neatly before him.

Keeping the level of reason in her voice, she slid the opened case

431

across the table. "I keep my own counsel on matters of my value—not in the eyes of others but in my own. But you are right, money and power can change the world of others . . . even buy and sell another's life and honor. I have come to take back my own and that of my family."

He listened to her, his face impassive. "You are here at my bidding, because at this moment you are my property. You are fortunate that I did not have you thrashed and dragged here."

"By whose law? I have discovered many things now that I have claimed my name. I do not recognize the *sung-tip* of the Golden One. Hers is a world that is past: The buying and selling of children is no longer permitted; neither is the smoking of opium."

He laughed at her presumption. "There is no price to be put upon my honor. What is this that you offer me?"

"The money is my only debt to you. It is three times that which you paid to Tamiko-san."

She paused for a moment. "I also have something more powerful than money—the truth. The case before you contains the private journals of my father, Captain Benjamin Devereaux, along with the journals of my grandfather. As you know, they both did business with the House of Ching. Our grandfathers became rich in the opium trade and shared many ventures together. But your father and mine became enemies, and a blood oath was sworn to destroy the male lineage of the Devereaux name. These journals were kept as protection against treachery."

The smile had left his face. Sing met his eyes squarely. "I have made it my business to learn what I can of Hong Kong's rule of law, though it is nothing to the law of the black society. But it might serve you to see what these documents contain."

He looked suddenly thoughtful. "What do you think you have discovered that could harm my name or my company?"

Sing sat forward in her seat, demanding his attention. "Your grandfather forced my grandfather, Jean-Paul Devereaux, to flee Shanghai with nothing but his infant son, my father. His wife, my grandmother, was Chinese of noble Manchu birth, but that did not save her from the revenge of the Yellow Dragon. My mother, Li-Xia, also died most hideously by the hand of a Boxer brave."

She stood up with the face and voice of a warrior. "So, tell me . . . why should I be afraid of you? What more could you do except to kill me too, and I am not afraid of that."

"Do you accuse me of involvement in the crimes you speak of?" Ching asked coldly.

She looked past the threat in his voice. "Of course not; my word would be nothing against the word of the taipan Ching. In this case are copies of the Devereaux family's records of its dealings with the House of Ho-Ching and the secret society of the Yellow Dragon triad. They expose the society's heritage as the family Ching, and its dragon heads as the eldest son of each generation. They prove without question that you are now the dragon head, overlord of the society's lodges all over the world."

Leaving the tea untouched, she rose from her chair. "I ask only that you read these pages and consider their value to you. The originals are held in my lawyer's safe, with copies in places even you will never find. If anything happens to me, my friends, or my future family, they will be delivered to the governor's office. If they are, the name of Jack Teagarden Ching will no longer be respected as a pillar of society and a public benefactor. You will be revealed as the traitor who tried to blackmail Colonel Pelham into a cowardly betrayal of his country. You will go to prison for a long time, and your ancestors will cry with shame."

He ignored the open case. "If I should agree to release you from the *sung-tip* and guarantee to end the blood oath, will the original documents be delivered to me with nothing withheld?"

"You have my word on it . . . but I can never be certain that another copy could have been made without my knowledge and used without my approval. There are many who care what happens to me." Sing placed the documents beside the banknotes, closing the case in readiness to leave. "Accept this payment or not . . . but I owe you nothing."

"You have overlooked one important thing, Topaz. In a matter of weeks this island will no longer be a British colony, but a possession of the Imperial Japanese Empire. The golden idols that allowed you to pass are Diabutsu, the Buddhas of Japan. I am well prepared. What good will your documents be then?"

Sing had descended the steps, but turned to look back at him, silent for a heartbeat. "If Hong Kong falls to the Japanese, then Britain and her allies will liberate it. If you do not believe this, then burn them if you wish. I think this is a risk you dare not take."

Ching studied her, then turned to look across the expanse of Victoria Harbor. "Is there anything more to this bargaining of yours?"

"There are two other people involved. Both are murderers. The one who caused my mother's cruel death was an elder brother, a *dai-lo* of the Yellow Dragon. He is known as Chiang-Wah."

The dragon head's face showed no change. "Chiang-Wah the Fierce is dead; he will trouble you no more. And the other?"

"The Forceful One, who licks your boots, is known to me since childhood. While he lives, my life and the lives of those I love will always be in danger. Warn him not to seek me."

Ching stood to indicate the interview was at an end. "I will have my lawyers look at these papers. If they are as you say"—he smiled more pleasantly—"and even if they are not, the blood oath sworn between the House of Ching and the House of Devereaux will be at an end. Our fathers are already at peace in the afterlife. Let us do nothing more to disturb them.

"Ah-Keung is another matter," Ching went on. "He fears no one, not even me. He obeys me while I pay him well . . . but I do not trust him. You must settle your score with him in your own way."

CHAPTER 34

The Amulet

S*ing hardly ever saw* Toby these days; he was working day and night as the Japanese moved ever closer to Hong Kong. She spent many hours with Angus learning the details of her business holdings, and started using the office above the godowns at Causeway Bay, where her mother had once checked the manifests and bills of lading from Double Dragon vessels. It was a small room with just enough space for a desk, wooden filing cabinets, two visitors' chairs, and shelves overflowing with ledgers. She found sheaves of port clearance certificates bearing the chop of Li-Xia, Comprador.

There was a knock at the door of the office one afternoon. Before she could look up, a man opened it and said, "Forgive me for coming unannounced, but I did not think you would see me if I asked permission. You are so important now." It was the voice of Ah-Keung.

He closed the door and seated himself before her, unbuttoning a black leather jacket. "The maker of pipes for the Japanese whoremonger has come a long way from the Emperor of Sausages, and the ballroom of old Moneybags Poon."

"What do you want of me?" Sing asked calmly.

Ah-Keung gave her a slow, sly smile. "Do not worry, Little Star, I have not come to claim my share of your success. I wish only to return that which belongs to you." From his neck he took the jade amulet of the crane and the tiger on its precious chain.

"I knew that you had lied, that it was not stolen by reed-cutters. They were afraid to enter his presence in life; they would never do so in death."

He spread his hands in a gesture of reason. "You were too young to wear it then. It was my duty to protect it for you." He held the amulet out to her. "It is yours by right. You were his last disciple, not I."

"I do not believe you," she said coldly. "Why did you not return it in the Nine Dragons?"

"If you had spoken to me privately as I asked, I would have returned it then." He shrugged. "But I have no wish to quarrel with you. Come, let us talk of our childhoods and remember the Place of Clear Water, where the old ones are at peace."

He looked at her with a smirk that suddenly made her see beyond the amulet to other lies. "The Fish was a Tanka," she said slowly. "She was born on the water. Like all boat people she knew the sea, the river, and the lake as one knows their own family. She was not one to drown in water no deeper than her belly."

The satisfaction on Ah-Keung's face did not change as Sing went on with a terrible certainty. "Master To was strong and knew the secrets of longevity. It was the contents of the gourd that killed him so easily. Do you deny this?"

His careful reply was mocking. "I kept many potions in many gourds when seeking and dispensing herbs. For years I found the gin-seng that made his tea. Sometimes I combined the venom of *yan-jing-shi* with the midnight berry to sell to the doctor in the village. Is it possible that the gourds became mixed up?"

He spread his hands helplessly. "Could I have made such a terrible mistake? This is something we may never know. As for the old woman, her heart was too tired to chase the mud crab. She died as she was given breath, on the water. There was no other way."

He shrugged again, then held the jade amulet up to the light from the window, its moss-green seams running like veins through its milky translucence. "See, does it not still hold the power of the crane and the wisdom of the sages?"

Ah-Keung leaned across the desk. "Allow me the honor of putting it where it belongs. Is this so much to ask? Have I not returned that which the master bequeathed to you?"

The flash of instinct that told Sing to spring to her feet passed as quickly as it had shot through her. This was not the time or place. *Let him replace it, then he will go*, a voice inside her whispered.

She felt his hands lift her hair, gently, with a long, stroking motion, then his fingers fastened the chain. They dropped to her shoulders and for seconds held them firmly. Sing felt his power pass through her like a current as she lifted her head, compelling her to look into his eyes and beyond them into those of *yan-jing-shi*.

A knock on the door broke the spell. Swiftly as a shadow, Ah-Keung moved to the window as Angus stuck his head around the door. "Oh, excuse me, I thought you were alone."

"It's all right, Angus. We've finished our business. I'll be with you in just a moment." Angus hesitated, then withdrew.

Ah-Keung remained at the window, looking down at the crowded causeway, He seemed suddenly harmless, his ungainly frame slouching, the arrogant swagger gone. Sing felt a twinge of pity at the sight of his angular face, the bristling hair cropped close to his large skull. At this moment he was no longer the Forceful One, but the unwanted boy with the twisted foot, who had found his way to survive and face his tormentors.

"Is it not in your heart to forgive the mistakes of a broken boy?" he asked humbly.

"I bear you no malice," she replied. "But we have chosen different ways. Let them remain apart."

"I have paid for my pride. The taipan no longer needs my services," he said tonelessly, "while you have found fortune and many friends. You are protected by the white-haired devil with the eyes of a pretty child; you may even have a child someday."

He shook his head sadly. "I am forced to live behind the walls of Ling Nam, the city of the damned. It is there that you can find me." He placed a folded slip of paper on the desk before her.

"Good-bye, Ah-Keung," Sing said quietly. "It is time for you to leave."

437

"Perhaps you are right," he replied simply. "I have done what I came to do. But I think you will see me again, Little Star." The door closed and he was gone.

Outside in the blazing sunlight Ah-Keung paused to wind several gleaming hairs from Sing's head into a tight curl. It glittered, bright and alive as copper in the sun, as he folded it into a square of red cloth and put it carefully in the pocket of his leather jacket.

Behind the well-guarded gates of the Villa Formosa, Sing Devereaux contemplated what she must do. She had always known the crane would have to face the tiger one day, and she was not afraid. But never had she thought that any life but her own might be in danger. Now she could not forget the quiet threat in Ah-Keung's words: "You have many friends; you may even have a child someday."

The words of Master To returned to her as well:

The crane was content to live quietly in the marsh, to build its nest in the rushes and to dry its wings on the sandbar. But the tiger came seeking the crane in the reed bed and tried to destroy her. She was ready, and defeated her attacker through the power of her wings and the steel of her feet and the blade of her beak. It will always be like this. The crane must be constantly vigilant. It was time for Sing to meet the destiny she had trained for on the Rock of Great Strength.

She sent a message asking Toby to come to the Villa Formosa as soon as he could be spared from his duties. They met in the Pavilion of Joyful Moments, where she tried to find the words that she must say. She took his hand. "There is something that I must tell you. I ask that you listen with your heart and do not question what I must do."

She lifted his hand, to hold it against her cheek. "The gods could not have chosen one more gentle or of greater strength than you. But I must take a path that none can follow, to a place no one can share. My only hope is that I may soon return to you."

His arms closed about her. "Then marry me, Sing . . . be my wife and let us take this path together, as Ben and his Li-Xia once did."

438

"It is not possible. This is not the time for happiness." There was no hesitation in her reply, and he knew it to be final. "If you would help me, please speak of this to Miss Bramble and to Angus. Thank them for their many kindnesses to me, but tell them I must complete a journey that was begun long ago."

She reached up to him, her fingers in the sunshine of his hair. "There are things from my past that are beyond your help. I love you too much to speak of it, so you must trust me." She took an envelope from the jade-ite table; it was sealed with the chop of the Double Dragon. "I shall be gone for one hundred days. If I do not return by then, you must give this letter to Angus. He will know what to do."

CHAPTER 35

Di-Muk

No *road led to* Po-Lin, the Temple of the Precious Lotus. Built a thousand years ago on Lantau Island, it was among the largest Buddhist temples in Asia. Its grandeur had been added to over the centuries, changing it from a humble mountain shrine and burial ground to a monastery housing over a thousand monks. Upon its mist-shrouded peak, the Pagoda of the White Pearl was seldom visited even by the monks of Po-Lin. Only the abbot and his chosen priests could enter its forbidden chambers.

It had taken under two hours for Sing to cross the water on the ferry and climb the thousand steps leading to the monastery. A nun approached her, a small birdlike woman in a faded robe once the rich color of fresh saffron. The little nun bowed a welcome as though Sing were expected, then showed her to an antechamber outside the main temple.

Sing waited alone until Abbot Xoom-Sai entered the chamber assisted by two sturdy elders, who set him down upon a bench of stone. His head shaven, his body swathed in a robe of deepest purple, he looked at Sing with a smile of welcome on a timeless face, his eyes curious and benign.

Sing kowtowed before him, placing at his feet the bamboo cylinder containing the eight precious scrolls. The abbot's face was in shadow as he unfolded the letter from Master To, inspecting the seal closely, running fingertips over the indented wax.

When at last he spoke, his words were for her alone, as though for that moment she was a child again, beneath the pear tree, listening to the patient voice of Master To. "Stand up, Red Lotus: You are a true disciple of the White Crane. Your master, To-Tze, was well known to me; he passes on his powers with great faith in you. This letter tells me that you were the only one to be trusted with the Precious Set of Eight; that you would find me when the time had come for the Crane and the Tiger to face each other."

He was silent for a moment, his eyes closed as though in a trance. "You must prepare well. Your enemy is very angry and very strong; his power is in hatred and his weakness is in rage."

He spoke as if he could see the scene unfolding before him. "First he will send *yan-jing-shi*, the snake. . . . In his heart he is a coward. Only if you prevail will the Tiger show himself."

"I ask that I may be allowed to reside here while I prepare, Great Lord."

"That you may do, Red Lotus. You will sleep in a place that is the battleground of the spirit. Your bed of stone will give no comfort, but you will find rest from the ninth hour until you are awakened by the voice of Buddha. The day begins at the hour of three, when the moon has reached its zenith, when body, spirit, and soul are open to all things. You will meditate alone, eat nothing except the food prepared for you by the nun Lu, drink nothing but water from the spring. You will train alone before the Pearl Pagoda. Call upon the spirit of the Crane and make ready to do battle with *yan-jing-shi*, who will come in the night."

⌖

It always began with the same dream. Cloud pictures skimmed over the lake from the Rock of Great Strength: Plank boats sailed peacefully beneath their piles of reeds; sampans sat still as grasshoppers in midsummer. Farther up the slope, the breeze sang to her through the bamboo like the harps of heaven. This place was the home of her soul. She stood transported by the joy of it.

The pale outline of the mountains suddenly darkened. The tree peonies closed their petals, to wither and drop as if in the path of a great fire. Birds lost their song in the groves. A shadow cast itself across the lake,

441

black as oil, swallowing her perfect world. She stood at its edge, safe at first, spellbound by its menace. Venom crept like acid, devouring the fragile lace of lichen on the ground. Her feet were bare, the feet of a child, firmly rooted upon the rock, connected to its hidden forces as they leaped and flew, spun and and turned, at one with the air . The voice of Abbot Xoom-Sai spoke to her clearly, calmly, telling her to stand her ground, reminding her that all things lived and were one in the Way of the Tao, that their energy was her energy, their strength, her strength.

At first the dreams were short and the blackness easy to repel, inching toward her and then slipping away like the tide of a dark sea. With every disciplined muscle in her body, she clung to the safe, sun-warmed surface of the rock. As if it sensed her power, the oily mass would withdraw, shrinking to become the glistening coils of *yan-jing-shi*.

Sing would see the poisonous white of its belly against the bile-green scales rising before her. Another voice would reach her . . . the voice of a boy, harsh with impatience to become a man. "See! I have tamed the foot well . . . faster and more deadly than the king of all snakes." She saw the snake's flicking shoelace tongue, the toadstool yellow of its gaping mouth, the blood-smeared jaws of the herd boy as he tore the spearhead-shaped head from the flailing body. "You owe your life to me, Red Lotus. One day I may claim it."

Suddenly, as though stabbed by a pin, Sing would wake up, her eyes wide and her senses sharp as an executioner's blade. The words of Ah-Keung lingered in the dark, the rock hard and cold beneath her whirling feet. The dreams came every night—closing in on her, cold as death against her feet, sucking the chi from her legs until they grew numb and she could no longer feel her connection to the rock. She was back in the typhoon, exposed to the sheets of lightning and the screaming winds; seeing the bloodied face of Ruby, her plastered hair and frightened eyes reaching out to her as they tumbled into darkness in each other's arms.

※

Ah-Keung seemed to float before an altar in a windowless room. The two yellow flames from the candles were motionless, lighting the contents of

442

a tray, as the Forceful One concentrated on the revenge he had carried in his heart for much of his lifetime. No matter how much the upstart girl had learned, the arts of Black Oath Wu had shown him more.

The force of the black Tao transformed night into day, light into darkness. It could turn quietude into chaos, poison the strongest mind with steady drops from the prettiest snuff bottle. It could weaken and devour the bravest heart, capture and possess a human soul.

Ah-Keung's lips moved soundlessly as he recited words from the suspended tablet only he could read, its characters long lost in the dungeons of a violent history. He was naked. The candlelight illuminated the intricate tattoo of the striking cobra that climbed the length of his spine, at its head the symbol of yin and yang turned upside down; on his chest the snarling face of a charging tiger.

He lost all sense of weight, transported in a state of mental levitation. In the tray of ash, drawn in the blackened remains of a flaming curse, a single character appeared: Red Lotus. Stretched across it, gleaming in the yellow buds of light, lay the strands of his enemy's hair. His body shook as they flared to flame, then curled to nothing. From the surrounding blackness a gust came, whirling the ash, obliterating the name forever.

⁂

A smudge of light began to appear in the horror of Sing's nightmares. The pale shape grew closer until she awoke, her heart racing as the face of Ah-Keung invaded her mind with the gold-ringed, lidless eyes of a cobra. Sing knew she was in grave danger. She heard the words of Master To: *Only you can break the link. You must withstand. To fall in the path of the Tiger is to perish.* She called upon all she had learned to combat the fear that threatened to wrap her in the sticky silk of the bird-eating spider, to feed upon her sanity as it had drawn the vivid colors from the hummingbird.

Food had become unnecessary, and when sense told her she must try to eat she could not force it past her throat. Her body lost all trace of energy. Inside, she turned to ice, but her skin was slick with sweat.

Dragging everything she could find to cover herself, she lay shaking in every nerve and muscle, every toughened sinew in her body disconnected from her wasting limbs. She could not rise, feeling the creeping warmth of her urine turn cold. At last she felt her link with the Rock of Great Strength snap like a single strand of silk; and she fell, silently screaming, into the maelstrom of Ah-Keung's making.

⁑

The elders carried Sing's unconscious body to the Pagoda of the White Pearl to do battle with the powers of darkness. The Abbot Xoom-Sai watched as she was carried up the narrow stone steps to the eighth and topmost chamber, and laid upon an ancient tapestry of mystic signs in the center of the circular space. A setting sun cast orange light through a small diamond-shaped window set in its walls.

Prayer cloths hung like flags from the high, domed ceiling. From a corner, lit bright as bronze by the fading sky, a statue of the Buddha in meditation looked down on the bed where she lay. On the small altar before it, an iron incense burner bristled with burned-out joss sticks. The abbot replaced them with eight fresh sticks, lighting each in turn, then passed thick candles to his trusted elders.

"She must be surrounded by light at all times, the flames lit with our prayers. It is in darkness of hidden forests that this evil dwells." Abbot Xoom-Sai began to pass his hands inches above Sing's shivering body. Through half-closed eyes he conjured her aura: The colors of her life-force were dimmed, oppressed by a malignant shadow. "This one has been cursed by the darkest of powers. It is filled with a great hatred. A powerful evil." His hands stopped above her forehead and his fingers began to tremble. "She has great strength, but her enemy is also great."

His low voice seemed to fill the chamber with faint echoes, his purple robe to blaze in the last of the daylight. One hand, still trembling with the force of the vibrations it had detected, moved to her throat, reaching to touch the jade amulet around her neck. The abbot's fingers closed around it until his fist shook violently and he let it go as though burned. Carefully, he unfastened the chain and held it dangling for them to see.

444

"The evil began here. It is this that has been used as a key to the door-way of her soul." He took it to the altar and laid it at the feet of the Bud-dha. "Send for the hook-maker . . . ask him to come without delay."

Sing remained in the Pearl Pagoda for thirty days and nights before she became conscious of her surroundings. It seemed to her that she had never known anything but the blackness of the pit, felt anything but its slimy walls, or seen anything but the eyes of the cobra. The darkness echoed only with the taunting laughter of Ah-Keung: "Tell me, Red Lo-tus, where are the powers of the White Crane now?"

Then, slowly, the blackness began to fade and the eyes of the snake grew dim. A pinprick of blue light appeared above her and gradually increased in size until it surrounded her in a bright bubble of pure light. She could feel it dry the damp chill of her sweat. The patch of summer blue became framed by a dome-shaped window. A single puff of white cloud floated in it, light and soft as a blown feather.

Sing felt the hot flow of tears and lay for a long time looking only at the little cloud. It seemed to grow bigger, to have movement of its own, coming closer and closer until she saw it was a great white bird whose wings rose and fell with dreamlike slowness. It soared and dived through the sky with majestic grace and boundless freedom.

She heard the voice of Master To calling to her and tried to rise. To her joy, she found she could move lightly as air. The pain that had come with the darkness was gone. The nun who sat beside her, spooning the foul-smelling mixture patiently into her mouth, saw the eyelids flutter and open. The taste of the herbal medicine was rank in Sing's mouth and nostrils. The nun wiped it from her chin and set the bowl aside. Even the slight rustle of her movement was comforting to Sing after the bedlam of the pit.

The abbot leaned over Sing, his brown arms and shoulders bare as he spoke to her quietly. "The worst of the battle is over, Red Lotus. Soon you will be strong enough to defend yourself. This is the one who will show you how." The abbot stepped aside.

The face that was lowered close to hers was so masked in wrinkles that only the searching brightness of its eyes showed life. "I am the hook-maker," a voice said in a thin whisper. "You are returned to the light. The amulet is purified. When you are ready to meet your tormentor, it awaits you at the feet of the deity in my hut by the sea."

⊱✠⊰

From the peak above the temple of Po-Lin, Red Lotus stood with her face lifted to the sky, using the power of her mind to surround herself with a golden light. Behind closed eyelids, she concentrated on breathing deeply the rarefied air off the sea, noting with satisfaction the unhindered ebb and flow of its circulation through her body. Lost to everything but the slight sounds of wind stirring the scant tufts of grass, she willed the oxygen through her lungs, following the upright channel of her spine and into her lower belly to energize her core, then back again to complete the cycle in gradual silent exhalation that would nourish her heavenly chi.

To stand so completely alone on this, the highest point in all the offshore islands of Hong Kong, the night breeze upon her limbs and in her hair, gave her soul the freedom it must have. She had meditated there since dawn, as she had each day for a month since climbing from the pit. The gentle movements of Pa-Tuan-Tsin, the Precious Set of Eight Silk-Weaving Exercises, restored flexibility to her limbs, returning new strength to every muscle and refreshing her bloodstream. At night, if thoughts of Ah-Keung came to her, she would surround his face with a ring of fire and watch his image be consumed by the flames of his own hate.

With each day Sing felt her powers growing to a level she had never known. She was ready.

⊱✠⊰

The hook-maker had lived on Lantau Island longer than anyone else, making fishhooks from the bones and claws of animals, barbs of seashell, and the beaks of birds bound into slivers of petrified driftwood, each one carved with ancient characters that, he claimed, no fish could resist. The fishermen believed his hooks were charmed, for they always caught the finest fish; and when a storm swept the islands, the sampan with his hooks aboard was sure to reach land safely. So great was his magic that some began wearing his hooks around their necks as talismans to attract good fortune and keep away demons. The hook-maker charged nothing for his work, accepting only fish and other food as payment.

His advice was sought on every problem and his blessing on every birth, marriage, or death among the boat people of Silvermine Bay. But it was in the destruction of evil spirits, the chasing of demons, that the hook-maker had his greatest power. So great were his forces for white magic that even the abbot of Po-Lin asked for his help in desperate cases.

Wood smoke from the hook-maker's hut was blowing on the offshore breeze as Sing approached it. She had run down the mountain to the sea without stopping, springing from rock to rock to rock in the plunging stream, taking the firm sand of the foreshore in long easy strides. Arriving at the hut, she greeted the hook-maker, watching the old man's crooked fingers fashion the delicate detail of a charm. He sat on a log of driftwood, its texture as seamed and weathered as his skillful hands.

He squinted up at her. "I see you are strong again, Little Sister. How can I help you?"

She seated herself on the log beside him. "The dream came again last night, *si-fu*. No longer in the form of *yan-jing-shi*, but as *lo-fu*, the tiger." She watched his gnarled hands carving with infinite patience. "I know the one who does this thing. He will not be so easily defeated."

"To defeat an enemy is never easy," the hook-maker said after a while. "I have come to know the heart of this Forceful One. He bears the venom of the cobra and the teeth of the tiger. Such a one knows only victory or death."

"I fear for those close to me. If he tests my strength and fails again, he may turn his venom on them, to bring me to him."

He nodded, setting aside his work and looking at her closely. "It may be so. You are strong again, but so is he."

"I must face him, *si-fu.*"

The old one nodded "This is his intention. What he cannot possess with the mind he must destroy. To him it is a matter of honor."

Sing withdrew a slip of red paper, unfolding it and laying it before him. "I have written this message in the old style. I ask you to lay your hands upon it. To bring him to me. There can be no peace for me until this is done."

He picked up the red paper filled with flowing calligraphy, reading it carefully. "You are indeed a maker of fine images. How can such a challenge be ignored? It is written in the way of tradition, from one disciple to another of the same master."

"I have come for the blessing of your protection and for the amulet, *si-fu.*"

"It is ready, Little Sister. Come inside." The inside of the hut was cool and almost dark, taking her back to the hut of Master To. The hook-maker crossed to a recess in the wall where the sparks of joss sticks illuminated the fiercely warlike figure of Kuan-Kung. From its neck, the hook-maker removed the amulet of the White Crane. Holding it between his palms, he bowed three times to the god of war, then turned and brought it to the light from the doorway.

"It is purged of the evil one's essence. Cleansed by the blessings of Po-Lin and imbued with the warrior spirit of Kuan-Kung. I have called upon all my powers to sanctify it."

He held the amulet high in the sunlight; for a moment it seemed to radiate pure light. He fastened it around Sing's neck.

"Remember, to the Forceful One all things are reversed. Night is day. Evil is good. The laws of the universe are turned upside down; only chaos reigns. Reverse the eight trigrams and you will triumph. Let the yin become the yang, black become white. When the strong become the weak and peace becomes war, then all things will be possible."

He handed back the folded red paper. "Send your message. It will find him and he will come to the appointed place at the appointed time."

※

Sing sat on the rock as the faint flush of sunrise turned the low moon pale as milky jade. Half an hour more and Ah-Keung would face her here. She could hear the words of Master To: *The crane can never match the tiger's strength and ferocity . . . but the tiger cannot guess the speed and cleverness of the crane. The tiger's power lies not in its jaws or its claws, but in the keenness of its eyes.*

As the sky lightened and threads of cloud stretched like strands of colored silk above the horizon, she sensed his presence and called out, "I am here, Ah-Keung. The sun is rising. I am ready to meet the Forceful One face-to-face in its pure light." The challenge echoed among the crumbling pagodas.

"I could think of no better place," his voice replied. "There is no one to know what happens here but the abbot and his thousand monks without a voice among them." His words were spoken quietly, yet echoed like those of a whispering giant among the rocky pinnacles, invading deserted burial vaults of pagodas from another age, to be lost among the great, dark pines that rose in sweeping tiers beside them.

Her heightened senses tracked down the voice to its source behind her. In the atom of time it took to turn and face him, Ah-Keung had stepped from the shadows of the Pearl Pagoda, wearing the loose black garb of the master *wu-shu* fighter, trimmed and cuffed with white, smiling at the element of surprise he had so cleverly created. "The crane becomes careless, she does not see the tiger in the reed bed nor hear its breath nor sense its smell." He drew a breath through closed teeth with exaggerated disapproval. "Have the comforts of fame and fortune made the Red Lotus less vigilant?"

As he spoke, he loosened the corded loops that fastened the jacket across his chest, laughing at her. "Did you think me a fool to meet you on ground I had not trod, in a place not known to me?" Without haste he folded the tunic and set it aside with a water gourd. "For eight days I have slept on stone as you have done, here in this Pagoda of the White Pearl. I have watched you call upon the old one, and heard you speak with him beneath the fading moon. I learned the movements of the crane, as you have studied the secrets of the tiger."

449

He sniggered, once again the herd boy from the hills. "You are a vision to watch in the sun's first light; it is a riddle yet to be solved that one so beautiful should be so dangerous. The same golden shell shines around you that once shone around our beloved master. He has taught you well." His tone was so even, his movements so normal, that the purpose that had brought them to this high place among the honored dead seemed suddenly unreal.

"I did not wish this day to come," Sing replied evenly, "but have always known that it must."

He stepped into the strengthening light, kicking the canvas slippers from his feet. "It is written in our stars, Red Lotus. We had no hand in it." He smiled at some inner thought too big to question, grinding his bare soles into the rock to find its texture. "From the moment my twisted foot led my family to cast me out, they left me with nothing but the heart of a survivor. The way of the warrior is the only path before me."

He picked up a piece of broken tile fallen from a pagoda roof, grinding it to dust between the millstones of his palms, not boastfully but in preparation for what must come. "And you, Little Star," he continued, dusting his palms and stretching the sinews of his neck. "Did the gods of happiness not turn from those who gave you life because they wore a different skin? What of the gods who spoke to the old woman who carried you to the lake? Was it not they who brought you into the world of the White Crane?" His voice had risen in anger, his eyes a well of sadness that made her silent heart reach out to him.

"If this time and place are not of our making, and its purpose none of our choosing, then why must we fight, Ah-Keung? There is great truth in what you say, but this irony has given us great strength. We two have the power to change the course of our stars. We have learned to take control of the sun and the moon of our existence—to defy the voices of destiny if we must. There is no dishonor in this."

He shook his head, and in that rare moment, the eyes that looked into hers were the eyes of a deserted child. "Such a decision will be blessed by the abbot," she said, "of less importance to the monks than a quarrel of

450

the hawk and the sparrow. No one else will know that we turned our backs to the face of karma." Was the child in him within her reach? "Must one of us die for the bad joss sticks of our parents? We have given our hearts and minds to the mysteries of earth and sky, devoted our lives in search of perfection in mind, body, and spirit. We can challenge the will of the gods, you and I."

Ah-Keung shook off her words as a dog sheds water from its coat. "We cannot change the Way of the Warrior. Once the path is taken, there is no turning back."

He padded catlike around her, in his wide-legged pants tied by a crimson sash. "We have waited far too long for the sun to rise upon a rock that knows no master. Our *si-fu* is not here to judge us; only you or I will know who leaves this place and who does not."

Sing made no reply, knowing her words had failed. Her eyes entered the black depths of his without fear, seeking the weakness she knew was there. *There is a fraction of time faster than a blink that shows the intention before the act. This is true of the cobra before it stikes. . . . We must not miss this fragment of eternity, or it may be our last. It is the infinite space between life and death. We must not allow this to evade us.*

There was a clatter of something tossed at her feet—the birth bracelet once worn by the Fish. "A pity the old witch can no longer advise her precious piglet." His words were now brutal in their mockery.

The threads of cloud had woven themselves into molten strands to celebrate the coming of daylight. "As our beloved master looks down from his temple in the sky, he will see Red Lotus, his last disciple, face the skills of Black Oath Wu."

She turned with him, never taking her eyes from his, as he moved in a wide circle. "He is here," she said coldly. "My *si-fu* lives through me. The amulet no longer holds the cobra's venom. You are a coward, Forceful One. The challenge of change is too great for you. You could not face the master on the rock, so you poisoned him. A defenseless old woman was easily felled with a single blow. Now you prepare to face a woman in mortal combat. There is nothing for you to be proud of, dog boy."

He seemed not to hear, but his smile had flown. "All great masters must eventually fall to the hand that once obeyed them. It has been the Way of the Warrior for a thousand years."

Sing answered with studied contempt. "Eye-to-eye and hand-to-hand, not by deception and betrayal." She played on his anger. "You are a thief and a liar, Ah-Keung. While I have pursued a life of hope and found my truth, you seek only the darkness of false gods. I am no longer the child afraid of spiders, but you are still the herd boy with a twisted foot."

Ah-Keung strutted before her, stretching and testing his limbs. "I have often wondered what he taught you that he would not teach me. Have you remembered? Do you practice the art of spiritual boxing? Do you fight me in your dreams?" His tone was confident, almost frivolous, a man speaking to a wayward child before punishment.

As he closed his fists, the muscles of his chest and abdomen twitched and the snarling face of the tiger seemed to spring to life. She stood perfectly still, silhouetted against the vivid sky. Time and distance dropped away for those alone upon the forgotten plateau of Lantau Island. The great temple bell boomed like the voice of Buddha, rising with a distant mantra, the shimmering vibrations of a thousand throats at prayer.

The tiger circled the crane, murmuring soft threats meant to unnerve her. They were meaningless words she did not hear, like the screech of gulls carried on the wind, as she awaited his first move.

It was a cautious move, merely testing her reflexes, and was easily repelled. They analyzed each other's strengths and weaknesses, attuned to the slightest sight or sound that might betray a flicker of fear; observing the steadiness of breath, the depths of stamina, the cycle of chi. In lightning strikes too fast to see, the claws of the tiger took the measure of the wings of the crane. Iron bone clashed with iron bone, as grasps and locks were evaded, grips broken, kicks that would shatter any ordinary limb or destroy an internal organ deflected and returned. The defensive dance of the crane rose with ease from the path of the tiger, its feet as deadly as tooth and claw, its lethal beak sheathed like a sword.

The words of her master were as much a part of her as the measure of her chi: *To take the upper part, first feign at the lower; to cut the lower part, first feign at the upper. To attack the left, be aware of the right; to attack the right, be aware of the left. Take care of both upper and lower parts; correlate the left and the right. Block and then attack at the first instance; attack and then block at the first instance. Defense should be accompanied by attack; attack should be accompanied by defense. It is an expert who wins without blocking in advance; it is the defeated who only blocks the opposing strike but does not attack simultaneously.*

Ah-Keung spun away, whirling to face his opponent at a distance of several paces. "We have tried each other for many precious moments, yet we hardly sweat." He grinned his slanted grin. "Perhaps there is something to be said for the barrel of a gun and the speed of a bullet to settle old scores."

Turning his back on her, Ah-Keung lifted the water gourd by its tasseled cord, pouring its contents over his head. He swilled water in his mouth, spurting some at her feet, tossing the gourd for her to catch. "Drink, Red Lotus. Taste the sweetness of water while you can."

Sing widened the space between them before pouring cold water into her open mouth. Her eyes left his for the sliver of time it took to lift the gourd, closing in less than a blink as the water splashed her face.

A blade sliced viciously through the air, so instantaneous she had no time to recognize the lethal buzz of the Shaolin Dart, only the silver blur of its passage and the scarlet streak of its flight. Too late she leapt high, but his timing was perfect. As if her ankles were bound by steel, she crashed to the rock with no hope of balance, striking her head in a blinding flash and rolling sharply into a chasm of blackness.

Ah-Keung's voice reached her from afar—from the Place of Clear Water, perhaps, or the shadowy corner of the herb shed. Her face was slapped from side to side until the warm, metallic taste of blood began to choke her. The slapping ceased, and his hard hand patted her cheek affectionately. "That's better, my Little Star. It would be an insult if you slept before I am finished with you." Consciousness returned to Sing in a wave she was careful not to show, as his fingers closed upon her throat.

She knew with absolute clarity what had happened. She had heard many times of the Shaolin Dart, a weighted blade kept straight by a swallowtail of red ribbon and secured to a length of twine supple as silk and strong as steel. Easily hidden by wide-legged trousers or about the waist in the folds of a sash, it was the tongue of the snake in the hands of an adept. That he would conceal such a weapon had not occurred to her, and she cursed herself for a fool. *That which the eye can see should not trouble you. It is what you cannot see that you should fear.*

He slapped her harder. "Wake up, Little Star. Did the old one not warn you to beware of tricks? I am disappointed. I did not think it would be so easy to overcome the Red Lotus." His thumb shifted from her jaw, probing behind the carotid artery. "But did you really believe that a disciple of the black Tao would allow a girl with the heart of a chicken to stand against him in the mortal combat of masters?"

As the ball of his thumb found the silent pulse that would paralyze her limbs but leave her senses heightened, she called upon the words of the hook-maker: *Let yin become yang, black become white; reverse the eight trigrams and you will triumph.* She feigned the tremor and wide-eyed stare of paralysis as he loosened the cord that bound her legs. She felt the garments ripped from her limbs, his knee forcing her legs apart. The pressure of his thumb increased; her vision swam as her life-force began to drain like blood from an open wound.

His breath was hot on her face as he searched her blank eyes with an ugly grin of triumph. "I have wondered for so long who would steal the precious cherry of the great Red Lotus . . . or would it be given freely? Was it the boys from the reed-cutters' camp? Did you yield to the Japanese whore and her wooden prince, or barter it for old moneybags at the Nine Dragons?" He shook his head wisely. "I do not think so. The taipan Ching would not pay so highly for soiled goods. So, has the one with golden hair and the eyes of a woman been there before me?"

He leaned closer, his foul tongue lapping at her face as he pulled the drawstring of his pants. "We shall see. If he has been the one to make you squeal, then I will kill him slowly." She felt his stiffened shaft jabbing, prodding to enter her. She called upon the source of her chi, the crucible of power reserved for just such a moment. The words hissed through his teeth in an ecstasy of hate. "When I have finished with you, the sun will be gone and you will think you have been mounted by a herd of mountain goats."

In his haste he did not detect the sudden movement of her cupped hands. They flew wide and with explosive force struck his ears simultaneously. A stream of bloody mucus shot from his nose, plastering his cheek like a weeping scar, his wide-eyed shock instantly eclipsed by a thunderclap of blinding pain. She knew precisely what he felt: The implosion of the blow within his brain cavity would rupture both eardrums in a sea of vivid stars; the vibrations would ring in his deadened ears and penetrate his head like a white-hot blade, crowding his skull like the boom of the temple's great bell, persisting with endless peals of pain.

The agony would take only seconds for one as trained as Ah-Keung to control—long enough for her to roll from beneath his weight and find her feet, kicking aside the loosened cord. The ear slap of the iron palm could have been fatal, but the keenest edge of her chi had been deflected by the pressure of his thumb. She had time to draw upon the pristine currents of mountain air, nourishing her internal strength with every vital breath.

The strike had left him unsteady, shaking his head to clear his vision, his nose flowing like a spigot as he drew a forearm across his face, flicking the bloodied flux from his fingers as he rose to face her. "You are clever, Little Star—your chi flows like a river." He grinned hideously, groping for the water gourd, his burning eyes absorbing hers, unblinking as he poured the remaining water over his head. "No longer afraid of the forest cobra." He spat copiously at her feet, smearing his chest with a bloodied hand. "Or the tiger in the reed bed . . . The old one taught you well."

Red Lotus was beyond the reach of hate, awed by the sense of power that welled within her like a boiling spring. Her heartbeat barely quickened, she felt humbled by the damage she had done with such immediacy and ease. She stepped away from Ah-Keung's advance. "It is not too late. You have struck, and so have I. None but the gulls will know we parted here."

He tossed the empty gourd away, its hollow rattle loud among the rocks, shaking his sodden hair as a wolf would shake a rabbit, as though he had not heard her. "I once thought of granting you a sudden and silent end—of letting you die with a warrior's dignity." His words were slurred as he dropped into the crouching tiger form, shaking his head to clear his vision. "But now I want to hear you scream. I want the monks of Po-Lin to stop their chanting, to search the skies for the hawk and the sparrow, and listen to you howl before I have done with you."

She breathed in his words as she would a sudden gust of sea air. Such naked fury could spell his downfall—all skill and discipline, all stealth and strategy, a lifetime of training tossed aside in the lust to kill.

Red Lotus waited calmly for the frenzied charge she knew must come. Her arms rose like arcs of steel, loosely erect, as the rising sun tipped the eastern horizon, flooding the oceans with its pure light, sweeping the rocky summit like a vast blade of fire. Red Lotus felt it hot across her back, reaching over time and distance to protect her with its radiant aura as it had done upon the Rock of Great Strength. She drank the air to replenish her chi, and drew upon the forces of the universe to enter her body through the Heaven Door at the top of her head.

Her feet were bare upon the rock, the grip of her toes summoning its ageless power to feed her roots—to anchor her, solidly, immovably . . . or to release her as lightly as the smallest feather is lifted by the slightest wind. The shadow of the crane grew in dimension, long and wide until it dominated the battleground like an avenging gargantuan, inviting the tiger's attack with open arms. She felt the great bird enter her, lifting her on rippling wings, surer, lighter, and higher than ever before, evading his wild rush with the mechanism that had been set and coiled within her for so long it had become a second sense . . . a force much greater than her woman's body that needed to be freed.

The full glare of the sun smote the twisted face of the herd boy as she heard the shrill cry of the crane echo through the old pagodas. Her arms arched higher, dropping with the swiftness and weight of the hammer that strikes the anvil. The right blocked the tiger's strike to her throat, absorbing the full shock of its power upon her forearm. She willed her chi into the marrow of the slender bone, turning it for that fraction of an

456

instant to steel, as her hooked fingers struck his dazzled eyes. Her blow drove deep, the heel of her hand breaking the bridge of his nose with a meaty click. She heard the words of Master To spoken from a place deep within, but as real as the burning stroke of the sun: *The power of the tiger is in its golden eyes.*

Ah-Keung mouthed a vicious curse, his left hand blocking her strike too late to deflect its impact. She sensed his crippling snap-kick to her upper shin before it reached her, lifting easily from its path. Her left hand flew in a wide arc, her arm supple as the neck of the crane, her fingers bunched and rigid as the lethal beak, under Ah-Keung's attacking arm, driving upward with the force of a sword point to a spot slightly below the armpit, allowing for the shifting of the pressure points, letting her senses guide her. Every ounce of her willpower and every second of her training went into the lethal strike of *di-muk*, the death touch she had practiced ten thousand times for this moment of truth.

She drove through vulnerable flesh between the muscles, penetrating tissue between corded cartilage, piercing taut sinew to reach the nerve juncture slightly above and behind the diaphragm, plunging with the force of a battle axe to the root of his lung; so finely tuned to his savage vibrations that she felt the electric spasm run up her arm like the ringing of steel upon steel. No sound escaped Ah-Keung's gaping jaws as he fought for his next breath, his damaged, blood-filled eyes staring at the burning sun.

In that splinter of time the voice of her *si-fu* spoke again: Yan-jing-shi *is unforgiving. We must strike him before he strikes us.* But she also heard him say in a quieter voice beneath the pear tree: *It is not easy to take a life and carry this forever in your heart. It is the heaviest of all burdens and leaves no place for happiness. To kill another is the end of freedom. . . . Sometimes it is the loser that wins.*

The aim of her blow shifted, avoiding by a hair's breadth the lethal spot deep behind the rib cage that separates the heart and lung from the liver and the gut, deflecting its full power from the lethal point of entry. Ah-Keung bent backward like a tautened spring, the bloodstained face of the tiger bared to a livid sky as he fought for breath. Every muscle in his body quivered, his hands flapping helplessly at his sides. One violent convulsion bucked him like a lightning bolt; blood flowed freely from his broken nose, seeping from his mouth where he had bitten through his tongue. Sing stepped back as he dropped to his knees, suspended by the shock of disbelief, to pitch forward at her feet.

Such a strike would have instantly killed any ordinary man, stopping any normal heart like a shaft of steel. She had spared his life, but the deflected blow had taken its toll; even a hardened warrior like Ah-Keung could not survive without lasting internal damage.

Sing Devereaux felt the spirit of Red Lotus leave her on the wings of the crane, along with all thoughts of violence and a threatened past. Turning her back on Ah-Keung the Forceful One, she saw only the herb gatherer who had swum the lake and roamed the hills in search of himself. She would never know if the decision to spare him came from her master's wish to save her from a deadly karma, or from her own sorrow for one who had faced an uncaring world with nothing but his strength and his courage to sustain him. She shed silent tears of regret for the abandoned boy whose cries to the gods had gone unheard.

Siu-Sing walked to the rock's farthest edge. Looking out over the clean colors of the sea at the glittering spray shattering like walls of green glass on the rocks far below, she felt the bond between her and the Rock of Great Strength part like a broken thread. The voice of Old To no longer whispered to her. Although Ah-Keung's injuries would improve with time, the strengths and passions of the warrior would never return to him . . . and never again would he threaten her or those she loved.

Lu, the nun, appeared beside her with a bamboo dipper of strong herbal tea. Her face said nothing and she did not speak, yet her gentle presence was like a calming hand. The threads of cloud had dissolved and the sun was clear of the sea, the keening of gulls unchanged. No word was spoken as Sing rose and took the steep path down toward the Temple of the Precious Lotus. There was no sign of Ah-Keung's body or of his blood. It was as though he had never been there. Monks worked silently side by side in the gardens . . . as though nothing had taken place in the shadow of the Pearl Pagoda.

Abbot Xoom-Sai had accepted the eighth scroll, along with the jade amulet, eight strands of Sing's hair plaited into its gleaming chain. Red Lotus was no more. It had taken one hundred days. "You were wise to spare the life of one so lost to reason; his is a karma that is heavy with hate."

The abbot's words were spoken in comfort, but Sing replied with a bitterness she could not hide. "I too was lost and belonged nowhere until I took his place upon the rock. He is not to blame. He has a right to hate me. It was I who entered the world of *yan-jing-shi* and stole from him his only dream."

The abbot shook his head. "It was the hand of To-Tze, the word of his *si-fu* that barred his way." He fluttered a frail hand. "This was decided before the soul of your ancestors had entered your body. You knew nothing of this world or its trickery." He sighed heavily. "Evil had claimed him before your feet had found the earth. His own heart is his greatest enemy. It is you who survives this *ku-ma-tai*. The eye of the tiger is forever closed and the venom of the snake is no more."

Abbot Xoom-Sai placed his hand upon Sing's head. "Go without regret, *siu-jeh*. He has many brothers here. Perhaps his troubled mind will find peace in stillness until he is laid to rest as one of us."

The skin of his hands seemed transparent, yet were surprisingly warm as he folded something in her palm no larger than a pebble. "Wear this in peace and harmony. The Precious Set of Eight and the jade amulet will be kept in sanctity and safety until the day you return for them." Four novice monks in bright saffron robes lifted the temple's palanquin as though it carried a child and the slap of their sandaled feet became a rhythm as Sing Devereaux descended from the heights of Lantau. Halfway down, she opened her palm to find a tiny golden Buddha glittering in the sun.

CHAPTER 36

Angel's Garden

In *the Pavilion of* Joyful Moments, Sing Devereaux sat in quiet contemplation. Her life seemed almost complete and the way ahead soon clear. Toby's duties kept him on the border or in the briefing room of Government House, but she had spoken with him on the telephone. The regiment, he had said soberly, was preparing to defend its territory.

Both he and Winifed begged her to leave Hong Kong to live with his parents in Surrey. She had laughed at the thought, but loved them both for their concern.

On the table before her was a file that had come with a note from Angus Grant.

> *I'll not ask where you've been, only thank the Lord that you're back. I have found one more lead in the search for news of your father. These papers include a bill of sale for a block of land on the Whangpoo River in Shanghai. The site is occupied by the Flying Angel Mission to Seamen, and the deed is cosigned with the name Agnes Gertrude Gates.*
>
> *I will be with you tomorrow. It is time to visit the English garden.*

There were photographs of her father beside a stout woman with a shock of white hair framing a face wreathed in smiles. There were also letters suggesting great warmth, humor, and trust between them. The official documents dealing with the property were stamped with the seal of the international organization of the Flying Angel Mission to Seamen.

460

Angus arrived after lunch on the following day, moments ahead of a delivery van. He supervised the unloading of a large flat item encased in a linen sheet, which two men carried carefully into the dining room. "I've a bit of a surprise for you, but first we'll take a look at the English garden. You'd best prepare yourself, but I think you're ready."

The overgrown gate was heavily chained and padlocked. Angus battled with the rust of years, finally opening it with a large iron key, handing it to Sing. "It's the only one. Ben made me swear that no one would know of this place but myself, Indie Da Silva, and you if you were ever found."

He forced a space for them to squeeze through. What was once a pathway through the spinney of birch and larch trees was knee-deep in weeds and undergrowth. On the edge of the treeline, overlooking the sea, was a mound smothered in wild violets. He crouched to pull away the growth of many years concealing the face of the tomb, wiping the rose-colored quartz face with his handkerchief and standing back for her to see the the deeply chiseled words inlaid with gold:

HERE LIES A SCHOLAR.
HER NAME IS LI-XIA DEVEREAUX.
1906–1924

She ran from no one and hid from nothing.

They stayed long enough to make some order of its surroundings. There were no tears, but Sing thanked Angus with quiet words and asked to be left alone for a while.

"Take your time, lassie. I'll be in the dining room when you're good and ready." Sing Devereaux sat beside her mother's grave until the sun had dipped behind the far horizon. No one would ever know what it was they talked about.

When she entered the dining room, she stopped at the French doors open to the terrace. At the far end of the long room, taking up most of the wall it was intended for and lit from above, hung the life-size portrait of Li-Xia and Captain Devereaux. "I had it cleaned and restored by experts. It's by Sir George Chinnery himself, painted just outside the door you're standing in."

Sing could scarcely find the words to thank him. When he had left, she sat at the shining table beneath the portrait of her parents and lost no time in writing to the English headquarters of the Flying Angel Mission to Seamen in England seeking information about Agnes Gates.

The response, when it came weeks later, was what Sing had been hoping for. The Shanghai branch of the organization was still an active mission, and Miss Agnes G. Gates had been its superintendent for the past thirty years. Sing wrote to her at once, and received an immediate reply urging Sing to visit her as soon as possible, indicating that she had important things to tell her of an extremely confidential nature.

She telephoned Angus immediately. "I must go to Shanghai. I believe this lady may be able to tell me what really happened to my father. Can you arrange a flight as quickly as possible?"

He sounded worried. Shanghai was in Japanese hands; even though the officials were easily bribed to arrange such a flight, her father had played very dangerous games with very dangerous people. Privately wondering what he would think if he knew of her battle with Ah-Keung, Sing thanked him for his concern but insisted that she must go.

There was a brief silence, after which he said, "Well, I suppose you could not be in safer hands; Aggie Gates was like a mother to him. If anyone knows of Ben's true fate, she will."

※

Sing was thrilled by her first flight in an airplane. The Catalina flying boat swept in low over the East China Sea, over the old treaty port of Ningpo to the vast mouth of the Yangtze, its crowded waters littered with Japanese warships. It circled the patchwork of rice fields and mangrove swamps that skirted the industrial enclave of Pudong, skimming the choppy brown surface of the Whangpoo River to the commercial canal of Soochow Creek.

Sing found the the mission little changed from the old glass-plate photographs in her father's files: a large, rambling, two-story structure, made of concrete with timber add-ons, and a corrugated iron roof, on which the emblem of the Flying Angel spread its rusted wings and raised its battered trumpet.

If the building was unlovely, the grounds made up for it, including several acres of thriving vegetable plots, where satisfied goats grazed among chicken coops and duck ponds. An abundant orchard spilled down to the water's edge; a jetty poked into the whirling currents of the broad commercial river where cormorants and gannets perched to dry their ragged wings.

Moments after she arrived at the mission, Sing found herself sinking into a cavernous armchair in Aggie Gates's upstairs parlor. "I hope you don't mind condensed milk. We're short of fresh cow's milk in Shanghai—we had a cow, but our Japanese friends ate it rather quickly." Aggie poured strong tea from a very large pot crowned with a knitted cosy. She turned her wonderful smile on Sing, unscrewing a half bottle of gin and adding a generous slug to her tea, offering the same to Sing with a raised eyebrow.

"Not for you, I don't imagine . . . but a blessing for old bones, believe me." She handed Sing a brimming mug and raised her own. "I am glad you were able to come; Shanghai is not an easy place to be these days. Fortunately, they tend to leave me alone." She smiled again. "I don't think they quite know what to do with me."

Aggie was as large and lumpy as her easy chairs and just as inviting. Her round ruddy face looked freshly scrubbed, and white wisps of hair were braided at her ears like a Swedish milkmaid. With her leg-of-mutton arms folded comfortably across a formidable bosom, she looked, Sing couldn't help thinkng, like a very large steamed pudding freshly liberated from its cloth.

"I had to see your face . . . look into your eyes to know you are truly his child. I see that you are, and it lifts my heart to say so. You stand as he stood, straight as a jack-staff and proud as his house flag."

463

She heaved herself from the chair to fold Sing into her motherly arms and to kiss her cheek. "God bless you . . . this is a day I thought would never come."

"My father was lucky to have such a friend as you," Sing replied with heartfelt respect. "I would be grateful for the chance to speak of him and to hear what you know of his death, and perhaps where he rests. . . ."

Aggie raised a hand to stop her. "I will not ask where you have been for these many years, or how you got to be here. You're here, and that itself is a miracle." She turned a beaming smile upon her visitor. "But then, everything about your old man is a blessed miracle . . .

"I want you to brace yourself, my child. There is something I have to tell you that no living soul can know but you." Sing looked patiently at her father's old friend.

"They said the river was alight that night—a tide of flame that spread from shore to shore. Under Japanese fire, *Golden Sky* and her cargo of munitions were split into matchwood and every man aboard went with it."

She shook her head at the memory. "Any other man would have died that night, but not Ben Devereaux—somehow he swam clear of that field of flames. They hauled him out of the creek at dawn, floating with the rubbish at low tide. There was enough left of him to give them my name, so they dumped him here more dead than alive."

Sing listened to the words as though in a dream. "He had burns like I've never seen on a living creature. Hospital? They'd have let him die— put him out of his misery. Lucky I know a thing or two about burns. Trouble was, gangrene set in. There was a Chinese doctor I knew took care of that the best he could."

Aggie faltered, as though losing track of thoughts that were too hard to bear. "We took care of him in there, in a tub of oil, for three months, then on a bed of cotton wool for the best part of a year." She nodded toward an adjoining room, its doorway hung with a curtain of threaded bamboo. "Couldn't touch him for most of that time . . . he just survived. A hundred times I thought he was gone. The pain he was suffering . . . forgive me, dearie, I prayed for the Lord to take him." She

464

sniffled hard. "Every time, he would open his eye, to let me know he wasn't ready yet."

Aggie suddenly sat forward, one work-reddened hand on each knee. "Well, he never was ready. He looked the Almighty in the eye and said no . . . not yet. I have a child to live for."

Sing could barely frame the question. "Do you mean . . . ?"

"That's right, dearie, your father is still alive . . . no more than spitting distance from where you're sitting now." She reached out to stop Sing from rising.

"Easy now, I'm not finished yet. We have to think about this. It was two years before he could leave that room. He didn't want anyone to see what was left of him, and made me give him my solemn oath that I'd tell no one that he still lives. No one but you, that is, not even his partner, Indie Da Silva."

Aggie's warm hands cupped Sing's face as though it were a precious flower. "I don't think he ever gave up waiting for you . . . he said that your mother spoke to him, told him you would come. So go to him gentle-like, but be ready . . . his body has failed him and he was terrible hurt."

Sing could no longer fight the tears she had denied for so long, whether of happiness or grief she could not tell. Aggie took her gently by the hand, drawing her to the window and pushing aside the chintz curtain.

"Down there, by the old jetty, there's a seat facing the river. He made it for me when he was a boy and it still stands strong. It's where he spends his time, listening to the voices of the river and feeding the birds." She ushered Sing to the door with another firm hug, her voice little more than a whisper. "I have to tell you he cannot see, but his spirit is still strong. All the fires in Hades couldn't burn that."

Descending the stairs alone, Sing was truly afraid for the first time in her life. Afraid of what she would see, what she would say, how she would say it, afraid of what he would think of her.

The hunched figure with its back to her sat motionless, except for a slight movement every now and again as he threw crumbs to a gang of marauding gulls. Wearing a faded oilskin jacket, the hood pulled up to cover his head, he half turned at the flurry of wings, as though sensing her presence.

"That you, Aggie? God's teeth, you know how to creep up on a man, for one who's built like a tugboat."

As suddenly as it had descended, Sing's uncertainty lifted. She saw his hand, with the top joints of his fingers missing, making a clean job of tossing crumbs to the birds. Light dancing off the water showed a glimpse of his face, so disfigured it made her catch her breath. She spoke with great tenderness.

"It is I, Father, your daughter. My name is Siu-Sing . . . it means Little Star." She took his hand, placing the finger jade in its palm, closing the crippled fingers around it.

※

For the next week, Sing and her father were inseparable. There was a pattern to their days together. Each morning at six, they ate a bowl of Aggie Gate's "burgoo," the nautical term for porridge with a sprinkle of salt, and swigged her hot, sweet tea. Afterward, Ben took his two black-briar walking sticks and, without help from anyone, found his way steadily through the fruit trees to the bench with Sing at his side. There they picked up where they had left off at seven o'clock the night before. At midday, Aggie brought them a basket of his favorite cheese and corned-beef sandwiches of a size that could choke a horse, and a flask of tea laced with rum, and there was fruit for the picking.

Drained of tears and grand emotions, almost beyond joy and laughter, they talked through each long and pleasant day. When she spoke of a doctor, his voice was harsh and definite. "You are all the doctoring I need." He gave a croak of a laugh. "So just tell me all there is to know; Li-Xia is smiling on us today and there is nothing I need to hear but the sound of your voice."

She told him of her life and what she knew of his: the childhood stories passed on by the Fish; Master To; the hut by the lake and the journey that had led her to this day. When she suggested that he should rest—he must be strong for the journey home to the Villa Formosa—he shook his head violently. He wasn't going anywhere, he said in a voice that held something of the man he had once been.

"I don't need to see the house I built for her. I know every brick and every stick of furniture in the place."

Sing spoke with gentle understanding. "Your beautiful home awaits you, just as you left it. And Ah-Kin has tended the gardens as his own. He loves and misses you so . . . and there is Indie, and Angus, all your old friends . . ."

He sensed her dismay; his voice lowered to a grumble. "Then why would I offend their eyes with this?" He threw back the hood defiantly.

Sing took his mutilated face in both her hands, brushing away his tears with her thumbs, as she would a child's. "It is your heart they remember, your courage and your love; they care nothing for the scars of battle."

He shook his head vehemently. "It's too late for revenge; why pour rum on wounds that won't heal? Why give the bastards that deserted me a look at this?"

He shrugged the hood back in place. "There's only one who'd be glad to see the way I look, and I took good care of Chiang-Wah before I left; even a Boxer can't stand up to three copper-nosed slugs from a Colt. 45 at close range."

He patted the bench and rubbed its familiar surface. "This bench will be my gravestone, and that's good enough for me."

Regretting his tone, he added more gently, "I need to feed the birds and listen to the water. This old river is where my true friends were put to rest for backing me—where we faced our fate side by side and took what came of it." He patted the smooth worn seat of the bench again. "This jetty was *Golden Sky*'s last berth before she sailed to kingdom come. If I listen hard, I can still hear their voices."

His words were defiant again. "Give me your hand and your word on it. I stay here, dead or alive. And you tell not a living soul that you have found me."

Sing took his hand and kissed it. "You have my word, Father."

He would not talk much about himself or his life with Li-Xia, but

467

could not get enough of listening to her as he sat facing the river, drinking in her words like draughts of cool, sweet water after a long and terrible thirst. Occasionally, he asked a question that proved that, in spite of all he had endured, there was nothing wrong with her father's mind. At first Sing would embellish the pleasant parts of her stories while minimizing the harsh, but he would stop her, urging her to give an honest account and leave nothing out to spare him. He detected every hesitation, preempted every omission, and chuckled deep in his chest at every triumph, great and small.

On occasion, his stiff, racked frame was seized by the unaccustomed mirth, bringing spasms of coughing and wheezing. When he found his breath, he turned his broken grin to her.

"Don't fret; I can feel your worrying," he gasped, still regaining his breath. "You wouldn't stop an old man dying of laughter."

⊠

Captain Benjamin Jean-Paul Devereaux died in his sleep on the seventh night of their reunion. Clutched in his broken hand, so tightly that nothing could take it away, was the orange-peel finger jade. Sing had sensed her father's weakening as the long days had flowed away with the river . . . but she had also sensed contentment. The week spent under the apple trees, telling him the true story of her life, feeling his laughter, feeling his pride in her, were the richest hours of her life.

"He passed away as peacefully as his personal gods would allow," observed Aggie Gates. "You brought him that peace, and as much happiness as he had left in him."

Two days later, the old seat by the jetty was carefully taken from its moorings and set aside, while the strong hands of those few who knew him dug Ben Devereaux's grave. He was laid to rest in the uniform he had worn only on the most special occasions. Sing herself had washed and dressed his body, draping over the casket the Devereaux house flag—the red and green dragons still bright on their flaming yellow background.

Sing watched without tears as a floating crane lowered a two-ton block of finest marble over the grave. The garden seat was carefully restored to its rightful place, with a new brass plate on its back:

Ben Devereaux rests here—disturb him if you dare.

❖

December 1941

The marriage of Sing Devereaux to the recently promoted Major Toby Hyde-Wilkins took place on the ocean terrace of the Villa Formosa under a crisp autumn sky. The brief private ceremony was performed by Colonel Pelham in accordance with some obscure rule in the military bible known as *King's Rules and Regulations*, with a guard of honor provided by Toby's brother officers forming a glittering arch of drawn sabers.

The bride was given away by Captain Rodriquez Da Silva, outrageously turned out in the antiquated regalia of a commandant of the Portuguese navy, his wild gray hair tamed and his beard hastily trimmed for the occasion. Angus Grant was best man, clad in the kilted uniform of his Black Watch Regiment of Reserves. Miss Winifred Bramble was matron of honor, with Lady Margaret Pelham in charge of catering and all formalities.

Sing wore a dress made of vibrant yellow silk found among the bolts stored in the Double Dragon godowns, a close replica to the one worn by Li-Xia in her parents' portrait, with a sash fashioned from her mother's happiness silk. Her bouquet was made from gardenias, ringed with Cornish violets against a spray of morning stars, proudly presented by Ah-Kin, who told her that these were her mother's favorite flowers.

Toby and Justin Pelham were turned out in full dress uniform, scarlet tunics and white doeskin breeches, with cavalry boots burnished to a chestnut gloss. Nearly all the male guests were in uniform, which not only gave the occasion a dash of color and flair, but made it hard to forget that the Japanese were marching on Hong Kong. Even Lady Margaret and Miss Bramble wore the uniforms of senior Red Cross officials. Already, the golf course in Fanling had been turned into a field hospital, as had the Happy Valley Jockey Club, the Hong Kong Club, and other grand facilities of the British colonial establishment.

After a splendid dinner, Sing stood with Toby breathing the evening air heavy with night-blooming scents off the gardens. He enfolded her in his arms, his lips brushing her ear. "I beg you again," he whispered. "There is a British destroyer anchored off Wan-Chai ready to evacuate British citizens. Please, my dearest, Justin has arranged a cabin. My parents are longing to meet you."

"Is Lady Pelham leaving?" his new bride asked.

"No. She is the commanding officer's wife."

"And I am now the adjutant's wife. I will be of use to her." Sing turned to look at the beautiful villa, its windows warmly lit, the sound of quiet voices from the dining room. "This is where I belong. Ben Devereaux and Li-Xia would not have moved from the path of danger." She laughed. "My father would turn in his grave if I were to leave the Villa Formosa out of fear of the future." Turning back to draw him close, she rested her head on his shoulder. "We have two days before you return to the border. When you come back, I must be here waiting. My mother lies here, and the spirit of Ben Devereaux is everywhere. I have journeyed too far to find them. I will not have them taken from me now."

❊

At dawn the next morning, Ah-Kin stepped from his house and looked up at the dawn sky, reflecting the silvery pinks and purples of a freshly opened pearl shell. Breathing deeply the perfumed air of his beloved Ti-Yuan gardens, he went to his toolshed and filled a small basket from the sack of fishmeal. His grass sandals made no sound as he crossed the first bridge. With the flood of pure light, lotus flowers were opening crowns of palest pink, and dew lay upon their leaves in perfect beads of crystal.

A movement caught his eye, and he saw the mistress standing in the Pavilion of Joyful Moments, looking out to sea. She began to move, her arms rising in a graceful arc, like the unfolding of wings prepared for

470

flight. With the slenderness of grass blown by a gentle breeze, she stepped as lightly as a finch in a pear tree.

Heavenly chi flooded Sing's body as sunrise exploded upon the China Sea. Her hair flowed about her, red brown as the sunlit coat of a moon bear on the slopes. She felt the presence of Li-Xia and two snow-white chow pups with tongues like crushed blueberries asleep on the cushions; of the Fish, pouring ginger tea. Across the path of the rising sun, she saw the topmasts of a fast-raked schooner under billowing sails, its dragon banners streaming in a flawless golden sky.

Read on for
exclusive reading group material:

RED LOTUS

by Pai Kit Fai

About the Author

- A Conversation with Pai Kit Fai

Behind the Novel

- Concubines and Bondservants: A Historical Perspective

Keep on Reading

- Recommended Reading
- Reading Group Questions

About the Author

A Conversation with Pai Kit Fai

Can you tell us a bit about how you decided to lead a literary life?

The short answer is that I was never much good at anything else. When the teacher spoke of mathematics I thought of poetry. Finding the right words to describe a walk by the river, or adventures to be found in an apple orchard, was far more enchanting to me than adding and subtracting truckloads of figures I felt I might never use. My mind just didn't belong behind a desk. It still doesn't.

I suppose I began writing then, at the age of seven or eight, looking out of the schoolroom window, listening for a cuckoo, transported by the smell of new-mown hay and the sun-warmed backs of Shire horses. For a child, even in the war-torn streets of London, or the bucolic joys of the rural counties, the world of letters and its search for words and sentences was considered a foolish waste of time. That didn't stop me.

What inspired you to write *Red Lotus*?

I traveled widely in the Far East in my early life. Every sight and sound, no matter how great or small, was a new experience for me, to be entered bravely and explored in full. The clamor of Oriental cities, never more than moments away from the most peaceful and enchantingly beautiful countryside, claimed me and my imagination completely.

Villages, too small to notice—where long lives were lived contentedly in the simplicity of faith under the kindly eye of some smiling god—offered an instant welcome and countless stories; such stories mingled with the unforgettable aromas of spices and herbs, produce grown a step from the door—stirred, mixed, tossed in sizzling woks over open flame, to some secret family recipe. Always by women, young or old, strong, capable women, stooped over endless terraces of rice, urging stubborn buffalo behind a wooden plow, or washing clothes at the village well. They always seemed so complete to me . . . until I learned how quickly and unjustly the gods could lose their smile.

Your protagonists, Li-Xia and Siu-Sing, are headstrong women who face seemingly insurmountable odds in a patriarchal society. You've mentioned your interest in women's rights in China. Can you tell us what spurred your interest, and how your story was imbued by your understanding of the issues?

I think my fascination with the courage and amazing strengths of heart and mind so often found in women the world over began during my early travels.

In male-dominated societies of the early twentieth century, underprivileged girls were arrogantly and often savagely exploited with no concept of dignity, spiritual freedom, or physical comfort. Nowhere was this more harshly followed than in China, where a girl child was considered of no more value than an unwanted kitten, to be drowned at birth in the paddy field and left for the ducks to squabble over.

Those unwanted daughters allowed to live were put to work as household servants, although slaves would be a better term, until old enough (usually six to eight years old) to sell as "cherry girls"— virgins whose innocence and chastity were bartered like a basket of fish or a fattened piglet—for about the same price and with the same degree of ceremony.

The *sung-tip*, or contract, bonded them for life to the buyer without payment or rights of any kind. The cunning and the ruthless among them, through the use of sex and manipulation, sometimes fought their way to a perilous position of power and success; but the vast majority were soon seen as disposable by the rich old men or whoremongers who owned them. Homeless and nameless, sold from one hideous situation to another, the future they faced was bleak beyond description.

Those few who forged their identity in such a cruel and unrelenting society through their own wits, decisions, and choices were sometimes clever enough to change their cruel destiny against the most formidable odds and by the most remarkable of adventures—to find a life and love of their own that led to great success. Theirs are the tales worth telling.

You are a master of the Chinese martial arts. Can you tell us a little bit about how you came to study martial arts? How has its practice enriched your life? How did you draw upon your knowledge of this ancient Chinese practice when writing *Red Lotus*?

Well, first, the title of master is often loosely used. It carries very different meanings in the many competitive schools, or forms, of martial arts throughout Asia and now the Western world. Today it is possible for a female to attain the degree of master, while for many centuries a woman adept was usually one of royal blood or noble birth, taught from infancy to evade the ever-present threat of kidnap and rape. That is, until a Buddhist nun created a form that was designed for the female disciple; it was called White Crane. So, there are many levels of master, or *si-fu*.

In China, especially the China of old, such a title was held in the highest possible esteem, earned by a lifetime of devotion in search of perfection, widely known as kung fu. This was often the rarified domain of novice monks cut off from temptations of the world by a life in mountain monasteries. An abbot or grand master may, if he deems it earned and well deserved, bestow the credit of *si-fu* upon one who teaches what he or she has learned.

While studying, in 1977, in the Philippines, I was faced with advanced cancer of the throat. As an alternative to radical surgery, my own Chinese master taught me a sequence of breathing exercises said to be eight hundred years old. When after five years of daily practice I was found to be free of the dreaded disease, he suggested that I teach the techniques to others. If the success of my books on the subject has helped share the benefits of ancient Chinese health systems with readers in the West, then I accept the compliment of *si-fu* within that context.

I have found that the study and practice of any discipline that seeks to harmonize the body, mind, and spirit is a path worth following—one that can lead to a world of endless fascination and undreamed-of achievement, in which anyone, with time and patience, can conquer the extraordinary.

You are a noted scholar of holistic medicine. Can you tell us a little bit about how you began studying holistic medicine? How did your understanding of the subject work its way into *Red Lotus*?

Again, the same could be said for the generous title of scholar: in the days of Li-Xia and her daughter, Siu-Sing, a scholar was a man or boy who could read and write with his fingers and had a mind fast and nimble as an abacus . . . or one who had mastered the art of the calligrapher's brush. Artists and poets were the ultimate scholars—but all were men. Education was strictly the domain of the male, not to be wasted in the worthless hands of the female.

If my books on this subject have provided the slightest understanding of traditional Chinese medicine (TCM)—if it is "scholarly" to research the subject of your story thoroughly, and to enjoy every moment of it—then I accept the title humbly.

What other research did you do when writing the story? How did you decide what to include and what to leave out? Did you scrupulously adhere to historical fact? To what extent did you take artistic liberty?

Most of my research was done over some thirty years of living and working in the Far East, much of it in Hong Kong and Macao. It is not difficult to absorb the way of life in such wild and wicked cities, or the unchanged territory that still surrounds them.

So, researching a story as like *Red Lotus* becomes part of one's life. There is no great need for historical facts; China is and always will be an unfinished adventure, its fabulous and often frightening past as alive today as it has ever been.

As for how it was decided what to leave in and take out—with a palette as rich as this with which to paint your picture, there is little need for artistic license, or censure, the truth lies around every corner and in every one of a billion faces.

You were born in England but married into a famous Hong Kong family. Can you tell us a bit about how you came to be called Pai Kit Fai, and what this name means to you?

If my impressions of China needed any qualification, this came as a treasure trove of information when I married into one of Hong Kong's founding dynasties, with branches in Shanghai and Macao. The Civil Library of Hong Kong was donated by the family, as were many of the colony's hospitals and colleges, so there was no shortage of history.

When a person of foreign blood takes up professional life in Hong Kong or on the Chinese mainland, he or she is automatically given a Chinese name to have printed on the flip side of their business card. A chop or seal bearing the adopted name is also carved from soapstone in the traditional manner.

The great honor of being received into the arms of a Hong Kong family, especially one of notable heritage, requires certain standards of behavior and acceptance of ancient customs on behalf of the foreign member. The most important of these is the choosing of a Chinese name by which he or she will be thought of by the family elders. The choosing of such a name is the responsibility of the patriarch or matriarch, and is taken very seriously. The newcomer is observed for weeks or months until a name is chosen to best translate his or her character and calling. In my case, an elderly aunt who had devoted her life to the education of Hong Kong's young people—a very dear lady with a doctorate from Cambridge University—provided me with the name of Pai Kit Fai, which loosely translated means something like "Person of Letters and Grand Ambition."

While I take the name most seriously, its interpretation is of less importance as it can differ with each new ear, eye, and tongue. A Chinese guest once took me aside at an important banquet to advise me (in a whisper) that my name could also be translated as "Large Mountain of Lup-sup," which I discovered was the Cantonese term for unpleasant garbage. Fortunately, I also discovered that the bearer of this disturbing news was a sworn enemy of the family and an uninvited troublemaker. So, Pai Kit Fai it is and always will be.

Behind the Novel

Concubines and Bondservants:
A Historical Perspective

For centuries before the early 1900s, there was a prominent male domination in China. Women were deprived of all rights and were present mainly to serve men. Women served as slaves, concubines, and prostitutes. What follows is a brief social history of the Chinese custom of female enslavement as portrayed in Red Lotus.

Although urban areas had seen progress in the condition of women's lives—in the abolition of foot binding and in professional and educational opportunities—rural women were scarcely affected. Their vulnerability was due not only to a perpetuation of patriarchal values but also to the absence of economic opportunities, which maintained the time-honored role with which women were still associated—to do with domesticity reproduction, as well as sexual services. Thus patriarchal dicta, coupled with the demands for unpaid domestic labor for prostitutes and concubines, plus Chinese women's lack of general economic independence, contributed to a disparate situation: While educated Chinese women clamored for political rights, women from the poorer social strata were still being sold into slavery.

Hong Kong was not only an entrepôt for inanimate goods between China and the rest of the world, but also for human beings. Girls of Chinese descent born in Singapore, in the Dutch Indies, in the Straits, and in Macao were brought to Hong Kong for profit; girls from Shantou, Shanghai, Tianjin, and the rural hinterlands were sold by way of Hong Kong to Southeast Asian markets. All these girls shared a background of poverty, whether rural or urban. Some girls could recall farms on which the whole family had eked out a living; perhaps at some stage the family lost its tenancy, drifted to the nearest city, and during the phase of alienation from what had constituted the family's rootedness in social and moral values, the sale of a daughter would occur. Disassociation from a supportive context of kinship relations eroded many of the social inhibitions parents might have had in selling their daughters into an unknown fate.

In times of greatest desperation boys, too, were sold, mostly to be adopted; but this was the last resort and an admission of ultimate defeat. Girls, being by cultural definition "outsiders" in a patrilineal society, sooner or later to be married off to another family, went first. Patriarchal evaluation of the female sex, supported by the absolute authority of the *pater familias* to decide the fate of his family, provided for an obvious solution in times of material crisis: to sell the daughter, and grant the rest of the family at least a temporary respite.

At these times of crisis, parents, when parting with their daughters, were not always indifferent or callous to their fate. With the same reluctance but resignation in the face of an unrelenting fate with which families left their home villages to face an unknown future in search of a living, they may have resorted to the next step in a downward spiral of despair—offering their daughters on the market.

Excerpted with permission from *Concubines and Bondservants: The Social History of a Chinese Custom* by Maria Jaschok (© 1988, Oxford University Press, East Asia)

Recommended Reading

World Without End

by Ken Follett

Tai-Pan

by James Clavell

Memoirs of a Geisha

by Arthur Golden

The Bonesetter's Daughter

by Lisa See

Falling Leaves: The Memoir of an Unwanted Chinese Daughter

by Adeline Yen Mah

The Talented Women of the Zhang Family

by Susan Mann

The Song of Everlasting Sorrow

by Wang Anyi, translated by Michael Berry
and Susan Chan Egan

Reading Group Questions

1. Discuss the similarities and the differences between Li-Xia and her daughter, Siu-Sing. What matters most to each of them, and what does each do to achieve and preserve it?

2. Pai-Ling tells Li-Xia to "gather your thousand pieces of gold wherever you may find them and protect them with all your strength." What do you think this means? How do Li-Xia and Siu-Sing gather their "pieces of gold" throughout the story?

3. What role does learning, from books and otherwise, play in the principal characters' lives?

4. Discuss the tradition of foot binding in Chinese culture. What are the deeper implications, aside from the obvious physical handicaps of the practice?

5. *Red Lotus* is the story of three generations of women, all of whom are faced with challenges. How does the experience of one generation influence the next? What does the novel have to say about continuity with the past?

6. Myths and legends are recurring elements in the story, and link generations with a common thread. How are stories used to explain the violent forces that barrage the lives of Li-Xia and Siu-Sing? What role does spirituality play in the characters' lives?

7. Although society in the novel is explicitly dominated by men, in what ways are both major and minor women characters able to assert some sort of power over their destinies? In what ways are they powerless? Although the position of women has obviously changed since that time, can you see any similarities to the role of women in contemporary society?

8. What motivates some of the women in the story to help their fellow women, while others try to thwart them?

9. Discuss the roles of the various men in the story, and Ben Devereaux's role in particular. What do you think Li-Xia finds most attractive about Ben? And how great a factor do you think his otherness plays in that attraction?

10. How does Siu-Sing's childhood, which is idyllic in some ways, prepare her for a world beyond the mountains? How does it leave her vulnerable?

11. As young readers we are taught that every story has a "moral." Is there a moral to *Red Lotus*?

12. *Red Lotus* is set in an exotic world that often seems to date back many centuries instead of less than a hundred years ago. What seems most alien to you about this world, and what, if anything, reminds you of life in our own times?